stripped

Also by Brian Freeman

Immoral

stripped

BRIAN FREEMAN

headline

Copyright © 2006 Brian Freeman

The right of Brian Freeman to be identified as the Author of
the Work has been asserted by him in accordance with the
Copyright, Designs and Patents Act 1988.

First published in Great Britain in 2006
by HEADLINE BOOK PUBLISHING

1

Cataloguing in Publication Data is
available from the British Library

ISBN 0 7553 2536 2 (hardback)
ISBN 0 7553 3163 X (trade paperback)

Typeset in Sabon by
Palimpsest Book Production Limited, Polmont, Stirlingshire

Printed and bound in Great Britain by
Mackays of Chatham plc, Chatham, Kent

Headline's policy is to use papers that are natural, renewable and
recyclable products and made from wood grown in sustainable
forests. The logging and manufacturing processes are expected
to conform to the environmental regulations of the country of origin.

HEADLINE BOOK PUBLISHING
A division of Hodder Headline
338 Euston Road
London NW1 3BH

www.headline.co.uk
www.hodderheadline.com

For Marcia

'Must crimes be punished but by
other crimes, and greater criminals?'

BYRON

Prologue

She slipped the robe off her shoulders, and the white silk gathered in a pool of accordion folds at her feet.

Her naked body became a riot of color, bathed by the neon sign that towered over the rooftop patio. Giant letters spelled out the name *Sheherezade* above her in flashes of green and red. The light spilled across her skin and painted psychedelic graffiti over the urns, fountains, and date trees that decorated the terrace like a Moroccan palace.

The city lived on light. Garish signs illuminated the valley, but their names told the truth of where they were. The Sands. The Dunes. The Frontier. Outposts in the middle of nowhere. Sanctuaries from the dust and sun.

Where the neon glow didn't reach, the roof of the Sheherezade was dark, like the black desert lurking on the fringe of the Strip. She didn't study the shadows. She didn't see the man waiting for her there.

The luminous blue water of the swimming pool invited her. She had showered after her performance, but the heat of the dance lingered, and she yearned for the cool shock of the water. With nothing on but her high heels, she glided along the marble skirting to the end of the pool. Hot, gritty wind blew across her body. She kicked off her stilettos and stepped onto the diving board. She sliced the water as gracefully as a mermaid, then sidestroked leisurely to the shallow end. When she stood up, water dripped from her breasts. She ran her fingers through her wet black hair.

This was paradise. She was meant to live like this.

Very soon, she would be able to live like this anywhere in the world. No more sweaty showrooms with chorus-line amateurs. No more playing the harlot in the closet. She had made the decision to escape months ago. Tonight was the last night. Tomorrow she would be free.

She wondered if she would miss it – the power she felt on stage, the hunger in the men's eyes as they screamed her name. 'Amira!'

1

Amira Luz. The Spanish beauty with the dark skin and teasing eyes. Her hair lustrous and long. Her nose sharp and angled like a blade. Her flesh full of sensuous curves. Amira Luz – goddess of the Sheherezade.

Yes, she would miss it. This was Las Vegas, where everything was sexy. Sinatra's voice. The diamonds on a woman's neck. Even smoke from a freshly lit cigarette. She could sashay through the casinos and hear whispers trail behind her. Here, she was a star. Once she left the bright lights behind, she couldn't come back. But she wasn't going to be a prisoner any more.

A loud splash startled her. Her heart pounding, she turned and saw a creamy form knifing toward her under the water. She was frozen with fear, and then, relaxing, she grinned. He had arrived early to surprise her. She felt a surge of desire and anticipation, thinking of their making love in the pool.

'You little shit,' she said playfully, as he emerged out of the water in front of her, solid and strong, naked like she was.

But it wasn't the face she expected to see. She knew him. He leered at her every day in the casino. A horny boy who wasn't worth her spit.

She knew why he was here.

Amira stumbled back and started to scream, but he was on her in an instant, his hand clamped over her mouth, his other arm snaking around her waist. He jerked her squirming body against him. He took his hand from her mouth, but before she could shout, he kissed her hard. Under the water, she kicked furiously, trying to dislodge him, but his legs were rooted to the tiled base of the pool. He lifted her effortlessly. She felt his erect shaft drag along her stomach.

First, rape, she realized.

And then murder.

Their mouths parted. She sucked in a breath and screamed for help.

'Shout all you want,' he told her, laughing. He ripped his arm from around her back and threw a stinging slap across her face, cutting off her cry. She tried to wriggle away, but he grabbed her again and shoved her whole body under the water. She felt his knee worming against her stomach, and then he jerked it upwards, compressing her lungs. Her mouth opened involuntarily, water rushing in. Air bubbles leached from her nose. Thrashing, panicking, she tried to lunge above the surface, but his hands held her in a vise.

There would be no freedom for her now, she knew. She would always be a prisoner.

Her wide-open eyes burned with chlorine. Through the distortion of the water, she saw the man's scrotum hanging like a huge pod, inches from her face. She had enough play in her arm to reach out and grab it, and as she tightened her grip and twisted, she dug her long, elegant nails into his testicles as if she was piercing a grape.

His animal wail carried to her ears through the water. He reared back, releasing her. She burst up with a splash and took several long, labored breaths, feeling the hot summer air rush back into her lungs. Her assailant was clutching his genitals and cursing. Furious, she laid both hands on his chest and shoved. His heels spilled out from under him, and he splayed back, landing flat on the water. Amira dove past him. She swam for the edge of the pool.

Behind her, she heard him scrambling to regain his balance. She felt his fingers scratch her leg as he clawed for her. Her left hand grazed the smooth marble, and she laid both palms flat on the tile, pushing herself up. She tried to pull her leg onto the skirting, but her foot slipped, and she lurched back into the water.

Quickly, Amira grabbed for the tile again, but she wasn't fast enough. He was right behind her.

He spun her around. She saw his eyes, contorted into dark little dots of fury, with a dirty stare that traveled from her face down to her full breasts and below the water to the black triangle between her legs.

'You won't be fucking anyone tonight,' she said, smiling at death, spitting the words at him.

'Neither will you,' he hissed, his voice filled with malevolence.

He yanked her long hair from behind, snapping her neck back. With a hand around her throat, he drove her skull into the sharp edge of the marble, where the bone split with a sickening crack. An electric charge erupted behind her eyes, agony flooding into every nerve end. Then, as quickly as it came, the pain was gone, and she felt nothing at all. Amira felt her body sinking, sliding, twisting, her limbs as powerless as a marionette. She stared peacefully at the night sky overhead and the fiery glow of the neon sign as the water closed over her face. It was her last glimpse of the city, living on light, dying on light. Her body corkscrewed down toward the deep end. Clouds of red trailed behind her. By the time she hit bottom, she was far away, on a wooden stage somewhere, her feet thundering to the flamenco beat as the crowd cheered.

'Amira!'

PART ONE

AMIRA

One

Elonda scanned Flamingo Road with the practiced eyes of a turkey vulture, lazily circling the desert landscape and hunting for prey. She spotted her quarry a half-block from the Oasis casino and sized him up.

He was tall and tan, like a surfer washed up in the city, with wavy blond hair that hung below his ears and wraparound silver shades. Young, maybe twenty-two. He wore a loud, untucked short-sleeve shirt with the buttons done wrong, a loose-fitting pair of white shorts, and dirty sneakers with no socks. His cocky walk told her he had money in his pocket. He wore sunglasses at night, and behind the shades she knew his eyes were on the hunt, too, just like hers.

His head swiveled in her direction. He saw her and grinned.

Her cop radar wasn't going off. Cops didn't walk – they pitched the girls from inside their unmarked, air-conditioned sedans. Only the newbies fell for them.

Elonda sauntered across the wide street, raising her hand to stop the speeding cars and flashing the drivers with her white teeth and a jiggle of her breasts. There was plenty of traffic at one in the morning. The city operated on jungle rules: feed under the cool cover of darkness, and find a patch of shade to sleep through the hot days.

On the opposite sidewalk, she ducked into the doorway of a magic shop. She pulled a bottle of K-Y from the back pocket of her jeans and squirted some on her fingers. Sucking in, she squeezed a hand inside her skin-tight pants and lubed up. She did a little dance, rubbing it in. A trick of the trade. *Oh, I am so wet for you, baby.* Although most guys weren't looking to pole her these days. They were too afraid of AIDS or too klutzy to get inside her standing up. So they went for the mouth music.

With the grease between her legs, Elonda flipped her hair back and listened to the rap of the multicolored beads dotting her corn rows.

7

She tugged on her feathered pink tube top until the black crescents of her nipples peeked through. Finally, she popped a wintergreen mint on her tongue. Another little trick. Guys loved the cool burn of the mint in her warm mouth.

She eased back onto the sidewalk and scoped out the street, looking for competition. But she was alone, just her and the bad boy. The lights of the Strip shone like fire across the freeway. On this side of I-15, where casinos spilled over from Las Vegas Boulevard like an overflowing box of popcorn, the Gold Coast and Rio shimmered on the north side of the street, and the Oasis tower loomed a block away. But where she was, Flamingo was dark, nothing but an empty lot and the old cinder-block magic shop butting up to the street.

Elonda leaned her shoulders against the shop window, her hips jutting out, and casually nibbled on one painted nail. Letting a slow smile creep onto her face, she turned her head and drank him in. He was headed right for her, his feet trampling on nudie brochures littering the street. No hesitation. This wasn't his first time.

As he got closer, her eyes narrowed. He looked familiar, but she couldn't place him. He wasn't a regular – she hadn't done him before. But she began to think she recognized his face, maybe from one of the tabloids. Behind the shades, it was hard to tell. But Elonda studied him long and hard, because a celebrity paying for sex from a Vegas hooker might be worth some serious cash from someone.

He stopped right next to her. 'Hey.'

His voice was young and carefree. Bored. Slurred.

'Hey yourself.' Elonda reached out and slid a finger inside his shirt, making a circle on his chest. 'Don't I know you, baby?'

'You ever been to Iowa?' he asked.

A hick with a familiar face, she thought. Damn. 'A lot of cows and corn there, right? And shit on your shoes? No thanks.'

Elonda cast her eyes up and down the street, looking for Metro patrol cars. The traffic came and went – Hummers, limos, pickups, beaters – but there was no one who would hassle her. A block away, near the Oasis, she spotted a man standing by a bus stop, looking bored, checking his watch. In the other direction, no one at all. The coast was clear.

'Suck or fuck?' she asked.

He didn't answer, but stuck out his tongue and flicked it at her. She smelled gin wafting from his mouth. Elonda gave him a price, and he dug out two crumpled bills from his pocket. She laid her palm on his chest and nudged him backward into the doorway of the magic shop. Elonda got on her knees and unzipped him. She glanced up.

8

His eyes were closed. She saw a couple days' worth of yellow stubble on his chin.

She began counting in her head. That was her little game, something to pass the time, like the office workers who listened to their iPods while they typed all day. One, two, three, four. No guy had ever made it to one hundred. Most didn't make it to ten.

He took a few seconds to stiffen. That was the gin, she figured. But she worked her magic, and his body responded. She heard a low rumble in his throat, a purr of pleasure. When she glanced up from her work, she saw his mouth had fallen open.

Thirty-two, thirty-three, thirty-four.

He was already close. She could feel his hips moving, starting to thrust, and she sucked harder and moved her head faster.

Thirty-nine.

Elonda heard something clip-clop nearby, the sound of heavy boots on the sidewalk. Someone was heading their way from the casino. She looked up again, but the farm boy was already on another planet, and he didn't hear a thing. Clip-clop, clip-clop. She didn't really care. She got peeped all the time and heard the shocked whispers from people who secretly wished she was on her knees in front of them. If he looked their way, let him enjoy the show.

Forty-five, forty-six. The farm boy was getting ready to blow.

The tapping of the boots came up directly behind her in the doorway, and then they stopped right there. Elonda heard a rustle of fabric and a strange metallic click. The john's eyes were still closed, and he moaned loudly.

It was creepy, that man standing behind her, watching them. She got a bad feeling. The hairs on her neck pricked up, and she knew he was still there, even though she couldn't even hear him breathing. She could feel his eyes. A cloud of menace engulfed her. It was the kind of sixth sense you got after enough time on the street.

Elonda let the man's shaft slip from her mouth. She bit her lip and looked up, but she wasn't going to look back, not for anything. Immediately, the john's eyes snapped open, his lips twisting into an angry scowl. Then she watched as he spotted the stranger behind her.

'What the—'

His anger became slack-jawed surprise. His eyes widened. She saw his face register disbelief.

Then he didn't have a face any more.

The loudest sound Elonda had ever heard detonated in her ears like the cap being blown off a volcano. The farm boy sprouted a third eye, and his head fell forward, so she could stare right at him and see up into the hole burrowed into his skull, a red river pouring out of it. As she watched, he crumpled into a pile and collapsed on top of her, pinning her to the ground. Blood streamed over her, rippling like worms across her skin and seeping into her clothes. She smelled urine and shit as his bowels evacuated.

Finally, Elonda remembered to scream. She closed her eyes and unleashed a screeching yell that went on and on until she ran out of breath. No one seemed to hear. None of the traffic stopped. All she heard was the sound of footsteps again, going away now, heading back down the street as casually as they had arrived. Clip-clop, clip-clop.

TWO

Fish out of water.

Jonathan Stride tried to concentrate on Elonda, who was slumped on the sidewalk, her body and clothes painted in dried blood. She talked a mile a minute, and he tried to keep up with her, but his eyes kept glancing over her head into the window of the magic shop. There was a black box inside, with a glass fish bowl on one half, filled with water. In the other half of the box, a goldfish swam back and forth. Outside the bowl. Seemingly in mid-air.

It was a hell of a trick, and Stride wondered how long a fish could survive in those conditions.

He tried to slow Elonda down. 'Take it easy, OK? We need your help.'

'You just get this bastard!' Elonda screeched, her arms waving, her corn rows clicking like plastic numbers strung in a pool hall. 'Son of a bitch probably left me deaf. Sounded like a bomb going off.'

Stride squatted down until he was eye to eye with Elonda, and he took one of her flyaway wrists firmly in his hand. 'Stay with me now. We're going to get you cleaned up, put you in some new clothes, and then you're going to eat yourself silly at the Rio buffet, all courtesy of Metro. OK? That sound like a deal? But I need you to give me some information first.'

'I like the Harrah's buffet better,' Elonda snapped.

'OK, Harrah's it is. Now are you ready to talk to me?'

Elonda pouted with her thick lips. She hugged her bare knees with her arms. Stride pushed himself to his feet and slid a notebook and pen from the inside pocket of his navy blazer. He wore the coat over a bone-white, button-collar dress shirt and crisp new black jeans. Serena had insisted that he start the new job with new jeans, and he had finally relented, although he hated to abandon the fraying pair that had fitted his body like an old friend for the last ten years in Minnesota. The

11

starched denim felt stiff, like cardboard, which was how he felt here in Las Vegas. A fish out of water. It was another universe compared to the Midwestern world where he had spent his whole life.

'The victim, did you see where he came from?'

'The Oasis,' Elonda said.

Stride eyed the casino and its slim, phallic tower. The hotel was hosting a Victoria's Secret fashion show, and a slinky lingerie model thirty stories tall stared imperiously back from a huge vertical banner that stretched nearly to the Oasis roof. She had white wings, like she might fly away and terrorize the city. King Kong with a D cup.

'Was he alone?' Stride asked.

Elonda nodded. 'Yeah. Headed my way like a fucking laser beam.'

'He say anything to you about himself? Tell you who he was?'

'Oh, sure, baby, we had a fine conversation. People meet me, they want to talk.' Elonda snorted. Then she added, 'He said he was from Iowa.'

Stride shook his head. 'He wasn't. His ID says Vancouver.'

'Fucker lied to me? Well, God'll get you for lying.' She grinned at Stride.

'Was there anybody else on the street?' he asked.

'Nobody.'

Stride glanced at the area surrounding the magic shop. The street was open and wide – you could see for blocks. He didn't think the killer appeared out of nowhere like one of the magic tricks in the window.

'You told me you heard the killer walk up to you. Where did he come from?'

'I don't know, man. There wasn't a soul.' She chewed a fingernail and idly scratched an itch between her legs. 'Wait, wait, hang on. There was somebody at the bus stop down there.'

Stride tapped his pen against his front teeth and squinted as he studied the bus stop, which was near the Oasis driveway about thirty yards away. No shelter, just a street sign and a notch in the pavement for the bus to pull off the street.

'What did he look like?' Stride asked.

Elonda shrugged. 'As long as he wasn't a cop, I didn't care.'

'Tall? Short?'

'Fuck, I don't know.'

Stride ran a hand back through his unkempt salt-and-pepper hair. It was wavy, with a mind of its own, and more salt and less pepper every day. He bit his lip, imagining the street empty, not a riot of police activity, just Elonda and the horny Canadian.

12

And a man waiting for a bus.

'Did you hear a bus?' he asked. 'You would have noticed if one went by right behind you.'

Elonda thought back. 'No. No bus.'

'How long were you in the doorway before the murder?'

''Bout forty-five seconds,' Elonda said.

'You sound pretty sure.'

'I count,' she said and gave him a broad wink.

Stride got the picture. No bus, and less than a minute before the shooting. He waved at one of the uniformed officers on the scene, a burly kid with a blond buzz cut and a stubble goatee.

'Go down to that bus stop,' Stride told him. 'Then time yourself walking back here. Don't hurry. You're just a pedestrian on the street, OK?'

The cop nodded. It didn't take him long. When he arrived back in front of the magic shop, he clicked his sports watch and announced, 'Thirty-two seconds.'

Stride squatted down in front of Elonda again. 'I'm going to need you to think real hard about that man at the bus stop.'

'That was the guy, huh?' Elonda said. 'Shit. I'm telling you, I don't remember him.'

'Let's try something,' Stride began.

He stopped when he heard a car horn blare sharply behind him, then heard the expensive purr of a sports car pulling up nearby, just outside the crime scene tape. A door opened, and Stride saw the cop with the goatee, who was still hovering nearby, mutter something foul under his breath. Stride glanced back in time to see a yellow Maserati Spyder peel off toward the Strip.

'Who's the tough-ass chick?' Elonda asked, looking over Stride's shoulder.

The Spyder had dropped off a woman who now stood surveying the scene, her arms folded over a large chest and one foot on the curb. Her hair was short and spiky, dirty blonde with black streaks. She was tall, probably only three inches short of Stride's own six foot one, and she looked strong and full-figured, with arms that filled out the sleeves of her tight white T-shirt. Her right arm sported a wolf's head tattoo. A gold police shield hung from the belt loop of her blue jeans.

'Don't worry about it,' Stride told Elonda. 'Right now, I want you to close your eyes. Just relax and think back to when you first spotted your customer.'

'You trying to hypnotize me?' Elonda asked. 'Can you make me stop biting my nails?'

13

Stride smiled. 'No, I just want you to remember. Picture it in your head, OK? You just saw your mark. You're crossing the street. Is the other man already waiting at the bus stop?'

Elonda started humming. Her head bobbed back and forth, following a rhythm. Then, abruptly, her eyes snapped open. 'No, he wasn't there! Hey, this is cool.'

'Close your eyes again. Keep replaying it.'

'Yeah, now the guy's behind him at the bus stop. I see him. Where the fuck did he come from?'

'What's he doing?'

'Checking his watch. Looking up and down the street. Real cool.'

'What's he wearing?' Stride asked. He thought about a way to trigger her memory and added, 'When he checks his watch, can you see his bare arm?'

Elonda pursed her lips, like she was puckering for a kiss. Her brow furrowed. 'A coat!' she said happily. 'He's got a windbreaker – tan, I think. And tan pants too, khakis maybe.'

'You're doing great. Is he a big guy?'

'He ain't so tall. Not real big either. But he looks, I don't know, tough. Mean dude.'

'How about hair color?'

'Dark,' Elonda said. 'Cut short. A beard, too. He's got a beard.'

'Elonda, you're beautiful,' Stride said, and he watched the girl beam with pride. He spent another ten minutes playing out the rest of the scene, but the closer she got to the murder, the more her mind blacked it out. When he was done, he called over the goateed cop and told him in a whispered voice what to do.

'Harrah's?' the cop asked in disbelief. 'You're kidding me. Sawhill will flip if I put this in for reimbursement.'

Stride shoved a hand into his pocket and fished two twenties out of his wallet. 'Here, take this, and get yourself something too. You're looking too thin.'

The cop rubbed his oversized neck and smiled. 'Whatever you say.'

'But hands off the girl,' Stride added.

When Elonda was safely in the back of a patrol car, Stride sought out his new partner.

It was odd, working the street again, a detective on the job. He had been the lieutenant in Duluth, a big fish in a small pond, and now he was just another investigator on the Metro Homicide Detail in Las Vegas. The closest thing he had ever had to a partner back home was Maggie Bei, the senior sergeant in his detective division.

Stride and Maggie had worked together for more than a decade, and the tiny Chinese cop with the sharp, sarcastic tongue had become his best friend. But Maggie was still in Minnesota, married and off the force, a baby on the way. Stride was in Sin City, the last place he could have imagined being.

Thanks to Serena.

He had met Serena Dial over the summer, while the two of them investigated a Las Vegas murder that had its roots in a teenage girl's disappearance in Minnesota years earlier. The investigation had upended his life in Duluth and destroyed his second marriage, which he knew had been misguided from the start. Maggie rarely missed an opportunity to remind him that she had seen divorce coming for him like a train wreck, and he had ignored her warnings.

But old things ended, and new things began. Meeting Serena had changed everything. She was beautiful, smart, and funny, despite the sharp edges that came with a troubled past. He fell for her fast and hard. When the investigation was over, he had followed Serena here, to this wild world, and wound up back on the street.

Now he had a real partner again, who looked like she didn't relish the task of playing second fiddle to a Vegas newcomer.

'Amanda Gillen,' she announced brusquely as he approached her, as if she expected him to challenge her. Her voice was husky. Or maybe she was just half asleep, as Stride was, after the phone call had dragged him out of bed, and out of Serena's arms, in the middle of the night. His first murder case in Vegas. A body on the street on Flamingo.

'I'm Stride,' he told her.

Amanda nodded and began nervously tapping her foot. Her lower lip jutted out, and she glanced around to make sure they were out of earshot. Her face was taut and unhappy.

'Look, I give everybody one free joke before I get pissed off, so do you want to make it now, or do you want to save it for a rainy day?'

Stride cocked his head. 'What?'

'You know,' she said sourly.

'You lost me, Amanda.'

Her eyes narrowed as she watched the puzzlement on his face. The wrinkles in her forehead went away, and her jaw unclenched. She gave him an odd, sparkling smile that was suddenly friendly and not at all closed-off. 'All right, maybe you don't know. Forget it. No big deal. It's two in the morning and I'm crabby.'

'You and me both.'

'That was nice with the hooker. The way you got her to talk. You're good.'

'Thanks,' Stride said. He added, 'I like your boyfriend's car.'

Amanda smirked. 'Oh, the Spyder. It's mine, actually. We were out dancing when I got paged. I told him if he puts a dent in it, I put a dent in his dick.'

'Yeah, that's an incentive,' Stride said. 'You win it at the slots?'

'Something like that.'

Stride watched her swallow hard, and a flush rose in her cheeks. She had a long face that tapered to a slightly protruding chin. Her lips were puffy and pale pink. She had thin black eyebrows and she had taken the time to apply her makeup with considerable care. Her Saturday night look, Stride guessed. Despite the wrestler chick bravado, she looked pretty when she smiled and vulnerable when she was nervous. Stride figured she was about thirty.

'Got an ID on the vic yet?' Amanda asked.

Stride nodded. 'Canadian driver's license. Probably a tourist whose luck ran out. Name is Michael Johnson Lane.'

Amanda did a double-take. '*M.J. Lane?*'

'That's right.'

She whistled and shook her head. 'Oh, shit.'

'You know him?'

'Check your spam folder once in a while, Stride,' Amanda told him. 'His bare ass is probably in half of the messages. Not to mention every issue of *Us* magazine.'

'My subscription lapsed,' Stride said.

Amanda studied his face long enough to realize he was joking, and a smile curled onto her full lips.

'Well, you're in Las Vegas now,' she retorted. '*People, Us*, and the *Enquirer* are more important reading around here than a DEA circular.'

Amanda walked over to the body. She wore ridiculously high heels, and Stride realized she was several inches shorter than he first thought. He noticed one of the ME staff look at her nervously and back up to give her space. Amanda didn't pay any attention. She bent from the waist until her hands were flat on the sidewalk, and she turned her head sideways to stare at the corpse's dead eyes. Stride found himself noticing her attractive, muscular ass and firm legs as her jeans pulled tight. He looked quickly away as she got up and announced, 'Yeah, that's M.J.'

'All right. So who is M.J. Lane?'

'Trust fund baby,' Amanda said. 'His dad's *Walker* Lane. You know, the billionaire producer in Vancouver.'

'Other than Daddy's money, what's his claim to fame?'

'He hangs with the right crowd. Hollywood connections. He was

16

low profile until he filmed a very nasty rendezvous with a young soap actress last year. Somebody stole it, and it wound up all over the internet. Bondage, anal sex, real kinky stuff.'

'A star is born.'

'Absolutely. Him getting popped is big news. You're going to get your picture in all the tabloids.'

'I'll whiten my teeth,' Stride said.

'So what do you think? Does it look like someone was stalking M.J.?'

'It feels like an assassination,' Stride said. 'A pro.'

'But he didn't kill the girl,' Amanda pointed out. 'A pro would take out the witness.'

'Yeah, true. He left the shell casing, too. A .357.'

'So maybe not a pro.'

'Maybe not,' Stride agreed. 'But he planned it well. Cool, in and out fast. The question is, was the guy specifically after Lane, or do we have some kind of moral crusader out to clean up the city's prostitution problem.'

'Or both,' Amanda said. 'M.J.'s not the first celeb to get his ice-cream cone licked around here. The perp could have been staking out the casino, looking to make a big splash, get some headlines with the hit.'

Stride nodded. 'Except from what you say about M.J., there could be plenty of reasons for someone to want him dead.'

Three

Pete, one of the valets at the Oasis, remembered M.J. Lane.

'He came in around ten o'clock,' Pete told Stride and Amanda when they quizzed him at the casino's porte cochère. Pete was young and as white as a tube of toothpaste, with brown hair slicked down to lie flat on his head. He wore black pants and sneakers, and a snug waist-length jacket in burgundy.

'Alone?' Stride asked him.

'Mr Lane? Not hardly. He had Karyn on his arm. Karyn Westermark. You know, the soap actress?' He fanned himself as if the cool night air had turned warm. 'You saw the video on the net? That was her. Hot stuff. Man, she's better than a porn star.'

'How'd they get here?' Amanda asked. 'Cab? Limo?'

Without answering, Pete broke off to attend to a gray Lexus sedan, opening the passenger door and then running around to the opposite side to take the car keys and hand the driver a parking stub. He returned, apologizing and pocketing a fifty-dollar tip. He cast a nervous eye as two more cars pulled into the driveway. Two in the morning at the Oasis on Saturday night was prime time.

'How'd M.J. get here tonight?' Amanda repeated.

'He drove himself,' Pete told them. 'He's got a condo in town, over in the Charlcombe Towers just off the Strip.'

'Why didn't he ask for his car when he was leaving?' Stride asked.

'I figured he was just going for a walk. You know?'

Stride cocked an eyebrow and leaned in close to Pete's face. 'Why'd he need a "walk" if he had Karyn with him?'

'Karyn left an hour before M.J. did,' Pete explained. 'I got a cab for her.'

'Did she look upset?' Amanda asked.

Pete shook his head. 'She looked bored. She told the cabbie to take her to Ra, over at the Luxor. She was just hunting for another party.'

'Did M.J. say anything when he left?' Stride asked.

'No, he looked pretty bombed. He headed straight down the sidewalk. I knew where he was going.'

'Did M.J. "walk" a lot?' Amanda asked.

The valet blanched. 'Not very often. A guy like him, he doesn't need to pay for it. But sometimes you want a little on the street, so you don't have to wake up next to her, OK?'

'Tell that to your girlfriend,' Stride said. 'Did anyone follow him out the door?'

Pete shrugged. 'I don't know. Cars were coming and going. I only noticed M.J. because he's a regular.'

A car horn blared noisily, and Pete waved and began dancing on both feet, anxious for his next tip. 'Anything else?' he asked impatiently.

'Who's head of security here?'

'Gerard Plante. Inside and straight back.'

'Thanks. We'll send a team over to check out M.J.'s car,' Stride added. 'Make sure no one gets near it before we do. You included.'

'Sure.'

Stride clapped a hand like a vise on the boy's shoulder. 'If I read in *Us* magazine about ribbed Trojans in M.J.'s glove compartment, I'm going to make sure the IRS comes knocking on your door about those fifty-buck tips. Got it?'

Pete's eyes widened, and he licked his upper lip, trying to figure out if Stride was serious. Then he gulped and ran for the next car.

'*Us* magazine,' Amanda said. 'Nice.'

'I thought you'd like that.'

Stride led Amanda through the revolving doors into the sea of noise and smoke inside the casino. The stale smell of cigarettes curled into his lungs like an old friend and, just like that, the craving was back. Funny how it never left. He hadn't smoked in more than a year, but he felt himself rubbing his thumb and finger together, as if there was a lit Camel between them. He took a deep breath, sucking it in and expelling it, wondering if Vegas had been dropped down in the desert by some sarcastic angel who wanted to test the willpower of ex-sinners.

He found himself getting aroused, too. It was auto-erotica, part of a mind-control game the casinos played. He couldn't pretend he was immune. He responded to the beating pulse in the city's bloodstream. Not greed, like most people thought. Hunger. For money, for flesh, for food, alcohol, and smoke – naked hunger, oozing, obsessive, and overwhelming. The casinos programmed it that way. Maybe the little

19

black half-moons in the ceiling weren't cameras after all, spying on every finger on a slot button or flip of a card. Maybe they were all spraying some odorless drug that unleashed the mania, which lasted until your money was all gone and you slunk back home.

The Oasis was among the most explicit of the Vegas casinos in using sex to sell its machines and tables, and to cultivate an image as the hip spot to rub shoulders with celebrities. Looking around the casino, Stride saw posters everywhere of impossibly gorgeous bikini-clad women, leering at him as they hyped slot tournaments, poker rooms, and crab leg buffets. It seemed to be working. The casino itself was relatively small, not a sprawling octopus like Caesars, but every machine was taken, and every seat at the blackjack tables was filled, with crowds pressing in to watch the action. It was a young crowd, dripping with women just as stunning as those in the posters.

Stride remembered what Serena's partner, Cordy, said about nights in Las Vegas. The time when breasts came out to play.

He had a hard-on. It pissed him off.

'Come on,' he growled. Amanda had a look of cool wonder. The drug was working on her, too.

They weaved their way through the rows of slot machines and found the security desk at the back of the casino, an imposing oak monolith staffed by the only woman in the casino who was ugly and severe. Talking above the thump of rock music blaring from the over-head speakers, Stride asked for Gerard Plante.

He held up his shield. She told him to wait.

Amanda sat down at a slot machine across from the security door and fed in a five-dollar bill from her pocket. The machine featured characters from some long-ago television show that Stride could remember watching when he was a kid in Duluth. He had an image of his bedroom window and of snow whipping past the glass.

Stride leaned against the machine and impatiently shoved his hands in his pockets. He leaned down to Amanda. 'So how did you get stuck with me?'

Amanda took her eyes off the slot reels and gave him a suspicious look. 'Excuse me?'

'The lieutenant thinks I should be back in Minnesota shoveling snow,' Stride said. 'You must have pissed him off to get stuck with a newbie like me who's on Sawhill's shit list.'

Stride knew that Sawhill was just angry at the world. He used to get that way himself sometimes when he was a lieutenant, during those stretches when everything that could go wrong did. Sawhill had lost his favorite detective when the man won the Megabucks jackpot and retired instantly, eight million dollars richer. Then Serena went over Sawhill's head to the sheriff to plug Stride, an experienced homicide investigator who just happened to be in town, available, bored, doing nothing but letting the city get on his nerves. And so Sawhill found himself with Stride crammed down his throat, and he had made sure Stride knew that he didn't think his newest detective was up to the task of big-city crime.

'Oh, now I get it,' Amanda said, half to herself. 'I was wondering what *you* did to get stuck with *me*. Now it makes sense. Sawhill has it in for you.'

Stride shrugged. 'I like you fine. You seem smart. You're something to look at, too. Seems like he's doing me a favor.'

'Not hardly,' Amanda told him.

'Want to fill me in?'

Amanda took a long look at him. 'You really don't know, do you? Serena didn't tell you?'

'I guess not.'

'You're not just playing dumbass games with me?'

'I haven't been in this city long enough to play games,' Stride said.

Amanda laughed, long and deep. 'Oh, that's good. That's really good.'

'Are you going to let me in on the joke?'

'I'm a non-op,' Amanda said.

'What's that?' Stride asked, genuinely confused.

'I'm a transsexual. A non-operative transsexual. I've had feminization surgery, and I take oestrogen supplements to promote development of breasts, soft skin, the right weight balance, that kind of thing. But I decided not to undergo SRS to remove the genitalia. Got it? I used to be a guy.'

Stride felt his face turn multiple shades of crimson. 'Holy shit.'

'So you see why I'm not exactly first in the rotation for potential partners.'

He couldn't help himself. He found himself glancing at the large breasts pushing out from Amanda's T-shirt and then at the crotch of her tight jeans, where his imagination seemed to freeze. He realized he was staring and couldn't think of a thing to say.

'Want to see?' Amanda asked.

'No!' Stride retorted, and then realized Amanda was giggling. 'I'm sorry,' he added. 'This really is perfect. Sawhill is sending me a message, you know. "Bet you don't have any non-ops back in Nowhere, Minnesota, hey, Stride?"'

'Is it going to be a problem?'

Stride thought about it. He had lived his entire life, until a couple of months ago, on the shore of Lake Superior, in a city that was liberal about labor unions and health care and conservative about religion and sex. But Stride considered himself strictly nonjudgemental about anything that went on behind closed doors, so long as no one got hurt.

He shrugged. 'Like I said, you're smart, and you're the prettiest guy I've ever seen.'

'I'm a girl now. But thank you. Most of the others on the force, men *and* women, haven't been so open-minded.'

'I bet.'

Stride had lots of questions for Amanda, but he wasn't ready to ask anything that would make him look even more like a fool.

He felt a hand on his shoulder. Stride turned and looked up into the olive-colored face of a very tall man who wore silver sunglasses even in the middle of the night inside the casino. His black hair stood up, a flat top cut to a perfect one-inch height.

'Detective?' he said. 'I'm Gerard Plante, Oasis head of security.'

Stride introduced himself, and Amanda stood up, doing the same. Gerard wore a navy suit whose fabric glistened under the lights. A burgundy handkerchief, embroidered with the Oasis logo, peeked out from his breast pocket. When he shook hands, his skin felt like the smooth leather of a hundred-dollar wallet.

'Let's go in the back, shall we?' Gerard said.

He guided them behind the security desk, and when the heavy oak door closed behind them, the noise of the casino seemed to vanish magically, replaced by a calming white noise. No soundtrack. No electronic pinging. This was where the volcanoes and white tigers vanished, where it was about nothing at all except money, the river that never experienced a drought.

Gerard led them into a vast office without windows, decorated in perfect taste and immaculate. Gerard obviously wasn't a man who believed in paper, because there wasn't a scrap to be seen anywhere in the office, and his desk and credenza were both glass-topped with triangular steel legs and not a drawer in sight. Stride couldn't pick out a smudge or fingerprint anywhere on the glass.

Behind Gerard, on the credenza, was the largest computer monitor Stride had ever seen, sleek and chrome, more like a plasma TV. A sliding drawer suspended underneath the glass top held a keyboard, mouse, and joystick.

Gerard motioned Stride and Amanda to two minimalist chairs in front of the desk and took his own seat in a black Aeron chair behind it. He moved with an arrogant grace. When he sat down, he inclined the chair, but his legs were long enough to remain flat on the floor. He carefully removed his sunglasses, folded them and laid them on the glass desk, and then steepled his fingers. His eyes were blue-gray underneath trimmed eyebrows.

'I assume this is about Mr Lane?' Gerard held up a hand before Stride could interrupt. 'I sent one of my security men there as a liaison when we saw the police arrive. He kept me informed about the incident.'

'Incident?' Stride asked. 'One of your guests was brutally murdered less than a hundred yards away from your door.'

'Yes. It's very unfortunate.'

'Because of all the bad publicity?' Stride remarked acidly, not sure why the man got under his skin. He had considered casino security himself for a day or so over the summer but had decided he didn't want to live in the lion's mouth.

Gerard smiled thinly. 'Not at all. The sad truth is, Detective, that publicity only helps us. Our gross will go up for weeks because of the murder. If it were all about that, I would have shot him myself. No, Mr Lane was a regular customer, and a generous one. We will miss him.'

'Did you know M.J. was in the casino this evening?' Stride asked.

'Of course. Mr Lane and Ms Westermark arrived together around ten o'clock and were escorted to a private gaming room to play black-jack.'

'Is this gaming room visible from the main casino floor?'

'No. The guests who play there don't wish to have an audience.'

'Was it just the two of them, or were there others in the same room?' Stride asked.

'It wasn't uncommon for M.J. to be part of a crowd,' Gerard said. 'But tonight it was just the two of them.'

'How long did they play?'

'About two hours. Around midnight, the two of them left the gaming room to visit her suite.'

'Did they go through the main casino to access her room?' Stride asked.

'No, there's a private elevator,' Gerard replied.

'Did you watch them?' Amanda asked.

Gerard didn't blink, and his voice was like honey. 'What do you mean?'

'I mean, we both know you have a camera in that private elevator. So we can sit here while you find the video clip, or you can tell us

23

that you got a call when M.J. and Karyn were leaving, and you tracked them in the elevator on that nice big monitor back there.'

Stride wasn't sure if Gerard was the kind of man who ever sweated, but he had to believe there was a sticky film gathering on the back of the man's neck. All three of them knew Amanda had scored a bullseye.

Gerard inclined his head slightly, like a politician conceding a point in a debate. 'They were frisky,' he acknowledged.

'But your valet told us that Karyn left early.'

'That's right. Ms Westermark left her suite after five or ten minutes, alone. Mr Lane followed a few minutes later. He looked agitated.'

'We know Karyn left the casino,' Amanda said. 'What did M.J. do?'

'He returned to the blackjack table and played for another hour. He was drinking heavily. Around one in the morning, Mr Lane told me he was planning to take a walk. I got the picture.'

'What did M.J. talk about after he came downstairs?'

'He mainly talked about Walker Lane, his father. It's no secret to anyone who knows Mr Lane that he and his father don't see eye to eye. I don't exactly get along with my father, either.'

'Have you had any unusual trouble with casino security lately?'

Gerard actually laughed enough to show a glint of teeth. 'Unusual would be a day when we did *not* have something unusual, Detective. Casinos run on money, alcohol, sex, and emotion. I don't have to tell you, it's a volatile combination.'

'But nothing involving M.J.?' Amanda asked.

'No. Our VIP patrons rarely cause that kind of trouble. They're more like children who play too hard. Sometimes their toys break.'

'We want to see some of the casino tapes from this evening,' Stride said. 'Can we do that from here?'

'Of course. But nothing odd happened in the blackjack suite, I assure you. And there's no sound on the tapes.'

Stride shook his head. 'I don't want the blackjack suite. I want the casino floor. If someone was following M.J. I want to know if he was in the casino.'

Gerard was proud of his eyes in the sky.

When he clicked a button on the mouse, dozens of thumbnail video feeds fanned onto his screen like cards dealt on a table.

'We were among the first casinos to go all digital in our cam system,' Gerard explained. 'Everything's burned for permanent storage. No more swapping out hundreds of tapes every day. You win more than

24

a thousand dollars at a sitting, we keep your face on file forever. And we can capture anyone's face in the casino and run a comparative search against our database and the Metro and Gaming Control files in a few seconds. Some of our technical staff used to work for the Bureau.'

He used the mouse to click on one of the thumbnails, and a larger image of a middle-aged Asian woman playing a Five Play video poker machine filled half the screen. The quality, Stride had to admit, was dazzlingly good. With a practiced nudge of the joystick, Gerard focused on the woman's hands and zoomed in until they could clearly see her stubby fingers selecting each button.

'Most people know we're watching,' Gerard said. 'But they don't realize the power of the technology.'

'Let's check the cam on the main doors around ten o'clock,' Stride said. 'You can do that?'

Gerard nodded. 'All of the images are time-stamped.'

'I want to see M.J. arrive and see if anyone follows him in,' Stride added.

Stride untangled himself from his chair, and he and Amanda crowded around Gerard, watching over his shoulder. Gerard slid his chair further under the credenza and brushed imaginary lint from his coat sleeve. He caressed the mouse like a lover as he swept the cursor around the screen at lightning speed.

'Here we are.'

Stride watched M.J. Lane and Karyn Westermark arrive through the revolving doors. Karyn wore an oversized purple football jersey, white short-shorts, and white high-heeled boots that hugged her calves and accentuated her long legs. M.J. was wearing the same grunge-cool outfit – untucked shirt and loose shorts – in which they had found him a few hours later. Not a care in the world. Stride always felt slightly nauseous seeing videotape of victims shortly before their deaths. Their faces were unaware, oblivious to the fact that the sand had almost run out of the hourglass. The black-hooded devil stood right behind them, polishing his scythe, and they smiled and laughed as if death were years away, not exhaling on their skin.

'Keep the tape going,' Stride said.

They followed the parade of people entering and leaving the casino for another two minutes. Then Amanda extended a finger, almost touching the screen.

'There,' she said. 'On the left.'

The man emerging through the left-hand door wore a faded blue baseball cap with the bill tugged down low on his face. He tilted his

25

head down, staring at the ground as he walked. They could only just make out the dark stain of a beard obscuring the lower half of his face.

'Tan khakis,' Stride said. 'Windbreaker. I think that's him. The son of a bitch is ducking the cameras.'

'Ten to one the beard's a fake,' Amanda said.

'We need to find him again,' Stride said, as the man disappeared out of camera range. 'He looked like he was turning toward the front desk.'

Gerard fingered the joystick. Less than a minute later, he tracked the killer down at a nickel slot. His hat was askew, at a casual angle to anyone who looked at him, but strategically placed to minimize the camera's view.

'He knows where we have the cams,' Gerard observed unhappily.

'Where's that machine?' Stride asked.

'Opposite the VIP lounge.'

Stride nodded. 'So he can see M.J. leaving.'

Gerard zoomed in, but the close-up footage didn't offer much more for them to see. Looking at the thick beard, Stride agreed with Amanda – it was a fake. And the man's cheekbones and nose looked as if he may have used putty to doctor his appearance further.

'We'll want a print,' Stride told Gerard, 'for whatever good it does us. And it would be great if you could have a tech review the other cameras and see if we get a better angle on this guy.'

'Of course.'

'Run the feed out,' Stride told him. 'Let's see what he does.'

Gerard accelerated the footage, but the killer's movements were so precise that it hardly mattered. He seemed frozen, with the rest of the action of the casino speeding behind him in a blur. Every minute, he played a single nickel from the twenty-dollar bill he had fed into the machine – so he could sit there for hours without exhausting his stake. He never appeared to be studying the entrance to the sheltered VIP area, but Stride recognized him instinctively as the kind of man whose eyes didn't miss a thing. Cool. Methodical.

Shortly before one o'clock, M.J. reappeared. Gerard slowed down the tape again. M.J. was obviously drunk now, and he weaved as he headed for the exit. The killer at the nickel slot stretched his arms lazily, betraying no interest. But he stood up, prepared to follow. Stride could imagine the adrenaline pumping, making the man hyper-conscious. M.J. was alone. The kill was close.

Then the man at the machine did something. It happened so fast that Stride wasn't sure he had really seen it.

'Stop, stop,' he said quickly. 'Back up. What the hell was that?'

Neither Gerard nor Amanda had noticed anything. Gerard backed up the tape and then, on Stride's instructions, let it go forward in slow motion, frame by frame. As M.J. disappeared in the background, the killer got up, every movement now jerky and unnatural, like an old penny movie machine.

Stretched. Pushed the chair in with his foot. Brushed past the machine as he moved to follow M.J.

Reached back with his hand.

'Son of a bitch,' Amanda said, seeing it.

'Freeze it!' Stride told Gerard.

As the killer walked away, he casually planted his thumb in the center of the slot machine's glass window and rolled it, leaving a perfect print.

Stride felt his stomach turn upside down, as if he had boarded a tunnel-of-love ride and found himself on the wild tracks of a roller-coaster instead. He felt the tingling chill of fear on his nerve ends.

'He must know he's not in the system,' Amanda whispered.

Stride stared at the frozen image on the screen. 'It's more than that,' he said. 'He wants us to chase him.'

Four

As Stride and Amanda climbed into his Bronco, he heard his cell phone ringing inside his blazer pocket. He had recently replaced a ring tone of Alan Jackson's 'Chattahoochee' with 'Restless' by Sara Evans, although it wasn't the same without Sara's amazing voice. But something about the song touched a lonely ache in Stride's soul every time he heard it. It was all about home, and for the past few months his sense of home, of where he belonged, had fled from him.

He flipped up the phone and heard Serena's voice.

'Bet you missed the glamour of this job,' she told him. He had crawled out of bed unhappily at one in the morning.

Stride felt himself relax. He had fallen so much in love with her that he felt it physically, deep in his gut, even though he wondered how the two of them could survive together in this city. Or how *he* could survive. She was his oasis, a dream to which a man lost in the desert could cling.

'Yeah, I missed being out with the night creatures,' Stride said. 'I think Sawhill enjoyed giving me a reminder.'

'Hey, you wanted back in the game, Jonny,' Serena teased him. 'I told you to stay home and be a kept man.'

Stride laughed. She was right. When he retired from the force in Duluth and moved to Las Vegas to join Serena, he was just like that Sara Evans song. Restless. His whole life had been in Minnesota. A beautiful first wife, his childhood sweetheart, now deceased. A second wife, recently divorced. Maggie, his partner and closest friend. And all the cold, vast spaces of the far north – the great lake, the endless stands of birch and pine. Home.

But after the last murder case he investigated – the case where he met Serena – his roots had been pulled up. He had been at loose ends for the last two months in Vegas, needing to work again. He had thought about getting a PI license, but he couldn't imagine himself

28

hiding in the desert brush, spying on cheating spouses. Then, with a spin of a slot machine wheel, a Vegas homicide detective had walked off the job with a fortune in his pocket. Suddenly, Stride was back in.

'Any regrets?' Serena asked. 'Wish you'd stayed in bed? Wish you'd stayed in Minnesota?'

Her voice was light, but he heard a pointed question there. Every now and then, she wanted a reality check on where they were.

'I definitely wish I'd stayed in bed,' he told her.

He didn't take the bait about Minnesota. He knew it was too early to tell about the job and Las Vegas and what that meant for their future. They hadn't really talked about it, because they both liked things the way they were and didn't want to screw it up.

'What's the case?' Serena asked.

Stride told her about the body and heard her whistle long and loud when he said the victim was M.J. Lane.

'How come everyone knows about this guy but me?' he asked.

'If you read my *Us* magazine in the bathroom now and then, you'd know these things,' Serena said.

Stride sighed. 'I've already been told that I'm culturally deprived.' He added, 'We're heading over to M.J.'s condo now.'

'You got a partner with you?'

'Amanda Gillen,' Stride said.

'*Amanda?*' Serena retorted.

Her voice was loud enough to be heard throughout the truck. Stride glanced at Amanda, who stared discreetly at the lights of the city as he drove. But he recognized a smirk twitching on the corner of her lips.

'Nice girl,' Stride said.

Amanda laughed out loud.

'Uh, Jonny, you do know . . . ?' Serena asked.

'Yeah, I know.'

'I hope this means I have nothing to worry about.'

'Never assume,' he told her. 'You're up early too. What's going on?'

'A cop spotted an abandoned car in the parking lot at the Meadows Mall. I'm picking up Cordy. The uni thinks it may be the vehicle used in the hit-and-run on the boy in Summerlin last week.'

'That's good. You needed a break.'

'Yeah.'

She sounded more tired than excited. Stride understood. Child killers were the toughest cases to handle, and the death of the boy, Peter Hale, had hit Serena hard.

'I should go,' Stride told her. They were nearing M.J.'s condominium.

'I know. Me too.'

Neither of them hung up. Even the silence of air on their phones felt like a lifeline, connecting them.

'Hey, Jonny?' Serena added. 'Watch your back. This isn't Duluth.'

Stride pulled off Paradise Road in front of the Charlcombe Towers condominium complex. He leaned forward and stared upward through the windshield. The old and the new, he thought.

The three forty-story white towers, gleaming and new, reached for the night sky on the west side of Paradise. The balconies of multi-million dollar apartments crept up the building walls like a stairway to heaven. A scant block away, crumbling and dark, was a vestige of old Las Vegas – one of the last of the 1960s-era casinos. A princess of its time grown tired and haggard. Still standing, but not for long. Stride had already learned that old didn't last long in this town.

Amanda pointed at the derelict casino, ready for implosion. 'Boni Fisso is launching a big new project called the Orient over there, once they detonate the old place. An Asian-themed resort. It's supposed to cost almost two billion dollars.'

'Why Asia?' Stride asked.

'Lots of whales in Japan and Singapore, I guess. And I think they figure China's the next capitalist up-and-comer. The outside's going to look like a Ming dynasty palace.'

'Too bad M.J. won't be around to enjoy the view,' Stride said.

He pulled up to the security gate and waved at the guards. Their faces were stony and suspicious, studying Stride's dusty truck.

'Should have brought the Spyder,' Amanda told him.

It took them almost forty-five minutes to talk their way past the guards and into M.J. Lane's one-bedroom condominium, which was midway up the northern tower on the twenty-eighth floor. Inside, Stride snapped on gloves but lingered in the wood-floored foyer. He wrinkled his nose. 'Pot,' he said.

He wandered down two steps into the living room, which featured a giant stone fountain in the center, two rich leather sofas, and an entertainment system that took up most of the west wall, including a seventy-two-inch high-definition television. The place was a mess, despite the tens of thousands of dollars that someone – M.J.'s father? – had plowed into chrome art, a cherrywood dining-room set, and chandeliers sculpted out of silver and crystal. M.J. treated it like a college dorm. A skin magazine lay open on one of the sofas. Dozens of DVDs spilled onto the floor in a messy pile in front of the television. Remnants of breakfast for two – cereal and soured milk, cold coffee – littered the dining-room table, along with the scent of a half-smoked joint that hung in

30

the stale air. He saw men's underwear and women's panties on the carpet near the open doorway to the master bedroom.

'M.J. had a guest,' Stride said.

'And it wasn't Karyn Westermark,' Amanda added.

Stride's forehead furrowed. 'How do you know?'

'No way Karyn wears underwear.'

Stride chuckled. He studied the unmarked DVDs on the floor and pushed the play button on the digital recorder. An image jumped onto the oversized television screen. Guttural moaning surrounded them from hidden speakers throughout the condo. Stride saw a man spread-eagled in bed, with a naked girl straddling him, her conical breasts dangling over his mouth. Stride thought for a moment that he was watching a porn film, but this was a home movie. The man on the bed was M.J. He didn't recognize the woman, but her wiry chestnut hair didn't match the straight-arrow blonde locks they had seen in the security footage of Karyn Westermark at the Oasis.

'Some guys don't learn,' Amanda said. 'You'd think winding up on the internet in your own nudie flick would make you a little more careful about this kind of thing.'

Stride stopped the playback. He noticed a phone and an answering machine on the glass skirt surrounding the gurgling fountain. The red light was flashing. When he tapped the button, an electronic voice announced that M.J. had three messages.

'M.J. it's Rex Terrell. I thought we could trade some secrets. I showed you mine, how about you show me yours? Give me a call, OK?'

Terrell left a number, which Stride jotted down in his notebook. The call had come in just after noon on Saturday.

'You know who Rex Terrell is?' Stride asked.

Amanda shook her head.

The next message was from Karyn Westermark, short and sweet.

'It's Karyn. I'm in town, baby. Seven o'clock at Olives. See you then. Love ya.'

'So we know they had dinner at Bellagio,' Amanda said. 'I wonder if Karyn knows about the brunette in M.J.'s latest porno movie.'

The last message began with several seconds of silence. The tape crackled. Stride heard movements in the background, a man clearing his throat, strains of classical music. Finally, the words came, in a growly voice split by halting, uncomfortable pauses. Gaps where he didn't know what to say. There was raw pain in his tone.

'M.J. it's Walker . . . please don't stop listening, don't delete the message. We need to talk . . . You're wrong . . .'

Stride hit the pause button. 'Walker?' he asked.

'Walker Lane. The producer. M.J.'s father.'

'What you've heard isn't true, and I wish there was something I could say to make you believe that . . .'

The last pause went on longer than the others, and Stride thought the message was over. But then the voice continued, softer, pleading.

'I wish you'd come home. I wish to God you didn't live there . . . I want to tell you the truth, face to face . . . I'm going to try your cell phone. If we haven't talked when you get this, call me.'

Walker Lane hung up the phone. The time stamp on the recording was midnight, right around the time that M.J. and Karyn were entering her suite at the Oasis. An hour before someone followed M.J. into the street and shot him.

Stride looked around the room again. He saw a few framed photos of M.J. with various celebrities, mostly women. There was a photo from years ago of a very young M.J. with a woman Stride guessed was his mother. But nothing of his father. Not a sign anywhere that Walker existed, except for the smell of money.

'I wonder if he called M.J.'s cell phone. That might explain why Karyn left early and why M.J. was upset.'

'That's not the voice of a man who paid to have his son murdered,' Amanda said.

'No. But I want to know what they were arguing about.'

They continued searching the condo. Stride found more drugs, inside a well-stocked liquor cabinet – a carved wooden box that contained a large bag of marijuana, a glassine envelope with several ounces of cocaine, and two prescription bottles with what appeared to be Oxycontin. The labels had been scratched off.

'He looks like a high-end user, but not a seller,' Amanda said.

Stride nodded. He began loading and sealing the drugs in an evidence bag.

'What's with the Maserati?' Stride asked, catching Amanda's eye. 'You didn't buy that on a cop's salary.'

Amanda shrugged. 'I had to sue the city last year. Discrimination. Harassment. You wouldn't believe the shit I put up with.'

'I think I would,' Stride said.

'Anyway, the city settled with me. The court made the brass say the right things, and most of the obvious crap went away. But they don't want anything to do with me.'

'Cops are all men, Amanda. Even the women.'

'Don't I know it,' she said. 'The settlement was pretty good. Low seven figures. Nobody ever dreamed I'd stick it out. I'm sure they thought I'd take the money and go away. But the hell with that. I bought the Maserati, put the rest of the cash in the bank, and kept on working. It drove them crazy.'

Stride laughed. He liked her in-your-face attitude. It reminded him of Maggie, his long-time partner in Duluth.

'It's been hard on my boyfriend, though,' Amanda added. 'I feel worse for him than for myself. We hooked up about six months after I made the change, and that was four years ago. And no, he didn't know, not at first. And yes, it was a shock. But he's come around.'

'I really wasn't going to ask,' Stride told her.

'Come on, you were curious. Everyone is. That's OK.'

'Guilty,' he acknowledged.

'You're lucky, you know,' Amanda said. 'With Serena. She's beautiful.'

'Yes, she is,' Stride said.

Serena's beauty had knocked him over when he first saw her. Long black hair that his fingers couldn't help but glide through. Emerald-green eyes that danced and teased him. Suntanned skin and just a few dry lines creasing her face that told him she was past thirty and cruising toward forty. A tall, athletic body that she worked like hell to keep trim.

Amanda saw it in his eyes. 'You love her, don't you?'

'I sure do,' he said.

'I love Bobby, too,' Amanda said. 'He takes a lot of shit, and he sticks around.'

'That's worth a lot.' Stride suddenly stopped dead and rolled his eyes. 'You picked the name, didn't you? *A man*-da.'

Amanda grinned slyly. 'Most people never get the joke.'

'Let's go in the bedroom,' Stride said. He added quickly, 'To search.'

The lush carpet in M.J.'s bedroom was black, and so was the furniture, all shining black lacquer. The left wall was floor-to-ceiling windows, with double doors in the middle, and Stride could see city lights through the wooden vertical blinds. M.J.'s California king was on the opposite wall. A checkerboard comforter, black and red, was half off the bed, and the burgundy sheets were a mess. Stride noticed a condom wrapper on the floor.

'Check the bathroom, OK?' he said.

Amanda disappeared through a doorway next to the bed. Stride turned his attention to the desk on the far side of the room, which was a war zone of unopened mail, bank statements, men's magazines, and receipts from restaurants and hotels. He sat down and began sifting through the piles.

'More pills,' Amanda announced when she returned. 'Lots of Ecstasy.

And take your pick – Levitra, Cialis, *and* Viagra. He could have played tennis with his cock.'

Stride winced.

'Anything there?' Amanda asked.

'I haven't found a date book or a Palm Pilot. He had upwards of ten million in his bank accounts, probably courtesy of Walker. He gambled a lot, all over town and in the Caribbean, too.'

'Stalkers? Hate mail? Lawsuits?'

'Not so far.'

'So what's our motive?' she asked. 'Why would anyone want to kill this guy?'

Stride rubbed his eyes, feeling the lack of sleep catch up with him. 'It doesn't look like he owed money to anybody. We might have a love triangle going on between Karyn and the mystery brunette in the video, but I think everyone cats around on everyone else in this crowd. Doesn't seem worth killing over, not with a hired gun. He did drugs, but what else is new? He was having an argument with his dad. That's as much as we've got, and it ain't much.'

'Unless we've got a psycho on our hands.'

Stride got up from the desk. He thought about the killer on the videotape, leaving his fingerprint for them. 'Yeah, that's something we have to consider.'

He saw a newspaper folded on the nightstand next to M.J.'s unmade bed and picked it up. The pages were already yellowing, and he saw when he checked the date that it was more than three months old. He read the headline:

Implosion to Make Way for 'Orient'

There were photographs covering most of the front page. Boni Fisso shaking hands with Governor Mike Durand over an architectural model of the lavish new resort. The showroom of the old casino in its heyday, forty years ago, with near nude dancing girls on stage. A billowing dust cloud from one of the earlier casinos that had been leveled in a few seconds with the efficiency of a bomb.

'Have you ever seen an implosion?' Stride asked Amanda.

'Yeah. I worked security when they brought down the last tower of the Desert Inn,' she said. 'It's awesome. An implosion always means a party around here.'

Stride nodded. He saw an old issue of *LV*, the city's monthly magazine, lying under the newspaper. There was a corner photo of the same old casino on its cover and a teaser headline beside it:

Amanda spied over his shoulder. 'He lives upstairs, you know, if you want to say hi.'

'Who?'

'Boni Fisso. He owns this whole complex, like the hotel across the street. I'm pretty sure his penthouse is in this tower.'

Stride knew Boni Fisso's reputation. He was one of a dying breed of Las Vegas entrepreneurs, a holdover from the mobbed-up days before the city went corporate. Fisso had to be over eighty, but he still looked suave and sharp in the newspaper photos, an old man who hadn't slowed down. He was short, barely five foot six, but built like a fire hydrant that you could kick and kick and never dent.

'What's your take on Boni?' Stride asked. 'Is his money clean?'

'That's hard to believe, but no one's ever proved otherwise,' Amanda said. 'Gaming Control has had him in their sights for years, but they never had the goods to put him in the Black Book. Either that, or Boni has juice with some politician on the inside. Either way, he's been able to play the game. Pretend he's like Steve Wynn, just an honest developer and philanthropist.'

'Does Boni have a connection to M.J.?'

Amanda shrugged. 'Not that I know of. Why?'

Stride gestured at the magazine and newspaper. 'It looks like M.J. was very interested in the new resort.'

'Well, his balcony looks right out on the implosion site. He was going to watch the Orient rise from the ashes for the next couple years if someone hadn't ventilated his skull.'

Stride nodded. He knew Amanda was right. It was nothing significant. But something niggled at him anyway. Little things did that to him – colorless pieces of the puzzle that didn't fit. M.J. had too many fish to fry in this city. Drugs. Parties. Women. Why keep a months-old magazine by his bed? What was it about the Orient project that was so important to him?

A two-billion-dollar development, underwritten by a man whom everyone suspected of mob ties – that was certainly worth killing over, if someone got in your way. But Stride didn't see how a playboy like M.J. could be a threat to a man like Boni Fisso.

Stride wandered across the bedroom to the double glass doors that led to the balcony. He unlocked them and stepped outside. A breeze made the vertical blinds slap and twist. There was no furniture outside, just a long stretch of iron railing and a view toward the north end of the Strip. He grabbed the railing. His heart fluttered a little in his chest at the height. He imagined M.J. standing here, high on cocaine, wondering if he could sprout wings and fly. The young are stupid, Stride thought. He realized that M.J. probably never came out here, probably never even opened the door. He had Karyn Westermark naked in his bed, and probably countless other women, and that was a better view than all the lights of the Strip combined.

Stride stayed outside. He wondered, just for the briefest moment, if *he* could fly. It was cool and beautiful up here, late September weather, when the worst of the heat was over and the nights had a taste of fall. To the east, there was a ruddy glow where the sun inched up to dawn above the mountains. But the valley was still wrapped in night – although night never really had a firm grip here. It was the land of the neon sun.

He stared down at Boni's old casino, across the street, its roof about ten stories below him. The building itself was black, stripped of life. On street level, a hurricane fence and a makeshift plywood wall gated off the property, no more hotel guests, no more high rollers. In the weeks since the property closed, the demolition teams had already moved inside, ripped out the guts, drilled holes in the walls to plant cylinders of dynamite. In another couple weeks, with a push of a button, a simple electrical charge, the whole house of cards would come tumbling down.

Stride thought of the photo in the newspaper. Girls on stage. Men in tuxedoes. Martinis. Money. All ghosts now.

He let his eyes travel across floor after floor, all of them quiet and dark.

Except for the roof. The roof was aglow.

It was such a Vegas thing to do, Stride thought, to leave the light on after the party was over.

A scalloped parapet stretched across the roof like a row of tiny onion domes. Where the roof notched downward in the very center of the hotel, he saw faintly the tiles and trees of what must have once been the garden of the casino's penthouse suite. All of it was reflected in the glow of the casino's sign, which still blazed out of the darkness in flashes of red and green neon that gave the ghosts inside a reason to believe they were still flesh and blood. No one had told them it was time to go.

Every few seconds, the sign would fade to black, and then each letter would illuminate again, one by one, like nothing had changed, like the floors below still pulsed with life.

One by one, letter by letter, until the entire name blinked on top of the roof.

Sheherezade.

Five

Serena could see that Cordy was down. When she picked him up at his apartment in North Las Vegas, he wore a hangdog expression, like a kid who had been forced to stand in the corner. As they drove back south through the city streets, he stared sourly out the window without saying a word. Even his hair was having a bad day. Normally, it was greased back on his skull like a jet-black lion's mane, but this morning there were tufts sprouting out in odd places like grass growing through the sidewalk. Not like Cordy at all.

'What's up with you?' Serena asked, while they waited at a red light. There was almost no traffic at Cheyenne and Jones. They were in the short stretch of dead hours when the midnight crowd was finally in bed, and everyone else was drowsily starting to come awake.

Cordy gave a long, dramatic sigh. 'Me and Lav,' he said. 'We're history.'

Lavender was a gorgeous black stripper who towered over Cordy by at least six inches. During the time Serena and Cordy had been partners, he had used up girlfriends like tissues, going from one to the next, each one tiny, blonde, and young. Lavender was different, and when they had started dating, Serena thought Cordy might finally have met his match.

'What happened?' Serena said.

Cordy rolled down the window of Serena's Mustang and spat. He cursed in Spanish. 'What do you think, mama? I fucked up. I screwed one of her friends. Lav found out.'

'Shit, you are a stupid man.'

'I blame it on this goddamned city,' Cordy told her irritably. 'All this fucking flesh. I mean, put a guy like me in a room full of sweet chillies, sooner or later I'm going to take a bite.'

'Only this time, the bite came out of your ass.'

She let Cordy stew silently as she turned onto Jones. She wanted

37

to tell him that the real problem was that he listened to his cock, not his brain. But he wasn't entirely wrong about Las Vegas. She knew that. You couldn't put so much sin in one place and not tempt people across the line.

Serena had spent more than two decades in Las Vegas, including ten years on the job as part of Metro. There were plenty of ex-showgirls on the force, and most people assumed Serena was one of them because of her tall, lean physique. But she had lived through a much less glamorous side of the city in her early days, arriving in the dead of night from Phoenix with her girlfriend Deirdre when she was sixteen.

There were about a thousand roads to ruin for young girls coming to Vegas. Stripping, hooking, gambling, drinking, stealing, fighting, doing drugs, filming porno, or just winding up in the wrong man's bed. All of them led to the same end, turning pretty young flowers into garbage floating amid the green algae of a swamp.

Like Deirdre. Her best friend, her savior, the girl she owed her life to, the girl who said she needed Serena more than anything in the world. Dead.

Sometimes it amazed Serena that she hadn't died, too. She had chosen a back-office job in one of the casinos when she could have made ten times that in the strip clubs, looking the way she did. She had stayed in school, first studying to get her GED, then working nights and weekends to get a degree in criminal justice at UNLV. It took her ten years to make it that far. When Deirdre died, the guilt sent Serena spinning into an alcoholic stupor that cost her two years of her life and almost everything she had worked for.

Eventually, she climbed back, dried out, and went back to college.

She wasn't sure where the determination came from. Maybe it was because, when she escaped from Phoenix with Deirdre, she had made a promise to herself that what she had gone through at home would not destroy the rest of her life.

But Cordy was right. Las Vegas didn't make it easy.

'I can make you laugh,' Serena told him.

'No way. I'm in mourning. I'm wearing black.'

Serena glanced at him. Cordy wore a black silk shirt with two buttons undone, tapered black dress pants, and buffed leather shoes. But that had nothing to do with Lavender. Cordy was a creature of style, a small but slick package. Serena herself liked to be casual, not fancy, wearing jeans, T-shirts, and weathered cowboy boots on most days.

When she dressed up, she knew she could pop men's eyes out. She remembered meeting Stride for the first time at the airport in Duluth, when she flew in as part of the investigation of a girl's murder in Vegas. On a whim, she had worn one of her hot outfits, baby blue leather pants, silver belt, midriff-baring T-shirt, black leather raincoat. That was the only time she had seen Jonny at a loss for words.

'Twenty bucks,' Serena said.

'You're on. I ain't laughing today.'

'Sawhill put Jonny on the street with Amanda,' she told him.

Cordy laughed despite himself. 'Oh, mama! Amanda? You know, her breasts are even bigger than yours.'

'News flash, Cordy. She's got equipment bigger than yours, too. Or so I hear.'

'It gives me the creeps just thinking about it.' He added, 'Hey, how do you know that Amanda's boyfriend is a couch potato?'

'I'm afraid to ask.'

''Cause he likes to turn on the TV!' Cordy laughed until he snorted.

Serena shook her head. 'Just keep that kind of crap between us, *muchacho*. Jonny seems to like her. And hand over twenty bucks.'

'Uh-huh. Speaking of which, there's a pool going on Stride. Most people think he'll crash and burn in a couple months.'

'Jonny's as tough as they come,' Serena said.

'Yeah, but this is Vegas.'

Serena didn't want to argue. Not because she thought Cordy was right, but because she could think of a lot of reasons why Stride might walk away that had nothing to do with the job.

'I suppose there's a pool on me, too,' she said. 'On whether Jonny and I will make it.'

'The odds on you are about as long as Keno,' Cordy said. 'Most of the guys, they still think you're Barbed Wire.'

Serena winced, but only because Cordy's words struck a nerve. Her reputation on the force – well deserved – was as the cool beauty, smart and unapproachable. Barbed Wire. She was the girl who cut men off at the knees, skewering egos with a sharp joke, and building a tall fence around her emotions. A sexy package that no one could seem to unwrap.

As far as Serena was concerned, that was OK. She had never trusted men. In Phoenix, as her mother sank into a cocaine addiction, her father had skipped town, leaving Serena to fall through the ground along with her mother. They wound up living in an apartment near the airport with a half-Indian drug dealer named Blue Dog. Most of the time, her mother owed him money for her drugs. Serena became the currency.

She didn't like to think about those days. The best defense was pretending they didn't exist. Like Pandora's box. Better to keep the lid closed and not see what was inside, because there was no going back. And so she became a closed book to anyone who wanted to get near her. At thirty-six, she had never had a serious relationship, never really missed it, never really wanted it.

Until Jonny.

She didn't know how Stride had broken down her walls so easily. Maybe because he was so unlike the men in Vegas, not slick, not a game-player who wore the face he thought you wanted to see. He was a cloudy pool of emotions himself, just like her, where you couldn't see the bottom. That depth attracted her immediately. When he let her inside his own walls, told her about losing his first wife to cancer, her heart cracked into pieces. They barely knew each other, and yet she knew he had fallen for her, the real way, the hard way. And she had fallen for him.

But it was one thing to make love on the beach at midnight in Minnesota. That was a fantasy. Back here, this was life. This was day to day.

Pandora's box was open. She didn't like what she saw. Goblins from her past, flying out, following her in the dark. She prided herself on being tough as nails, but lately she sometimes felt like a frightened teenager again. Frightened about love, about sex, about the future. She was more confused than she had been in years.

She had only told Jonny bits and pieces about her past and about what was happening to her now. Partly, she was used to relying on herself and dealing with her problems alone. She didn't want help. Partly, she didn't want to scare him away by showing him that she wasn't solid to the core, that her armor had been pierced.

Besides, she knew he was struggling too, trying to find his way. Homeless. That was as much as he'd been able to say to her. He felt homeless. Serena understood how he felt, being displaced from the only life he had known, but hearing him talk like that set off all kinds of warning bells in her mind. As if one day he would decide that home was somewhere else, away from Vegas, away from her.

Serena pulled into an open-air lot on the north side of the Meadows Mall. It was her mall, just a few miles from her town home; she had shopped there for years. No talking statues and giant aquariums, like at Caesars. No stores catering to celebrities who dropped a hundred thousand dollars a visit. It was just Macy's and Foot Locker and Radio Shack, the kind of ordinary stores where ordinary people shopped. Serena loved it, because the whole mall felt normal, as if it could be dropped into any other suburb in any other city. There was nothing Vegas about it.

At five in the morning, the parking lot was a vast, empty stretch of pavement, just a handful of lonely cars spread out like pins on a map. The street lights were still on, throwing pale circles of light on the ground. But dawn was near. Halfway across the lot, a patrol car was waiting for them. Its headlights were on, its engine running. As they pulled alongside, Serena saw that the officer at the wheel had his window rolled down, his arm dangling outside, a cigarette smoldering between his fingers. The car they had come to see was parked twenty yards away, a midnight-blue Pontiac Aztek.

Seeing them, the policeman scrambled out of his patrol car and reached back in to stub out his cigarette. He was gangly and tall, and his uniform was baggy at the shoulders. His blond hair was cut as if his mother still sat him in a chair and clipped him with a bowl over his head. He kept picking at his long chin as if he had a pimple that wouldn't go away. Serena didn't think he could be more than twenty years old, and she realized that he was both terribly earnest and terribly nervous.

Serena got out of her Mustang. 'Good morning, officer,' she said. 'You got us out here pretty early.'

'Yes, ma'am,' he told her, with a Texas twang in his voice. 'I do realize that, and I'm real sorry. I'm Officer Tom Crawford, ma'am.'

Serena introduced herself and Cordy, and Crawford did everything but curtsy.

'How long have you been on the force, Tom?' Serena asked.

'Oh, coming on a month, I guess.'

Pretending to rub his eye, Cordy glanced at Serena and mouthed, 'Shit.'

Serena shook her head and sighed. Rookies.

'Well, Tom, you've got a blue car here. We had a witness who thought they saw a blue car speeding away after the hit-and-run on the boy. But that was in Summerlin, which is several miles and a few tax brackets away from here.'

Crawford nodded, still scratching his chin. 'Yes, ma'am, I read the incident report about that boy Peter Hale and the hit-and-run in Summerlin. Terrible thing. Word for word, I did. And I've had my eyes open all week for a blue car. See, we got a call overnight from the security company that patrols these lots, and they said this here car hadn't been touched in at least a week or so, and they were figuring it was abandoned. They were planning on having it towed, and they wanted to know if we wanted to take a look at it first. The overnight

41

super, he thought we should just let them yank it. But I heard it was blue, see, and we're just a whiz straight down the parkway from Summerlin. And that accident was just about a week ago. So I thought it was worth checking out.'

'It took the security company a week to call it in?' Serena asked, shaking her head.

'Yes, ma'am, I'm afraid so. They rotate a lot, is what I think, and the guy who made the rounds tonight hadn't been in the lot since last weekend.'

'Go on,' Serena told him, yawning, and hoping she hadn't been dragged out of bed for nothing.

'Well, when I came out here, the first thing I did was check the front of the car. And sure enough – well, let me just show it to you.'

With loping strides, Officer Crawford guided them around to the front of the Aztek and used the big steel flashlight on his belt to illuminate the car. Serena sucked in her breath. The dead center of the hood was bowed, the grill punched in. The shell of the bumper was cracked and the license plate twisted like it was on its way to becoming a paper airplane.

Crawford got down on his knees. 'If you look real close here, you can see fibers stuck on the grill. And there's other stuff, too, could be skin and blood.'

Serena had seen half-eaten corpses in the desert without her stomach turning over. But something about the damage to the car – not much damage at all, really, for what it had done – left her swallowing back bile.

'Good work, Tom,' Serena told him somberly. Cordy was silent, but his copper skin paled. He kicked the ground with the toe of his shoe, his hands shoved in his pockets. Only Crawford seemed unaffected and even enthusiastic about what he had found. But he was young, and this was a big deal, the kind of story he'd be telling the other rookies for the next year. He hadn't been in the Summerlin street last Friday afternoon to see Peter Hale's broken body, blood puddling under his head. To hear his mother wailing. To see the vacant, dead grief in his father's eyes.

It was an upper middle-class neighborhood, the kind where both parents had good jobs, and twelve-year-old boys were latchkey kids, taking the bus home after school, letting themselves inside to watch television and play video games. Linda and Carter Hale thought they were lucky. Linda Hale didn't work. Peter had someone to open the door for him after school. He had been playing outside in the driveway, tossing a tennis ball against the door and catching it in his mitt, when Linda

42

Hale heard the thump all the way inside the kitchen. And she knew, the way any mother knows that something catastrophic has happened. She found Peter outside, half on the sidewalk, half on the street. No one around. No witnesses. The most they found was a maid three blocks away who caught a glimpse of a blue car racing through the neighborhood around the time of the accident. The lab was dragging its feet figuring out the model from the blue paint and the pieces of grill. But Serena knew that didn't matter now. It was an Aztek. It was this car.

'Did you search inside the car?' Serena asked.

'No, ma'am, I sure didn't,' Crawford assured her. 'The car was locked, and that wouldn't be procedure anyway. I didn't touch a thing.'

'How about running the plates?'

'Well, that I did do. Yes, ma'am. The car is registered to Mr Lawrence Busby. He doesn't have a sheet. Thirty-four, African American, six foot two, two hundred forty-five pounds. Or that's what his driver's license says. Mr Busby reported the car stolen at eight thirty last Friday night.'

'Several hours after the accident,' Serena said. 'Isn't that convenient?'

Crawford offered her a shy, country-boy smile. 'I thought so myself. A little too convenient. That's why I offered Mr Busby a free ride over here to collect his vehicle.'

'You did what?' Cordy asked.

'I got the supervisor to send a patrol car over to Mr Busby's home on Bonanza. You know, in case he decided to make like a prairie dog and scamper. Then I called him. Told him we had found his car and we'd be happy to bring him over to the scene. He should be here in a couple minutes.'

'You're one smart Texan, Officer Crawford,' Serena told him.

'Thank you, ma'am. That's what my mama says. My wife, she's not so sure.'

'How did Busby sound on the phone?'

'Well, the first thing he asked was whether there was any damage,' Crawford said. 'Guess that's natural, but I thought it was interesting. I told him it was nothing a good body shop couldn't make go away.'

Serena thought about it, trying to put herself in Busby's shoes. He's just killed a kid. He's afraid someone saw the car, or that he left evidence behind at the scene that would lead them right to his doorstep. Another perp who watches too much *CSI*. So he ditches the car at the mall, then hops the bus home and reports it stolen. If he's lucky, no one ever connects it to the accident. If they do, he's laid the blame on someone else.

But something didn't smell right. The Summerlin neighborhood in which the Hales lived was lily-white, and she figured that a black man the size of Lawrence Busby would have attracted somebody's attention. She also couldn't understand why Busby, who lived a couple miles from downtown, would be speeding around a residential neighborhood on the far west side of the city.

'Open the car for us, will you, Crawford?' Serena asked. 'I'd like to take a look before Busby gets here.'

'Don't we need a warrant for that?'

Serena shrugged. 'That's a stolen vehicle, according to Mr Busby. We need to look for evidence of who stole it.'

Crawford popped the trunk of his patrol car, pulled out a stiff narrow wire with a loop at one end, and disengaged the lock on the driver's side door of the Aztek in a few seconds. Taking care not to disturb any prints, he gingerly swung the door open.

Serena peered inside, then squeezed behind the wheel. She looked around. Busby had cleaned up after himself. The interior was spotless, vacuumed clean, no papers or trash. With the tip of a pen, she opened the glove compartment, but found only the owner's manual inside. She pulled open the ashtray. It was unused.

She heard the back door open.

'Anything up front?' Cordy asked.

'Zip.'

'I'll check under the seats.'

Serena saw a flashlight beacon scooting like a searchlight on the floor. Cordy whistled.

'Come to papa,' he said. 'Got a piece of paper here. Looks like a receipt.'

Serena got out of the car and watched Cordy maneuver his arm under the seat. He emerged triumphantly a few seconds later, clutching a two-inch by three-inch white slip in the tiny jaws of a tweezer. He shone the flashlight on the paper, and Serena leaned in with him to get a better look.

The receipt was from a convenience store somewhere near Reno, more than four hundred miles to the north. Six Krispy Kreme doughnuts and a Sprite at eight in the morning. Breakfast of champions. The receipt was dated more than two weeks prior to the accident.

'I reckon that's Mr Busby now,' Crawford said, as a second patrol car pulled silently into the lot.

As the car drew closer, Serena could see what looked like a grizzly bear in the front passenger seat. His driver's license stats didn't do him justice. Lawrence Busby had to weigh three hundred pounds. He had a moon-shaped face, black hair cut as flat as a pan on top of his skull, and jowls that drooped like the face of a bloodhound. Serena could see a sheen on the man's ebony face. He was sweating.

'I bet *his* breasts are bigger than yours, too,' Cordy said, winking.

Serena fought back a grin. She saw Busby reaching for the door handle, and she held up a hand like a crossing guard stopping traffic in its tracks. The woman cop inside the car spoke sharply to Busby, and Serena saw the whites of his eyes get bigger. He put his hands back in his lap. Now he was sweating and scared.

Cordy crooked a finger at the cop in the patrol car, who got out and joined them. Serena approached the car and climbed into the driver's seat. She left the door open, then used a button to roll down the passenger window. Cordy came over on that side, leaning his elbows on the door.

The car stank. Busby was wearing a gigantic Running Rebels T-shirt, and odor wafted from the wet stains at his pits and under his neck. His legs, like tree trunks, grew out of white shorts. Shifting nervously, he passed gas, then mumbled an apology. His eyes darted back and forth between Serena and Cordy.

'Mr Busby?' Serena asked. 'Is that your car there?'

Busby nodded. His chins swayed.

'How long have you owned it?'

''Bout two months,' Busby mumbled. For a large man, he had a voice so soft that Serena had to strain to hear him.

Cordy jutted his face through the window. 'You fit in that car, man? I wouldn't think you'd fit in that car. What do you do, steer with that gut of yours there?'

Busby looked like he was about to cry.

'That's enough, Cordy,' Serena said sharply. 'What do you do for a living, Mr Busby?'

'I'm a chef at the Lady Luck downtown.'

'A chef!' Cordy hooted. 'They ever wonder why the guests look hungry and you got a big smile on your face?'

Busby meekly shook his head. 'I don't steal nothin'.'

'Do you work any other jobs?' Serena asked. 'Anything to bring in a little extra cash?'

'No, I've been full-time at the Lady Luck for five years.'

'You ever been to Summerlin, Mr Busby?'

'That rich place out west? Don't think so. No reason to.'

'You didn't go out there last Friday afternoon?' Serena continued.

'No. Like I said, I've never been there.' He wiped his forehead with a hand the size of a football. 'What's this all about?'

45

'This is about the kid you killed, you lying sack of shit,' Cordy told him.

Busby shook his head furiously. His eyes got even bigger and whiter. 'I never killed nobody.'

'You ran down a little boy,' Cordy insisted. 'Then you ran away like a piece of pussy, didn't have the balls to tell his mother what you did.'

'You're crazy,' Busby murmured. He turned to Serena. 'He's crazy. I didn't do that. No way.'

'You want to tell us how your car got stolen?' Serena asked coolly.

'I parked in the Fremont Street lot downtown last Friday. When I came back, it was gone. I called it in. That's what happened.'

'This was about eight thirty in the evening?'

'Guess so,' Busby replied. 'Sounds about right.'

'And what were you doing downtown?' Serena asked. 'Playing the slots?'

'I wasn't playing, I was working,' Busby said. 'Like I told you, I cook sausage and eggs at the Lady Luck.'

'When did you get to work?' Serena asked. She didn't like where this was going.

'Around noon, like always.'

'You mean you parked the car in the Fremont ramp before noon?' she repeated, just to be sure.

'Course. That's what I do every day. That's what I'm saying.'

Serena closed her eyes, feeling sick again. This time it was because she knew they were wrong. He had an alibi. She thought about Cordy teasing the man about his gut and then remembered, too, the tight fit as she slid into the Aztek to search. Wrong, wrong.

'Anybody work with you?' Serena asked. She knew she was wasting her breath. He wasn't the one.

'Well, yeah, you've got a bunch of other cooks and waitresses in and out all day.'

'Did you take any breaks? How about a lunch break in the afternoon?' She was grasping at straws, and she knew it.

'No, I don't take a lunch break. I work straight through.'

Serena couldn't help smiling. She eyed the man's whale-like physique. 'Come on, Mr Busby. No lunch break? You?'

Busby smiled too, for the first time. 'The fact is, I'm trying to cut back. And, well, I guess I do have a little snack from time to time on the job.'

Serena sighed. 'So tell us what happened to your car.'

'Not much to tell. I left work at the usual time, went back to the

46

lot. No car. I always park in the same spot, so it's not like I could have lost it. It just wasn't there.'

'Any relatives have keys to your car?'

'I don't have much in the way of relatives,' Busby said. 'Mama's dead, Daddy's in the nursing home. Nobody wanted to marry me looking like this.'

Serena nodded. She felt like shit now, putting this poor man through the ringer. A sad, lonely life, and all she could do was sprinkle in a little more pain and fear. And she was going to have to tell him that he couldn't have his car back tonight.

She gestured to Cordy, and the two of them huddled. Cordy popped a piece of gum in his mouth and began chewing loudly. 'He didn't do it, did he?'

'Nope.'

'So what does that mean?' Cordy asked.

Serena stopped and thought about it. The more she did, the less she liked the implications of what they had found. It didn't feel like an accident any more. It felt like something much worse.

'Somebody steals a car downtown, and then just happens to get into a vicious hit-and-run in a suburb the same afternoon?'

'He killed the kid deliberately,' Cordy concluded.

'It sure feels that way.'

Serena remembered the receipt for the Krispy Kreme doughnuts. She returned to the patrol car, where Busby was waiting, and leaned inside.

'Did you go to Reno last month, Mr Busby?'

Busby frowned. 'No, I've never been to Reno. Not ever.'

Six

Stride waited in Lieutenant Sawhill's office, swirling coffee in his mug and staring down through the third-floor window at a black cat slinking across the street outside and disappearing into a garbage-strewn backyard. Not long after, a policeman sped by on a mountain bike that looked several sizes too small. His ass hung over the seat, and his knees were almost at his chin. The cat and the cop, both patrolling for rats.

The Homicide Detail operated out of the Downtown Command, Metro's flagship building, modern and beige, its entrance lined with palm trees. The city fathers had located it in one of the city's uglier neighborhoods, a few blocks from the downtown casinos, as if the presence of the police headquarters might somehow bring down the surrounding crime rate by osmosis. It wasn't working.

Stride checked his watch and saw it was almost noon. His stomach was growling. He wasn't sure what he wanted to do more, sleep or eat.

Behind him, the office door opened and closed. Stride nodded at Lester Sawhill, who frowned and pointed a finger at the chair in front of his desk. The phone rang, and Sawhill picked it up. The lieutenant settled himself into his own leather chair, which was so large compared to his small frame that it made him look like a child visiting Daddy's office. Stride took a seat too, and waited.

'Good morning, Governor,' Sawhill announced, looking unimpressed, as if he talked to the governor every day.

Serena said she couldn't remember ever being in Sawhill's office when he wasn't on the phone with a politician. He liked an audience. It reminded everyone of where he stood in the pecking order.

In Minnesota, Stride had reported to the deputy chief, a leprechaun of a man named Kyle Kinnick – K-2, they called him – who had elephant ears and a reedy voice that sounded like a clarinet played

48

by a six-year-old. Sawhill wasn't much taller than K-2, but he was a smoother piece of work. He seemed to get a haircut every five days, because the neat trim of his balding brown hair never changed at all. He had a narrow face like a capital V, pockmarked cheeks, and half-glasses that he wore on a chain around his neck when they weren't pushed down to the little round bulb at the end of his nose.

Sawhill wore a modestly priced gray suit, old but well kept. His uniform. It didn't matter if it was a July day under the blistering sun, according to Serena. Sawhill never went so far as to open the collar button of his shirt or loosen the knot in his tie. He never raised his voice, which was toneless but utterly in control. He didn't seem to have any emotions at all, at least none that made their way onto his face or that lit up his brown eyes.

'That's a very nice gesture, Governor,' Sawhill said into the phone. He had a pink stress ball on his desk that he squeezed rhythmically, his slim fingers tensing. Every now and then, he studied a fingernail, as if it might need filing.

Stride may as well have been invisible, listening to the one-sided conversation.

It had taken years for Stride to trust K-2, because deep inside Stride always believed that moving up the ladder in the police bureaucracy meant being a smart politician and giving up the things that made you a good cop. But K-2 was different. For him, the cops came first. Stride respected him for his loyalty.

Maybe someday Lester Sawhill would convince him that he, too, was on the side of the angels. But Stride didn't think so. That wasn't to say that Sawhill was a bad man. He wasn't. Stride knew he was intensely moral. A Mormon, like so many senior officials in Sin City. No caffeine. No tobacco. No alcohol. And lots of kids – at least seven, Stride figured, counting up the photographs he saw propped on the bookshelves behind Sawhill's desk. But Sawhill put God and Vegas first, not his cops.

Stride didn't know how Sawhill and the other Mormons survived here. They could work in the casinos, but not gamble. They were religious in a godless town. He found it strange and a little hypocritical, like a bartender who thinks drinking is evil but doesn't mind watching others pour poison down their throats.

Sawhill hung up the phone. 'That was Governor Durand,' he explained, in case Stride had missed it. 'That should give you an idea of the concern that exists over this homicide.'

'I'm aware of that,' Stride replied.

'This is a very public case, Detective,' Sawhill added. 'A celebrity murder. The communications department is already fielding press inquiries from around the world.'

Stride could translate Sawhill's meaning easily enough. If the lieutenant had known it would turn out to be such a high profile case, he would never have turned it over to his black sheep, the untested detective from Minnesota and his transsexual partner. Not in a million years. But it was too late to yank them. Unless Stride gave him a reason by screwing up.

'And that reminds me,' Sawhill continued. 'Direct any media inquiries to the PR office, OK? You've got a case to solve. I don't want you wasting your time with reporters. That goes for Amanda, too.'

Amanda most of all, Stride thought. Sawhill didn't want either of them representing the city or, worse, snatching the limelight.

'What's the status of the investigation? I need to tell the mayor something.'

'We have the perpetrator on film,' Stride said. 'He left us his fingerprint. Deliberately. That's a pretty ballsy move. And not like a hired gun who's just doing a job.'

Sawhill narrowed his eyes. 'Were his prints in the system?'

'No. We couldn't get a good read on his face, either. He knew where the cameras were. All in all, one cool customer.'

'But you're sure he was after Lane? This wasn't a random thrill kill?'

'It wasn't a typical hit. But random? No. He was after M.J. Tracked him and killed him.'

'You have a line on a motive?' Sawhill asked impatiently.

'Drugs, gambling, women. Pick one, you've got a motive. But so far no reason to think any of them got him killed.'

'So how do you plan to crack the case?' He was the inquisitor now, probing for a weakness, looking for Stride to give him an excuse to pull him off the murder.

'We're doing a sketch from what we've got, which isn't much. The Oasis is reviewing their entrance tapes for the last month, to see if he was inside casing the joint and may have been a little less careful about keeping his face hidden. We're backtracking M.J.'s route that day and using the sketch to see if anyone spotted the perp when he picked up M.J.'s tail. Amanda and I are talking to everyone who knew M.J. or saw him recently, to see if we can pick up a thread on who he might have pissed off. And I want to talk to M.J.'s father. There was something going on between them. It may be nothing, but it's the only sign so far that anything was amiss in M.J.'s party-boy life.'

Sawhill shook his head. 'It might be better if I talked to Walker Lane myself.'

'Why is that?' Stride asked, struggling to betray no irritation in his voice.

'Walker Lane is a wealthy, influential man,' Sawhill said. He sounded like a teacher lecturing a slow student. 'The governor himself was the one to break the news to Mr Lane about the murder. I assume you're not suggesting Mr Lane is a suspect?'

'I have no reason to think so,' Stride said. 'But there was a dispute between Walker and M.J. We think they talked an hour before he was killed. It's possible that M.J. was involved in something that led to his death, and Walker might know what it is.'

Sawhill drummed his fingers on his desk. He nodded, looking unhappy. 'All right, fine. You do the interview. But tomorrow, not today.' Stride began to protest, and Sawhill waved it aside. 'Let's give Mr Lane a decent time to grieve. You've got plenty of other leads to follow. And kid gloves, Detective. He's a powerful man who just lost his son.'

'Understood,' Stride said.

'How are you and Amanda getting along?' Sawhill asked. His face was stony, but Stride wondered if the man was hiding a smile.

'No problem. She's smart. I like her.'

'Ah. Good.'

He sounded disappointed.

Stride barely had time to return from Sawhill's office when Amanda poked her head around his cubicle wall.

'We've got company,' she told him brightly, her eyes twinkling. 'Karyn Westermark in the flesh. And I do mean flesh.'

Stride followed Amanda to the third-floor conference room, which sported large windows looking out on the rabbit's den of cubicles that made up the detective squad.

'Why'd they put her in the fishbowl?' Stride asked.

Amanda just grinned, and Stride understood when he reached the windows and saw that Karyn wore a white dress shirt, unbuttoned, with its flaps tied in a loose bow beneath her breasts, which were in serious danger of spilling out each time she leaned forward. Stride also noticed that most of the detectives had found reasons to take the long way to the kitchen to buy soda, a route that steered them past the windows of the conference room.

He went in and told Amanda to close the blinds.

'Sure, make me the bad guy,' Amanda muttered under her breath.

Karyn stood up and reached across the desk to shake his hand, offering another expansive view of her cleavage. Stride didn't dare let his eyes drift south, and he saw faint amusement in Karyn's face, as if she were enjoying his struggle.

'I'm Karyn,' she said, pronouncing her name as if it were spelled Corinne.

Stride wasn't familiar with her as an actress, but Amanda had already prepped him. *Us* magazine, Amanda told him again. Karyn was an up-and-coming soap star, trying to make the leap to the big leagues. She was LA stunning, with straight blonde hair that reached well below her shoulders and glowed like a summer wheat field. She had a model's long face and cool blue eyes, which reflected the sharp intelligence of someone who knew exactly how much power she had simply because of how she looked. Through the glass table top, he saw a red skirt that ended at her mid-thighs, and then a long, silky expanse of bare legs.

'Thanks for coming in to talk to us, Ms Westermark,' Stride said. 'Can I get you a cup of coffee?'

'A skinny no-foam latte would be great,' Karyn replied.

'I'm afraid we have black coffee, and we have white powder with little plastic spoons,' Stride replied. He added, 'The powder goes in the coffee.'

Karyn smiled at him, but there was ice in her eyes and the barest nod of appreciation. 'No coffee.'

'I'm very sorry about M.J. It sounds like the two of you were close.'

'I don't think I'd go that far,' Karyn replied.

'No? We heard you spent a lot of time together. Including last night at the Oasis.'

'We were fuck buddies,' she said with a shrug. 'We'd hook up when we were both in Vegas. Party. Gamble. Screw. That's all.'

'Were you shocked to hear he'd been murdered? Right after you left him?'

'Sure.'

Stride didn't think she was likely to break down crying.

'Do you have any idea who killed M.J.? Or why?'

Karyn shook her head. 'None at all.'

'When the two of you got together, was it usually at the Oasis?'

'Most of the time. But we'd go other places, too. The Hard Rock. Mandalay. If there was a fight or a concert, we'd be there.'

'How long had you known him?' Stride asked.

'A couple years. I met him at a party at the Oasis. You know, he was young, cute, threw money at everyone. What's not to like? He had a limo with him that first night, and we went for a ride, and I guess that's how it all got started.'

'You had sex with him?' Stride asked.

Karyn leaned forward. Her breasts grazed the tabletop. Through her smile, he saw a glint of her cherry-red tongue. 'I made a bet with him at the party that I could make him come using nothing but my right nipple.'

Don't ask, don't ask, don't ask, Stride told himself.

'Who won the bet?' he asked.

Shit.

Karyn's eyes danced. He could see gold flecks in a sea of blue. 'We had a bottle of Krug at Spago that night. M.J.'s treat.'

Stride cleared his throat and tried to stay on track. 'Was this a serious relationship?'

'What, like marriage? No way. I didn't want to sign an eighty-page pre-nup.'

'Did M.J. see other women?'

'I'm sure he did.'

'Like who?' Stride asked.

'I didn't really keep track, Detective. The only one I knew about was Tierney Dargon.'

Stride wrote down the name. 'What can you tell me about her?'

'Tierney likes to pretend she's part of our crowd. But she was just a cocktail waitress who got lucky and married some rich old comedian.'

'Comedian? You mean Moose Dargon?' Stride asked.

'That's the one.'

Stride had heard of Moose Dargon, a comedian from the Rat Pack days who had a reputation as a bad boy in his prime. He had seen him on television a couple times and remembered almost nothing from his act except that the man had an amazing set of eyebrows, which rippled on his face like giant caterpillars. He hadn't even realized that Moose was still alive.

'What does Tierney look like?' he asked, thinking of the brunette in the video they had seen in M.J.'s condominium.

'Brown hair, sort of kinky. Thin. Pretty.'

That description fitted the girl in the video, as well as half the women in Las Vegas, Stride thought.

'Moose must be in his eighties,' he said. 'How old is Tierney?'

'Maybe twenty-five.' Karyn laughed. 'I'm sure it was a love match, Detective.'

'Was Tierney around last night?'

'I didn't see her. But M.J. said Tierney was always hanging on him. He was looking to get rid of her. I mean, she's got a tight little body, but she's still just a waitress.'

'Did Moose Dargon know that M.J. was having an affair with his wife?'

'You'd have to ask Moose,' Karyn said.

'If M.J. was seeing other women, what were you getting out of the relationship?' Stride asked.

'He was rich,' Karyn replied. 'I like to live that way. Besides, whenever I was with him, the paparazzi usually hung out. I'm not at a point in my career when I can afford to find that annoying. I need them.'

'But there were no photographers last night,' Stride said.

'I only got into town that afternoon. I guess they hadn't smelled us out yet.'

'Who else knew the two of you were going to be together that night?'

Karyn thought about it. 'My assistant. She's in LA. And my parents in Boca Raton.'

'Who did you tell here in town?'

'Well, the people at the Oasis when I checked in. I also used a bodyguard while I was shopping in the afternoon, but I told him I wouldn't need him for the evening. And I made reservations in our names at Olives.'

'Who do you think M.J. would have told?'

'I really don't know, Detective. I didn't know much about the other parts of his life.'

'How about the videotape of you and M.J.?' Stride asked. 'The one that wound up on the internet. How did that happen?'

'You mean, why did I make it?' Karyn asked, licking her glossy lips. 'Or do you want me to autograph your copy?'

'I mean, how did it get stolen?'

Stride thought he saw a ghost of a smile on Karyn's face.

'I have no idea,' Karyn said. 'But I'm sure glad it did. I got more ink from taking it up the ass in that video than I would have got with an Academy Award.'

'How did M.J. feel about the tape getting out?' he asked.

'He thought it was cool. No one knew who he was before that.'

'Let's talk about the parties at the casinos. Any drugs there?'

Karyn's eyes narrowed. 'I'm starting to feel like I need a lawyer.'

From the doorway, Amanda broke into the conversation. 'This is Vegas, Karyn. What happens here, stays here, remember? We're not

54

out to bust you for anything. We just need the real dope. So to speak.'

Karyn noticed Amanda for the first time and gave her a long, careful look. She nodded approvingly.

'OK. Sure. We've been known to take the occasional snort.'

'Who supplied?' Stride asked. 'You or M.J.?'

'I don't want to know where it comes from, OK? If it's there, then I'll be a recreational user like anyone else. But I don't buy, I don't sell.'

'And M.J.?'

'Supply was never a problem with M.J.,' Karyn said. 'I don't know where he got it.'

'Any ideas?'

Karyn shrugged. 'There are always hangers-on. People at the fringes. Maybe it's a driver. Or a waiter. When you've got the kind of money M.J. did, and you lead the kind of life he did, you don't have to worry about it. Those people find you.'

'Did they find M.J. last night?'

'Not that I saw.'

'What kind of life did M.J. lead?' Amanda asked. She was doing her best to look cool and cynical, but Stride thought that Amanda was a little star-struck by Karyn's presence.

'He was the life of the party,' Karyn replied, pinning Amanda with her blue eyes. 'It's fun being in the fast lane, you know. You should join us sometime, Detective.'

'I've got more than you can take,' Amanda replied, laughing.

'What, because you're a tranny?' Karyn asked. She smiled as Amanda's mouth dropped open in astonishment. 'You can pass with a lot of people, Detective. But a real woman knows the difference. Not that I have a problem with it. A lot of people in our circle would find it a turn-on.'

Stride interrupted. 'Here's the problem I have with all this, Ms Westermark. M.J. may have been the life of the party, but someone followed him and put a bullet in his brain. So somebody had a beef with him.'

'I don't know who,' Karyn said, reluctantly breaking eye contact with Amanda and turning back to Stride. 'M.J. was the gravy train. He was the one paying all the bills. Who's going to mess with that?'

'He never lost his temper?'

'M.J.? No. He was a little kid. He wanted everyone to like him. The only time I ever heard him arguing with anyone was with his dad. They went at it all the time.'

'His dad is a movie producer in Canada, right?' Stride asked.

'Sure, like Tom Hanks is some actor,' Karyn replied dismissively. 'Everyone in the business knows Walker Lane. Hell, I admit it, I first came on to M.J. because I thought he would put in a good word for me with the old man. But I learned fast enough that M.J. didn't want anything to do with Walker, except take his money.'

'He tell you why?'

'No, but it was always something. They argued about money. They argued about his mom. They argued about M.J. living in Vegas. I was at M.J.'s condo a few weeks ago when Walker called. M.J. went ballistic. Took the phone and threw it against the wall. I'd never seen him like that.'

'Do you know when he last talked with his dad?' Stride asked.

'Sure. Last night.'

'What were they talking about?'

Karyn shrugged. She played with a scrap of paper on the desk, rolling it into a ball and rubbing it between two long nails. 'I don't know. But M.J. was pissed. So was I. We took a break from the black-jack tables and went up to my suite to fool around. I was really in need of a good fuck, you know? But we barely got started when M.J.'s cell phone rang. It was Walker. They yelled at each other for a few minutes, and M.J. wasn't in the mood any more. So I left. I told him to grow up.'

'Then what?'

'Then nothing. I went to a club, was there until almost five. I hear M.J. went back to the tables and kept drinking. And then he went out to find a hooker. Bad choice, huh? If he'd stayed with me, this never would have happened.'

Or you'd be dead too, Stride thought. 'I'd really like to know what he and his father were arguing about,' he said.

'And like I told you, I don't know. You'd have to ask Walker. But here's something for you. I mean, I heard something M.J. said to his dad. Pretty ironic, given what happened to him.'

'What did he say?' Stride asked.

Karyn gave him a cat-like smile. 'He called Walker a murderer.'

Seven

Serena felt it as soon as Linda Hale let her inside her Summerlin home. Grief.

It hung in the air, multiplying like a virus. It clung to the furniture, gathered in the deep carpet, and threw a blurry film over the lights. Each room carried a tiny echo of loss, unmistakable, heartbreaking. There were toys still littering the floor in the den. A kid-sized Wilson football. PlayStation cartridges. A Harry Potter book. No one had picked them up, Serena knew, because no one could bear to touch them. You'd get grief on your fingers.

The silence was the worst of all. It wasn't meant to be a quiet house. Twelve-year-old boys made noise. Shouted. Turned up the volume on the stereo. But there wasn't a sound any more. Right now, a marching band could have come down the hallway, and Linda Hale would have smiled.

They sat around a solid oak breakfast table, in a porch off the kitchen that looked out on a small, carefully landscaped cactus garden. Mrs Hale clutched a mug of coffee with both hands. There were family photos, a lifetime collection of memories, strewn across the table, dumped from an old shoebox.

'We found the car used in the hit-and-run,' Serena told her.

Mrs Hale nodded but didn't react. She was staring at the photos, shiny eyes moving from one to the next.

Like Serena, she was in her mid-thirties. Her blonde hair was cut in a short bob, a functional cut for a stay-at-home mom, quick out of the shower and off to Peter's soccer practice. She didn't need much makeup, but she wore silver earrings and a slim silver chain around her neck. She wore a stylish Kuhlman shirt with the cuffs folded back.

'Your husband is an executive at Harrah's, is that right?' Serena asked.

'Yes,' she replied softly. Her mind was still on the photos. On the past.

The house was large for a family of three. Linda Hale kept it well appointed, frequent trips to Pottery Barn, every china knick-knack carefully placed and dusted. Precise. Ordered. She probably used to have trouble getting Peter to pick up after himself. Once upon a time, it must have driven her crazy.

Serena studied the photos. They spanned decades. She picked up one, staring at a little boy's glowing eyes. He was at the beach.

Linda Hale brightened. 'That's Cocoa, on the east coast of Florida. We took Peter with my mom to Orlando five years ago.' She slid another photo in front of Serena. 'Here he is with Mickey. He was so scared at first. Then he gave him a big hug.'

More pictures. Peter on a bicycle with training wheels, his dad beside him. Peter in a soccer uniform. Linda's mother – it had to be; the resemblance was striking – nose to nose with her grandson at Christmas. Husband and wife in a hospital room, Linda looking tired, holding her new baby.

'Peter looks happy,' Serena told her. It was something to say.

'Very.'

'You look a lot like your mom,' she added, hating small talk, especially with a mother who had lost her son.

'I know, everyone says it. But I'm not glamorous like her. She has showgirl looks, like you.'

'Maybe a decade ago I did,' Serena said, smiling.

'No, no. You've got it, of course you do. So does Mom. Me, I just get older.' She shuffled through the pile and found an eight-by-ten print among the family photos. It was a black-and-white publicity shot of a dancer in full costume, wild with silk and sequins. The girl in the photo, who looked about twenty years old, was a dead ringer for Linda Hale.

'See? Forty years later, and my mom still can have any man she wants.' She laughed. 'Usually does, too.'

'Is your dad alive?'

She shrugged. 'Oh, yeah. Somewhere. Mom's on number four now. Number one was a lot of years ago. Stepdad two was as close to a father as I got. That's one of the reasons my husband and I worked so hard to give Peter a normal upbringing. Why I stayed home with him.'

She took a sip of coffee and put it down on a wooden coaster. She was distant again. Asking questions, Serena thought. Talking to God. Why us when we did all the right things. Made the sacrifices.

'You said you found the car,' Linda said. Serena watched her emotions shift. Despair became anger, and her jaw hardened. 'Does that mean you know who did this?'

'It's not that simple.'

'I don't understand,' she replied.

'The owner of the car wasn't driving it at the time Peter was killed. He has an alibi. Someone stole his car and then abandoned it after the accident.'

'What does that mean?'

Serena explained. 'One possibility is that Peter was struck while the driver of the car was fleeing from somewhere, or rushing to get someplace. Another is that we're dealing with a psychopath, who set out to kill someone, and Peter was in the wrong place at the wrong time. And the other – well, the other is that Peter was the target. That someone killed him deliberately.'

'But that's crazy! He's just a little boy.'

Serena nodded. 'I know. We have to consider the possibility that someone was trying to inflict pain on *you*. That's why I wanted to ask whether it was possible the two of you had any enemies.'

'Enemies who would murder our child?' She shook her head. 'There's nothing remotely like that.'

'I know it's hard to believe. But a mother in Texas hired a hit man over her daughter's cheerleading squad. People are capable of anything. So it would be helpful to know about any disputes, even ones that may seem trivial to you.'

Linda sat back in the chair. Her hands dropped to her sides. 'This is too insane.'

'I know it seems that way. But if there's anything—'

'That's just it, there isn't. We're your average middle-class family. We keep to ourselves. We're not in the public eye. My husband is an accountant, for heaven's sake.'

'Has he dealt with any funny numbers lately? Or received any threats?'

'No, no. This isn't the old days. It's all public companies and SEC filings now. If a casino exec picks up a quarter from the floor, you can find it in a financial statement somewhere. Everything's out in the open.'

'How about the personal side?' Serena asked. 'Please don't take this wrong. I have to ask. Are there any problems with drugs? Money?'

'Sorry, I don't have a secret life. What you see is what you get. Same with my husband.'

'You two are happy? Have there been any sexual issues? Affairs? Things like that.'

Linda's face screwed up. 'Once a week on Friday night is enough for both of us. I hope you don't need to know our favorite position.'

'I'm sorry,' Serena said. 'I know this is intrusive.'

'I just don't see how our sex life is going to help you find out who killed Peter.' Her voice rose sharply.

'I understand your impatience. But this is a very unusual hit-and-run. Most accidents like this involve someone local, often someone who was drinking. They're scared, and they flee the scene. Usually, within a few days, a friend or family member turns them in, or the guilt overwhelms them, and they come in voluntarily. There's no motive. No intent. But what happened to Peter no longer feels like an accident.'

'I realize that, but I can't help you,' Linda insisted. 'We don't have any skeletons in our closet. I'd tell you if we did.'

Serena watched her eyes. There was nothing furtive behind them. 'Do you have any ties to Reno? Have you visited there recently?'

'Reno? Not in years. There are plenty of casinos around here if I want to drop a nickel in a slot. Why?'

'We think whoever did this was in Reno a few weeks ago. We found a receipt in the car. There may be a connection. Do you have friends or family there?'

'No, I'm sorry.'

Serena nodded. 'If you think of something, or if anything unusual happens, I hope you'll let me know.'

'Of course I will. But I really think you're wrong about this. I just don't see why anyone would deliberately hurt our family.'

'That's what scares me,' Serena acknowledged.

'Why?'

'Because it means we may not find this person before he kills someone else.'

Eight

Stride and Serena both made it home separately just before midnight on Sunday. He had been awake for almost twenty-four hours, but he was still too wired on caffeine simply to tumble into bed and sleep. The two of them barely turned on the lights before leaving again and taking Stride's Bronco west into the hills. It had become a night-time ritual for them. They followed Charleston until the houses ran out, before the road wound into Red Rock Canyon. He steered the Bronco off the paved road and climbed a rocky slope to the high ground. They turned around and parked, doors open, windows open, with the night air blowing through the truck and the expanse of the Las Vegas valley stretched out below them. The tracts of suburban homes inching up the street, eating more of the empty space week by week, were dark.

Even in July, when the daytime heat was ferocious, the night cooled in the hills, enough for the breeze sailing down over the peaks behind to make it bearable. Now, in the early fall, there was a hint of chill, like a Minnesota evening without the fragrant scent of pine. He could see literally the entire city, its myriad lights creeping out like vines in all four directions until they finally ran out in the darkness of the desert. Cutting through the middle was the fiery glow of the Strip, taller and brighter than anything else around it, a multicolored, bedazzling belt across the city's fat belly.

From far away, without the sunlight, the valley sparkled. There was no orange rim of smog floating over the city like a smoke ring. The casinos were jewels.

Stride twisted his upper body and stared at Serena's face in silhouette. He knew she felt him watching her. This was the time when it was just the two of them, peaceful, in love, free of the city. 'You are way, way too beautiful,' he told her.

'If you want sex, you're going to have to do better than that,' Serena replied, laughing.

'But that was my best line.'

He smiled and stroked her dark hair, in a way that told her he wanted her. He knew, when they got home, they would be too tired to do anything but sleep, and he very much wanted to make love to her.

She leaned across and kissed him. 'Haven't we proven it's not safe for a man in his forties to do it in a truck? Last time, you almost threw your back out.'

'It was worth it.'

'Don't say I didn't warn you,' she told him.

Serena pulled her T-shirt over her head. Her hair was mussed and sexy. She unhooked and wriggled out of her bra, then stretched her shoulders back. She reclined her seat and began peeling down her jeans. Her skin was firm, her breasts milky white like oyster shells in the pale light. He climbed over her and felt her fingers on his clothes.

He was back in his own seat a few minutes later, sweaty and sore. 'Ow,' he said.

'Your back?'

'Back, arms, legs.'

'I told you so.'

Stride dangled his foot out of the truck and rubbed it against the loose dirt. He hoped that a scorpion wasn't scuttling nearby, or that a rattlesnake wouldn't choose that moment to slither from the rocks. Those were the real night creatures, doing what came naturally, unlike the human ones below them in the valley.

Serena lay next to him, bare and disheveled. She made no effort to repair her clothes. Her eyes were lost, focused into the hills. She touched her skin idly with her fingertips. 'Think the novelty of this is ever going to wear off?'

'Us having sex?'

'Yeah.'

'I hope not.'

'I'm ready to go again,' she told him.

'You're on your own.'

Serena gave him a mock sigh. 'Did it ever wear off with Cindy?'

Stride smiled as a picture of his late wife flashed in his brain. 'No. She was like you. She couldn't get enough.'

'Oh yeah, I'm a sex fiend. I'm just glad vaginas aren't like piercings.'

Stride looked at her. 'What?'

'You know. Closing up from lack of use.'

He threw his head back and laughed, and Serena joined him. Her head fell against his shoulder, and he slipped an arm around her. They sat silently for a few more minutes, lulled by the wind.

The longer they sat, the more he felt her go away somewhere. That was how it usually happened. When they got close, and she felt safe with him, she took another step into her past and pulled another ghost from her closet.

It was a compliment, she told him. She had never done that with anyone else. Her secrets were like notes plugged up in bottles that she had long ago tossed into the sea. Now, one by one, they were drifting back to shore.

He knew only sketches of what she had gone through. Raw facts. She had told him what had happened to her as a teenager in clinical terms, like a doctor reciting from someone else's file. Her mother used her as a whore to pay for drugs. She got pregnant, she had an abortion, she ran away. End of story. Only those kinds of stories never ended.

'What's on your mind?' he asked.

Serena took a long time to reply, and he wondered if she would drop it and go back to something safe, like work or music or the lights in the valley.

'I've been thinking a lot about Deirdre,' she said.

Deirdre was the girl who had come to Las Vegas with Serena when she escaped from Phoenix at the age of sixteen. Serena had never told him much about her. Only how she died.

'Strange, huh?' she went on. 'I really haven't thought about her in years. But she's been in my dreams lately. I fall asleep, and there she is.'

'She got AIDS. That wasn't your fault.'

Serena rubbed her shoulders as if she were cold. 'The thing is, I never went to see her. Maybe there was nothing I could do, but I didn't have to let her die alone. I mean, she saved me. Back in Phoenix? She saved me. I was being abused night and day, and she helped me escape. I loved her, Jonny. I really loved her, those first few years we were together. But I just let her die.'

'You don't need me to tell you that isn't true, do you?' Stride asked.

Serena shrugged. 'No. But it keeps coming back to me. You'd think by now it would all be gone, dead, not a big deal. But I can't switch on part of myself with you and keep the rest shut off.'

Stride frowned. 'How can I help?'

'I'm not sure you can.'

'So I guess one alternative is to shut me off, too,' he said.

'Sure it is. But that's not what I want. I just have to learn how to deal with all this. And keep you around.'

'I'm not going anywhere.'

She turned to him, unconvinced. 'I know how you feel about this place. I'm worried that you'll hate this city more than you love me. You'll go back home to Minnesota, where your heart is.'

'My heart's here with you.'

Serena took one of his hands and kissed his fingertips. 'Thank you for saying that.'

But he wasn't sure she believed him. He wasn't sure he believed himself.

He went to reach for her again, but somewhere on the floor mat, where her jeans were crumpled, they heard her cell phone ringing. Serena laughed, setting the tense moment aside, and found the phone.

Stride heard a man's voice. Serena brightened. 'Hey, Jay, hang on a second.'

She quickly covered the phone and whispered to Stride. 'Jay Walling is a detective I know in Reno. Sixty years old and very dapper. Watches too many Sinatra movies.' She spoke into the phone again. 'Jay, I've got another detective with me. I'm going to put you on speaker.' She pushed a button, and then continued, 'Jay Walling, meet Jonathan Stride, and vice versa.'

'How are you, Jay?' Stride said.

'Excellent, thanks.' His voice had a smooth elegance. 'So, Serena, is this the man you're playing house with? Or did Cordy finally get arrested on a morals charge?'

Even in the darkness of the car, Stride could feel Serena flush with embarrassment.

'Nice to see the rumors have made their way across the state, Jay. Yes, Jonny and I are an item, and no, the women of Las Vegas are still not safe from Cordy. Mind if I ask who told you about us?'

'My lieutenant, actually,' Walling said. 'He's tight with Sawhill.'

'Great, just great.'

'Don't be offended, darling. My wife will be relieved. She's been looking for someone to fix you up with since we worked that case together last year.'

'Don't make it sound like the impossible dream,' Serena snapped.

'Nonsense. You just have high standards. Detective Stride, my congratulations. Serena is one of my favorite people in the whole world, so treat her nice or I'll have to have you rubbed out.'

Stride laughed, and Serena groaned. 'Jay, if you don't shut up, I'm going to have *you* rubbed out. Now did you run down that receipt for me from my hit-and-run car?'

Walling chuckled. 'Six Krispy Kreme doughnuts and a Sprite. At least we know your perp isn't diabetic.'

'Funny.'

'I tracked down the store, but it was a cash sale, and the owner doesn't remember a thing.'

'No surprise. That's what I figured. Thanks for trying.'

'Yes, but there's something else. I was hoping you might be able to fly up to Reno tomorrow.'

'Oh? Why?'

'Because I don't like coincidences,' Walling said. 'The same day your perp got his sugar fix in Reno, a woman got murdered on a ranch a few miles south of here. Someone cut her throat.'

Nine

Stride began to do research on M.J.'s father, Walker Lane, following dozens of links on the web from the computer in his cubicle. There was no official home page about the man, just gossipy sites that rehashed the same dry facts from his Hollywood biography and spiced up the written record with hints about his reclusive lifestyle in Canada.

There was plenty of information about Lane's early days in the 1960s when he was a *wunderkind* producer-director who struck it rich with his first self-funded film. From the beginning, he was about money, not art. *Cherry Tree* featured a fifteen-year-old newcomer, sort of a Hayley Mills with breasts, whose huge eyes and innocent sex appeal won over audiences, despite a lame spy story about a teenager helping George Washington win the Revolutionary War. Two more family comedies followed, both hugely successful, and Lane won a reputation as Frank Capra-lite, the boy with the golden touch. Because he hadn't thrown in his lot with the big studios, he reaped the financial rewards himself.

Scandal dogged him, mostly because there were rumors on the set that he had been having an affair with his under-aged star since their first film together. Lane denied it, but he didn't hide his playboy ways, partying in LA and Vegas, and leaving a trail of photographs of himself with starlets on his arm.

Then came the big disappearance.

As far as Stride could tell, it happened in 1967. Lane left Hollywood, moved to Canada, and essentially vanished from the public eye. From a distance, he continued to build his reputation as a mover and shaker. He chose and funded a series of monster hits throughout the next three decades, deftly moving in and out of comedy and drama as public tastes changed. He never directed again, not as far as Stride could tell, but he became a huge force, a star-maker, without ever stepping foot out of his estate in British Columbia. He was executive producer behind two of the twenty highest grossing films ever.

He became almost fanatically private. Actors and directors who met with him signed non-disclosure agreements. Like Howard Hughes, he seemed to run his empire primarily by phone. Stride couldn't find a photograph of the man taken in the last twenty years. There were rumors of a disabling illness that left him in a wheelchair and of facial degeneration that had ravaged his once handsome, boyish looks – which resembled M.J., Stride realized, looking at Walker's early photos. There were also rumors of a scandal that had driven him out of the country, but as far as he could tell, no one had pierced the veil and uncovered the real story.

He married a young actress in the early 1980s, when she interviewed for a role in a science fiction film he was bankrolling. She didn't get the part, but she got Walker, and two years later, M.J. was born. There were no public details about the relationship between Walker and his twenty-something wife, but somewhere along the line, it went badly wrong. Stride found news reports from 1990 about the woman's suicide. There was no public memorial, no photographs of a grieving Walker Lane, and no public comment. She may as well not have existed.

Stride couldn't find any evidence that Lane had given an interview in decades. That wasn't a good sign. He didn't expect the man to open up and discuss all his father-son secrets with a police detective from Las Vegas.

'You ready for your close-up?' Amanda asked, dropping into the chair squeezed inside his cube. She looked scrubbed and rested, which made him feel old. He had taken Serena to McCarran to catch an early flight to Reno, and two cups of coffee hadn't dented the haze in his head. On the other hand, his body still had the pleasant ache of cramped, sweaty sex with Serena a few hours earlier.

'I'll be lucky if he takes my call,' Stride said.

'He's still a father with a dead kid. He's got to be anxious to find out what happened.'

Stride shrugged. 'Maybe. Sounds like Sawhill practically had to beg the governor to get Lane's number. Nobody wants me to make this call.'

'Except me, because I want to hear what the big guy sounds like. So make it.'

'Let's go in a conference room.'

They took over a small, windowless office and shut the door behind them. Stride had another cup of coffee with him, and Amanda had a cruller and a glass of orange juice. They sat down on opposite sides of the conference table, and Stride dragged the phone to him. Amanda had a yellow pad in front of her. He punched the hands-free button and dialed the number.

He expected to go through five layers of secretaries, personal assistants, and senior aides. Instead, almost immediately, the man answered his own phone.

'Walker Lane.' His voice sounded exactly like it had on the answering machine in M.J.'s condo, but flat, without the emotional pleading. It was a terrible voice, as gritty as sandpaper, an old hound trying to bark like a fierce dog in its prime.

Stride couldn't help but think of the photo he'd found of Walker Lane in the 1960s: absurdly tall, a mop of blond hair, Clark Kent glasses. Cocksure, as if he would someday own the world, which he pretty much did today. But the price he'd paid was chiseled in his voice.

Stride introduced himself and Amanda. Lane didn't sound surprised. Stride wondered if the governor had tipped him off about the call.

'Do you have any idea who killed my son?' he demanded.

Stride explained what they had found on the casino videotapes and the steps they were taking to retrace M.J.'s movements. 'We were wondering,' he added, 'if you had any idea who the killer might be or why he wanted your son dead.'

'No, I don't. I just want you to find him.'

'Did M.J. talk to you about any problems he was having?' Stride asked.

'No.'

'Do you know of anyone in Las Vegas he was particularly close to?'

'No,' Lane repeated.

'What about women in his life? Did you know who he was involved with?'

'I didn't ask.'

Walker Lane didn't waste unnecessary words. Stride realized he was just going to have to lay down his cards.

'Mr Lane, we heard the message you left for M.J. on his answering machine. We know you talked to M.J. shortly before he was killed. There was obviously a significant disagreement between the two of you. Can you tell us what it was about?'

This time there was a long pause.

'That's a private matter, Detective. It has nothing to do with his death.'

'I understand you feel that way, Mr Lane,' Stride said, choosing his words carefully. 'But sometimes we find connections in ways we don't anticipate. Or we can pursue more productive areas of investigation because we can cross things off the list.'

In other words, we'll keep digging until we find out, Stride wanted to say.

Lane didn't take the bait. He didn't say a word.

Stride finally gave up after the silence stretched out too long. 'How long had M.J. lived in Vegas?'

'Since he turned twenty-one.' Lane's tone was clipped, unhappy.

'You didn't approve?' Stride asked.

'No.'

Stride began to understand why the man had never made a movie longer than eighty-seven minutes. 'Why is that?'

'Because the city is a sewer,' Lane snapped. 'It's immoral. A wasteland. There are only two kinds of people living there, users and suckers.'

Amanda casually held up one hand and extended her middle finger at the phone. Stride shrugged.

'When were you last here?' he asked.

'A lifetime ago, Detective.'

'A lot's changed since then,' Stride said.

'Nothing's changed. Nothing at all. Now if you have nothing else, let me go back to my job, and you can go back to yours. Finding out who killed my son.'

'I do have a few more questions,' Stride said.

Lane's impatience crackled through the phone line. 'What?'

Stride was running out of ideas to make the man talk and decided to take a wild leap. 'M.J. seemed to be very interested in that new casino project near his building. The Orient project that Boni Fisso is launching. Do you know why?'

'I have *nothing* to say about Boni Fisso,' Lane hissed.

Stride and Amanda looked at each other. Boni's name had obviously struck a raw nerve.

'Was M.J. somehow involved with the Orient project?' Stride persisted.

Lane exhaled in disgust. Stride wished he were there in person to read the man's body language.

'M.J. didn't care about the *new* casino,' Lane retorted. 'All he could talk about was the Sheherezade.'

'Why is that?' Stride asked.

There was another stretch of silence.

'The Sheherezade,' Lane said. 'When I read it was coming down, I thought finally it would all be over.'

He paused, but Stride could hear the fissures in the dam grow wider. Lane wanted to tell them. Just like he had wanted to tell M.J.

'Boni couldn't just drop it in the dead of night. Let everyone wake

69

up and find a pile of rubble. All its secrets leveled, ready to be carted away. No, no, make it another goddamn tourist attraction. The governor's going to push the button. Half the Congressional delegation will be there applauding. Like it was something noble. Like they were saying goodbye to something sacred.'

'What happened there?' Stride asked.

'Las Vegas killed me, that's what happened,' Lane retorted. 'And now it's killed my son. Both of us. My God, it never ends. Sins live forever in that city. I just never believed it could reach out and destroy me again.'

Stride waited until he was done. He could hear the man gasping for breath.

'You sound like you think you know why M.J. was killed,' Stride said. 'Does it have something to do with Boni Fisso?'

'No, Detective, I don't know why. The past is the past, and I have no reason to think what happened then has any relevance to what happened to M.J. Or any connection to Boni. I don't see how it could.'

'Still—' Stride began.

'Still you want to know. You're curious. That's your lot in life. But I'm sorry. I've said more than I should have already, and I can't say any more.'

Amanda leaned closer to the phone. 'But if it was so long ago, Mr Lane, why not tell us?'

'No, I can't. I'm grieving over M.J. I'm wishing I had been a better father. That's enough pain without dredging up mistakes I made when I was a young fool.'

'Mr Lane,' Stride said, 'we know that M.J. called you a murderer.'

'Yes, he did.'

'Why?'

Lane sighed. 'You'll have to ask Rex Terrell about that, Detective.'

Stride remembered the answering machine message in M.J.'s condo. He quickly checked his notes.

M.J., it's Rex Terrell. I thought we could trade some secrets. I showed you mine, how about you show me yours?

'Who is Rex Terrell?' Stride asked.

'He's a writer,' Lane replied, his voice curling around the word with contempt. 'He's the one who dragged this trash up about the Sheherezade and put ideas in M.J.'s head. Ask him to tell you what I did, and maybe you can find a way to kill me again. I've died many times, Detective. What's once more?'

70

Ten

Serena sped south out of Reno in a rented Malibu, gulping in the sweet mountain air that whipped through the car, and cranking Terri Clark on the stereo until the speakers of the Chevy vibrated.

'I think the world needs a drink,' Terri sang in her Canadian twang.

People sometimes told Serena she looked like Terri Clark, without the cowboy hat. Both tall, with silky dark hair. Maybe that was why Serena liked her so much.

Like the song on the radio, Serena realized that she needed a drink. When she licked her lips, she could still imagine the taste of vodka, although it had been more than a decade since she quit. A drink was a no-no, off limits, *verboten*. She imagined it was like Jonny and cigarettes. It didn't matter if it was one year or twenty, the desire could come back in an instant and take your breath away.

Her mother's face flashed in her brain. She tried to will it away by gazing out the window at the crown of Mt Rose in the distance. But her mother may as well have been hitchhiking by the side of the road like some old episode of *The Twilight Zone*. Appearing over and over, following her. Of all the things her mother had done to her that she couldn't forgive, the worst was passing along her addictive genes. For her mother, the demon was cocaine. For Serena, the demon was alcohol. For two years in her early twenties, she had drunk her way into deadness. She was grateful for AA and for a crowd of strangers who had pulled her back.

Those were the two years after Deirdre died. Funny that she didn't start drinking when the two of them left Phoenix, when the flashbacks of the drug dealer's dirty hands on her breasts still visited her every night. Or that she didn't start when Deirdre began having sex with men for money and encouraging Serena to do the same. No, it was years later, when Deirdre was out of her life. A week after her funeral. One drink became two, two became ten, and ten bled so easily into hundreds.

71

Someone had told her that Deirdre weighed sixty-eight pounds when she died. Serena shivered in the car. The girl she had known was so different, so alive. Red, kinky hair. A trashy way of dressing and walking that men loved, like they loved the tattoo above the crack of her ass, a coiled serpent that seemed to wriggle with pleasure whenever her shirt rode up. She had pale skin, not made for the southwestern sun. Her whiteness set her apart in a town of bronzed bodies. When she was naked in the shower, she almost seemed to glow.

The truth was that Deirdre and Serena were never from the same world. Deirdre was fast in a fast town, a perfect fit. For the first few years, Serena was grateful that Deirdre had plucked her out of the lion's mouth, but sooner or later she was bound to split off and go her own way. Eventually, she left Deirdre and moved out.

They never talked again. When Deirdre died, the guilt came crashing down on Serena, and she filtered it through bottles of Absolut.

She remembered how amazing it was to her that she could put bottles in the freezer and let the alcohol get colder and colder and colder, and still it didn't freeze.

Sixty-eight pounds. God.

Following the directions that Jay Walling had given her, she pulled onto the shoulder at the end of a long dirt track off old 395, near the house where the murder had taken place. She got out of the car and enjoyed the silence. The sounds she did hear were crisp and clear, like the crunch of gravel under her feet and the distant rumble of a plane climbing over the hills out of the Reno airport. A hawk pinwheeled above her, scanning the fields, but otherwise she didn't see another living soul anywhere around her.

A handful of old ranch houses dotted the overgrown fields. Farm machinery lay rusted and unused nearby, and telephone wires sagged between poles. She saw the tall mountains to the west, with evergreens climbing the sides and patches of snow clinging to the very peaks. Closer by, the foothills were covered with auburn down, which would turn green when the rains came.

The house she had come to see was modest, a gray two-story with an RV parked on the side. Its closest neighbor was a half-mile away. There was a large white-fenced meadow in which she expected to see horses, but it was empty, its bitterbrush bending in the cool breeze. The air was fragrant with wild flowers.

She had picked up a large cup of coffee at a convenience store a few miles back. She sipped it while she waited, leaning against the hood of the car. Fifteen minutes later, she watched a white Ford Taurus pull up behind her. It was glossy, as if it had just been washed. Serena figured that Jay Walling probably took personal offense at any dirt particles that had the audacity to affix themselves to his car. She knew Walling well. They had worked a nasty homicide the year before, in which a body had been found in the Las Vegas desert and its head had turned up in the ball rack of a Reno bowling alley. Who said murderers didn't have a sense of humor?

'What say, Jay?' Serena said as Walling got out of the car. 'What's with the bird crap on your coat?'

He looked down in horror, and Serena laughed. Walling wore a black shearling overcoat that must have cost him two thousand dollars, and he pampered it like a baby. He also wore a black fedora that made him look like a holdover from 1950s Manhattan. He was tall, with a long face and a boxy mustache.

'I've missed your sense of humor, sweetheart,' Walling told her. 'I hope my phone call last night didn't interrupt a little love fest between you and Detective Stride. I was truly figuring I would get your voicemail.'

'Ten minutes earlier and you might have heard some heavy breathing.'

'Ah, good.' Walling looked a little uncomfortable with the details. 'So is it serious?'

'I think so,' Serena admitted. 'He seems to think so, too. I'm trying not to screw it up.'

Walling, who knew some of Serena's history, nodded thoughtfully. 'Well, I appreciate your coming up here. Can you tell me more about this receipt you found?'

Serena gave Walling a quick summary of the hit-and-run case in which Peter Hale had been killed and about their discovery of Lawrence Busby's car in the parking lot of the Meadows Mall. 'The receipt was under the driver's seat,' she said.

'No line yet on who stole the car?'

Serena shook her head.

'Shame. This could all mean nothing, but it smells funny. That receipt of yours was from a little convenience store less than five miles away. About two hours after those half-dozen Krispy Kreme dough-nuts got sold, a woman was murdered at this ranch. And then the receipt shows up in a stolen car used in a hit-and-run in Las Vegas.'

'I don't like it.'

'No, neither do I.'

'So what happened here?' Serena asked, inclining her head toward the ranch house.

Walling tugged at his mustache and then removed the fedora. He smoothed his carefully trimmed gray hair.

'Brutal killing. We don't get cases like this very often. Albert Ford came home from a golf game and found the front door open and his wife lying in the foyer. Clean cut across the carotid. Near as we can tell, she opened the door, and the perp dropped her right there. Bloody mess.'

'Motive?'

'We don't have one,' Walling said. 'Nothing was taken from the house. It doesn't look like he even went inside.'

'And no witnesses?'

Walling shrugged and gestured at the empty landscape. 'Out here? Not many neighbors. The road dead ends to the east. We haven't found anybody who saw a thing.'

'What do we know about the woman who was killed?'

'Salt of the earth,' Walling said. 'Both of them. The Fords are multi-generation Reno residents. Both retired. Albert Ford bred horses for decades and sold out a few years ago. His wife Alice was a schoolteacher – third grade. She put in thirty-five years and retired around the same time that Al unloaded the horses.'

Serena shook her head. 'A third-grade schoolteacher?'

'Exactly. It makes no sense.'

'And Al is in the clear?'

Walling nodded. 'His golfing buddies gave him an alibi. Alice had been dead for several hours when he found her.'

'They have kids?'

'Four. All grown. The youngest is in her early thirties.'

'Any of them in Las Vegas?' Serena asked.

'No, two in Los Angeles, one in Boise, one in Anchorage. All clean. Alice has a brother in Reno, but that's it within the state. Al's the only one left in his family.'

'I don't suppose the brother is mobbed up,' Serena said.

Walling laughed. 'Retired director of an adoption agency. He's in a retirement home now.'

'So we have a twelve-year-old boy run down by a car and a retired schoolteacher with her throat cut,' Serena said. 'Nothing similar about the MO, nothing similar about the location. And the only thing we have to tie the cases together is a few doughnuts. Maybe we're just blowing smoke here, Jay.'

'Except both vics do have something in common,' Walling said.

'Oh?'

'We can't find a reason why anyone would want to kill them.'

Eleven

Rex Terrell was thirty minutes late.

It was five o'clock, and Stride and Amanda had a booth in the corner at Battista's, underneath a wall of vintage celebrity photos that spanned the decades. They had already shooed away the accordionist, who was ready to serenade them, and turned down the house wine that came with dinner. But they had finally agreed to accept two bowls of penne with meat sauce, on the house.

Terrell had picked the place, which was on a side street behind the Barbary Coast. 'Real Vegas,' he said. 'A landmark.'

Stride had Terrell's number from M.J.'s answering machine, and he had finally reached him in the middle of the afternoon. It turned out that Rex Terrell was a freelance writer who did gossipy features for entertainment magazines, including *LV*. Stride wanted to know what Terrell had told M.J. Lane about his father and the Sheherezade.

They waited impatiently. Amanda stabbed a few noodles with her fork.

'So what's it like in Minnesota?' she asked.

Stride smiled. 'Are you thinking of moving?'

'Who knows? I know how this sounds, but I wouldn't mind living somewhere a little less strange. Bobby and I have talked about getting out.' She added, 'And it would be nice to be someplace where not everybody knew. My little secret, that is.'

Stride nodded. 'Minnesota is cold.'

'Cold? Is that news? Here's a hint, Stride. That white stuff that hangs around up there for six months? That's called snow.'

'That's not what I mean,' Stride said. 'I don't care about the weather. I used to live right on the shore of Lake Superior. I'd watch the big ore freighters come and go from my patio.'

'So why'd you leave?' Amanda asked.

He hesitated, wondering how much to say, and then realized he was still doing it. Being a Minnesotan, locking everything away. 'I began to realize it was a cold place. Minnesotans are hard to get to know. They don't let you inside. You won't find nicer people anywhere, but you can live with them for decades and never really know them on the inside, where it counts. They don't open up.'

'That sounds a lot like Serena,' Amanda said.

Stride shook his head. 'Don't get me wrong. I'm that way too. And yeah, that's Serena. But we've been able to get to each other in a way that no one else did. I found out I liked it. So to me, that was worth moving for.'

'But you miss Minnesota,' Amanda said.

'Sure I do.'

'What about Vegas? If it's too strange for me, I can't imagine what you think of it.'

Stride let his eyes wander around the restaurant. Terrell was right. This was Vegas in all its kitschy, bitchy glory. He thought about Walker calling the city immoral and about executives like Gerard Plante at the Oasis calmly manipulating his guests. But then there were the mountains and the blue waters of Lake Mead. And Serena. And something irresistible and terrible about all of it together.

He looked up, and fortunately he didn't have to answer.

Rex Terrell was waving at them as he crossed the restaurant, his other arm draped around the back of the maître d'. He wore a lime-green shirt, untucked, over expensive black silk slacks. His blond hair was gelled, sticking up in jagged spikes, and he wore narrow black sunglasses. He was about thirty years old, medium height, and muscular. He carried a lowball glass with a coppery drink that sloshed over the side as he approached.

'Rex Terrell,' he said, jutting out his hand. 'And you're detectives? What a trip. A real murder investigation. This is so *CSI*.'

Stride shook his hand, which was moist, and introduced himself. Amanda did the same.

'Amanda Gillen?' Rex stripped off his sunglasses and leaned into her face. 'Oh my *gawd*, I know you. What delicious headlines. "Metro Sexual: Pre-Op Cop Says Her 'Equipment' is No Big Deal."' He giggled, spilling more of his drink. 'Remember that one?'

'Fuck off,' Amanda said.

Terrell sat down and picked up a fork. He plucked a mouthful of pasta from Amanda's bowl. 'Oh, no, no, I loved it! Your lawsuit? I was with you all the way. I cheered when you won. And look at you, you are so hot! Tranny is definitely the new gay.'

Stride saw the ice in Amanda's eyes. She was holding a glass of water with such force that he thought the glass would shatter in her hand. 'You're poking the bear, Rex,' he told him.

Terrell blathered on. 'Listen, honey, how about an article in *LV*? And we could do a photo spread with it. I don't mean chicks with dicks, not that kind of thing, although wouldn't *that* drive up our numbers! But very tasteful, very erotic, cleavage, maybe a bulge in the right place. I'm talking artistic here.'

Amanda grabbed Terrell's jaw and clenched it until he shut up. She yanked his face toward her. 'Focus, Rex. Listen carefully. I am not a freak show. I am not a circus performer. I'm Amanda. I may be a little different from most people, but all I want to do is lead an ordinary life. What I don't want is people invading my privacy. So leave me alone, or the operation that I chose not to get, I'm going to give to you right now with a butter knife. Got it?'

She pushed Terrell away, and he rubbed his jaw. 'Ow, ow, ow.' He looked at Stride. 'She's a pistol. But I like that, I really do.'

'Maybe we can get down to business,' Stride said.

'Oh, absolutely. I smell a story here. M.J. murdered? I want the dirt.'

Stride shook his head. 'No story, Rex. This is off, off, off the record. And the conversation goes one way. You tell us what you know about M.J.'

'Start by telling us where you were on Saturday night,' Amanda added.

'You think *I* killed him? How exciting. But no. David and I got to Gipsy at ten, and we were there, like, all night.' He winked at Amanda. '*You* can call David and check if you'd like, but not your partner here, because David has a teensy weakness for the strong, silent type.'

'M.J.,' Stride prompted.

'Well, what can I tell you?'

'How did you meet?' Stride asked.

'He called me after the story appeared. Very upset. But who can blame him for that, right? I mean, if it was *my* father . . .'

'What story?' Amanda asked.

Terrell clapped a hand to his heart. 'Best thing I've published in *LV*. I was sure I was going to get death threats, but not a one. I'm disappointed. But I named names, and no one else did. Two big names in particular. Walker Lane and Boni Fisso.'

Stride remembered. There was an issue of *LV* magazine on M.J.'s nightstand, underneath the newspaper story about the implosion.

'What was the story about?' Stride asked.

'It was called "The Dirty Secret of the Sheherezade". Does that give you a clue?'

'M.J. called his father a murderer,' Stride said. 'Is that what you said in your story?'

'He is. Scandalous, isn't it?'

'We talked to Walker Lane. He says you were putting ideas in M.J.'s head.'

'You talked to Walker? And he mentioned *me*? Oh, now that is too much. I wondered if he would hear about it. Walker Lane telling people about Rex Terrell. God, David is going to flip over this.'

Stride and Amanda shared an exasperated glance.

'Tell us about the story,' Stride said. 'The short version, please.'

Terrell nodded. His drink was empty, and he waved the glass in his hand at a waitress.

'The Sheherezade was Boni Fisso's first big place,' he said. 'Now that was Vegas. The real stuff. Like Battista's here. Authentic. I mean, look around most bars in town now, it's all fake. You got your celebrity photos there, sure, but it's all Tara Reid and Lindsay Lohan, and ten years from now people will look at them and go, who's that? Sinatra, he was authentic. Alan King. Rose Marie.'

'Rex,' Stride said, through gritted teeth.

'I mean, I'm a Vegas baby,' Terrell continued. 'How rare is that? Born and raised. I'm authentic. These days, everyone is from California.'

Amanda picked up a butter knife and began slapping it against her hand. Terrell blanched.

'All right, all right. For you, I'll leave out the good parts. Back in nineteen sixty-seven, the Sheherezade was *the* hot place in the city. Right up there with the Sands. Part of the buzz on the joint was its showroom, see? They had an amazing dancer. Amira Luz. Spanish beauty, dark hair, spitfire. Absolutely a sex machine, and I am not lying. She did a nude dance that filled the seats, SRO every night. I mean, in those days, there were plenty of boobies jiggling on stage, but it was all chorus-line stuff, deathly dull. Amira did a flamenco number and stripped down like a thousand-dollar call girl. H-o-t.'

'So?' Stride asked.

Terrell leaned forward and whispered. 'So one hot July night, they found Amira at the bottom of the pool in the high roller's suite on the roof of the Sheherezade. Someone had bashed her skull in.'

'And you think it was Walker Lane?'

'Absolutely. Everyone knew back then, but no one was going to say a word, not in *those* days.' Terrell twisted his index and his middle finger together. 'Boni Fisso and Walker Lane were like this. Walker was Boni's whale. He was there at the casino every weekend. Staying in that very same high roller suite where Amira was killed. He was a party boy, couldn't get enough of Vegas, liked rubbing shoulders with the mob.'

'That doesn't mean anything,' Amanda said.

Terrell put on a look of faux astonishment. 'Oh now, don't play innocent with me. I talked to people who saw Walker in the casino that weekend, but the official word is, he wasn't in town. He wasn't in the suite. I mean, come on. Walker was a horny little dog. He wanted to hump Amira's leg and move up to her fur. People told me he was obsessed with her, and Amira wasn't interested. Turned him down flat. But Walker wasn't about to hear the word *no* from some Spanish stripper. Crack, pow.'

'Apparently, the police didn't think so,' Stride said. 'Walker was never arrested.'

Terrell sighed dramatically. 'The police? This was nineteen sixty-seven, Detective. You don't think Boni could make the police go away? Puh-leez. The detective in charge of the case was Nick Humphrey, and Nicky was in Boni's pocket. Everyone knew it. So Boni spirited Walker out of town. I mean, the man did a Roman Polanski and left the whole fucking country. And Nicky looked the other way. A murder in a high roller's suite, for heaven's sake? How easy should that be? But all the police could come up with is that some fan climbed down into the garden from the maintenance area of the roof and killed her.'

'What was Amira doing in the suite?' Amanda asked.

'The story was, she had seduced a key out of one of the desk clerks, and she liked to go up there for a nude swim after her shows, when the suite wasn't occupied. Again, that was the official word. I mean, as if.'

Stride shook his head. 'You put all this in your story? Get ready for a lawsuit, Rex.'

'Oh, we had a lawyer read every word,' Terrell replied, rolling his eyes. 'We added lots of maybes and allegedlys and other weasel words like that. And anyway, you think Walker wants to make the story even bigger by suing? I think not. Walker wants this to go away. So does Boni, so he can put up his new slant-eyes baccarat palace.'

'What about M.J.?' Amanda asked. 'How does he fit into this?'

'Hang on, honey. My butt's vibrating. Damn cell phone. I swear, it goes off so often I could have an orgasm if I kept it in my shorts.' He slid a wafer-thin phone out of his back pocket and checked the caller ID. 'Oh, her again. Never mind. Some little blonde flack, never has any real stories to sell. Probably bangs her clients.'

'Rex, we're running out of time,' Stride said.

'Chill, Detectives. Like I said, M.J. called me when he saw the article. He asked about my sources, which I could *not* tell him – duh – other than to suggest he ought to check out the archives at the library. Most of it was tucked away in the gossip columns back then if you could read between the lines. Dishy stuff. He asked me honestly if I thought his dad had killed the girl, and I told him honestly, yes I did. End of conversation.'

'But you called and left a message on the day he died,' Stride said.

'Surely. In my business, I give you a little, you give me a little. Which reminds me that I'm giving you guys a lot, so hello, don't forget your friends. I figured M.J. could feed me some dirt about Karyn Westermark but, oh well, somebody popped him first.'

'And do you have any idea who would have wanted him dead?' Amanda asked.

'Other than Walker and Boni?' Terrell grinned. 'No, M.J. seemed like a decent enough celeb. Pretty vanilla if you ask me. He poked it around a lot, though, so maybe you ought to find a jealous husband.'

'Like who?' Stride asked.

'Well, all I have is gossip. Rumors.'

'Tell us,' Amanda said.

Terrell glanced around at the other tables. 'I *do* know that Moose Dargon's wife, the little twenty-something waitress, hangs with a lot of celebs at the Oasis and likes to hook up. I heard she was very impressed with M.J.'s performance in that sex tape with Karyn. Word is that Moose can't plump the wiener any more, even with Viagra. And you know what kind of temper Moose has. In the old days, he was in and out of the jails around here for busting people up.'

'His wife is Tierney, right?' Stride asked. He remembered that Karyn Westermark had already mentioned her as one of M.J.'s flings.

'Tierney.' Terrell groaned. 'Puh-leez. I mean, whatever happened to ordinary names? Did you hear, one Hollywood actor thought it was such a riot and named his daughter Tinkle?'

'What does this Tierney look like?'

'Brunette. Kind of a bottlebrush look. She did *Playboy* last year. Breasts look like the pyramids in Egypt. Know the type?'

Stride did. He realized they had seen Tierney and her cone-shaped breasts on the video in M.J.'s condo. He wondered what someone like Moose Dargon would do if he saw his wife fornicating on camera and whether it would be enough to make him hire a professional killer.

'What else can you tell us about Moose?' he asked.

'He's still a riot and a half, even with one foot in the grave,' Terrell said. 'He's mostly retired, but he still does charity stuff, fundraisers for the gov, that kind of thing. His jokes are dirty, dirty, dirty, and they are hysterical.'

'He still have a temper?'

Terrell's face lit up, and he leaned in and whispered, 'Oooh, like would he blow M.J. away for condomizing little Tierney? Isn't that a delicious idea. Well, it would be very *ironic*, you know.'

'Why?' Stride asked.

'Because Moose used to be a regular at the Sheherezade back in the nineteen sixties. And who was he banging at the time? None other than Amira Luz.'

Twelve

Sawhill was on the phone with Governor Durand again.

Stride and Serena sat in the two chairs in front of Sawhill's expansive desk, while the lieutenant affixed his lips electronically to the governor's ass. Cordy was leaning against the wall, hands in his pockets. Amanda stood there too, and Stride smothered a smile as he watched her play games with Cordy. She kept inching closer, and Cordy, looking pained, kept shifting further along the wall, trying to keep his distance. Then she took a deep breath that swelled her breasts and lazily stretched her arms upward. Cordy couldn't help but stare.

Sawhill saw the game too and snapped his fingers at them.

'I'm meeting with my team right now,' Sawhill told the governor, his voice casual and familiar. 'No, no, I can assure you that line of inquiry is closed. You can pass the word along.'

Stride didn't like the sound of that. Sawhill was staring directly at him while he said it, and Stride had a sinking feeling that his hands were about to be tied.

It was no secret that Sawhill was aiming for big things in the department, with an eye on the sheriff's job. Stride had to give Sawhill credit. The lieutenant knew how the game was played and understood the political connections he would need to leapfrog the competition. The current sheriff had already announced his retirement for the following year. At least two Metro veterans who were older and more senior than Sawhill had made noises about campaigning for the job. But no one was ruling Sawhill out. A sheriff's election was more about endorsements than votes, and Sawhill had spent the last decade cultivating friends in high places.

Most of all, he knew that murder headlines made bad politics.

Sawhill put down the phone. He picked up a copy of the Tuesday edition of the Las Vegas *Sun*.

'I have two murder investigations on page one,' he told them. 'The governor doesn't like that. I don't like that. That's why I wanted all of you here to tell me what you're doing to get these cases *off* the front page.'

He said it as if somehow the four detectives in the room did like it and were basking in the media glow.

'Serena,' the lieutenant continued, pushing down his half-glasses so he could stare at her above the frames. 'You go first. Tell me more about the murder near Reno and whether this ties in to the hit-and-run on the boy in Summerlin.'

'A schoolteacher named Alice Ford had her throat cut at her ranch home,' Serena explained. 'Jay Walling and I spent an hour and a half with the victim's husband. We couldn't find any connection between Alice Ford in Reno and Peter Hale's family in Summerlin. There's not even a hint of a common motive for both victims.'

'So maybe there's no connection,' Sawhill concluded. 'You're talking about a major artery between Reno and Carson City. It may seem like a backwater compared to Las Vegas, but you've got thousands of cars on that highway every day. Just because our perp in the hit-and-run bought doughnuts up there the same day Alice Ford was killed, it doesn't mean he did it.'

'I don't like coincidences.'

'Neither do I, but they happen. Other than the receipt you found, there's nothing to tie these cases together.'

'That's true,' Serena admitted.

'What about a hit man?' Amanda suggested from the other side of the room. 'It could be two separate jobs, and you stumbled across a way to tie them together.'

'Sure, it's possible,' Serena said. 'Except who hires a pro to kill a twelve-year-old boy and a retired schoolteacher?'

Sawhill made a chopping motion with his hand, cutting off the conversation. 'Let Reno worry about Reno,' he told Serena. 'The crime that concerns me is right here. What else do you have?'

Cordy cleared his throat, then squealed and practically jumped in the air, as if he had looked down and found a tarantula crawling across his foot.

'What's wrong with you, Cordy?' Sawhill demanded.

Cordy blushed furiously. 'Nothing,' he murmured. 'Sorry.'

Stride saw Amanda struggling to keep a straight face.

Cordy tried to regain his cool. 'We did another run through the neighborhood in Summerlin. I thought now that we know it was an Aztek, we might jog some memories. The thing's butt ugly, who can miss it?'

'And?' Sawhill asked.

'We got a hit. A neighbor remembered seeing a blue Aztek parked across the street, a few minutes before the hit-and-run. It means our guy was lying in wait. He wanted a shot at the kid.'

'Did the witness see the driver?' Sawhill asked.

Cordy shook his head. 'She was on the second floor. Couldn't even see if someone was in the car.'

'So what's next?'

'Jay Walling sent me a pile of receipts from the store that sold those Krispy Kremes,' Serena said. 'Credit card purchases in the last two months where the person ordered doughnuts and Sprite. Plus other people who were at the same store within an hour of our man. I could use some help making phone calls.'

Sawhill nodded.

'We're also running a search on other hit-and-run deaths in the southwest where a child was involved,' she continued. 'Maybe this guy has done this before. And we're expanding our background checks on the family and friends to see if anyone might have been carrying a grudge about something.'

'Use discretion,' Sawhill reminded her. He extended a slim finger at Cordy. 'You too, Cordy.'

They both nodded. Stride knew he was next.

'Detective Stride, you're new in this department,' Sawhill told him. 'But Governor Durand already knows your name.'

'I'm flattered,' Stride replied pleasantly. Serena kicked him.

'Don't be. He added a few expletives in front of it. Walker Lane called him, complaining that you seemed more interested in a forty-year-old murder than in finding out who killed his son.'

'I didn't know anything about the murder of Amira Luz when I talked to Walker. He was the one who steered us to Rex Terrell.'

Sawhill snorted. 'Rex Terrell has turned *LV* magazine into the *National Enquirer*. He writes gossip and trash. It has no place in this investigation.'

'But there *was* a murder at the Sheherezade.'

'Yes, I'm familiar with the crime, Detective.'

'I'd like to talk to the detective who ran the investigation back then,' Stride said. 'Nick Humphrey. Is he still alive?'

'He is, but that would be a waste of time.' Sawhill leaned forward and stripped his glasses off. 'What Rex Terrell probably did *not* tell you is that the murder of Amira Luz was solved.'

Stride hesitated. He hadn't pulled any files on Amira's death yet. 'You're right, I didn't know that.'

'The murderer killed himself,' Sawhill replied crisply. 'He was a stalker. An unemployed gambling addict from Los Angeles. A month after Amira Luz was killed, he was found hanged in his LA apartment. He had pictures of the girl all over his bedroom wall. And he had a receipt from the Sheherezade the night she was killed. I imagine Rex left that out of his little story.'

Stride felt his cheeks growing hot. 'Things still don't add up. Terrell says he talked to people who saw Walker in Las Vegas that day. And then he left the country and has hardly come back since. Why?'

'Maybe he likes Canadian bacon. Maybe he always wanted to be a Mountie. I have no idea, Detective, and I don't care. Walker Lane didn't kill anyone.'

'M.J. thought he did.'

'M.J. was wrong. Rex Terrell was wrong. *You* are wrong. There is no connection to M.J.'s death, because there is no mystery here. Move on. Is that clear?'

Stride nodded. 'Perfectly clear.'

But his doubts lingered. He was willing to admit that Rex Terrell might have spun a fairy tale for them, more fiction than truth. If nasty rumors had followed Walker Lane after the girl's death, he might have chosen to leave town, even if he was innocent. But there was another name that had popped up in the middle of the story, like a bathtub toy that wouldn't sink.

Boni Fisso.

Boni, who owned the Sheherezade and had ties to both Amira Luz and Walker Lane.

Boni, who had two billion dollars on the line in the Orient casino project. *Worth killing over.*

Sawhill wasn't stupid. He could read Stride's eyes. 'You don't sound convinced, Detective. So you tell me, what connection could there possibly be between the death of Amira Luz and the murder of M.J. Lane?'

Stride shook his head. 'I can't think of a thing,' he admitted.

'Good. Let's look for a more plausible theory of the crime. And I really hope you have one.'

'We know that M.J. was having an affair with Tierney Dargon,' Stride said.

'Moose's wife?'

Stride wondered how many Tierney Dargons there could be in Las Vegas. 'There was video in M.J.'s apartment of the two of them together. We heard about the affair from Karyn Westermark and Rex Terrell, so the word was out.'

Sawhill leaned back in his chair and tugged at his pointed chin. 'Moose is a wild man. He always has been. I wouldn't put it past him to go into a rage and kill someone. He's come close a few times.'

'Except this wasn't a rage killing,' Amanda pointed out. She came forward and leaned over the desk. 'This was planned.'

'And unless he's dropped several decades and a hundred pounds or so, the killer wasn't Moose himself,' Stride said.

'So he could have hired someone,' Sawhill said. 'The two of you will talk to Tierney?'

Stride nodded.

'What about the video archives at the casino? Did we get another look at the killer?'

'If he was there, he didn't look like he did on Saturday night,' Stride said.

'All right, keep me posted.' He waved his hand, dismissing them, and picked up the phone again. He grabbed the pink stress ball on his desk with his other hand and squeezed it. Stride hoped he used a lighter touch with his wife's breasts. 'I want your teams on both of these cases day and night. Get them off the front page. Or get me the perps. And Stride, I don't want you talking to Walker Lane again without consulting me.'

'Understood,' Stride said.

The four of them made a beeline for the door. Stride pulled it closed behind him as they left. Cordy shot an evil glance at Amanda, who winked at him and gave him a tiny wave with a crook of her index finger. He stormed away.

'What did you do to him, anyway?' Stride asked.

Amanda giggled. 'I pinched his butt.'

Thirteen

Amanda drove over to the south side of McCarran and parked in a lot where she could watch the jets landing on runway 25 Left. She was driving her used Toyota rather than the Spyder, which she reserved for weekends and road trips. She turned her radio to the frequency of the tower and listened to the chatter between the pilots and the traffic controllers. Tierney Dargon's United flight from San Francisco was scheduled to land in half an hour.

There were a few other plane nuts parked around her. Some people made checklists of the incoming and outgoing flights and ticked them off as they watched the planes come and go. Amanda wasn't that extreme. She just liked to sit here with a latte and a cigarette. She didn't smoke often, not any more, but she allowed herself one cigarette when she came here and kept a pack in the glove compartment for those occasions. Something about the smoke and the sweet coffee, and the roar of engines and the smell of jet fuel made time stop for her, like a kind of hypnosis, when her mind could wander. She didn't even take Bobby here. This was her place.

She had found it when she came to the city from Portland five years ago. Back when she was Jason Gillen, a smart Oregon cop who became a smart Vegas cop. Back when she was thinking about killing herself. She remembered sitting here with her gun on the seat beside her, wondering if she had the guts to do it, and finally realizing that it took no guts at all to run away. The courage was in sticking around and facing down the people who were afraid of her because she was wired differently.

So Jason died, and Amanda was born.

She took the cigarette out of her mouth, exhaled a trail of smoke out the window, and smiled as she saw the lipstick ring on the white wrapper.

People always thought that it was about sex. That to be her, the

87

way she was, she had to walk on the wild side. That she could only do that to her body, and gulp down hormones every day, if she were obsessed with sex. They never believed her when she told them that she and Bobby were pretty conservative at heart, in or out of the bedroom. *They* were the ones who were obsessed with sex. They were titillated by her. Aroused by her. Men and women alike. They wanted to know how she did it, in what positions, and how often. They wanted to see her. Taste her.

The worst were the he-men on the force. People like Cordy. She got under their manly skin. They were so scared of the fact that she turned them on that they ran like hell from her. It used to bother her. Now she had fun with it. It was her way of showing them that she did have guts, that she wasn't going away. And maybe it was a little payback, too.

She knew the jokes hadn't stopped, just gone underground, because the brass had told the other cops to stay cool. Seven-figure settlements had a way of making people behave, at least to her face. No one wanted her around, though. She knew that. They ignored her, talked behind her back, and waited for her to take the money and run. It killed them that she stayed.

She had been worried about Stride. She could deal with the others for the most part, but a bad partner could make your life miserable. Worst of all, he was a heartlander, from the Midwest. She thought of people from the ag belt as narrow-minded, quick to judge. She figured he would look at her like an alien. But Stride surprised her. She understood what Serena saw in him. He was attractive, no doubt about that, but he also seemed to have a soul a mile deep. Once he got over the shock, he simply treated her like a person. He was curious – everyone was curious – but she felt respect from him for what was in her brain, not what was between her legs.

That was rare.

Beyond the fence, a Southwest 737 angled gracefully upward and soared toward the sky. She knew that most of the people on the plane were going home, with lighter wallets, leaving the fantasy world behind and winging back to reality. To her, it looked like freedom. One day, she might really take the money, climb into the Spyder with Bobby, and run. Not because she couldn't take it, but because she wanted to be somewhere where no one knew her, where people didn't stare.

Bobby deserved that, too. He probably didn't tell her half the shit he got for living with her, or the abuse he took. But he had stood by her and slept beside her for more than three years. She had avoided sex with him for months when they were dating, because she had assumed she would lose him as soon as he found out the truth. When she finally told him, she *had* lost him, at least for a couple weeks while he came to grips with what he felt. Then he had come back, and he had stuck around, never once asking her to be anything but what she was.

She had never wanted to have the SRS surgery, to take the final step. She was afraid that things would go wrong, that the parts wouldn't work, that she would be left with no sexual sensation whatever. She didn't need it to define her as a woman. But she had wanted to have it for Bobby, to make herself a little more *normal* for him. Except he said no, that he didn't want it, not unless she wanted it for herself. She loved him for that.

It sounded so appealing, to run away with him someday, to escape all the cruelty. San Francisco maybe, where Tierney was coming from. No one would give them a second look there. Not in the City by the Gay.

Amanda tossed the cigarette butt out of the car. She laughed at herself and shook her head. She was as guilty of fantasy as the people on the plane. The truth was, she would never leave.

The radio crackled to life. United 1580 was cleared to land.

Amanda fired up the engine. Tierney Dargon was coming home.

She spotted Tierney in the baggage claim area, standing apart from the crowd, a cell phone wedged between her shoulder and her ear. She was stick-thin and pretty, with a loose pink top that let her breasts sway and rose-colored tight pants. But other than her Vegas body, she wasn't making any effort to look glamorous. Her brown hair hung limply to her shoulders in a mess of curls. She hadn't put on makeup or jewelry, except for a gold bracelet that she twisted nervously around her wrist with her other hand. The whites of her eyes were lined with red.

Amanda began to approach her, but found her way blocked by a giant Samoan in a Hawaiian shirt, obviously a bodyguard. She discreetly flashed her badge. The man asked if she could wait, then lumbered over to Tierney and whispered in her ear. The girl studied Amanda, murmured something to the Samoan, and went back to her phone call.

'Mrs Dargon wonders if she could talk to you in her limo,' the bodyguard told Amanda. 'It's waiting outside. There's a picture of Mr Dargon on the door.'

Amanda shrugged. 'OK.'

She found the limo without any problem. Samoa had obviously radioed to the driver, who was waiting for her with the door open. He was in his sixties, and he tipped his black hat to Amanda as she got in.

'There's champagne if you'd like,' he told her. 'And we have muffins, too, but don't take the blueberry oatmeal muffin. That's Mrs Dargon's favorite.'

Amanda smiled. 'She eats carbs?'

The driver laughed but didn't reply. He closed the door with Amanda inside.

She had never been in a stretch before. Her ass slid all over the leather seat as she tried to get comfortable. A television was built into a corner unit toward the front of the car, with a stereo and DVD player on shelves underneath. A rap video was playing, with the sound muted. The opposite corner included a refrigerator and a circular glass serving tray with sweets, fruits, an open bottle of champagne, and a carafe of juice.

There was a portrait of Moose Dargon on black velvet, stitched into the middle seat on Amanda's left. He looked twenty years younger, with wild wavy black hair, caterpillar eyebrows, and a bulbous red-veined nose. Amanda clucked her tongue in disbelief. Elvis had not left the limo.

She chose to sit on Moose's face, because she could get some traction on the velvet. There was a series of wooden drawers built into the lower half of the seats. She glanced through the limo window, then slid open the drawer between her legs.

No surprise. Drugs. And a six-pack of Trojans. Amanda removed the envelope of cocaine.

She felt the car rock as the driver got out. A few seconds later, the rear door swung open, and Tierney slipped inside. She took a seat opposite Amanda and brushed her dirty curls out of her face. She wasn't smiling.

'This is about M.J., huh?' Her voice was girlish and made her sound even younger than she was.

Amanda nodded.

'Sorry, I must look like a mess,' Tierney apologized. 'I've been really upset about what happened.'

'You look fine.'

Tierney gave her an embarrassed smile. 'That's nice of you to say.'

It was amazing, Amanda thought. In Las Vegas, even murder was no excuse for not looking your best.

'I guess you found the video,' Tierney added.

'Yes, we did.'

90

'God. I can't believe I was so stupid. But M.J. thought it was hot doing it on film. If this gets out, Moose is going to kill me.'

Amanda raised an eyebrow. 'I hear he has a temper.'

'No, no, I didn't mean literally. Moose would never touch me. But he'd be upset, humiliated. I never wanted that.'

Her defenses were up. Amanda decided to go another way. 'When did you go to San Francisco?'

'Sunday morning. As soon as I heard about M.J. My family's there, and I told Moose I wanted to spend some time with my parents. But mostly I stayed in a downtown hotel and cried. I didn't want Moose to see me that way. He'd wonder why.'

She was on the verge of tearing up. Amanda realized that Tierney wasn't cold, like Karyn Westermark. This girl actually felt something for M.J.

'Were you in love with him?'

'Who, Moose?' Tierney asked, misunderstanding. 'Of course. I know what everybody thinks, that he wanted a bimbo on his arm and I wanted his money. It's not like that. We care about each other.'

'He does have a lot of money,' Amanda pointed out. Moose lived in Lake Las Vegas, a gated resort community on the other side of the mountains.

'Sure, but I won't see any of that. I'm with him because he's funny and sweet, and he treats me nice. I was nothing before him.'

'What about M.J.?'

Tierney stared blankly at the television screen in the limo for a long time before saying anything. 'I'm twenty-four, OK?' She said it as if that was enough to explain everything.

'You have a reputation as a party girl. Lots of hook-ups.'

'Well, that's crap,' Tierney retorted. Her brow wrinkled in annoyance. 'I've only slept with a couple guys. Lately it was just M.J.'

Amanda wondered about the pack of condoms in the drawer under her feet. 'Did Moose know about M.J.? Or the others?'

'It was more like don't ask, don't tell. He knows there are things he can't give me.'

'But what if he did find out? Moose has put a few people in the hospital in his time.'

'That was years ago! He's nearly eighty, for God's sake.'

'But would he hire someone to send a message? He might not hurt you, but what about M.J.?'

'You think Moose had M.J. killed?' Tierney shook her head vehemently. 'No way. First, he wouldn't do that. I told you, we have an arrangement. And second, he didn't know about M.J.'

'Come on, Tierney,' Amanda scolded her. 'Don't be naive. People knew. We didn't recognize you from the video. We asked someone who M.J. might be sleeping with, and yours was the first name that came up.'

Tierney's mouth fell open. 'Oh, shit. I can't believe this.'

'Did you love M.J.?'

'Love him? Yeah, a little, I guess. I don't sleep with people I don't care about, whatever you think.'

'Well, if Moose thought you had feelings for M.J., that might make him feel pretty vulnerable. Like you might leave him.'

'You're wrong,' Tierney insisted. 'Moose knows I would never do that. He's sick. Cancer. He doesn't have a lot of time left, and he knows I'll be there for him. M.J. was – well, I kind of wondered about the future. After.'

Amanda was having a hard time deciding whether Tierney was a sweet, lonely girl, or a shrewd gold-digger with her eyes on the next prize. If she was putting on an act, it was a good one.

'Did you know about M.J. and Karyn Westermark?' Amanda asked.

Tierney pressed her full lips together until they formed a thin line. 'Yes.'

'Did that bother you?'

'We did a threesome once. That freaked me out. I didn't want to do it again. M.J. wanted to, though.'

'Were you with M.J. on Saturday morning?'

She nodded. 'And Friday night, too.'

'Why'd you leave on Saturday?'

'I had a thing with Moose on Saturday night. A party.'

'Where?' Amanda asked. She jotted down the details as Tierney told her. 'Were you with Moose the whole time? Did he make or receive any calls on his cell phone?'

Tierney shook her head. 'He was schmoozing. It was a political thing for the governor. You know, it's re-election time. I was with Moose the entire evening.'

'Did you know M.J. was with Karyn that night?'

'I figured,' she said unhappily.

'You sound jealous.'

Tierney tucked one of her curls around her finger and played with it. 'Karyn is the big leagues. I know that. I'm just a cocktail waitress who was in the right place at the right time. I try to fit in with M.J. and his crowd, but I don't, not really. I know they laugh at me.'

'So why hang out with them?'

'What else do I have? My old friends, they can't deal with who I

92

am now. Because of Moose. You know, living by the lake, the body-guards, the limo. It doesn't matter that I'm still who I was. If you're young and you've got money, you just wind up at the Oasis. And there are all the same little cliques in that crowd. It's like high school.'

'What clique was M.J. in?'

'Karyn's. That's how I met him. He was at the casino with Karyn about six months ago. She was really friendly to me, and I only realized later it was because she wanted to get me in bed with them. But I liked M.J. so I did it. We started going out after that, just the two of us.'

'How did Karyn feel about that?'

Tierney shrugged. 'I don't suppose she cared. She still slept with M.J. whenever she wanted.' There was a hint of bitterness in her voice.

'Karyn says M.J. was planning to dump you,' Amanda said.

Tierney was shocked. 'She said that? No way. I don't believe that. M.J. wouldn't do that.'

'Do you have any idea who might have wanted to kill M.J.?'

'No, I don't,' Tierney said. 'I can't imagine. But not Moose. Definitely not.'

Amanda asked, 'Do you know if M.J. had anything to do with Boni Fisso? Did they know each other?'

'Boni? Not that I know of. He never mentioned him.'

'How about Moose? Does he know Boni?'

Tierney nodded. 'Well, sure. Moose played the Sheherezade all the time in the old days.'

Amanda wasn't sure it meant anything. But Moose was a volatile man, despite his age and health. If someone like Moose did want to hire a hit man, it was easy to imagine him talking to Boni.

She thanked Tierney and reached for the door to the limousine. Tierney took her arm in a soft grip. Her hand felt small.

'Does this have to become public? Me and M.J.?'

'I can't make any promises,' Amanda said. 'And like I said, it's already an open secret.'

Tierney nodded. Her eyes drifted to the drawer on the other side of the limo, which wasn't fully closed. She glanced back at Amanda, then looked away. 'You took my stuff, huh?'

'Yeah,' Amanda told her. 'But I'm not vice. It gets flushed. You know, it's none of my business, but you don't seem cut out for the fast lane, Tierney. Maybe you should think about making some changes.'

'Thanks.' Tierney took a jaded look around at the limo and gave her a half-smile. 'Believe it or not, there's a part of me that wishes I

93

was still slinging drinks at the Venetian. Sometimes it's easier being on the outside, looking in.'

Stride leaned back in the uncomfortable wooden chair and stretched his arms. The knotted muscles in his back tugged and strained. He felt a pain behind his eyes, and he closed them, hoping to tame his headache. He had been staring at the fiche reader for three hours, squinting at fuzzy forty-year-old images, feeling himself transported to 1967. The year Amira Luz was killed. It was odd, looking at headlines from newspapers back in those days, knowing how history turned out. The young girls in the ads were old women now. There was a photograph of Robert Kennedy. Everyone had cigarettes hanging off their lips.

Things weren't so different then. Las Vegas still floated above the times, corrupt and somehow incorruptible. He saw articles about desperate times for blacks in North Las Vegas, and a few pages later ads for the black entertainers headlining on the Strip. He saw names from the past, in their prime: Red Buttons, Milton Berle, Ann-Margret. Mini skirts were in. The latest Bond movie, *You Only Live Twice*, was in the theatres that summer. Connery was cool.

He tried to imagine what it was like to live back then, to be a part of those days. From a distance, it looked old-fashioned, like the pencil drawings of models and the washed-out color in the photographs. Sophisticated but naive. He felt the pull of nostalgia, the yearning for the good old days. But nostalgia was nothing but sadness over times past. The good old days weren't so good. He saw headlines about labor strikes and bribery scandals. The death of a Cosa Nostra leader thousands of miles away in New York made the front page in Las Vegas. The rumor of dark things was in the papers along with Frank's old black magic, like shadows of clouds passing overhead.

He picked up a copy of the first article he had printed. It was dated 18 June:

AMIRA MAKES TRIUMPHANT RETURN

Fresh from a six-month stint in the Montmartre district of Paris, Spanish dancer Amira Luz got a roaring welcome home on Saturday night from a packed crowd at the Sheherezade, where she introduced a risqué new show entitled 'Flame'.

Like other shows now in vogue in casino showrooms, 'Flame' features a cadre of lavishly dressed topless showgirls, as well as a riotous comedy performance by Strip veteran Moose Dargon. But Luz is the star. Her showstopper is a flamenco striptease, where the stage is lit by dozens of candles and a single guitarist provides accompaniment as she sheds her fiery red Spanish costume . . .

Stride retrieved another article from the third week in July. Amira was on the front page:

SHOWGIRL MURDER SHOCKS STRIP

Las Vegas police confirmed today that Amira Luz, star of the hit show 'Flame' at the Sheherezade, was murdered on Friday night in a luxury suite in the popular casino. While police offered few details, sources inside the casino say the dancer was found early Saturday morning in a rooftop swimming pool, her skull crushed. Luz was last seen on stage on Friday during the late performance of 'Flame'.

Detective Nicholas Humphrey declined to speculate on a motive for the crime or on any possible suspects. In a prepared statement, casino owner Boni Fisso declared 'profound sadness' over the death of Luz and vowed 'complete cooperation with the police in tracking down the deranged individual who defiled our property in order to perpetrate this heinous crime'.

One day after Luz was killed, and already Boni was laying the groundwork to pin the blame on an outsider. Stride wanted to talk to Nick Humphrey.

As he re-read the article, Stride felt experienced hands massaging his shoulders. He glanced up as Serena leaned down and put her face next to his.

'This is your idea of a lunch date?' she asked him. 'The library?'

'Just don't stop,' Stride told her. 'That feels great.'

Her fingers continued to knead and separate the tissues in his back. She looked at the newspaper articles over his shoulder and at the stack of microfiche boxes.

'Maybe I heard wrong,' she teased him. 'Didn't Sawhill say the case was closed?'

Stride smiled. 'Did he? I must have misheard him.'

Serena dragged another chair across the worn gray carpeting and set it down next to him. Stride noticed several of the men in the library watching her. The midday crowd in the library was almost all men, unemployed, in jeans and baseball caps. Some made a show of reading the newspaper. Others simply stared into space.

'Find anything?' Serena asked.

Stride shrugged. 'You have to read between the lines. It's mostly rumor and innuendo. There was a gossip column back then that dropped some broad hints. I think that's where Rex Terrell picked up a lot of the details for his story in the magazine.'

'Don't get me wrong, Jonny,' Serena told him. 'I trust your instincts. But I'm not sure I see the connection. I don't know how you take a nineteen sixty-seven murder that was supposedly solved and draw a line to M.J.'s death today.'

'Maybe you don't,' Stride admitted. 'There may be nothing in this. But I'm like you. I don't like coincidences.'

'Such as?'

Stride leaned back in the chair. 'Here's what I have. M.J. starts nosing into the murder of Amira Luz, because he reads allegations in *LV* magazine that his father was the one who killed her. Shortly thereafter, M.J. winds up murdered himself. The murder of Amira took place at a casino owned by Boni Fisso, who may or may not have ties to organized crime and who is set to break ground this year on a new two-billion-dollar development project. How'm I doing?'

'You have my attention,' Serena said. 'First question: who was Amira Luz, and why was she killed?'

Stride nodded. 'Amira was a nude dancer and *very* good at it, according to the papers. They called her Spanish, but I found a bio that said she was actually half Spanish. Her father was a Spanish diplomat, and her mother was the blonde bombshell daughter of a Texas Congressman. When Boni Fisso opened the Sheherezade in late nineteen sixty-five, Amira was eye candy, twenty-one years old, in a show built around a comedian. Guess who?'

'Moose Dargon,' Serena guessed.

'Exactly. Another interesting coincidence. Anyway, Amira is a big hit. By May of nineteen sixty-six, she has her own show, Lido-style, backed up by a chorus line of wannabes. Toward the end of the year, Amira went off to dance in Paris for six months. Or maybe she was over there planning her next act. Regardless, by June of sixty-seven, Amira is back in Las Vegas at the Sheherezade in a whole new show called *Flame*, and she's bigger than ever.'

'Until someone kills her,' Serena said.

'Right. A few weeks after the show opens, Amira winds up murdered in a penthouse suite at the Sheherezade. By the way, Moose wound

96

up as a supporting act in Amira's new show and lost his solo gig. I don't imagine he was too happy about it.'

'Go on,' Serena said.

'Now let's look at Walker Lane. He filmed one of his movies in Vegas during the spring and got hooked on the city. Soon he was a regular, flying here every weekend from LA. His favorite watering hole was the Sheherezade. Walker was tight with Boni Fisso. And Rex had it right, too: the gossip columns in June suggested that Walker had his eye on "a Latin beauty regularly seen on the Vegas stage". Amira.'

'So what's the theory?' Serena asked. 'What happened to Amira?'

'Try this. Walker gets carried away in his suite when Amira rejects him. Or maybe rough sex gets out of hand. She winds up dead. And then Boni helps Walker get away clean and finds a patsy in LA to take the fall.'

'Why'd Walker stay away after the police closed the case?' Serena asked.

'I don't know. Maybe Boni had a secret deal with the cops back then that Walker wouldn't set foot in Vegas again. Anyway, it's ancient history until Rex Terrell drags the story into *LV* and brings up all the old rumors about Amira, Walker, and Boni. Then M.J. gets hold of it and starts asking questions.'

'And gets killed.'

Stride nodded. 'I keep coming back to Boni's plan to implode the Sheherezade and launch the Orient project. The last thing you want to deal with when you've got that kind of money on the line is a skeleton in the closet from forty years ago. Like Amira's murder.'

'I hate to point this out, but Sawhill doesn't want you asking questions about this. What are you going to do?'

'Ask questions about this,' Stride said.

Serena laughed. 'You could wind up the fastest hired, fastest fired detective in Metro history. Come on, let's get out of here, and you can buy me lunch.'

'Deal.'

Stride gathered up his copies and shoved them inside his blazer pocket. He stacked the boxes of microfiche together and balanced them unsteadily. 'Can you grab that copy of *LV*? That's the one with Rex Terrell's article.'

Serena picked up the magazine. One of the pages had a Post-It note, and Serena opened it to look inside.

'That's Amira,' Stride told her.

There was a large black-and-white photograph in the magazine from the 1960s, with Amira in a sexy Spanish black dress, her black hair spilling across her sweaty face, her hand pulling up her skirt to reveal her bare, muscular leg. Behind her, in white, another showgirl struck a similar pose.

Stride dropped off the boxes with the librarian. He looked back and realized Serena hadn't moved. She was holding the magazine in her hands, staring at it.

'What is it?'

Serena didn't seem to hear him. Then she folded the magazine back and pointed at the photo.

'This girl in white behind Amira. That's Peter Hale's grandmother. The boy who was killed in the hit-and-run.'

PART TWO

CLAIRE

Fourteen

Breaking into the car was child's play.

He waited in the back seat of the Lexus, parked in the shadows of the underground ramp at the Fashion Show Mall. His gun, a Sig .357, was on the seat beside him.

The Lexus was near the entrance to Nieman's. Of course. She was a fashionable lady. Seventy-five years old, widowed. Thin as a bird. She parked in a handicapped spot, because she had arthritis in her legs. The windows of the car were smoked, and no one could see inside. But he could see out and see her when she came.

He caught a glimpse of himself in the rear-view mirror. He found himself staring back at his own dark features: thick black hair, heavy beard line. And his eyes, so deep brown they appeared to have no color at all. He scared people with his eyes. He always had. It was as if, when they looked into his eyes, they were inside a closet, black, without light, with the walls closing in.

He was like his eyes. Without emotion. Focused only on his goal.

Except he knew that wasn't true when it came to the boy. Peter Hale. He had felt something then, despite all his training, despite the soldiers who had shown him how to view pain and death through the lens of a microscope. Study it. Learn from it. But feel nothing.

He had felt something about the boy, so much so that he had changed his plans in the middle, which he *never* did. He changed targets.

His plan had been the mother. He took the boy instead.

No one would know about his lapse except himself. But it bothered him. He didn't like to think that he was a creature of anger any more, not like in the old days. Those creatures made mistakes. He was a strategist, a mercenary in the field, with a goal and a plan.

He saw the doors that led to the ramp elevators open, and the old woman came out, shopping bags in both hands. She walked gingerly.

Each time her right foot came down, she winced, feeling pain in her joints. He could see her clearly, but she couldn't see him, not when she approached the car and put the bags in the trunk, not when she fumbled with her keys by the driver's door. The ramp was dark, and the car was dark. Even when she pulled open the door and maneuvered her frail body inside, she didn't see him. She pulled the door shut. He was right behind her, watching her. He heard her exhale, sighing, the pressure finally off her feet.

She hunched over, struggling to fit the key in the ignition. When she finally did, the engine turned over, and light classical music filled the car. She settled back, resting her head against the cushion, relaxing.

Then she glanced in the mirror and saw him.

His hand was already around her face, clamping off her scream. He didn't bother with his gun. There was no need. Instead, he leaned forward, his quiet voice at her ear, soothing her.

'We're just going for a little drive,' he said.

He didn't want her dropping dead of a heart attack, and he needed her calm for what she had to do. The old woman had to get him through the security gate at Lake Las Vegas. She lived there, alone, in an estate where he could wait safely for night to fall.

He knew this was the hard way. If it was only about killing the girl, there were easier ways to get it done. She partied at the casinos. She stripped off at the spa. He could take her in any of those places. But he was sending a message. Security doesn't mean a thing.

I can strike anywhere.

I'm coming for you.

Fifteen

Linda Hale told them to take Bonanza Road east until they wanted to become Mormons. That was where her mother lived.

Her mother, Peter's grandmother, who had been a dancer on stage with Amira Luz.

Stride didn't understand the reference to the Mormons until he and Serena took the drive. Where Bonanza ran out, on the border of the eastern mountains, they were less than a block from the city's giant Mormon temple, its white spires visible throughout the valley. In the neighborhood surrounding the temple were lavish homes with Jaguars parked in the driveway, rock gardens landscaped with tall saguaros, and kidney-shaped clear blue swimming pools.

Linda's mother, Helen Truax, had a house of luminous white stucco almost directly opposite the temple, with a view down the valley that Stride figured was worth at least two million bucks. According to Linda, her mother was no Mormon, and she enjoyed having her wealthy religious neighbors know about her past as a barely clad dancer.

When Helen Truax opened the door, she looked nothing like any grandmother Stride had ever seen. She was dripping wet, with a diaphanous white robe slipped over her shoulders, open, revealing a one-piece teal swimsuit underneath. She was barefoot and at least as tall as Stride himself. He knew she was sixty years old, but she could have passed for forty.

'Please, come in.' She smiled at Stride, and her teeth were snowy white. She held a bell-shaped glass of white wine and had the dirtiest blue eyes he had ever seen.

'Your daughter said you had showgirl looks,' Serena told her. 'She was right.'

Helen laughed. 'I'd love to tell you this is all original equipment, but it's not. If it starts to sag, I lift it. If it starts to wrinkle, I tighten it.' She cupped her full breasts in her hands. 'Without help, these babies would be pointing at my toes by now.'

She turned on her heels. The robe didn't stretch to the bottom of her swimsuit, and Stride watched the rhythm of her ass as he followed her. Serena landed a sharp elbow against his ribs.

Helen's house was sparingly decorated. There were large empty walls, painted in glossy white and soft pastels. The same honey-gold carpet spread from room to room. Where there was art, it was Italian, mostly hand-blown glass and landscape oils heavy on sienna and umber. In a wide corridor leading to the rear of the house, however, Stride saw a series of photographs hung in slim frames. Helen, elaborately costumed, with Sinatra. Helen with Wayne Newton.

Helen with Boni Fisso.

She noticed Stride admiring the pictures. 'Helena Troy,' she said. 'That was my stage name. Don't you love it?'

'It looks like you knew all the big stars,' Stride said.

'Why, of course. It was a small town back then. Everyone knew everyone among the entertainers. Las Vegas was like our personal playground. The world was our stage. The tourists who came, they were like children with their noses pressed against the glass, watching us, and wanting to catch a little bit of the glamour.'

'But it's not that way any more?' Stride asked.

'Oh, no. People don't appreciate the magic of those times. The sixties were our golden age. There was such a sense of class. But today everything is corporate. It's Disneyland with a topless Minnie Mouse. There's none of the star quality the town had in the past. Ma and Pa Kettle come here from Kansas, and they dress like they're taking the kids to Six Flags. Even the celebrities who stay here now are so crass. I miss the old days, I really do.' Helen sighed.

She led them into a sunken family room overlooking the valley. The east wall was made of rough-cut stone and featured a large fireplace. There was a wet bar on Stride's right and a mirrored display of crystal behind it. Helen took them through French doors that led to the outside patio. She pulled out three chairs from around a glass table and angled the umbrella to block the sun.

Stride noticed two deckchairs placed side by side next to a forty-foot swimming pool. Two sets of wet footprints were drying quickly in the afternoon sun. Obviously, Helen had a guest who wasn't invited to the interview.

'Linda was very upset when she called me,' she said. 'She made it sound like you thought I was in some way responsible for Peter's death.'

'It's nothing like that,' Serena assured her. 'We're exploring whether there's a connection between Peter's death and the murder of M.J. Lane over the weekend.'

'Who?' Helen asked. There wasn't any guile in her voice. She noted their surprise and added, 'You'll probably think I'm old-fashioned, but I don't use my television set other than to watch old movies. And I don't read the newspapers. Too much bad news.'

'M.J. Lane was murdered near the Oasis casino,' Stride said. 'He was the son of Walker Lane.'

Helen blinked and looked uncomfortable. 'All right, I knew Walker Lane. But that was forty years ago. I don't see what possible connection there could be to Peter's death.'

'We've had two murders in the space of a week under unusual circumstances,' Serena said. 'Both victims had family relationships to people who had connections to the Sheherezade casino in nineteen sixty-seven, and specifically—'

'Specifically, a relationship with Amira Luz,' Helen said, finishing the sentence.

'That's right,' Stride said. He played a hunch. 'You talked to Rex Terrell, didn't you? He mentioned you in his article in *LV* as one of the people whose careers benefited from Amira's death.'

Helen nodded.

Stride leaned forward, his elbows on the table. 'Why don't you tell us exactly what happened back then?'

Helen stared off into the valley, then turned back to Stride with a hardness in her face. 'I have a nice life. My husband is an international lawyer, and he makes a great deal of money. And he's away a lot. I'm sure you understand.'

She knew Stride had spotted the footprints.

'It's one thing to gossip with a reporter on background,' Helen continued. 'It's another to be a witness for the police. We're talking about a murder at a casino owned by Boni Fisso. Boni has a long reach and a long memory.'

'Have you been threatened?' Serena asked. 'Do you think someone was sending you a message by killing your grandson?'

'No,' Helen said flatly. 'Not at all. I haven't heard from anyone. Certainly not Boni. The idea that Peter's death could somehow involve me or what happened in the past – that's a complete shock to me. I don't see how or why.'

'That's why we need to know what happened in nineteen sixty-seven,' Stride told her. 'To find the connection.'

'It may be the only way to find out who killed Peter,' Serena added.

'Peter,' Helen murmured, struggling with her reluctance. 'I can't believe what happened to him. I've never been a very emotional person, Detectives. I'm not one to believe that attachments last forever. You can ask my ex-husbands about that. But I loved that little boy.'

She drummed her nails on the patio table and bit her lip.

'I guess the first thing to say is that I feel like I have blood on my hands, too. I hated Amira. I was insanely jealous of her. When she was killed, I have to say I was glad. Funny, how petty it seems in retrospect. But I was barely twenty-one then, and ambitious, and Amira was standing in the way.'

'What was she like?' Serena asked.

'Amira? She was scandalous.'

'In what way?'

Helen gave them a wicked smile. 'You two are too young to understand the times. It was the sexual revolution, but there was still a lot of the nineteen fifties about the world back then. Big hair. Ugly black glasses that made us look like librarians. Lots of ridiculous hats. Flouncy little mini skirts where you could practically see our pussies, but we were still supposed to look virginal.' She laughed. Stride thought she was pleased to see that her language surprised them.

'There was plenty of flesh back then,' she added. 'You had Lido at the Stardust, the Folies at the Trop, Minsky's at the Slipper. All of them bare-breasted, but pretty tame. Even so, we took a lot of heat. We had some councilmen in Henderson who thought a few tits on stage meant the end of civilization as we knew it. They wanted the girls wearing pasties, elevated stages, all sorts of nonsense like that. Fortunately, no one listened to them. Like I said, the nudity was pretty innocent.'

She took a sip of wine. 'But then Amira came along. Looking back, I can admit it now. Amira had something special, something I didn't. She was utterly uninhibited. When Boni made Amira the lead dancer in our nudie show, she was a sensation. And that show was pretty conservative. But *Flame* – my God. Everyone thought she was a prima donna going off to Paris for six months. But when she came back, she unveiled *Flame*. No one had seen anything like it. Amira wasn't stripping. She wasn't dancing. She may as well have been masturbating right there on stage. For nineteen sixty-seven, my dears, *that* was scandalous.'

'What was Amira like as a person?' Stride asked.

'Cold. Ambitious. Selfish.' Helen traced the top of her wine glass with a painted fingernail. 'Does that sound harsh? I admit, I was biased against her, because she treated me like shit. She treated all the

106

other dancers that way. Most of us would pal around, look out for each other. But not Amira. She was only interested in herself.'

'Do you know how she wound up in Vegas? How she got her start?'

'If you were a young girl with stars in your eyes, you went one of two places back then,' Helen said. 'Hollywood or Vegas. I don't think Amira liked the idea of being a movie star. She fed off the crowd. She liked performing in front of an audience. And she was all about sex. Vegas was a natural for her.'

'But you don't just walk into town and become a star,' Serena said.

'Most of us, no. But Amira wasn't like most of us. The first thing she did was have an affair with Moose, and he put her in his show. That gave her an audience. From there, her sex appeal carried her.'

'How did she get involved with Moose?'

Helen laughed. 'Moose wasn't exactly playing hard to get in those days. He told me later that Amira was the greatest fuck he ever had. Of course, he didn't realize the little bitch would turn around and put a knife in his back. Take over *his* show.'

'He must have been angry,' Stride said.

'Furious. Which for Moose is saying a lot. He trashed his dressing room when Boni told him he wouldn't have his own show any more and would be a variety performer in *Flame*. Boni had to have Leo talk to him.'

'Leo?' Serena asked.

'Leo Rucci. Boni's right-hand man. He ran the day-to-day operations at the casino.'

'What do you think Leo said to Moose?'

'I think Leo told him he'd be out on the street with a rearranged face if he didn't shut up.'

'So Moose was nursing a major grudge against Amira,' Stride said.

'Sure. Most of us were. Amira didn't care who she trashed to get what she wanted.'

'Did Amira have a boyfriend?' Stride asked. 'After Moose, that is.'

'Not that I ever saw. In fact, I don't really think she had many friends at all. Amira rarely hung out in the casino when she wasn't on stage. The rest of us liked to gamble and drink with the other stars. Amira did her act and disappeared. I think that was part of how she cultivated her image. She was unapproachable. It made men want her.'

'Tell us about Walker Lane,' Stride said. 'We heard he wanted Amira, too.'

Helen's eyes twinkled. 'Well, he wanted *me* first.'

'You slept with him?' Serena asked.

'Once. He was filming his Vegas movie that spring. *Neon Nights*. Remember that one? Well, it was forgotten quickly, but it made a lot of money at the time. A few scenes were filmed at the Sheherezade, and I got to know him when he came to the show. Over the course of a couple months, I think he fucked all the dancers.'

'Was Amira one of them?'

Helen shook her head. 'She wasn't back from Paris at that point. But when *Flame* started up that summer, Walker fell for her hard. Every weekend, he flew in from LA and was in the front row. Like a puppy dog. But as far as we could tell, Amira didn't give him the time of day.'

'It's a long way from unrequited love to murder,' Serena said. 'Sounds like Moose had a better motive. Or you, for that matter.'

'That's true,' Helen acknowledged. 'Then again, we didn't leave town right after the murder. Why else do you think the word went out that Walker wasn't in Vegas that night? Boni was covering for his whale. But Walker was there. I saw him at the first show.'

'Tell us what happened that night,' Stride said.

'I don't know, not really. We did our two performances of *Flame* that evening, at eight o'clock and then eleven o'clock. Amira was in both shows. She left around one in the morning. I saw her leave the backstage area. There was nothing unusual about it. But by the next morning, the word was all over the casino that she had been killed.'

'Did you see Walker at the second show?' Stride asked.

'No. He usually attended both shows when he was in town. But he was only at the first show that night.'

'Did you see him in the casino at all after the first show?'

'I never saw him again, period. Ever.' Helen raised her eyebrows as if to say, that's what I've been telling you.

'What did you do after the last show?' Serena asked.

'I went to one of the hotel rooms. Leo met me there, and we sweated up the sheets for an hour.'

'Leo Rucci? The casino manager?'

Helen nodded. 'That was what he called himself, a manager. He was mostly just dumb muscle for Boni. He managed people by bullying and threatening and beating them up when he needed to.'

'So why sleep with him?'

Helen seemed amused at their naivety. 'Well, first, I was ambitious, like Amira. I knew whenever she decided she wanted more money somewhere else, I'd have a shot at the lead role. I thought Leo could put in a good word for me with Boni, and he did.' She winked. 'But it wasn't just that. Leo also had the biggest cock I'd ever seen. Nine inches and fat like a sausage. I could only do him after a show, because there was no way I could dance after having that thing inside me.' She said it matter-of-factly. Stride got the feeling that Helen liked being outrageous. He tried not to blush but felt his face growing hot.

'How long was Leo with you?' Serena asked, coming to his rescue.

'About an hour. That was about two o'clock in the morning. Normally, I could count on Leo for a couple go-rounds, but he had to leave.'

'Why?' Serena asked.

'Mickey called him. There was a problem outside.'

'Who's Mickey?'

Helen shrugged. 'One of the lifeguards. There were always students who took summer jobs to make money and screw some of the wives while their husbands were at the tables. Mickey told Leo some guy was drunk near the pool and trying to start a fight. Leo went outside to break the guy's nose.'

'That was how Leo solved most of his problems?' Stride asked.

'Oh, yeah. He was a vicious son of a bitch. Huge, like a linebacker. He slapped me a couple times, too, and that was the end of it for me.'

'Did you hear anything more about the fight?' Serena asked.

'Not a word. I assume it was some nobody. If it was Dean or Shecky, that would have been news. As it was, the next day all the talk was about Amira.'

'And you didn't see Leo again that night?'

'No, not until the next day.'

'Did he tell you anything about the murder?' Stride asked.

Helen smiled. 'Only that I should keep my mouth shut and not ask any questions. The other girls got the same story. If anybody asked, we didn't know a damn thing.'

'What about the detective who was investigating? His name was Nicholas Humphrey. Did you ever speak to him?'

'Sure. He interviewed all of us together, and Leo was there, too. No one said a thing. If you ask me, Nick didn't look too disappointed. I'm not sure he was all that interested in the truth.'

'Nick?' Stride asked. 'You knew him?'

'He was a regular at the Sheherezade,' Helen replied. 'Sometimes he had private security gigs for the stars.'

Stride began to think that maybe Rex Terrell was right, and the fix was in. 'Did Nick Humphrey ever provide security for Walker Lane?' he asked.

'Well, it's possible Nick helped him out on *Neon Nights*. I'm not sure.' Helen leaned closer to them. A few drops of water from her swimsuit landed on the patio table. 'Can I ask you something? How does this involve me? Or Peter?'

'Our first thought was that someone was trying to keep you quiet,' Serena said.

'But no one threatened me,' Helen insisted.

Stride watched her closely. He could see age there, no matter how much she tried to hide it with plastic surgery and makeup. He saw vice, too, plenty of it. But not deceit. Not fear. She wasn't hiding from anyone, or covering up the truth.

'Right now, we don't know who's doing this or why,' Stride admitted. 'But in the meantime, please be careful. Until we know what game this person is playing, we don't know his next move.'

Sixteen

Being up here, Stride thought, was like being on top of the world, staring down. Jagged, barren mountain tops of red-orange rock were set against a blue sky that seemed as tall as heaven. Streaks of erosion on the cliffs looked like grooves that had been carved into the hills with a knife. It was stark, surpassing beauty, ringing the valley.

The late afternoon weather was warm, but not hot, although he could feel even in the waning glow of the sun how easily it could turn ferocious. He remembered the summer and how he had baked then, barely able to take a breath, feeling super-heated grit clog his lungs. There were none of the lake breezes or storms from Minnesota, no electrical shows of thunder and lightning, no cool dampness. Just an oven, set on broil and left to cook for three months.

He took a last look at the whitewashed stucco of Helen's palatial home.

'So how do you think she is in bed?' he asked, glancing at Serena with a smile.

'I think she's more than you could handle,' Serena replied.

'You got that right.'

His cell phone rang. Sara Evans again. Restless.

'This is Sawhill.' Stride imagined him with his stress ball in hand, squeezing rhythmically.

'Hello, Lieutenant,' Stride replied.

Serena drew a finger across her throat and mouthed, *He's going to cut us off.*

'Cordy tells me you think there may be a connection between M.J.'s murder and the death of Peter Hale,' Sawhill said.

'It looks that way.' He explained how they had discovered the link between Helen Truax and Walker Lane, and what Helen had told them about Amira Luz.

'I thought I told you that line of inquiry was dead,' Sawhill said.

111

Stride chose his words carefully. 'You did, sir. And it was. This was professional curiosity, nothing more. It was simply luck that Serena recognized the boy's grandmother in a photo that ran in *LV*. In Rex Terrell's article.'

'Professional curiosity,' Sawhill said, repeating the phrase as if he was tasting sour wine. 'Tell me, Detective, do you expect me to believe that story?'

'Not for a moment,' Stride replied.

Sawhill actually laughed. 'All right. I fire cops who think I'm an idiot. I respect a cop who follows his instincts, even if it lands him in hot water. Which this still may, Stride.'

'I realize that,' Stride acknowledged.

'What about the murder in Reno?'

'Serena talked to Jay Walling. So far, it doesn't look like the woman who was killed, Alice Ford, or her family had any connection to the Sheherezade or Amira. But he's going to keep digging.'

As he talked to Sawhill on the street, Stride heard Serena's cell phone ring. He watched her take the call and cup her ear, moving several steps away.

Sawhill kept talking. 'For the time being, we keep this out of the press. Got it?'

'Agreed.'

'My restriction still stands. Don't talk to Walker Lane again without clearing it through me.'

'Fair enough,' Stride said. He didn't mention that Walker Lane was already back on his list, along with another name that would drive Sawhill crazy: Boni Fisso. This investigation had all the makings of a political tornado, sucking people into the updraft.

'What's your next move?' Sawhill asked.

'I want to talk to Nick Humphrey,' Stride said. 'The detective who handled the original investigation of Amira's death.'

'All right, I'll get you his address,' Sawhill replied. 'He still lives in the city.'

Stride heard the clicking of keys, and then Sawhill rattled off an address in North Las Vegas. Stride jotted it down in his notebook.

'Step carefully, Detective. I'm willing to let you run because it looks like your instincts were right. But keep your professional curiosity on a short leash.'

Sawhill hung up the phone. A few feet away, Serena did the same.

'A reprieve,' he told Serena. 'Sawhill thinks the connection is tenuous, but he's not shutting us down. Yet.'

Serena was smiling. 'He's a lying bastard.'

112

'What?'

'That was Cordy,' Serena said. 'There's nothing tenuous about the connection. We ran the Aztek for fingerprints, and there was a beautiful print left for us on the inside of the front windshield. It matches the print you guys found on the slot machine at the Oasis. It was the same guy.'

'Son of a bitch,' Stride said. 'Sawhill knew?'

'Cordy just left his office.'

'And to think I was actually polite to him.' Stride laughed.

They climbed into the Bronco and headed down the long stretch of Bonanza back to the city. The elegant estates disappeared behind them as they descended into the valley, replaced by drab middle-class housing behind gray walls. Stride pulled up to a stop light, and he turned and stared thoughtfully at Serena. They were working the same case again. Like the murder of Rachel Deese that summer, when they first met. It gave him a jolt of adrenaline.

'So we have the same killer,' Serena said. 'And the guy is leaving his calling card behind at each crime scene.'

'Did Jay Walling run a match for prints at the scene in Reno?'

Serena nodded. 'No match.'

'So maybe there's no connection,' Stride said.

'Or we haven't found it yet. It's possible the perp didn't think about leaving a print behind until the hit-and-run. Then he decided he wanted to lead us on a merry chase. So he left the receipt as a clue to tie in the murder of Alice Ford at her ranch.'

'Except Helen and Walker Lane are both mentioned in Rex Terrell's article in *LV*. They have a connection to Amira Luz. The Fords don't, as far as we can tell.'

'You think the article by Rex is the connection?' Serena asked. 'That's what got this started?'

'Maybe,' Stride replied. 'No one cared about Amira for years before he started nosing around. Rex may have got someone's attention.'

Seventeen

As they climbed up Nick Humphrey's driveway, a little blur of white came streaking like a comet from next door. They stopped as a West Highland terrier sped around their feet, dancing on its hind legs and then flopping over on its back. Serena laughed and crouched down, rubbing the dog's belly. It closed its eyes, in heaven.

An elderly black man limped over from the neighboring house. 'I'm sorry about that.'

The dog leaped up and began jumping for attention at the man's legs, wanting to be picked up. He bent over with a groan and scooped her up. 'Some watchdog you are,' he grumbled at her. The dog kissed his face.

'What a sweetie,' Serena told him.

'Yeah, she loves people,' the man replied. He added, 'I'm Harvey Washington. You coming to see Nicky?'

They nodded.

'He's inside. Probably watching ESPN. Me, I prefer the History Channel. I love it when they do those dinosaur shows.' He put the dog down, and the dog sat and stared up at him. 'You wouldn't have liked those days, huh, missy? You would have wound up an appetizer for one of them T-Rexes.'

The dog looked unconvinced. It pawed at Serena's leg and then flopped over on its back again.

'Oh, you're a lady, for heaven's sake,' Harvey said. 'Don't go offering up your tummy like that. You want people to think you're easy?'

Harvey had gray curly hair and a broad nose. His chocolate skin was wrinkled and hung like ill-fitting clothes on his arms and legs. He wore navy blue shorts and a white polo shirt.

'Have you know Nick long?' Stride asked.

'Oh, for years. Long before both of us moved here.'

'Were you on the force, too?' Serena asked.

114

'No, nothing like that. I can see you two are on the job, though. You both have that look. I'd know it anywhere.'

Stride saw a twinkle in Harvey's eyes and wondered if the man knew the police from personal experience. He wouldn't have wanted to be a black man in Las Vegas in the old days.

'I won't keep you,' Harvey said. 'I'm sure you've got ground to cover with Nick. When you see him, ask him if he's taking his Lisinopril. The man's blood pressure could pop a champagne cork.'

He waved goodbye with his dog's paw and shuffled back to his yard.

A small plane floated overhead, its engine whining. They weren't far from the North Las Vegas Airport. Nick Humphrey lived on a street of tract houses just off Cheyenne. There was still a lot of open land out here. Stride could hear the rumble of bulldozers digging up the rocky soil somewhere, giving birth to another lookalike development like this one, where each unit was cheap and without any soul, painted the same mute beige, dropped next to one another like part of a build-by-numbers master plan. Stride was sorry to think that this was the best Humphrey could afford, after several decades on the job.

Stride and Serena continued to the front door and rang the bell. Humphrey answered immediately, as if he had been waiting for them. His eyes were hooded with suspicion. Stride explained who they were and that they wanted to talk to him about an old case, but his granite expression didn't change.

'Amira Luz,' Stride added.

'Yeah, I thought as much,' Humphrey said. With a shrug, he let them in.

Humphrey had a shock-white crewcut and a goatee. He was bulky for his age, and when he shook their hands, his grip was crushing. He wore jeans and slippers, but no shirt, and a green terry robe tied loosely at his waist. He led them into a small living room, trailing an aroma of Ben-Gay.

'You guys want a beer? If anyone asks, I can just say it was bottled water.' They declined, and he didn't seem surprised. He added, 'That's OK. No one would believe I kept bottled water in the house anyway.'

His living room had the look of a bachelor's house, messy and unorganized. Prescription pill bottles and beer cans were strewn across a coffee table, its wooden veneer scratched and dotted with water rings. Books and newspapers sat in stacks on the floor. Stride took a seat on a sofa and heard its sagging frame squeak through the cushions. Stuffing spilled out through the ripped floral fabric on the arms.

115

Stride saw an old baseball on the coffee table. He picked it up and noticed the ball was autographed in a faded blue scrawl. *Willie Mays.*

'This must be worth a lot,' Stride said.

'Yeah, so what, I'm not allowed to have some nice things?'

'I never said that.'

Humphrey snorted. 'I'm a collector.' He took a seat in an old leather recliner across from them. 'So I hear Sawhill is in charge of homicide now.'

'That's right,' Serena said.

'Bunch of Mormons running Sin City,' Humphrey said, curling his lip. 'Ain't that a fucking joke? But I suppose you got the Indians raking in the gambling bucks everywhere else. Take your pick.'

'Did you work with Sawhill?' Serena asked.

'Sure. Ambitious but smart. Politics first, God second. I hear he's got his eyes on the sheriff's campaign next year.'

Serena nodded. 'But the word is that the sheriff will endorse someone else.'

'Don't be so sure. He's going to feel a lot of heat. Sawhill's got a brother who's a top aide to the governor, and he's got a sister who does political ads and worked on the mayor's last campaign. And the old man, Michael Sawhill, is a big-shot casino banker. The whole family's connected.'

'You didn't sound surprised that we were here about Amira Luz,' Stride said.

'I saw the article in *LV*,' Humphrey retorted bitterly. 'That little snot Terrell all but accused me of being on the take. I called a lawyer who told me there wasn't much I could do. Too bad. A libel suit would pay for a few upgrades around here.'

'A lot of people back then seemed to think Walker Lane was involved in the murder,' Serena said.

Humphrey shrugged. 'There was no evidence he was involved. And there was plenty of evidence that this guy in LA did it.'

'But Walker was in Las Vegas that night,' Stride said.

'Hell, I know that. It was that goddamn article that said we were clueless about it. But I had six people who told me that Walker Lane left town before the second performance of the show. He drove back to LA.'

'Could they have been lying to you?' Serena asked.

'Sure they could. But if they were, they got their stories straight.'

'Did you talk directly to Boni Fisso about what happened that night?' Stride asked.

Humphrey shifted uncomfortably and tugged at his groin. 'Boni

116

talk to the cops? Fat chance. I dealt with Leo Rucci. He was the fixer, Boni's boss on the casino floor. Everything went through Leo. Meanest asshole I've ever met.'

'We heard Leo Rucci was involved in breaking up a fight in the middle of the night on the night of the murder. Did you investigate that?'

'Fight? I never heard a word about it. Rucci never mentioned it. His alibi was he was balling one of the dancers, and she confirmed it. Besides, Rucci didn't usually break up fights, he caused them.'

'How about a lifeguard named Mickey? He was the one who called Rucci. Did you talk to him?'

'Nah. Pretty boys by the pool were a dime a dozen.' Humphrey pushed himself out of his chair. 'I got to take a leak,' he said. 'Prostate. What a bitch. Bet mine's the size of a fucking orange by now.'

He left the room, and Stride got up from the sofa, shaking his head. 'It's hell getting old,' he said.

'So you tell me,' Serena said with an impish grin.

He did think about it sometimes, the age difference of almost a decade between them. He worried about a day when she might wake up and ask herself what she was doing with an old man. He didn't feel any older or younger than his years, but he wasn't a superman. He was in his mid-forties, and some of the original equipment was a little worn. He felt better physically away from the Minnesota cold, suffering from fewer of the bone-deep pains that the frigid lake winds brought.

Serena, by contrast, was physically in her prime, at least in his eyes. It was her soul that felt older, and that was what held them together. It was as if she had started bruising and weathering it at a young age. He only wished she would tell him more about it. She had begun to offer him little glimpses, like opening the windows in an Advent calendar, but there was still a lot he didn't know about her.

He studied Humphrey's living room, looking for clues to the man. There were sports sections littering the floor near his recliner, not just from the Las Vegas paper, but also from Los Angeles, Chicago, and New York. Sports book, Stride thought to himself. Humphrey probably spent a lot of time trying to beat the spread.

The recliner itself reeked of menthol. The whole house was dank, as if the windows had been closed for too long. He also picked up a remnant of Cajun smells in the air, as if someone had been spicing up a pot of jambalaya.

'Look at this,' Serena called to him.

She was looking at several framed photographs on the wall. They

117

were publicity shots of old Vegas stars, similar to the ones that Stride had seen at Battista's. He recognized Dean Martin, Elvis, and Marilyn Monroe.

'All of these are autographed,' Serena said.

Stride shrugged. 'So he collects memorabilia. He told us as much.'

'No, they're autographed to him,' Serena said.

Stride joined her at the wall and realized she was right. Each photograph bore Nick's name and a personal message in addition to the star's signature. 'Helen said he did private security gigs,' Stride said.

'Yeah, but look at Marilyn's message,' Serena told him.

Stride leaned closer to the smiling photograph of the platinum blonde. Across one bare shoulder, in black marker, a feminine hand had written: *Nicky – What a night. I needed you, and you were there. Love and kisses, MM.*

'She was a hell of a girl,' Humphrey said as he re-entered the living room behind them. He held a lowball glass with a large shot of what looked like whiskey.

'Come on, Nick,' Stride told him. 'Maybe you could get by with Willie Mays and Dean Martin. But not Marilyn. I'm not buying it.'

Humphrey was smug. He put down his whiskey and rummaged through a pile of paperbacks on an end table. He pulled one out and tossed it across the room to Stride. It was a biography of Marilyn Monroe.

'There are some photographs after page seventy-two,' he said. 'One of them shows a letter she wrote to DiMaggio. Now you tell me if that's not the same handwriting.'

Stride and Serena both found the page and held up the image of Marilyn's old letter to the photograph on the wall. Humphrey laughed as their faces fell. Stride had to admit that the handwriting looked like a dead-on match.

Humphrey sat back down in his recliner, picked up the whiskey, and grinned at them, enormously pleased with himself.

'So you guys want to tell me why you're really here?' he asked. 'I don't imagine Metro has the resources to be digging up forty-year-old murders.'

Stride and Serena sat back down. He found himself stealing glances at Marilyn's photograph and still thought Humphrey was pulling one over on them.

'Two close relatives of people who were mentioned in Rex Terrell's article have been murdered in the last two weeks,' Serena said. 'Same perp. We want to know if these murders somehow are tied back to the death of Amira Luz.'

'Forty years is a long time to wait to start a vendetta,' Humphrey replied.

'Even so, you might want to take precautions,' Stride suggested. 'Tell your family to do the same.'

Humphrey shrugged. 'Never married, no kids. I'm the end of the blood line.'

'Do you have any idea who might be doing this or why?' Serena asked.

'None at all,' Humphrey said. 'I hope you don't think it's me. A geriatric serial killer, now that would be a new twist. They could show that one on *Law and Order: Nursing Home Unit*.'

'Then what do you think is going on?' Stride asked.

'Look, you already mentioned his name,' Humphrey said. 'Boni Fisso. He's got a big new project going up, right? Couple billion dollars in play?'

Stride nodded. 'That was our first thought, too. Boni might be afraid that the truth about Amira's death would come out. We thought he might be sending a signal to people who were involved back then. Keep your mouths shut.'

'Boni wouldn't bother with relatives and signals,' Humphrey said. 'He'd simply take them out.' The old detective shook his head, as if he had already figured it out. Stride realized, watching the man's mind work, that Humphrey had been a smart cop. Which made the gaps in the investigation of Amira's death smell even worse.

'Turn it the other way around,' Humphrey said. 'Maybe someone wants to derail Boni's big new casino as a kind of weird justice for Amira. So he starts killing people. Leaving breadcrumbs for you guys to follow. And all of it leading into the past.'

Breadcrumbs, Stride thought. Like fingerprints. 'Did Amira have relatives?'

'None that I ever found. She was an only child, parents both dead. But it wouldn't have to be someone who was related to Amira. Boni made plenty of enemies in his day.'

'The question is, where do the breadcrumbs lead?' Stride asked. 'If you're right about this guy, he seems to think there's more to Amira's death than ever came out.'

'He's wrong,' Humphrey insisted. 'We closed the case.'

'Listen, Nick,' Serena said cautiously. 'Don't take this the wrong way. Word is you were a regular at the Sheherezade. You did a lot of private security gigs there.' She gestured at the photographs on the wall. 'Looks like you've got the pictures to prove it, too.'

Humphrey's eyes got as cold as the ice in his drink. 'So?'

'So it was another time. Different rules. This was an outlaw town. What we're wondering is—'

'You're wondering whether I was paid off,' Humphrey said, his voice rising sharply. 'Right? Fuck, you're as bad as Rex Terrell.'

'No one said that,' Serena replied. 'But there are a lot of questions, and you seem too smart to have missed them. We want to know whether you got pressure from somewhere to go easy on the investigation.'

Humphrey stared at them, and Stride thought he saw the pain of a compromised man. The retired cop looked down into his drink and drained the last of the whiskey in a single swallow. 'There was no pressure,' he croaked, his throat constricted.

Stride saw movement out of the corner of his eye. Harvey Washington from next door stood in the doorway of the living room, his dog in his arms, his eyes sad. The dog squirmed to be put down.

'Nick, why don't you tell them the truth? We're old men. No one gives a rat's ass about us any more.'

Humphrey didn't show any surprise. 'Shit, Harvey, I could still get in trouble. We both could.'

Harvey shook his head and put down the dog. It immediately scampered across the room, jumped into Humphrey's lap, and curled up for a nap.

Serena blinked. 'He's *your* dog?'

'Do you guys want to tell us what the hell is going on?' Stride asked.

Harvey folded his arms and waited. Humphrey scratched the dog's head and refused to look up. He gave a petulant shrug. 'You do what you got to do,' he told Harvey.

'Oh, don't be a child,' Harvey said. He pulled a rickety wooden chair out from the wall and sat down. 'There was pressure,' he told Stride and Serena. 'But it's not what you think. Nicky never took a dime. He went soft on those guys because of me.'

Stride didn't understand. 'You?'

'We've been partners for almost fifty years.'

In the recliner, Humphrey took a deep breath. If there had been a closet in the room, he would have crawled back into it. 'Leo Rucci knew. I don't know how. Those guys back then, they knew everything about everybody. He made it clear that if I pushed in the wrong direction, the department would find out I was gay. That would have cost me my job.'

'And the wrong direction was Walker Lane?' Stride asked.

Humphrey spread his arms wide. 'What do you think? I knew it smelled. But I was fucked.'

120

'It was more than that,' Harvey added. 'Nick was protecting me. He would have lost his job, and I would have wound up in jail. Me and the law, we haven't always seen eye to eye about things.'

Stride looked at Marilyn Monroe smiling at him from the wall. 'You're a forger,' he guessed.

'He's an artist is what he is,' Humphrey insisted.

Harvey ducked his head modestly. 'I imitate things. When I was younger, sometimes I wasn't all that fussy about people knowing what was real and what wasn't.'

'But not any more?' Stride asked, picking up the Willie Mays baseball.

Harvey grinned. 'I give Nicky presents from time to time. It's a game for us. These days, I can sell my imitations on eBay and still make pretty good dough. Mind you, I advertise them as imitations, not the real thing.'

'And I'm sure your buyers are always equally honest when they re-sell them,' Serena said.

'That ain't my problem,' Harvey replied pleasantly.

Stride couldn't believe it. A gay cop and a lover who happened to be a con artist. The result was that someone – Walker Lane? – got away with murder, and some poor chump in LA got killed to close the case. And forty years later, another round of murders had begun.

'Is Leo Rucci still alive?' Stride asked. 'We need to talk to him.'

'He's alive,' Humphrey said. 'But Rucci was just the arms and legs. Boni was always the brains. He's the only one who really knows what went on that night.'

'Except Boni's not likely to talk to us without a warrant and seven lawyers vetting every question,' Stride said.

'See if Sawhill can get his dad to make a call,' Humphrey said. 'The old man has done money deals for Boni and a lot of the other casino owners for years.'

'Sawhill has connections to Boni?' Stride asked.

'It's a small town,' Humphrey replied.

'You could talk to Boni's daughter, too,' Harvey suggested.

Serena looked up, surprised. 'I didn't know Boni had a daughter.'

Humphrey nodded. 'Claire Belfort. She took her mother's name. Claire and Boni had a big falling out years ago. She's a folk singer at one of the joints on the Boulder Strip.'

'Why would she help us?' Stride asked.

Humphrey shrugged. 'She might not. Probably won't. But if anyone can get you to Boni with a single phone call, it's Claire.'

Eighteen

He parked the Lexus on the lake road in front of an estate where the windows were dark. Whoever owned the mansion was away in the city for the evening, or maybe cruising through the calm waters of the Greek islands. That was what the people in Lake Las Vegas did. They could afford to go anywhere and do anything.

It didn't really matter if someone was inside. If they looked out and saw a Lexus parked in front of their house, it wouldn't arouse any suspicion. Just one of the neighbors taking a night-time stroll by the water. After all, strangers couldn't come here. You couldn't get in without passing through the security gate on the south shore.

The old woman had played her part well. Smiling at the guard, laughing as if nothing was wrong, as if no one was behind her in the back seat, with a gun. Roll up the window, and drive through the gate, as she did most days. The only telltale sign, which he could see from behind her, was the frantic quivering of her fingers on the steering wheel. Not from Parkinson's, as anyone might expect from an old woman. This was terror.

He had spent the late afternoon with her in her house, watching her fear grow, watching the sun set. She was tied to a chair and gagged, eyes wide, following his movements as he went back and forth to the window. When it was night, he was finally ready. He knew she was waiting for him to kill her, and he wondered if her heart finally stopped racing when he simply left the house, took her car, and drove away.

He didn't drive far. Just a few blocks down to the lake, where the largest of the estates hugged the water. He had a vantage from here to the big house dominating the street.

Waiting.

He wanted a cigarette but didn't dare open the smoked windows of the car. Better to let it look deserted, if anyone drove by. He sat, almost motionless, watching the large estate, observing the lights that

122

went on and off from room to room, seeing occasional silhouettes moving behind the curtains. He used a miniature pair of binoculars to see inside and confirm that both of them were still home. Just the two of them.

Every now and then, his eyes flicked across to the lake. The lights of the resorts twinkled like a fairyland. That was what they peddled here. Illusion.

He cleared his mind. He had done this many times, and he wasn't nervous. But the mental lapse with the boy still worried him. He had allowed himself to get angry, to have his emotions spill over. It hadn't been a problem with the others. He didn't want it to be a problem again. Not tonight. Not with the rest in the days to come.

He saw motion in the rear-view mirror of the car. Headlights. A long black limousine glided by the Lexus, continuing down the lakeside street and pulling into the driveway of the estate he was watching. The driver didn't turn the engine off, or switch off the headlights, or toot his horn – it was simply the time for him to be there, and with celebrity assignments you were always there at the right time.

The door of the estate opened.

He raised his binoculars and watched the big man leave the big house and proceed to the rear door of the big limousine. Everything about the man was larger than life. The driver had jumped out and was waiting there, tipping his hat, smiling.

The car door closed. The front door closed. He watched the limo back out of the driveway and retrace its course along the lake road, passing the Lexus as it went.

He gave it another ten minutes, sitting in silence and darkness. The street remained deserted. Finally, he turned on the car, leaving the headlights off, and rolled the Lexus quietly down the remaining stretch of pavement until he was in front of the large estate. He put the car in park, set the brake, but left the engine running. This wouldn't take long. He was always surprised to hear about the mistakes that other professionals sometimes made, such as turning the car off and finding, when they got back from the scene, that the car wouldn't start again. A little thing like that could mean twenty-five years to life.

He studied the mirrors one last time and got out of the car. The Sig was almost invisible in his right hand.

As he walked up the driveway, he felt a glimmer of hesitation, which he tried to quell. Then he understood – he knew her. In almost every other case, he had faced a stranger, whose story he didn't know. But he had been with her and liked her. She seemed lost, a victim, a little like himself. He came up to the oversized front door, rich with wood and brass, and thought how small she seemed in these giant surroundings.

It didn't matter in the end. Everyone was a victim sooner or later. That was what the voice said, the one that had always been there, guiding him.

Amira.

He rang the doorbell. A few seconds passed. He grew uncomfortable, bathed in the porch light. His gun was sheltered behind his right thigh.

She labored to open the door, and when she did, she smiled at him, recognizing him. There wasn't any fear in her face.

'Oh, hi,' she said in her girlish voice. Pretty. Vulnerable. 'Didn't you get the message?'

Those were her last words. When she saw the gun, she only had an instant to become confused and then afraid, and then it was over. You couldn't afford to hesitate when you had any doubts. Ten seconds later, he was back in the Lexus, with the windows open to disperse the acrid smell of smoke, driving back toward the hills that led into the city.

Nineteen

Serena ordered a bottle of sparkling water and a champagne glass. She found a table for two near the stage and tipped the waiter twenty dollars to remove the other chair.

She hated being in a casino by herself, where she had to fend off drunken passes all night and watch drinks being poured that reminded her of what she couldn't have. But Stride had suggested that Boni's daughter Claire might respond better to her, one on one in the casual setting of the club, than to the two of them together.

The Boulder Strip casinos mostly attracted locals, people in the know, who assumed their odds here were better away from Las Vegas Boulevard (not likely) and that they could be higher rollers with more perks on a smaller stake out here (true). Serena knew that Cordy was a fixture at Sam's Town, the largest of the Boulder casinos, a few miles to the north. He poured thousands of dollars into their greedy hands each year, but they treated him like a king in return.

The joint where Claire sang, called the Limelight, wasn't in the same league as its bigger cousins like Sam's Town, Arizona Charlie's, or Boulder Station, and didn't include an attached hotel. It was on the deserted southern end of the highway, where there were still acres of dirty, open land, interspersed with RV parks, adult superstores, and pawn shops. A few housing developments had begun creeping in at the edges, as the suburbs expanded their hold on the desert.

The Limelight had been recently renovated over the skeleton of a long-shuttered roadside casino, a beer-and-nickels joint where fights used to break out nightly and down-on-their-lucks gambled away their last few dollars. No one was sorry to see it go. The Limelight wasn't upscale, but it was one of the few venues in town that featured live country music for the price of a couple drinks. She and Stride had dropped in once or twice. It was barely more than a bar, with a matchbox gaming room for tables and slots and a claustrophobic showroom with green walls, a long bar with video poker machines, and about fifty circular tables squeezed without much breathing room in front of a narrow stage.

Serena sipped her water and watched the tables filling up quickly. Claire Belfort obviously had a reputation. Anyone could fill the club on Saturday night, but it was Tuesday, and that meant the crowd was coming to see her. Serena had been ready to assume that Boni's money had paved the way for his daughter's career, but now she wasn't so sure. The Limelight was a dive, but the people who came to the shows knew music.

At nine o'clock, Claire's band took their places. It was a typical country arrangement, with fiddle, bass, drums, and steel. The lights went down in the showroom, and overhead cans lit the stage. The band opened with a keening, melancholy tune, and Serena recognized it immediately as one of her favorite songs – 'You'll Never Leave Harlan Alive' – a bitter elegy about the plight of Kentucky coal miners. Serena had heard Patty Loveless sing it, and Patty was a tough act to follow.

But from offstage, she heard a smoky voice wrapping itself around the lyrics and weaving all the pain in the world into the music. Claire's voice could have stood up to the demands of the blues. It was strong and filled with emotion, but with a nuance in her expression that Serena had only heard in the most mature country singers. She sounded a little like Allison Moorer, with a voice so sorrowful and hypnotic that Serena found it arousing to listen to, and irresistible, like one of the Sirens.

Claire walked into the light from the corner of the stage. She kept singing, as applause erupted and then turned into a hush as people listened to the song. She had long, strawberry-blonde hair, with wavy ends that swished around her shoulders. Her face was angular, with hard edges and dimples in her cheeks, and a small birthmark in the hollow of one dimple that made her face both imperfect and attractive. She had piercing, intelligent blue eyes. She wore an untucked pink silk shirt, with its top three buttons undone, black pants that clung to her slim legs, and razor-thin stiletto heels. Light glinted on her gold hoop earrings.

She came to the very front of the stage, directly above Serena, singing a poignant story about a grandfather in the nineteenth century who went back into the coal mines to feed his family, only to die there like so many others. The music was haunting. Serena found herself staring up at Claire on the stage, enraptured. Their eyes met, and a strange, electric sensation passed between them. Serena passed it off as her imagination, but it felt real and intense.

126

When the song ended, with Claire whispering the last few lines over and over like a ghost, Serena found herself on her feet, applauding. She saw the flush in Claire's face and the way she thrived on the energy of the crowd.

Claire moved on to another country ballad and followed it with a rockabilly foot-stomper, then a medley of bluegrass covers. But all of them were sad songs, with lyrics about loss and surrender and death, the kind of songs that would ring false with a lesser singer. Claire brought them to life, made them real and sorrowful. In every tragedy she sang about, she found an inner longing that Serena could relate to and remember.

Her eyes kept coming back to Serena. Speaking to her. Teasing her. This wasn't Serena's imagination. When they looked at each other, Claire's lips would crease into a small smile, not of humor or irony, but of kinship. It was almost as if Claire was singing *to* her. Or that was how it felt.

Serena found herself being seduced.

It was a sensation from long ago that she hadn't felt for years. She wasn't drinking anything but water, but she felt drunk anyway. The music and smoke made her light-headed. Claire's voice felt like soft hands on her body, and Serena felt naked and exposed.

It was electrifying.

An hour later, Claire opened her dressing-room door with the same dark smile. Her skin glowed with sweat from her performance. Her eyes, seeing Serena, were bright and curious.

'I'm Serena Dial,' Serena told her. 'I'm a homicide investigator with Metro. I'd like to talk with you.'

Most people folded and became putty when they heard what she did. Claire just arched an eyebrow to show her surprise and opened the door a little wider, so that Serena could squeeze past her.

The dressing room was small and dreary. Yellowing linoleum stretched across the floor. The ceiling was made up of water-stained foam panels, and a couple aluminum pie pans were on the floor, catching occasional drips that plinked like music. There was a sleeper sofa on the right and a card table with several chairs around it. A clothes rack on wheels held hangers with Claire's costumes. She had a refrigerator, a sink, and a bathroom at the rear.

Claire gestured to the sofa and the card table. 'Take your pick.'

Serena sat in one of the card table chairs.

'Can I get you a drink?' Claire asked. When Serena shook her head, she added, 'I guess it would be bad form to offer a joint to a cop.'

127

Serena laughed. Claire retrieved a bottle of water from the refrigerator and slouched into one of the other card table chairs, her long legs stretched out, her elbow on the table. She opened the water bottle with slim, delicate fingers. 'Serena Dial,' she said. 'Great name.'

'Thanks.'

Claire leaned over and combed her hand through Serena's black hair. 'I love your hair, too. What do you use?'

Serena told her, feeling embarrassed that it was just a cheap shampoo.

Claire nodded and rocked back in the chair. 'I guess detectives don't talk about those kinds of things. You're tough, right? Detectives are tough. Shouldn't you be fat and wear a bad suit, instead of being gorgeous?'

'This is my after-hours look,' Serena said with a smile. 'During the day I'm fat and wear polyester.'

Claire smiled. 'Did you like my show?'

'I thought you were amazing,' Serena told her honestly. 'Why aren't you in Nashville?'

'What, this isn't glamorous?' Claire replied. She caught one of the drips from the ceiling in her hand. 'I don't do this for the money, and here I can sing whatever I want, whenever I want. In Nashville, people would want to control me.'

'Like your father,' Serena said.

Claire pursed her lips. 'Yes, like my father. Am I supposed to be impressed that you know about him? It's not a secret.'

'But you don't advertise it.'

'No, I don't. He probably likes it that way too. Is that why you're here? To talk about Boni?'

Serena nodded. 'In part.'

'What's the other part?' Claire asked, taking a drink of water.

'To tell you that you might be in danger.'

'That's intriguing,' Claire said. 'Will you be the one to protect me?'

'This isn't a joke. Two people are dead.'

Claire nodded. 'I never said it was a joke. But why would anyone want to kill me? Because I'm Boni's daughter? We may be estranged, Serena, but someone would have to be a fool to do that. I know my father, and you're a cop, so I guess you do, too. Boni would eradicate them. Torture them. They'd wind up in a corn field like Spilotro.'

'I don't think whoever is doing this cares about that.' Serena explained about the deaths of Peter Hale and M.J. Lane, and the connection that had brought them back to the forty-year-old death of Amira Luz. She added, 'Have you ever heard of Amira?'

'No,' Claire said. 'Boni never mentioned her. But I wasn't born until later that year.'

'How about Walker Lane?'

'I know of him, of course, but that's it. I wouldn't have been able to tell you he had anything to do with my father.'

'Why are you and your father estranged?' Serena asked.

Claire didn't answer. She put her bottle of water between her lips and drank again. Then she took one of Serena's hands in hers and turned it over, palm upward. Serena didn't pull away. Claire used her middle finger to lightly trace a line down along Serena's palm to her wrist. Claire's finger was moist from the condensation on the bottle.

'I can read palms, did you know that?' she said, with mischief in her voice.

Serena played along. 'What do you see?'

'Well, we already know you're tough.'

'Right.'

'You're a cop, so I'm going to hedge my bets on your life line. Your love line is broken, I'm sorry to say.'

'Is that so?'

'Definitely.'

'I can also see that you had a passionate affair with another woman when you were young.'

Serena yanked her hand away. 'What the hell is this?'

Claire raised her own hands in surrender. 'Easy, OK? It was a joke.' She added, 'But methinks I touched a nerve, Serena.'

Serena realized her heart was pounding. 'No, you just surprised me.'

'Well, don't worry about it,' Claire replied smoothly. 'I was reading my own palm. That's my story. I'm gay, if you hadn't noticed.'

'Did Boni not approve?'

'That's part of it.'

'But only part?'

Claire sighed. 'I spent my first twenty-eight years with Boni running my life, like he runs everything around him. I'm his only child, and he wanted me to follow in his footsteps. I went to UNLV, got a master's degree in hotel administration, all so I could take over the business whenever he was ready to hand it over. That's what I wanted, too. He bred all his ambition into me.'

'So what happened?' Serena asked.

Claire's face was emotionless. 'He had to make a choice between me and the business. The business came first. Big surprise.'

Serena guessed that she was covering something up.

'What about your mother?'

'She died giving birth to me. It's always been just me and Boni. At least until I walked out. I decided I wanted to be my own person, not some clone of my father.'

'You sound pretty tough, too,' Serena said.

'I told you, I was reading my own palm. Anyway, that was more than ten years ago, and we've hardly spoken since. He makes overtures from time to time, but I'm on my own now. I don't want him to buy me. It drives him crazy. I'm the only person in the world he hasn't been able to dominate.'

Serena knew at some level that Claire must be very much like her father. Stubborn. Dominant. She imagined that they must have had titanic fights over the years. It impressed her that Claire had stood her ground. That was what she had had to do herself, along the rocky road from her mother to Deirdre. People who promised to save her, and then betrayed her.

'You've made it hard for me to ask what I wanted to ask,' Serena admitted.

Claire shook her head. 'Not at all. Ask me anything. But I may ask for some of your secrets, too.'

'I need to talk to your father. We think he may know what's going on, and why. If it involves what happened to Amira, he's the only one who may be able to put the pieces together.'

'And you want me to call him,' Claire said.

'That's right.'

'I'm sorry, Serena. I'm not ready to do that. If it puts me in his debt, I won't do it.'

'I understand. But lives are at stake. Maybe yours, too.'

'Do you really think I'm in danger?' Claire asked.

'Yes, I do.'

Claire nodded. 'I need to think about this,' she said. A moment later, she added, 'I can't give you an answer now, OK?'

'Don't take too long,' Serena urged her. She found a card in her pocket and handed it to her.

Claire took it and tapped the card lightly on the table. 'You tell me something,' she said.

Serena smiled. 'OK.'

'Was I right?'

'You mean, about me?' Serena knew exactly what she meant. The affair. Touching a nerve. 'That's none of your business.'

'I forgot, you're tough.' Claire stood up and stretched her arms languorously over her head. 'I'm going to take a shower.'

Serena scraped her chair back along the linoleum and began to stand up. 'I'll go.'

'No, it's OK.' Claire waved her back to her seat. 'We can keep talking.'

She took a couple of steps to the dressing-room door and turned the deadbolt. She began unbuttoning her blouse. When she was done, Claire left her blouse hanging open, her cleavage and midriff on display.

'Do you sing?' Claire asked her.

'Me? No. I clear the room on karaoke night.'

'So how do you express yourself? You must have something.'

'I take pictures,' Serena said. 'Desert photos.'

Serena watched her carefully remove her earrings, using two hands as she unhitched the gold hoops. Claire put the earrings on the table, then ran her hands back through her hair, gently separating the strands.

'I'd like to see them,' Claire told her.

She nudged the blouse off her shoulders. The silk rubbed up along her skin, then separated and fell down her back. Her breasts were bare, perfect white globes with erect red nipples. She gently tugged the sleeves off each wrist and turned away to hang the blouse on the clothes rack. Her spine rippled, dipping into the hollow of her back.

'Would you like to have dinner?' Claire asked, without turning around.

'Sorry, I can't.'

Claire slid a zipper down the side of her black pants. She pushed them down over her ass, past her thighs, and then bent each leg to step out of them. She was now wearing only a black thong.

She turned back. 'Too bad.'

Serena knew she had an opportunity to say something, to make a joke, to leave. When she sat there, not moving, not even breathing, Claire stripped the thong off her body, exposing her auburn mound, which was trimmed to leave only a wisp of curly light hair. She stood there for a brief moment and then disappeared into the bathroom. The water in the shower began running.

Serena got out of the chair. She looked at the locked door to the dressing room and knew she should simply leave. But Claire returned, a towel slung around her neck, reaching low enough to cover her breasts but not the rest of her naked body.

'The water takes forever to heat up,' she said.

Serena nodded and tried to moisten her lips with her tongue, but her mouth was dry.

131

Claire walked up to within a few inches of Serena, too close for comfort. 'You could join me.'

'No. I couldn't do that.'

'You're very beautiful,' Claire told her.

'So are you,' Serena admitted, before she could stop herself.

'I'd like to see you again.'

'I'm not gay,' Serena said.

'Does that matter? I'm attracted to people, I don't care whether they're men or women. I'm attracted to you.'

'I'm involved,' Serena said. She added, 'With a man.'

'But you're attracted to me, too.'

Serena wanted to deny it, but she didn't. 'Look, this isn't going to happen.'

Claire reached out and touched Serena's face with the back of her hand. 'Don't hide it from him. You're keeping a secret now.'

'I'm sorry.' Serena pulled away. 'I sent the wrong signals.'

'They weren't wrong. You want me so bad you can taste it. What's wrong with that?'

Serena's cell phone rang. She backed up as if the room had caught fire and dove into her pocket to retrieve it. She heard Stride's voice, and she felt a wave of guilt crashing over her. She couldn't believe what she was doing, what she wanted to do. Not since Deirdre, she thought to herself.

'What is it?' she asked, and she hated herself because her voice was husky with arousal.

Stride brought her down to earth.

'There's been another murder,' he said.

Twenty

Amanda choked back tears as she stared at the body of Tierney Dargon. It surprised her. She had steeled herself to death over the years, but the bodies she saw day in and day out were rarely people she had known when they were alive. They were corpses, flesh, wounds, devoid of personality. But Amanda had seen Tierney so recently that she could remember her perfume and hear the girlish intonation of her voice. She had liked her. Felt sorry for her. Tierney was a decent kid lost in the Vegas high life. But no more.

Now she was like M.J., eyes wide with shock and fright, trails of blood streaked on her face from the gaping bullet wound in her forehead. Dead in the foyer of Moose's sprawling house, like Alice Ford in Reno, with no time to react or scream. Open the door, see the face of death, and bang. Her brain was gone before it had time to react. Instantaneous.

Amanda looked beyond the foyer into the mansion and realized that, even alive, Tierney would have looked out of place here. She was young, and this was a rich old man's house. Moose had made it into a shrine to his past, with bookshelves filled with awards, decades-old posters advertising his shows, and dozens of photographs of himself on stage. He was larger than life, and so was his estate, both of them gaudy and giant-like. The living room was decorated like a lavish casino, with tall Roman columns, gold trim, a grand piano, and – most impressive of all – a second-story indoor swimming pool with a translucent bottom, so visitors could look up and see the blue water. Moose had one of the prime locations in Lake Las Vegas, in the MiraBella development, hugging the golf course and the resort's private manmade lake, with the moonscape of the desert hills stretched out in the distance.

No one would hesitate to open the door here, even to a stranger. Lake Las Vegas was located a few miles east of the city, over the mountains on the road to Lake Mead. There was only one narrow road in or out to MiraBella and the other south shore developments, with a guard station to keep out strangers and gawkers. If you made it in, you were safe.

But not this time.

Amanda wondered how the killer had made it past the south shore gate.

'Where's Moose?' she asked one of the uniforms on the scene. She saw the cop's eyes cloud over with disgust and felt her hackles rise. Nothing ever changed.

'Guard at the gate said he left in the limo around six,' he said. 'I assume someone is tracking him down.'

'You assume?' Amanda retorted. The cop shrugged, and she added sharply, 'Don't assume. Find out, and let me know.'

'Yes, sir,' he replied acidly. Amanda felt her mood sour further as he left.

There was a large team on hand to work the murder. That was one advantage of getting killed in a place like Lake Las Vegas, which was usually immune to this kind of crime, unless it was a rich wife shooting a rich husband. A body out here got plenty of attention. The call had come in from a neighbor who heard the gunshot. He was a hunter and knew the difference between the report of a pistol and the crack of a target rifle, which wasn't an uncommon sound in the desert hills. When he went to investigate, he found the door wide open and Tierney just inside.

Amanda's cell phone rang. It was Stride.

'Where are you?' she asked.

'I'm parked outside, next to your car,' Stride said. 'I thought you didn't use the Spyder at crime scenes.'

Amanda was puzzled. 'Usually I don't. But I love to take it on the mountain roads. So what?'

'Come out here, OK?'

Amanda swallowed back acid and felt a pit of worry in her stomach. She slapped her phone shut and headed for the front door. As she passed two of the crime scene techs, she heard a whispered comment and a laugh behind her. She wheeled round, but couldn't tell who had spoken. She gave them a fierce glare, then bolted past Tierney's body into the warm air outside. The curving driveway was being scoured for evidence. She took a circuitous route through the garden rocks and past the cluster of patrol cars on the edge of the crime scene tape. Beyond the house was the deep darkness of the lake and sparkling lights from the resort hotel on the opposite shore.

Stride was leaning on his Bronco, next to her Spyder, about twenty yards away. He was standing under a street light. His arms were folded over his chest. When she joined him, he nodded at the driver's door of her sports car. Amanda saw it and swore.

The car was desecrated. Someone had chiseled the word PERVERT into the door of the Spyder in large letters.

'I didn't want you to find this alone,' Stride said.

Amanda felt her emotions battling between rage and humiliation. 'Fuckers,' she muttered. 'It never stops. Thanks for telling me.'

'I asked around,' Stride said. 'No one admits seeing anything.'

'Big surprise.' Amanda ran her fingers over the ruts in the paint. In some ways, it was like being raped. As if that was what they would do if they got her alone.

'Don't take this shit lying down, Amanda,' Stride told her.

'I never have before.' Amanda wondered, though, how much more she could take. It didn't matter how often she proved herself, they kept coming for her, trying to drive her away. She stared at the word again. Pervert. She could feel the hatred of whoever had written it. This wasn't a mean joke, a taunt. It was primal and ugly.

'You OK?' Stride asked, watching her.

She shook her head. She wasn't OK. 'I could have caught the Green River Killer and the headlines would have been about my cock. I mean, is it really such a big deal?'

Stride laughed. Amanda realized what she'd said and laughed too. Some of the tension drained out of her. 'OK, it is a big deal,' she said slyly. Then she added, 'I know what people think, it just hurts to have it constantly thrown in your face.'

She spent another few seconds feeling sorry for herself. Stride waited, not pushing her, and she felt a surge of warmth for him. She remembered what Serena had told her – that Stride had swooped in out of nowhere and become a lifeline for her. Amanda felt a little like that herself. Not in a romantic way, because she loved Bobby, and she knew Stride loved Serena. But it made her feel less alone on the force to have him there, as if she finally had an ally, a friend. That hadn't happened, not since she was Jason. Her friends from back then had peeled away, one by one.

'Tell me something,' she said to Stride. 'Why don't you hate me too?'

'Come on, Amanda. That question's not worthy of you.'

'You're right. It's stupid. Someone else asked that, not me.'

Stride was all business again. 'You said Tierney had a bodyguard, didn't you? Where was he?'

135

'Who, the Samoan? I think he's just rent-a-muscle. There was no one else in the house.'

'Shouldn't there be live-in staff at a palace like this?' Stride asked. 'A butler, six maids, a few gardeners to water the rocks?'

'Not according to the neighbor who found the body. I talked to him. He says there's day staff only. Apparently Moose likes to walk around naked at night.'

'Thanks for putting that image in my mind,' Stride said.

'What I'm wondering is how the perp got in here. He sure as hell didn't walk from the highway at night.'

'Is there a log of all the vehicles in and out?'

Amanda nodded. 'I've got uniforms tracking down every car in the security log, starting with the cars that left after the time of the murder.'

'Did he leave the shell casing again?'

'Yes, a .357, just like with M.J. I'm betting if we can recover the bullet, we'll get a ballistics match. Although I doubt we'll even need it. He's not trying to cover his tracks. I'm having them dust for prints to see if he left us another souvenir.'

'Three murders,' Stride said. 'Four, if there's a tie-in with Reno. He's picking up the pace.'

Amanda saw headlights approaching down the lakeside avenue where Moose and a handful of other wealthy neighbors kept their homes. As the vehicle passed under the first street light, she recognized the limo in which she had sat with Tierney Dargon. When Tierney was alive and young.

She pointed at the car. 'Moose,' she said.

Stride could see where the comedian got his nickname. He was amazingly tall and seemed to be all legs, like a circus magician on stilts. He had a shaggy head of long hair, unnaturally black and thick for a man his age. It flopped across his face as he sat with his elbows propped on his knees and his long, spindly fingers cupping his face like tentacles. His tuxedo fitted loosely. He had undone his bow tie, which lay like a squashed bat on his ruffled white shirt.

He was alone with Stride and Amanda in the rear of the limo. His feet almost touched the other cushions of the stretch.

'My beautiful girl,' he said. 'I should have left her where she was. I'm a selfish bastard. I wanted someone to take care of me. To bury me. Now I have to bury her instead.'

He looked up at them, his dark eyes haunted. Stride noticed his trademark eyebrows, furry and wild, which he was able to curl and twitch at will. They were part of his act. He could make his eyebrows dance, and crowds died laughing. Stride had seen him in a stand-up routine on television almost twenty years ago. His humor was black and self-destructive, filled with jokes about drinking, divorce, and strokes, drawn from his own life. But his eyebrows lightened everything, as if they were twin dummies, and he was the ventriloquist.

Tonight, though, they sat motionless above his eyes like sleeping dogs.

'Can you tell us where you were this evening, Mr Dargon?' Stride asked. He was polite but firm.

Moose slowly focused. He seemed genuinely numb with grief, but Stride had been disappointed too many times by suffering spouses. Too often they turned out to be perpetrators, not victims. And Moose was a performer.

'I was entertaining at a fundraiser,' he said, pointing to a re-election button for Governor Durand on his tuxedo lapel.

'Why didn't Tierney go with you?'

One of Moose's eyebrows sprang briefly to life. 'I'm a beast when I have a show to do. I don't talk to anyone before or after. Tierney would have had to sit by herself with a table full of gassy lawyers. Listen to them telling her about their latest Daubert motion while checking out her tits. She would have hated it.'

'Who else knew she was going to be home alone?' Stride asked, putting a faint emphasis on the word *else*.

'I can't think of anyone,' Moose said. 'Usually, Tierney goes out if I have a show. She's young. But today she decided to stay home and watch some movies.'

'Did she tell anyone about her plans?'

'Just the security company. She called them around noon and said she wouldn't need an escort tonight.'

Stride glanced at Amanda, who was already scribbling in her notebook. He asked Moose for details about the security company he used, which was called Premium Security. Stride remembered that Karyn Westermark also used a bodyguard when she was in Vegas, and he jotted down a reminder to find out whether she used the same firm.

Amanda leaned forward. 'Mr Dargon, did you know M.J. Lane?'

Moose's face was blank. 'Walker's son? The boy who was murdered last weekend? I knew the old man back in the sixties, but not M.J. Why?'

'There's no way to be delicate about this,' Amanda told him. 'Tierney was having an affair with M.J.'

'Oh.' Moose rested his head back until he was staring at the ceiling of the limo. 'Now I see. You think I'm a jealous cuckold. First I had her lover killed, and now my wife.'

'You have a reputation,' Stride said. 'A temper.'

Moose looked down and gave them a sad smile. His eyebrows rippled. Stride noticed the gray pallor on the man's skin, how the bones of his face formed the outline of his skull. He had seen the look before, when his wife Cindy was dying of cancer.

'Once upon a time, sure. But we were all bad boys then. We drank, we partied, we got out of hand. We were colorful, and that's how people liked us. I used to piss into the fountains at Caesars. I'd egg on pretty boys until they took a swing at me, and then I'd break their jaws. I'd dance on blackjack tables. That was part of the show. When I went too far, they'd throw me in a jail cell until I sobered up, and then I'd have bacon and eggs with the cops in the morning. I knew the first name of every cop in the city, and I went to most of the birthday parties for their kids.'

'So your mean streak was just an act?'

'I'm saying I was what everyone wanted me to be. Look, I could blow up with the best of them. I was a son of a bitch sometimes. But I'm eighty years old, Detective. I'm on my way out. I'm a squealing little pig with his nuts cut off. My devil days, when I had a temper and liked to use it, were a very long time ago. I didn't marry Tierney for sex, and not even to have a pretty young thing on my arm. Believe it or not, we liked each other. We were friends. I encouraged her to see young men if she wanted to, because I knew she'd have to go back to that life after I was gone. I didn't ask for details, so I had no idea she had a relationship with M.J. or anyone else.'

Stride listened for a false note and didn't hear one.

'Do you remember Helen Truax?' Stride continued. 'Her stage name was Helena Troy.'

'Sure. She was a dancer at the Sheherezade.'

'How well did you know her?'

'Well enough to have a drink now and then,' Moose said. 'But that was it. She was Leo Rucci's gal, so I kept away from her. Where are you going with this?'

'Less than two weeks ago, Helen's grandson was killed in a hit-and-run,' Stride explained. 'Then Walker Lane's son. And now your wife. We think the same person was responsible for all three murders.'

Moose sat up. 'You think this is all connected to the Sheherezade?'

'All three of you were mentioned in the article Rex Terrell did about the murder of Amira Luz. Did you talk to Terrell?'

Moose's upper lip and eyebrows seemed to curl in disgust at the same time. 'Me? Talk to a fucking worm like Rex Terrell? No way.'

'Rex says you, Helen, and others benefited from Amira's death.'

'I won't deny I wasn't too sad to see the little bitch dead and gone,' Moose said. 'She played me. Used me to get to Boni and then kicked me in the balls.'

'Helen says you told her Amira was the best lover you ever had,' Stride said.

'That was no secret. We were involved. That Spanish blood, it runs hot. But she was no better than a hooker, using me to make her way up the ladder.'

'Where were you the night Amira was killed?' Amanda asked.

Moose laughed. 'Drunk. In jail. Like I said, that happened a lot in those days. As it turns out, it was fortunate that I had an alibi.'

'So you don't know what happened that night?'

'Just the rumors,' Moose said.

'You mean Walker Lane?' Stride asked.

Moose nodded. 'Everyone assumed he did it. That story about a stalker, that was pretty convenient. I figure they wanted a fall guy. Like I said, I'm glad I had an alibi, because I would have made a sweet target.'

'So you believe Walker did it, too.'

'It makes sense,' Moose said. 'But it surprised me.'

'Why?'

'I never thought Walker would have the balls for it. He was soft. He liked to dance with the devil, but he was just an LA rich kid. Killing Amira, that took guts. I can't believe he's still alive after doing that.'

Stride and Amanda looked at each other. 'What do you mean?' Stride asked.

'Most people didn't know. But I knew, because I knew Amira. She told me, just to rub my face in it. And Walker would have known. He *had* to have known. I know he loved her act, went to all her shows. But he would have gotten word from Leo Rucci that the high roller amenities didn't extend to Amira.'

Stride's eyes narrowed. 'Why?'

Moose's eyebrows did a little dance, like caterpillars wriggling to the music of the Sugar Plum Fairy. 'Amira Luz was the sole property of one man and one man only,' he said. 'The man you didn't mess with. Boni Fisso.'

Twenty-one

Serena parked in her driveway at home. She didn't get out of the car. She turned off her cell phone and sat silently in the darkness.

She remembered the first time it happened with Deirdre, when she was eighteen. She was in the shower. Deirdre knew that she went into little fugues sometimes under the water, letting it pour over her head as the memories came back, hoping it would somehow rise above her mouth and drown her. In Phoenix, she used to take showers after Blue Dog, her mother's drug dealer, was finished with her. Brown water, lukewarm, then cold.

She wasn't sure how long she had been standing there. Frozen. Lost. She felt like a quadriplegic, aware of her surroundings but unable to move or react, helpless to stop what was happening to her. Forced to rewind her past and watch it recurring over and over. As if, in the two years since she had escaped from Phoenix, she had not escaped at all but been consumed by a single, silent scream.

Then she felt someone else crawl inside her cocoon. Without a sound, out of nowhere, Deirdre was there with her. Behind her, in the shower, naked flesh against naked flesh. Deirdre's lips were by her ear, and she was cooing over and over, 'It's OK, baby.' Deirdre's hands encircled her stomach and held her gently, nurtured her, saved her. Serena leaned back against her, and something seized inside. A coffer dam of fear and shame began to grow fissures and give way. Serena sobbed. Her whole body trembled, and she was indescribably cold, frigid to her soul, except for the warmth of Deirdre behind her. The more the tears fell, the more Deirdre held her and soothed her.

It's OK, baby.

Serena turned around and buried her head in Deirdre's shoulder, and still Deirdre held her, letting her cry herself out. She didn't know how long they stood there as she climbed out of her flooded cave and back into the light. The water of the shower was still on; it was cold, but they

140

were warm. When Serena finally looked into Deirdre's eyes, she felt free. She stared with exhilaration into Deirdre's damp, beautiful face and felt love and gratitude overwhelming her, morphing into passion. Deirdre began, and Serena didn't stop her. She joined in. Their lips came together. Their slippery bodies seemed to merge. She felt Deirdre relishing her touch, and the more Deirdre responded, the more Serena strove to give her pleasure. Kissing her. Massaging the hollow of her back. Hearing her whispered pleas to go further. Sliding fingers inside her, everywhere, front and back, deep and probing. Wanting to climb inside her.

In her memory, they seemed to glide, dripping, from the shower to the bed. And then to spend hours together as night fell outside, making love to each other over and over in the squeaking twin bed where Serena usually slept alone. Then, finally, when they had sated each other, falling asleep, exhausted, entwined.

They spent six months as lovers. She knew that Deirdre wanted it to stay that way. In the beginning, so did Serena. She was afraid of men and felt safe in Deirdre's arms. She had no mother, and Deirdre played that role for her, too. That was enough for a while.

But as Serena's confidence in herself came back, she realized that their relationship was built on sand. She loved Deirdre, but she didn't want to be her lover any more. She wanted to see what she could build for herself, on her own, not leaning on anyone or running to someone to rescue her.

They argued about it. Deirdre became hysterical. It finally dawned on Serena that Deirdre was the frightened one, the one who needed love and was afraid of men. Deirdre was the one who couldn't live without Serena.

But Serena ended it anyway. That was how Deirdre's new life started. The dive into prostitution and drugs. She always thought Deirdre did it to get back at her, to throw it in her face. Serena still blamed herself. Her fault. Her guilt. Deirdre had been there for her at the worst time in her life, and in the end Serena walked away when Deirdre needed her help. She just let her die without going to see her, without trying to comfort her.

Serena sat in her car, watching the memories play out in her head. She was eighteen again. That was how it felt. When Claire walked out on that stage, Serena saw Deirdre. When Claire touched her, she felt Deirdre's hands. They were nothing alike, but that didn't matter. Claire was right. Serena wanted her. She wanted to follow Claire back into that shower, strip, kiss, touch, and find a way to make love to Deirdre again. To tell her how sorry she was. To tell her everything would be fine.

It's OK, baby.

Twenty-two

'What's next?' Amanda asked. They stood outside Moose's house.

'I'm calling Walker Lane again in the morning,' Stride said. 'I don't care what the hell Sawhill says.'

'Walker won't admit killing Amira.'

'No, but he may know who's doing this and why. This isn't some random vendetta. It's personal.'

'If Walker did kill Amira, why didn't Boni erase him?' Amanda asked. 'Assuming Moose is right about Boni and Amira being lovers.'

Stride thought about the penthouse suite in the Charlcombe Towers and Boni Fisso looking down on his old casino. And his new Orient project. 'It's one thing to kill members of the family. But a CEO and a celebrity like Walker – that's a lot harder to cover up. If Walker Lane was murdered or disappeared, people would ask questions.'

'Walker did disappear,' Amanda said. 'He ran to Canada.'

Stride nodded. 'Maybe he was running from Boni. Maybe he's still running.'

He heard his cell phone ringing. He grabbed it, expecting a call from Serena, but he didn't recognize the number on the caller ID.

'Stride,' he answered.

He heard a man's voice, flat and unemotional. A stranger. 'Have you found her yet?'

Stride knew without having to ask. From the moment he had seen the killer leave the fingerprint for them at the Oasis, he had suspected that a moment like this would come. The man would find a way to make contact. To make it personal.

He snapped his fingers sharply at Amanda to alert her. She read his face as he gestured at the phone. He punched the speakerphone button. 'We're at Moose's house now,' he said.

'Not her,' the voice retorted impatiently. 'Not the girl.'

'Who are you talking about?' Stride asked. He mouthed to Amanda: *Another victim?*

'You're going to have move faster, Detective. I don't have time to spoon-feed you clues. I drove out in a silver Lexus. That should narrow it down.'

Stride listened for gloating in the man's voice and didn't hear it. He didn't sound unbalanced, like a monster. 'Why call me now?' Stride asked.

'I'm doing your job for you, Detective. I'm going to catch a murderer.'

'Why commit murder to catch a killer?' Stride asked him sharply. 'These people, the ones you killed, were innocent. Why not just come in and tell us what you think you know about Amira's death? Let us get justice for her.'

'Like you've done for forty years?' the man asked.

'You killed a little boy,' Stride snapped. 'That's worse than anything that happened back then.'

There was a long silence in which he thought he'd succeeded in finding a vein and drawing blood. He heard the man's breathing become more rapid and harsh.

'You don't understand what happened back then,' the man said finally.

'Explain it to me,' Stride said. 'And tell me what all of this has to do with you.' He wasn't talking to an older man – at most, maybe someone his own age. There was no way he had been a participant in the events that happened at the Sheherezade.

'Are you there?' Stride added when the man didn't reply. 'Hello?'

The silence stretched out into dead air. He checked his phone and found the call was over. The caller had disconnected.

When he punched a button to redial the number, it rang and rang without being picked up.

'Shit,' he said. 'There's another body here.'

But this one was alive.

Half an hour later, they found Cora Lansing, a 75-year-old widow, tied to an oversized walnut chair in her dining room, in another house not far from Moose's MiraBella estate. A strip of duct tape was pasted across her mouth. Her eyes were wide with fright, and she had soiled herself, throwing a stink into the lavender-scented home. But she hadn't been harmed.

They called in a medical team, who gave the woman oxygen and carefully removed the tape from her mouth. It left behind a rash and sticky residue that she picked at with irritated flicks of her fingernails. She was bird-like and frail, but she was hopping mad, even after a

143

shower and change of clothes. Stride poured a large glass of Remy Martin from her liquor cabinet to calm her down.

They soon extracted her story. She had been shopping at Nieman's and returned to find a stranger in her Lexus. The man forced her to drive back through the hills to the south shore entrance to Lake Las Vegas, and he hid in the back seat while she greeted the guard. He made it clear that if she tried to alert the guard, he would shoot them both, and his tone was such that Cora had no doubt he would do it.

She drove him to her home, where he tied her up, gagged her, and waited until night fell. Then he took her car and left.

'Did you see what he looked like?' Stride asked.

'I certainly did,' Cora replied immediately, surprising him. 'I'll never forget his face.'

Stride felt a rush of excitement, mixed with apprehension. He told Amanda, 'Get a sketch artist down here.'

Stride looked at Cora and thought to himself what he would never say to the woman aloud. *Why the hell are you still alive?*

'Can you describe him for me?' he asked.

Cora swiftly painted a man similar in build to the man Elonda had seen at the bus stop before M.J. was killed: not as tall as Stride, lean but very strong, with short dark hair and an angular face. Either he had shaved his beard, or the one he had used on Saturday night was a fake. Cora provided enough detail for the police artist to do a solid rendering. Stride glanced around at the tasteful, expensive art in Cora's house. She had a good eye.

'Did he say anything to you?' Stride asked. 'About who he was or why he was doing this?'

Cora shook her head. 'Not a word. He hardly said anything. But he was very intense, very scary.'

Stride thanked her and tracked down a policewoman to sit with her while they waited for the artist to drive in from the city. He left Cora's living room and made his way back outside. The killer's phone call was vivid in his mind. He wished it had lasted longer, because he wasn't sure the man would call again. He had said what he needed to say, enlisting Stride in the hunt. But the hunt for what?

Amanda joined him. 'You don't look happy,' she told him. 'Isn't this what we call a break? A lead? That's a good thing, right?'

'We've only got it because he gave it to us,' Stride said. 'He could have killed that woman, and we wouldn't have a damn thing. But now he wants us to know what he looks like. Why?'

'Maybe he's an arrogant bastard. He wouldn't be the first serial killer to get tripped up by his own ego. Look at BTK. They never would have nailed him in Wichita if he hadn't started sending letters to the papers again after thirty years.'

Stride shook his head. 'He knows he's taking a risk. He knows we might find him. His picture is going to be all over the papers. Someone could spot him.'

'He may think he's covered his tracks so well that it doesn't matter.'

'I don't think so, Amanda. I'm sure he's covered his tracks, but I don't believe he'd give us something this big if it wasn't part of his plan. Hell, he could have killed Tierney in the city any time he wanted. He didn't need to figure out a way to get inside the security out here. And he sure didn't need to give us his face.'

'He was showing off,' Amanda suggested.

Stride thought about it. He heard the killer's voice in his head again. Cool, focused. Complaining about spoon-feeding them clues. As if the police were interfering with his schedule.

'Or sending a message,' Stride said.

Twenty-three

Serena appeared in the doorway of his cubicle on Wednesday morning. He was leaning dangerously far back in his swivel chair, and he had his feet propped on the laminate desk.

'Hey, stranger,' he said. He had arrived home long after Serena went to bed, and he had been up and out at dawn, leaving her to sleep.

'Hey yourself,' she said.

'You really should try the perp power breakfast,' he added. Serena gave him a confused look, and he gestured at the desk. Her brow unfurled, and she laughed, seeing a sack of Krispy Kreme doughnuts and a large plastic bottle of Sprite.

Serena came in and sat down, but Stride could see that her body language was uncomfortable.

'Something wrong?' Stride asked.

He was glad that she didn't try to bullshit him with a fake smile and pretend that he was imagining things.

'Something happened last night,' she said.

'Oh? Are you OK?'

'Yeah.' She hesitated and added, 'I'm not really ready to talk about it yet.'

Stride was good at poker. Nothing showed on his face.

'Should I be concerned?' he asked.

'No. Maybe. I don't know.' She shook her head. 'Clears that right up for you, huh? Sorry about that.'

He stared at her for a long while and tried to see behind her eyes and understand what she was hiding.

'I'm here when you're ready,' he told her. 'But don't push me away.'

'You're not that lucky,' Serena told him. She winked, trying to make everything fine again. It made him feel a little better.

Amanda came around the cubicle wall with a sheaf of white paper. 'Here's our perp,' she said. She handed each of them a copy of the

146

sketch the police artist had produced from Cora Lansing's description. Stride was immediately drawn to the man's eyes, which were dark but remarkably expressive. He thought if he hung it on the wall, the eyes would follow him as he walked around the room.

'We've got uniforms re-working each of the neighborhoods where the murders took place, to see if anyone recognizes him,' Amanda said. 'I faxed it to Jay Walling in Reno, too. Sawhill's going to be releasing the sketch to the media at a press conference this morning.'

Stride smiled, knowing that Sawhill loved the limelight. He'd make it seem like this was the product of brilliant investigative work by his division. Not a gift from the killer.

'Did you call Walker?' Amanda asked.

'Sawhill wanted a couple of hours to confer with the politicians,' Stride said. 'I told him if I didn't hear anything by noon, I was just going to pick up the phone.'

'How about Boni? We make any progress there?'

Stride turned to Serena. 'Did you talk to Claire?' he asked.

She nodded. 'They're estranged. I don't think she'll call him. But she didn't close the door entirely.'

'What's she like?' Amanda asked.

'She's fiercely independent. She didn't seem to care that she might be in danger. As a singer, by the way, she's exceptionally talented. And charming. I think, like her father, she's driven in getting what she wants.'

Stride spoke to Amanda. 'We need to warn people. Fast. There were a couple of other people mentioned in Rex's article. They or their families might be in danger. And let's track down Leo Rucci, too. He was Boni's right-hand man at the Sheherezade, the one who was sleeping with Helen. Anyone who started looking at what happened to Amira would find Leo's name.'

'He's already on my list,' Amanda said. 'Maybe I can sweat him about Amira's murder, too.'

'Yeah, I'm sure he's a talkative guy. If you can, find out about that fight the night of the murder. And that kid Mickey. That bothers me.'

'Right.'

He turned to Serena. 'Can you or Cordy run down a lead for us? Tierney used a security agency in town. Premium Security. I don't know if Karyn Westermark used them too but she told us she had a bodyguard with her during the afternoon, before she met M.J. It's worth taking a sketch of the perp down there. Maybe this guy had access to inside information about the schedules of the victims.'

'Sure, you got it.' Serena grabbed a handful of the sketches and was about to walk out of the office. Then, with a smile at Amanda, she bent down and gave Stride a long kiss.

'That help?' she asked him.

'That helps.'

She winked again as she left.

'If I were you, I'd sue for harassment,' Amanda teased him.

'Not a chance.'

The phone on his desk rang, and Stride snatched it up. He was still a little breathless from the kiss. 'Stride.'

'It's Walker Lane, Detective. I understand you want to talk to me.'

Stride recognized the wheezing voice. He leaned back in his chair and gathered his thoughts. 'Yes, I do, Mr Lane. Do you have a few minutes?'

There was a long pause on the line, as he had come to expect from Walker. 'I had something else in mind. I thought we could meet personally.'

'Are you coming to Las Vegas?' Stride asked, surprised.

'No, no. You know how I feel about that city. I'm sending my private jet for you, Detective. You can meet it at McCarran at two o'clock, and it will take you to Vancouver. Will that be acceptable?'

Twenty-four

The secretary at Leo Rucci's Henderson office told Amanda that Rucci always spent Wednesdays on the golf course. Amanda hung around long enough to find out that Rucci owned a successful chain of fast oil change shops throughout Nevada and southern California. He was a multimillionaire, divorced, with one son whose primary occupation, like M.J.'s, seemed to be spending Daddy's money.

It wasn't hard to tell who had set Rucci up in business. There was a large photograph in the office lobby of Leo Rucci and Boni Fisso together at the ribbon-cutting ceremony for his first quick-lube station.

But Rucci wasn't welcome in Boni's casinos any more. Or any casinos. He was in the Black Book – the state Gaming Control Board's list of persons whose ties to organized crime and other illegal activities got them banned from so much as using the bathroom in a Nevada casino. According to Nick Humphrey, Rucci had taken the fall for Boni in the 1970s when the feds raided the Sheherezade on the hunt for evidence of tax evasion. Boni walked away in the clear. But the feds needed a trophy, and Leo was it. He spent five years in prison on tax fraud charges but never sang a note about his boss.

When he got out in the early 1980s, Boni set him up in a legitimate business. Loyalty pays, Amanda thought.

Along the way from Henderson to I-15, she made her usual stop for coffee and a cigarette in the parking lot near McCarran. She watched the planes and thought more seriously about chucking her job and escaping the city. She and Bobby had had a long talk overnight, when she got home from the crime scene in Lake Las Vegas. He always stayed up to greet her. It was sweet. But when he saw the slur scraped into the door of the Spyder, he threw a fit and wanted to storm down to City Hall. He was tired of the harassment, and she was, too. She knew it would never change. As long as she stayed in Las Vegas, she would be a freak, hated and unwanted.

149

The trouble was, she loved her job. She didn't like the idea of being bullied out of town.

She stubbed out her cigarette and drove to the Badlands golf course in the northwest corner of the city to find Leo Rucci. The clerk at the pro shop told her that Rucci's foursome would be somewhere on the Diablo nine, and he let her take a golf cart to find him. As she followed the cart paths, she fell in love with the city again, like she always did. The fairways were lush emerald green, dropped in narrow strips amid the giant estates and golden brush of the desert and dotted with pure white sand traps. The razor peaks of the red rock mountains loomed overhead a mile to the west. The temperature was in the mid-eighties, but the rushing wind on her face kept her cool.

She found Rucci and his three partners on the green of one of the later holes. Their rough laughter carried on the wind. She waited until they had putted out and were on their way back to their own golf carts, then drove up and parked behind them. She got out with the police sketch flapping in her hand.

'Leo Rucci?' she called.

All four of them stopped and studied her suspiciously. One of the younger men slipped a hand inside his windbreaker, and Amanda wondered if he was armed. Rucci waved the others off and approached her, twirling his putter in his hand. He was obviously the alpha male, the tallest and biggest of the group. He was in his late sixties, but he was physically imposing, with a shaved head and a neck that looked like a tree trunk. He wore sunglasses, a charcoal and black Tehama wind shirt, and khaki shorts. She could easily imagine him as a younger man, busting heads for Boni as the casino manager of the Sheherezade.

'Yeah, I'm Rucci. So what? Who are you?'

'I'm Amanda Gillen, from the homicide division at Metro.'

Rucci's face didn't move. 'Cop, huh? So what do you want with me?'

Amanda handed him the sketch. 'I'd like to know if you recognize this man.'

Rucci took the sketch without looking at it and wadded it up, then tossed it in the air and let the wind blow it away. 'No, don't know him.'

'Thanks for studying it so carefully,' Amanda said.

'I don't like cops. That means I don't like you. You want to put someone away, you do it without me.'

'This man may be trying to kill you,' Amanda said. 'Or your son.'

Rucci reached into his pocket and took out a golf ball. He put it between his two huge hands and laced his fingers together. With his elbows up, he squeezed. His fingers turned red, but the muscles in his face didn't contract, as if he were making no effort at all. Amanda heard a crack as the casing of the golf ball split. He opened his hand and peeled the cover off the ball, then tossed the remnants away, along with the core.

'No one messes with Leo, sweetheart. If somebody wants to come after me, I don't need your help.'

'How about your son?' Amanda asked. 'Do you watch his back, too?'

'My boy Gino can take care of himself,' Rucci said.

'Well, you better warn him that somebody might be painting a target on his back. Three people are dead, including a little boy. They all had family connections to the Sheherezade and Amira Luz. Like you, Leo. So you or your boy Gino could be next.'

'Thanks for the advice, Detective.' Rucci turned on his heels and headed back to his three stone-faced colleagues.

'Hey, Leo,' Amanda called after him. 'Who killed Amira?'

Rucci stopped. He turned back and leaned on his putter. 'It was some nutcase in LA. Why don't you ask Nick Humphrey about that? He was the cop on the case.'

'Some people think Walker Lane killed Amira.'

'Some people think Castro killed Kennedy. That don't make it true.'

'I guess it would have taken balls for Walker to kill Amira. I mean, she was Boni's mistress, wasn't she? Did Walker know that?'

Rucci came toward her with an ugly snarl, brandishing the putter like he might take a swing at her. Amanda involuntarily stepped backward. 'Boni Fisso has done more for this city than all the cops and politicians put together. Got that? He's one of the guys that made this town great. So don't you go fucking around about him with me, OK? Boni's farts are worth more to Las Vegas than anything you'll ever do.'

Amanda recovered and stepped inside Rucci's shadow. She was half a foot shorter than he was, and she knew damn well he could snap her in half with little effort. But she shoved her face close to his anyway. 'Where were you when Amira got killed?'

'You know where I was,' Rucci retorted, grinning for the first time. 'And you know what I was doing. I was balling one of the dancers. She could hardly walk straight when I was done with her. Maybe you'd like to know what that feels like, Detective.'

'Or maybe I'd just cut it off and use it as a paperweight, Leo,' Amanda said, smiling back. 'Tell me about the fight that night.'

151

'What fight?'

'The dancer you were sleeping with, Helen, says you got a call from one of the lifeguards. Kid named Mickey. There was a drunken fight outside, and you went to break it up.'

Rucci shook his head. 'Helen's wrong. She should be keeping her mouth shut and not talking to cops, if she knows what's good for her.'

'You threaten a witness, Leo, and you're going to regret it.'

'I don't need to make threats. There was no fight. There was no phone call. Helen's memory is fucked up. That happens. She's an old woman now, underneath all the Botox and plastic. We had drunks get rowdy all the time, and I used to break their noses and send them back where they came from. But not that night.'

'You think Mickey would tell the same story?' Amanda asked.

'You find him, you ask him,' Rucci said.

'Any idea where I can find him?'

'Sure. I stay in touch with every fucking kid who spent a summer at the casino helping girls out of their bikinis.'

'What was his last name?'

Rucci grinned. 'Mouse.'

He lumbered back to his cart and slammed his putter back into his bag. The foursome drove off in their two carts, and as they left, one of them looked back and extended his middle finger at Amanda.

She waved back at them.

Twenty-five

Serena let Cordy drive his PT cruiser to the offices of Premium Security. She sat in the passenger seat and stared out the window, trying to figure out which emotion would get the upper hand. She was angry at herself for dwelling on the past, confused about her feelings for Claire, madly in love with Jonny, and horny as hell. Take your pick.

Cordy had a Spanish-language radio station on, and he was pounding his fingers against the steering wheel to the annoying, thumping beat of a song she didn't understand. When Serena couldn't take it any more, she reached down and clicked the radio off.

'What's eating you, mama?' Cordy asked.

'Nothing. I'm just not in a mood to do *La Bamba* now, OK?'

'Yeah, sure, whatever.'

They pulled up to a stop light, and Cordy kept humming the song without the music.

'Tell me something,' Serena said. 'You had a good thing going with Lavender. Why'd you screw it up?'

Cordy pointed out the window. A leggy brunette was on the corner, jogging in place as she waited for the light to change. 'You see that? That's a sexy *muchacha*. I see her, and the first thing I do, I peel off her clothes in my head. What color are her nipples? How big are they? You know, quarter, half-dollar, bigger? What kind of panties is she wearing? Bikini, thong, maybe nothing at all. Then I wonder what she likes in bed, OK? Her, I'm thinking—'

'That's enough,' Serena said, interrupting him.

Cordy shrugged. 'You asked.'

Serena hoped he would drop it, and he did. She didn't need a man's advice anyway. What was going on in her head wasn't about lust. Or not only about lust.

She wondered if she was bisexual. She hadn't thought that in years. Even when she was with Deirdre, she had never thought of them as girl on girl, just as two friends who used sex to comfort each other. She had never dated any other women. Her experiences with men, until Jonny, had been rocky at best, but she chalked that up to her aggressive defenses, born of the hell she went through in Phoenix.

Nothing happened with Claire, she told herself. But she couldn't take much comfort in her willpower. When Claire tried to seduce her, she had been on the verge of giving in, and only Jonny's call had broken the mood and given her an excuse to leave.

'Here we are,' Cordy said, turning into a grungy strip mall on Spring Mountain Road that looked like it would blow down in a stiff breeze. They were a couple miles west of Las Vegas Boulevard.

Serena looked up and frowned. 'This is Premium Security?'

Cordy pointed at a sign on the glass door in front of them, which advertised the name of the agency in flaking white paint. The windows were blackened so that no one could see inside. Serena took note of the other occupants in the tiny mall, including a fast food gyros joint, an auto parts store, and a pawnshop advertising handguns.

'Low overhead,' Serena said.

'Uh-huh.'

They got out of the car and approached the door, but found it locked. Serena saw a buzzer and pressed it several times. She peered into the darkened windows, not seeing anything, but she suspected they were both on camera. A few seconds later, she heard a soft click, and she pulled the door open. They entered a claustrophobic vestibule, about four feet by four feet, with another locked door on the other side. She had been right; there was a camera pointed down at them.

She heard a female voice through an overhead speaker. 'Please let the outer door close behind you.'

Cordy let it shut, and this time they heard two locks click in place. When he tugged on the door again, it was locked from the inside. They were trapped.

'How can we help you?' the disembodied voice said.

Serena explained who they were and held up her shield in front of the camera. There was another click, and this time the inner door swung open for them.

They entered a surprisingly plush waiting area, which didn't fit at all with the surroundings in the rest of the mall. Big band music played gently overhead. There was a cherrywood welcome desk with a large vase of bright yellow daffodils. A petite blonde sat behind the desk, and Serena caught a waft of her perfume.

'Have a seat,' she said with a big smile. 'Mr Kamen will be with you in just a moment.'

Serena and Cordy sat on an overstuffed sofa that seemed to swallow them up. In front of them, a coffee table sported current issues of the *Economist*, the *New York Times*, and *Variety*. They waited almost ten minutes before the door to an inner office opened behind the receptionist, and a man emerged to greet them. They both struggled to extricate themselves from the sofa and shake his hand.

'I'm David Kamen, the president of Premium Security.' Kamen was dressed in a black knit turtleneck and gray pants. He was in his mid-thirties, tall and good-looking, with sandy blond hair and a freckled, Southern California complexion. He wore boxy black glasses that had been out of style for so long that Serena assumed they were hip again.

Kamen guided them into his office, which was as attractively decorated as the lobby. Serena noted that the door was heavy and closed behind them with a solid thud.

'Before we sit down, may I see your identifications, please?'

Serena and Cordy both presented their shields, and Kamen studied them carefully. He handed them back with a polite smile and gestured for them to sit around a circular oak conference table. Inlaid wood. More daffodils.

'We have some ex-Metro personnel on our team,' Kamen informed them.

Serena nodded and rattled off two names. She wanted Kamen to know they had done their homework. He gave her a small nod of appreciation.

'You're a shooter, huh?' Cordy asked, pointing at a photograph on the wall that showed Kamen in camouflage, a rifle in his hand. It was one of the few pictures on a wall with dark, metallic wallpaper.

He nodded. 'Afghanistan.'

'A sharpshooter with glasses?' Serena asked.

Kamen winked. 'You caught me. My vision is perfect. Better than perfect. The glasses make people think otherwise, and I like it like that. Besides, they're cool, don't you think?'

'Long way from shooting ragheads to guarding models in Vegas,' Cordy said. 'How'd you wind up here?'

'I was recruited.' Kamen folded his hands together and smiled, not offering details. He wasn't the kind of man who volunteered information. He waited for them to continue, keeping a polite expression on his face, but glancing at the clock on the table.

Serena saw Cordy reaching for the police sketch inside his sport coat, but she gently reached over and took his arm, restraining him. She wanted to hear what they could coax out of the man before putting the killer's face in front of him.

155

'You know that Tierney Dargon was murdered last night,' she said.

'Of course. Terrible thing.'

'Your firm provided security for her, right?' Serena asked.

'Mrs Dargon often used our security personnel when she was in Las Vegas. Moose is an extremely wealthy man, and they were concerned about kidnapping attempts. But they felt secure while they were at MiraBella and didn't use us there.'

'Bad move, huh?' Cordy said. 'Guess they should have had some of your boys around.'

Kamen didn't reply.

'Did Tierney call and cancel security arrangements with you yesterday?' Serena asked.

'Yes, she did.'

'What were the original arrangements?'

'She was going to spend the evening at one of the Strip casinos. One of my men was going to pick her up and escort her. But she contacted us around noon and indicated she was planning to stay home that night and would not need our services.'

'Did you talk to her directly?'

Kamen shook his head. 'She talked to our receptionist.'

'You work with a lot of stars, I bet,' Cordy said. 'Must see a lot of wild things. Guess it's like the Secret Service, you have to keep your mouth shut.'

'We're very discreet.'

'How about that soap star? The one that did the porno with M.J. Lane. You ever work for her?'

'Karyn Westermark is one of our clients, yes,' Kamen acknowledged.

'But not M.J. Lane?'

'No.'

'How about last Saturday?' Serena asked. 'Was one of your men with Karyn?'

He nodded. 'Ms Westermark contacted us when she arrived in town, and Blake, one of our people, stayed with her while she shopped in the afternoon. She prefers shadow security, where we stay in the background, not with her. We're there if needed, but we're not obvious.'

'Was Blake with her on Saturday night, too?'

'No. She dismissed him when she was going to meet M.J.' Kamen added, 'I hope you're not suggesting that any of my people could be involved in the string of murders. Or that we released information about the schedules of our clients.'

'We're just looking for connections,' Serena said. 'When two of

156

our murder victims have ties to the same security agency, we get curious.'

'We work with hundreds of clients, Detective, including many of the most famous people in the city. If someone decides to murder celebrities, or people close to them, there's a good chance we'll have a relationship. There's nothing odd about it.'

Serena knew he was right. Tracking celebrities in Vegas was like shooting fish in a barrel. They were everywhere.

She raised the other names with him – Linda and Peter Hale, Albert and Alice Ford – and wasn't surprised to find that neither of those middle-class families had anything to do with Premium Security. Kamen looked relieved.

'Do you have any other celebrity clients that have ties to the Sheherezade casino?' Serena asked.

She saw a flutter of hesitation in his eyes. 'I'm sure there are many,' he replied cautiously. 'The Sheherezade has been around for years. Why?'

'There may be a link between the victims and the casino.'

'What kind of link?' Kamen asked.

'We're not talking about that publicly yet,' Serena replied. 'You sound like you're holding out on us, Mr Kamen.'

He was silent, pursing his lips and studying her intensely. Serena had the uncomfortable feeling that this was the same look he used on victims through the scope of his sniper's rifle.

'Mr Kamen?' she prompted.

'We don't have any actual ties to the Sheherezade,' he said.

Cordy leaned forward. 'Actual ties? How about un-actual ties? Sideways ties? Give us a clue, Dave.'

Kamen looked as if he would rather chew glass. 'The agency is owned by Mr Fisso,' he said.

'*Boni Fisso* owns Premium Security?' Serena asked.

'He owns many businesses,' Kamen said. 'Slot manufacturing. Direct marketing. Golf apparel. He has no active day-to-day role in our operations. It's simply an investment.'

Cordy's white teeth shone as he grinned at Kamen. 'So you're telling me that you and the boys never do any private work for Mr Fisso? Teach a few slot cheats that they're messing with the wrong guy?'

'Nothing like that,' Kamen said through tight lips.

Serena didn't buy that for a minute. A security agency owned by Boni Fisso was a great way to get muscle on demand and cloak their shadier services under the guise of a legitimate operation. It also explained the low-rent location, to keep the entire agency under wraps.

She wondered whether any celebrity secrets made their way back to Fisso as grist for influence and blackmail.

But she knew they didn't have enough, just based on the ties to Karyn and Tierney, to get a warrant to open up their books and go digging. Kamen and Boni were safe for the time being.

'If someone else gets killed and we find out you had information that might have prevented it, we're going to be taking a long, hard look at Premium Security,' she said. 'Is that clear?' Serena knew it was an empty threat, but she made her voice cold and hard.

'Of course, Detective.' Kamen wasn't intimidated.

Cordy reached inside his jacket pocket to retrieve a copy of the police sketch and handed the paper across the desk. 'Now it's time for show and tell, Dave.'

'We want you to take a look at this sketch and then show it around to your men,' Serena added. 'If anyone has seen this man, we need to know about it immediately. And tell them to watch out for him around your clients.'

'Naturally,' Kamen said. He unfolded the sketch and laid it face down on his desk, using his thumbs to smooth out the creases. He turned it over, and the dark eyes of the killer stared up at him.

Serena watched his face turn to ash.

Twenty-six

Stride had never been in a private jet before. It beat hell out of flying cattle class, where he spent most of the flight with his knees almost under his chin. The Gulfstream cabin offered seating for eight in rich ivory-colored recliners that seemed to swallow up his body in leather and cushiony foam. He was the only passenger, just him, two pilots, and a middle-aged flight attendant who smiled at his overawed expression. He had his choice of sitting at a maple dining table or lounging in front of an entertainment center with satellite music and movies. When the flight attendant, whose name was Joanne, described a lavish lunch, he chose to sit at the dining table, read the *Wall Street Journal*, and watch the desert terrain giving way to the Rockies forty thousand feet below him. It was easy to pretend for a few minutes that he was one of the super rich, and he realized it was a lifestyle that would be easy to get used to.

He changed seats after lunch and settled in with a cup of black coffee that tasted dark and smoky, exactly how he liked it. Joanne showed him how to navigate the remote control, and he found the country music station on satellite radio and boomed it through the cabin. He figured it was the first time that anyone on this plane had heard Tracy Byrd singing 'Watermelon Crawl', but Joanne was kind and didn't complain. His plan was to review his notes on the case and plow through more of the research he had done on Walker Lane. But despite the coffee, the heavy lunch and the bouncing of the jet as it passed over the mountains acted like a sedative. Several days of stress and sleeplessness caught up with him, and he wound up reclining the seat and closing his eyes.

His dream took him back to Minnesota. He was on the beach in front of his old house on a finger of land jutting out between Lake Superior on one side and the placid harbor water on the other. He was in a dirty plastic lounge chair, watching the lake waves crash on

159

the shore, and his first wife Cindy was in a matching chair beside him. They held hands. Every hand had a different feel, and he could actually touch hers again and feel the prongs of her emerald ring scratching his skin. She didn't talk. There was a part of him that knew it was a dream, and he wanted to listen to the sound of her voice again, which had faded in his memory over the years, but she was quiet, staring at him, loving him. Eventually, in his dream, he fell asleep, and when he awoke, he was alone on the beach. Her chair was gone. There had been children playing by the waves, running in the sand, but they were gone. There had been an ore ship moored out on the water, the kind of ship on which his father had worked until a winter storm washed him into the lake, but the ship was gone, too.

Stride woke up as a thermal jostled the plane, and he heard Montgomery Gentry singing 'Gone' on the satellite radio. That was how the dream made him feel. Long gone.

Joanne told him they were getting ready to land, and Stride looked out to see snowy peaks looming beyond the downtown Vancouver skyline. He knew why he had dreamed of Cindy. They had been to Vancouver together once, several years earlier, when they took a cruise of the Alaskan inner passage. They had spent a weekend in the city after the cruise, and it had been magical, jogging together through the fog of Stanley Park in the early morning, and eating Dungeness crab meat from the market on Granville Island on a bench by the water, surrounded by hungry gulls. He remembered thinking on that trip that he had never been quite so happy in his life. But it wasn't long after they returned that a teenage girl named Kerry McGrath disappeared, launching one of the darkest investigations of his career. In the midst of it, his beautiful Cindy was overrun by cancer, so swiftly and appallingly that he barely recognized her in the end. He figured later that the cancer had already taken root while they were in Vancouver. He wondered what that said about life. He wasn't sure he wanted to know.

Stride was anxious to see Vancouver again. He liked the city, and he wanted to face his demons, or maybe just wallow in them. But when they landed, he realized it wasn't to be. There was no car to take him to Walker Lane, but rather a helicopter waiting for him after he was cleared by a customs official who met the plane. It swooped him up and took him south, away from the city, toward the gulf islands north of Victoria. He was a little nervous flying over the water, not in a float-plane but in a rock that would simply hit the water and sink if its rotors stopped turning. At least it was a calm, cloudless day. They flew for what seemed a long time, but was probably only twenty minutes, before Stride saw islands dotting the blue water below them. He saw fishing villages and large bands of oak and fir trees covering the hills and sweeping down to narrow stony beaches. As they passed over one of the smaller islands, the pilot began to descend, perilously close to the treetops. Beyond the crest, on the southern shore of the island, Stride suddenly saw a clearing where a massive estate clung to the beach. The water seemed to lap almost to the windows overlooking the sound. The house itself was Victorian in design, with numerous gables and a large main tower topped by a cone-shaped roof. The coloring was dark and gothic.

The pilot flew over the home itself and gently set the helicopter down on a concrete circle amid the rear gardens. He cut the engine, and Stride climbed out. An attendant greeted him and guided him back through a maze of topiaries and fountains into an expansive rear porch, with heavy antique furniture and ceramic tile the color of crème brûlée.

'Mr Lane will be right with you,' the woman told him and left him alone to wait.

Stride stood near the doors and felt the cool cross-breeze cutting across the island. He wondered what to expect from Walker Lane. All he had seen were photographs from decades ago, when Walker looked very much like his son M.J., with unruly hair and a gangly look, like a kid whose limbs had grown too far too fast. Even then, he had been a millionaire, and over the years he had traded the 'm' for a 'b'. Stride had never met a billionaire. From Walker's voice over the phone, he imagined the man to be tall and severe, imperially gray, wearing a sweater and cupping a glass of port.

He was right about the sweater, and that was it.

'Welcome to Canada, Detective,' Walker said, as he rolled onto the porch in a wheelchair operated from a joystick in his right hand. 'I'm glad you agreed to join me here.'

Stride found himself staring. He recognized the voice, which sounded like a stormy gale, but not the man. Half of Walker's face was strangely rigid, as if he had lost control of it in a stroke. The man's right eye was fixed, and it took Stride a moment to realize the eye was fake, made of glass. His nose was misshapen, broken and reconstructed. When he smiled, his teeth were pristine and perfect, and Stride guessed that those were fake, too.

'Not what you expected?' Walker asked drily.

Stride was too surprised to answer. He extended his hand, and Walker shook it. The man's grip, at least, was strong and tight.

'I don't advertise my disability, Detective,' Walker added. 'I hope I can count on your discretion. Most people who come here sign non-disclosure agreements. I didn't do that with you because I want to trust you, and I want you to trust me.'

Stride was still unsettled by Walker's appearance and by the fake eye that seemed astonishingly real. 'I understand,' he said.

'Do you know who killed my son?' Walker asked pointedly. He sounded like the impatient man Stride had talked to on the phone.

'Yes, we do.' Stride saw surprise bloom in Walker's good eye, and he reached into the slim folder he carried to retrieve the police sketch. 'We haven't arrested him, but we have his face. This is the man who killed M.J.'

'Let me see it.'

Stride handed him the sketch, and Walker took it eagerly. He held it far enough away in his right hand for his eye to focus.

'Do you know him?' Stride asked.

'No.' Walker shook his head, disappointed. 'He's not familiar to me.'

'I'll leave the sketch with you.'

Walker turned the sketch over and put it in his lap. 'Would you like a tour before we get down to business? Not many people get to come here, you know.'

Stride had come halfway across the continent to see the man, and he was curious about the estate, which was the kind of home he was never likely to see again. 'Why not?' he said.

'Good.'

Walker spun his wheelchair around and led him from the porch into the main body of the house. For all the antique décor, it was electronically sophisticated, with every feature controlled by computers and operated from the control pad on Walker's chair. Windows, lights, doors, curtains, skylights, everything could be opened, closed, turned on and turned off with a flick of the keypad. They passed from room to room, and each one felt like something out of a European palace, huge and elaborately decorated, but sterile, like a museum. Stride knew the house couldn't be more than a couple of decades old, but it felt like a relic from another century. It didn't feel as if anyone lived here.

The house was generally warm, but some of the dampness of the region still made its way inside the walls, and the heat sometimes seemed to dissipate into the high ceilings. Stride found himself shivering and pulling the button closed on his suit coat. In just a few months, he thought, he had changed from a Minnesotan impervious to cold to a desert dweller chilled when the temperatures dipped below eighty.

'I rarely leave the island,' Walker told him. 'I'm sure you know that. But I can do almost anything from here. I see just about every movie made right in here.' He guided Stride into a full-sized movie theater that had a handicapped access row directly in the center. They may as well have been in the upscale multiplex in Las Vegas. Stride realized the theater here was probably always empty, and Walker sat here, alone, analyzing movie after movie. He began to feel sorry for the man.

Walker sensed his emotions. 'Don't feel bad for me, Detective. I'm not Howard Hughes, you know. People visit me all the time – actors, directors, editors, agents. I am intensely engaged in every aspect of every one of my movies. When they're being filmed, I have the dailies transferred to me electronically right here, and I review them and get my feedback onto the set by morning.'

'Why not go there?' Stride asked.

'First, I don't need to. I can do it from here, and you have to admit, I have one of the most beautiful locations anywhere on earth.'

Stride nodded. That was true. Every time they passed a window, he saw the island, the sound, or the gardens, and each one was a view to get lost in.

'Second, I'm intensely private. I'm not a partier, not any more. To be very candid, the way I look makes people uncomfortable. I hate that. The people who come here generally know me well enough not to be put off by who I am and they respect my privacy.'

He took Stride through the living room at the front of the house, with chambered windows looking out on the water, and then out onto a deck that led down toward the boat dock below. Stride could see a ferry passing by well offshore on its way to Victoria. The trees closed in around the estate, and he saw several eagles circling overhead.

'This is wonderful,' Stride told him honestly.

'Thank you, Detective.' Walker seemed to recognize that the compliment was genuine, and it pleased him. 'You want to know about M.J., don't you? How things went so wrong between us?'

'I do, yes,' Stride admitted.

Walker rolled his chair to the very edge of the balcony, where he could stare down at the waves slapping gently on the rocks. 'Does it surprise you that many women want to marry me?'

Stride shook his head. 'Not at all.'

Walker used his one eye to give him a knowing stare. 'Very smooth, Detective. But of course it's my money. Actresses – hell, plenty of actors, too – seem to become very enlightened about wheelchairs and physical appearance when they think about all that cash in the bank. They tell me it's love that matters. You really have to be from LA to make that line work.'

Stride laughed. Walker did, too.

'But M.J.'s mother was different. Terrible actress – all the desire in the world, but none of the talent. I think the director must have known she and I would hit it off, because he certainly didn't send her to me because of her audition. Or maybe he just thought I needed a good lay. She wanted to be in this movie I was casting, and she was ready to do anything – I mean anything – to be in it. When I declined, she fell to pieces, crying. She was very unstable, but there was something oddly appealing about her, she was such a waif. I guess I wanted someone I could take care of. Much to the surprise of a lot of people in Hollywood, we got married. I guess you could say we were co-dependent for a while.'

'I understand,' Stride said. He thought about his second wife, Andrea. Their relationship was similar. Two people who needed each other but didn't love each other.

'M.J. was born a couple years later. I didn't realize she was falling into a deep depression. People didn't really talk about those things. I just thought she didn't love me any more and didn't love the boy. I was a fool.'

Stride had read newspaper articles about Walker. His wife had killed herself a few years after M.J. was born. 'I think I know the rest,' he said.

'Yes, her suicide made the news. But you don't know *why*, Detective. M.J. understood it eventually, or he thought he did. He realized that my wife couldn't stand the competition. She was fragile and neurotic, and I only made it worse. Because I couldn't let go of the past, you see. M.J. realized it too. That's why this business about the Sheherezade was so upsetting to him.'

Stride felt his senses shift as he heard the name Sheherezade. He tuned out his emotions and hardened his heart. It was a shame, because he found himself liking Walker Lane.

'You said your wife couldn't stand the competition,' Stride said. 'What do you mean? What couldn't you let go?'

Walker sighed. 'Yes, that's what you've come for, isn't it? To hear the real story.' He turned the wheelchair around and pointed up at the tower rising above the house. 'Do you see it, Detective?'

Stride looked up, confused. He saw only peaked roofs and stone, and dozens of windows opening on the water. He saw the tower overhead, with a circular balcony at the top like a widow's walk. 'I don't . . .' he began, but then his eyes finally lighted on the five stones different from the others in the tower. They were gray slate like the rest, but someone had carved a letter into them. There were other stones between them, so they were spread out, forming a word horizontally that stretched from one side of the turret to the other. Years of Pacific rain had washed down their edges, but he could still read it: AMIRA.

He stared down at Walker, not understanding. Walker was lost in thought, studying the letters with his one eye as if he could caress them.

'You named your estate after her,' Stride murmured. 'Why?'

'Why? Detective, you're not a romantic.'

'You *killed* her,' Stride said. The words slipped out.

Walker shook his head. He didn't seem angry, just intense and heartbroken. 'No, no. Never. Don't you understand? I'd sooner kill myself. There are many days I've thought about doing that, just to be with her. I *loved* Amira. She loved me. We were going to be married that very night. The night that Boni Fisso murdered her.'

When they returned to the porch, Stride saw that the cloudless sky had dissipated into patches of darkness. It happened so quickly here, the changes from rain to sun, sun to rain. Drizzle began to dampen the garden outside and streak the windows. It grew colder. Walker called one of his staff, who stacked logs in the fireplace and started a blaze that quickly warmed the room. He opened wine, and Stride gave up his inhibitions and accepted a glass. Walker sipped the pinot noir and stared into the fire.

'I wish I could explain about Vegas in those days,' he said. 'I think it had the same kind of allure that Hollywood did in the thirties. It was young, electric, glamorous. Millionaires rubbing shoulders with showgirls. Entertainers playing craps on the casino floor at two in the morning. Everyone dressed up in jewels and tuxes like they were going to the Met. I remember it seemed to me that everyone there was beautiful. Everyone was rich. It was illusion, of course. Sleight of hand. That's what the town is so good at. But you couldn't walk into one of the casinos then and not get caught up in it. Maybe that's because the real world seemed so far away. Walk a hundred yards in any direction, and there was nothing but desert, an utter wasteland. I remember driving there on this two-lane nothing road from California, spending hours in the darkness without a glint of light anywhere. And then you'd see a glow like fire on the horizon, and you'd come over the crest of a hill and find this neon island blazing out of the night.'

'Helen Truax said the town had star quality then,' Stride said.

'Yes, she was right. That's exactly what it was.'

Stride added, 'Helen was one of the dancers with Amira.'

Walker shook his head. 'Was she? I don't remember her.'

'Her stage name was Helena Troy. She says she slept with you.'

Walker looked embarrassed. 'I don't doubt it. I played the game. I was young and rich, and I liked to sleep with lots of girls in those days. Vegas seduced me like so many others.'

'What about Amira?'

'Yes, her, too. She seduced me. Have you read about *Flame?*'

Stride nodded.

'Words can't do it justice,' Walker said. 'I think I fell in love with Amira the very first time I saw it. I had had plenty of flings, but Amira was different. I fell for her, head over heels. Maybe I'm flattering myself, but I think it was the same for her. Perhaps she just wanted my money, or wanted an escape, but I believe she loved me just as passionately.'

'But Amira was Boni's mistress, wasn't she?' Stride asked.

Walker's face, the part of it that moved, showed his pain. 'Foolish, wasn't I? Naive. I was playing with gangsters, and I thought it was just another one of my movies. The tough guys in suits and fedoras looked like actors. But this was real.'

'What happened?'

'We thought we could keep it secret,' Walker said. 'No one would know how we felt until we were long gone and married.'

Long gone, Stride thought again.

'I wasn't good at hiding my feelings. I was young, and love was written all over my face. Everyone knew it. They knew when I showed up every weekend at her shows. Boni knew too, of course. Leo Rucci told me how it was; he told me Amira was Boni's property, like a chair or a dog. That made me furious, but I pretended it was just a crush, nothing serious. Amira was the better actor. She never so much as looked at me in public. She told Boni if I ever laid a hand on her, she would knock me flat. Boni laughed about that, she said. So you see, we thought we were getting away with it. After her performance, in the middle of the night, she'd slip up to my suite on the roof, and we'd be together. It was our secret.'

'There aren't many secrets in Vegas,' Stride said.

'No. Later, I realized he probably bugged my suite. We thought we were so smart, and he knew all along what was going on between us.'

'Tell me about that night.'

'That night,' Walker murmured. 'That horrible, horrible night.' He brought his right hand up and touched the frozen side of his face, rubbing it, as if he might feel something there. 'After her last show, we were going to Europe. We planned to get married and spend six months traveling the world.'

'But Boni knew?'

Walker nodded. 'He and I spent the evening together in his office. We did that a lot. I always thought Boni was charming. We had fun together. But the hours wore on, and there was something wrong. There was something different about him. As it got later, I knew Amira would be waiting in my suite, and I wanted to go to her. But Boni kept finding excuses to keep me there, and I just watched the clock. Then Leo Rucci arrived. Boni's enforcer. He always scared me, because you knew he was nothing but a vicious thug underneath his suit. Boni asked Leo to escort me back to my suite, and I protested, but Boni insisted. And as I left, Boni kissed me on both cheeks. I remember what he said. "God be with you, Walker." Right then, I knew. I knew it was going to be bad.'

Stride didn't say anything. He remembered standing on the balcony of M.J.'s apartment, looking down at the rooftop suite of the Sheherezade.

'Leo followed me into the suite. I tried to stop him, but he just laughed. I expected to find Amira there, but it was quiet, and I thought she had come and gone. And then – I could see the door to the patio was open. I had this terrible feeling. I went outside.' Walker choked up. 'She was in the pool. The water was red and cloudy. I just stared down at her. And all I could think was that I was the one who had killed her. By falling in love with her.'

'What did they do to you?' Stride asked, guessing what had happened next.

Walker looked down at his useless limbs in the chair. 'Leo took me into the basement and put me in a limousine. He said they were taking me to the airport, and I was to leave the city and never come back. But that wasn't enough for them, of course. The two men in the car – they took a detour into the desert. Do you know what it's like to have your knees broken with a baseball bat, Detective? Or to have your skull fractured by brass knuckles? I would have given them any amount of money to kill me. But they were very careful about that. Boni didn't want me dead. He wanted me to know what he had done to me.'

Sitting in his wheelchair, Walker Lane, billionaire, began to cry.

167

Stride felt himself getting angry.

He was angry at Boni Fisso, a man he had never met. He was angry at Las Vegas for the lives it left in ruins. He felt a strange kinship with the killer in that sketch, trying to find justice for Amira in his own immoral way. He began to realize that the killer had been ahead of them all along.

This was never about Walker.

It was about Boni.

Twenty-seven

'His name is Blake Wilde,' Serena told Stride. 'Or at least, that's the name he's been using. He was one of the bodyguards at Premium Security. The guy who runs the agency, David Kamen, recognized Blake from the sketch. He's our perp, and he's disappeared.'

It was night, and Stride was in Walker's private hangar at Vancouver airport, waiting for the return of the Gulfstream. The jet was grounded in Denver by bad weather. It was raining on the coast now too.

'How long has he worked there?' Stride asked.

'Just a couple months. Kamen claims they did a background check on Blake, and it came up clean. But his personnel file is gone. They say Blake must have lifted it. I wonder if Kamen sent it to the shredder.'

'You think they knew each other?'

'Kamen has a military background. A sharpshooter for the Marines in the Gulf. But I made some calls, and the rumor is he had ties to a lot of other groups in the Middle East, including smugglers and mercenaries. If you were Blake Wilde and you wanted to make a landing in Las Vegas, wouldn't you look up an old friend?'

'The question is why Blake came to Las Vegas,' Stride said.

'To kill people.'

'I know, but why. Why him? Why now? I suppose his address was a fake.'

'A house in Boulder City,' Serena said. 'Mormon family, five kids, a Beagle. They never heard of Blake Wilde.'

'How about his SSN?'

'It traces to a boy in Chicago who died at age five.'

'He had to get paid,' Stride said.

'He cashed his checks at local pawnshops. A different one each time. It cost him ten per cent, but no cameras and no questions asked.'

Stride stared through the door of the hangar at the rain falling

169

outside. 'So this guy was with Karyn Westermark on Saturday afternoon?' he asked. 'He was running her security?'

'Nice, huh?' Serena replied. 'It explains the disguise that night. He didn't care about hiding from us, but he didn't want Karyn recognizing him.'

'How about Tierney Dargon?'

'Yes, Kamen says he worked with her, too. No problem getting her to open the door in Lake Las Vegas.'

Stride couldn't believe they were this close, and it still felt like they had nothing.

'There's got to be something more,' he said. 'What about expense vouchers, something with a credit card number or a bank account?'

'Zip,' Serena said. 'Everything he gave them was faked. Nice jobs, too. I called Nick Humphrey's next-door neighbor, Harvey Washington. Call a forger to find a forger, right? He had a couple names for me. Other local con men. Cordy's checking with some of his snitches on the street, too. But this guy's smart. I'm betting he didn't have it done locally.'

'He probably has a back-up identity ready as well,' Stride said.

'We're getting in touch with all of the people that he did security for. We're warning them to take care in case he shows up, and we're interviewing them to see if Blake tipped anything about his personal life while he was with them. Where he shopped, where he ate, anything that might narrow down the area for us.'

'The sketch is on TV?'

'Yeah. We're getting calls, but nothing solid so far. What did you get from Walker Lane?'

Stride quickly reviewed his day with Walker and what Walker had told him about the connections between Amira's death and Boni Fisso.

'Do you believe him?' Serena asked.

'It plays either way,' Stride said. 'Either Walker really did kill Amira, and Boni had him worked over as punishment. Or Boni took it out on both of them because Amira and Walker were trying to run away. That's what Walker says, and I think he's telling the truth. The man has more money than God, and he still looks afraid of Boni.'

'There's more,' Serena said. 'Boni owns Premium Security.'

Stride shook his head. Boni Fisso had his tentacles wrapped around the neck of every person in the investigation. 'So that means David Kamen has already told Boni everything that's going on.'

'Count on it,' Serena said. 'I wonder if our perp, Blake Wilde, knew that the company had Boni's fingerprints on it. Maybe that was part of the game, worming his way into one of Boni's shadow companies.'

170

'I think Blake Wilde knows Boni a hell of a lot better than we do,' Stride said. He added, 'We've got to talk to Boni. He must know what the hell is going on. This all gets back to him. And maybe to his Orient project, too.'

'Sawhill says he tried to get us in to see him,' Serena said. 'He even asked his dad to call Boni. No luck. The most we can get is an interview with Boni's lawyer.'

'Goddamn it,' Stride swore. 'I'm not going to arrest the son of a bitch. I'd love to, but I can't. He's not a suspect in any of these murders, so why the hell won't he talk to us? The one murder we think he *did* commit was forty years ago, and we won't be able to touch him for that.'

'Boni keeps his hands far away from the dirt,' Serena said.

'There's only one way in. You've got to talk to Claire again.'

Serena was silent for a surprisingly long time. Finally, she said, 'I don't think that will work. She won't talk to him.'

'You said she didn't close the door entirely. We need her help.'

'It's a waste of time,' Serena insisted.

Stride didn't understand. 'You can talk anybody into anything. What's the problem?'

'Claire made a pass at me,' she said.

He almost laughed. 'Well, so what's the big deal? Guys make passes at you all the time. If she gets fresh, you have my permission to deck her.' He tried to understand what he was missing, why this had knocked Serena off her feet. Finally light dawned. 'Unless it was a completed pass,' he said.

'No,' she told him. And then, embarrassed, 'Not really.'

'Not really? That sounds like being a little pregnant.'

'Nothing happened,' Serena insisted. Then she went on. 'But I wanted it to happen. I mean, it came out of nowhere for me. I was ready to jump into bed with her. That's what scared me. Shit, I can't believe I'm telling you this.'

Stride was at a loss for words. He tried to let his brain catch up with his emotions, but he had no idea what he felt. Betrayed. Jealous. Aroused. All of those things.

'Just what are you telling me, Serena?'

He had stumbled into a conversation for which he wasn't prepared, and the last thing he wanted to do was have it by cell phone, a thousand miles apart.

'I don't know what I'm telling you.' Her voice was becoming part of the static. He strained to hear her. 'There's a lot you don't know about me. There's a lot I don't know about myself.'

'You're making too much of this. You got caught off guard. You're not made of ice.'

'It was easier when I was,' she said.

'So tell me this, do you love me?' he asked. He held his breath, because he was suddenly not sure what she would say.

'*Yes.*'

'Has Claire changed that?'

'No, no, that's not it. But now I have to see her again.'

Stride thought about it. 'You know you can use her attraction to you as a way to get her to call Boni.'

'Of course. That's what I have to do. But I'm worried about getting in over my head.'

'The attraction is that strong?'

'Yeah, it is.'

Stride stared into the mist that hung like halos around the lights of the airport. His sense of homelessness had never been keener. He wanted to leave, start walking into the downpour, and disappear somewhere.

'Look, I can't tell you what to do,' he said.

He was talking to air. The signal was gone, lost in the rain. For the time being, they were in different universes. He knew it was going to be a long wait and a long flight home through the dark sky.

Twenty-eight

'Hello, Serena,' Claire said. 'I'm glad you called.'

Serena slipped past her into the one-bedroom apartment, passing through the honeysuckle fragrance of Claire's perfume. Their eyes met.

'I'm sorry to come so late,' Serena said. 'They told me at the Limelight this was your night off.'

'You're not interrupting anything,' Claire said. 'Just me and some chick lit.'

The lights in the apartment were dimmed, and several candles were lit, giving off a vanilla aroma. There was an indentation on the sofa and a blanket where Claire had been sitting with her book. A Tiffany lamp on the end table gave her light to read. There was a glass of white wine, half filled, on the coffee table. Soft jazz played from speakers discreetly hidden around the room.

'I love your apartment,' Serena told her. It was small but warm, with an old-fashioned feel, nothing metal or modern. The wood furniture looked antique but beautifully kept, and Serena wondered if Claire had done the restoration herself. There were collectibles everywhere, inlaid wooden boxes, glass angels, and stone animals.

'Can I get you some wine?' Claire asked.

'No, I don't drink,' Serena said. She added deliberately, 'Once I start, I can't stop.'

'I understand. I'm sorry. How about some mineral water?'

'Sure.'

Claire disappeared into the kitchen, and Serena sat in the love seat. She knew she was playing a dangerous game. She was volunteering information, spilling secrets that gave up who she was. That was her strategy. Claire liked her. If she could balance their relationship on a high wire, close but not too close, Claire might do what she wanted. Call Boni.

But she knew that high-wire artists sometimes took a long fall. She

173

remembered what a divorced friend had told her about having an affair. You want to see how close you can get to the line without going across, and then one day you look back and realize the line is half a mile behind you. Serena wondered if she had made a mistake, believing she could get what she wanted from Claire and still hold on to herself.

Claire came back and offered her a champagne flute, filled with bubbling water. She had also refilled her own wine glass. Claire sat back down on the sofa and pulled her legs underneath her. She was relaxed and comfortable in her body, like a cat. She wore worn-out blue jeans and a black satin V-neck top. Her feet were bare.

'I owe you an apology,' Claire told her.

'Oh?'

'For coming on to you like I did. It's not like me to be so forward. I must have seemed like a shark, and that's not me.'

Serena wondered if that was true, or if this was just phase two of the seduction. 'You caught me unprepared, that's all.'

'I'm sorry. Blame it on my romantic imagination. I thought there was something between us.' All the time she was talking, her blue eyes never left Serena and never even seemed to blink. Her voice, too, was mellow and inviting, like warm sake that went down smooth and washed away your defenses.

The ball was in her court, Serena knew. To say something. To deny it. Instead, she danced closer to the edge of the line. 'You didn't imagine it.'

Claire didn't look surprised. She took a sip of wine. 'I'm glad.'

'But nothing will ever happen between us,' Serena added.

'No?' Claire asked, giving her a mock pout.

'No.'

'Too bad.' She studied Serena thoughtfully, drumming her wine glass idly with her fingers. 'Who was she?'

'What do you mean?'

'The girl I remind you of,' Claire said with a knowing smile. 'Somewhere in your past, there has to be a girl. I don't flatter myself that I'm so stunning that straight women suddenly climb the fence when they see me.'

'OK, yes, there was someone else,' Serena admitted. 'It was a long time ago.'

'Why don't you tell me about it?'

Serena took a breath. This was what she wanted, the chance to draw Claire into her story. Build a kinship between them. But it was easy to lose track of where her strategy ended and where her own catharsis began. She had wanted to talk about Deirdre to someone for years, but she never had. Not to her therapist. Not even to Jonny. She had told him a little bit, but never the whole truth.

Serena put down her champagne glass, and the words spilled out. The memories were vivid, despite twenty years in between. She told Claire about meeting Deirdre, who was two years older, at a diner in Phoenix where they were both waitresses. As the abuse from her mother and the drug dealer named Blue Dog became more horrific, Deirdre became her lifeline, giving her a place where she could escape. Deirdre held her hand when she got the abortion, an ugly one, far too late. They had talked about going back and killing them, her mother and Blue Dog. But freedom sounded better. Escape, go, get away. The two of them ran to Vegas and lived together, working and partying. They were best friends, and eventually more than friends.

Lovers. She had found ways to rationalize it over the years or pretend it was something other than what it was. But they were lovers. Serena realized, as she was telling the story, that she wanted to feel some of that sexual power again. She wanted to be the one to arouse Claire, and she knew, watching Claire shift her limbs on the sofa, that she was turning her on. She could have this woman. She could make Claire do anything to her. She could get back anything that she wanted.

It was a heady sensation, as if she were drinking again.

Even when she told her about leaving Deirdre, and the destructive cycle that led to Deirdre's death, she no longer felt close to tears, as she usually did. She was strong, because she had to be.

'That's a lot of guilt to carry around,' Claire said when Serena was finished. 'But I forgot, you're tough.'

'I was cruel.'

'Do you think you can make it up to Deirdre by making love to me?' Claire asked. She was too smart to be fooled. 'Because you can't. I don't want that.'

'What do you want?' Serena asked.

Claire didn't miss a beat. 'I want you to fall in love with me.'

'That's not going to happen,' Serena said, although the fact that Claire could say it so calmly almost took her breath away. 'I wasn't in love with Deirdre. We were lovers, but I was never in love with her.'

'I'm not Deirdre.' Claire tossed her strawberry-blonde hair back, but it fell across her face anyway, covering one eye. 'What do *you* want, Serena?'

'I want you to get me and Jonny in to see your father,' Serena said. 'That's what I want. That's all I want.'

175

Claire looked as if she had known that all along. 'What if I do? Would you spend the night with me?'

Serena thought about Jonny and poker. She kept a stone face, even though a flutter of wind would have knocked her off the high wire and into Claire's arms. 'No. And besides, you said that's not what you want.'

'I think maybe you're not so tough,' Claire said. 'I think if I kissed you now, we'd end up making love. You're hoping I don't try to find out.'

They were playing a game of chicken, and Serena tried to steel herself and not blink.

'I want you to call Boni,' Serena repeated.

Claire reached languidly down to the coffee table, and Serena saw a cell phone there. Claire flipped it open, tossed her hair again, and looked at Serena long and hard. 'Do you know what a big deal this is for me?'

'Yes, I do.'

'You'll never know what he did to me. How he betrayed me.'

'I understand. Maybe someday you'll tell me.'

Claire punched one button on the phone. She still had Boni on speed dial. It was after midnight, but her father answered immediately. 'It's Claire,' she said, still staring at Serena on the opposite sofa. 'I need you to do something for me.'

Twenty-nine

An express glass elevator – smoked windows, bulletproof glass – took them to the rooftop suite in the northernmost building of the Charlcombe Towers. To Boni's lair.

Stride thought about M.J. as they shot upward, watching the earth recede below them at a dizzying speed. M.J. had lived in the same complex as Boni Fisso and looked out on the same casino where his father's life had been destroyed. Where Walker Lane's lover had died under the glow of the Sheherezade sign. Stride wondered if M.J. had ever met Boni, if he had even a glimmer of the titanic conflict between Boni and his father. It was little wonder that Walker was so desperate for his son to move.

He looked at Serena, who was quiet, staring out at the Strip. All the way home, listening to the hum of the Gulfstream's engines, he had asked himself how he felt about her and Claire. He still didn't know. He had half expected her to be gone, but she was in their bed, awake, when he arrived home in the middle of the night. Without him asking, she had blurted out that nothing happened. Then she made love to him, as intensely and passionately as he could ever remember, and he couldn't help wondering if some of her attraction to Claire was spilling over into their bed.

Not that he was complaining about it right then.

The elevator doors slid open.

They stepped out into a small, brightly lit foyer. A whitewashed wall blocked the way, with mammoth double oak doors in the center. The floor, too, was white – marble, shiny and spotless. Stride noted a total of four original paintings lining the wall on either side of the door, all of them done by realist painter Andrew Wyeth, from the Helga series. He guessed it was meant to soothe visitors while they waited for admittance to the inner sanctum. And perhaps to send the message that Boni was about class, not just money. If Steve

Wynn could put Picassos at the Bellagio, Boni could build a gallery too.

Stride had heard the stories about Boni, although it was hard to know which were true and which were spin. Like the rumor that he used to keep a rat, trained to chew the balls off casino cheats. Then he made the would-be thieves eat the rat's droppings. Stride thought that one smelled like an urban legend. Or the story that half the politicians in the state had worked in his casinos when they were young and ambitious, and that Boni owned their souls. He figured that one was probably true.

Rex Terrell had done a long profile of Boni in *LV* a year ago. Bonadetti Angelo Fisso had been born in New York in the mid-1920s. His father made pennies driving trucks in Manhattan but managed to send his oldest son Boni to Columbia (with help, it was said, from the mob bosses). With degrees in law and business, Boni emerged from Columbia smart, polished, and clean. He ducked the draft with a seventy per cent hearing loss in one ear, and in the boom following the Second World War began buying and selling businesses up and down the east coast. The rumors clung to him that his stakes were funded by the mob, and that Boni's companies were a laundry service for blood money. But several generations of FBI agents had devoted a lot of taxpayer money to proving Boni was dirty and wound up with nothing but wrist slaps for little fish in Boni's empire – people like Leo Rucci.

Boni arrived in Las Vegas in 1955. He took over a series of low-roller casinos, added hotel rooms, lavish shows, and half-naked cocktail waitresses, and turned them into profit machines. He also nurtured an image as a grand benefactor, building hospitals, landscaping parkland, and paying college tuition for the children of long-time casino employees. In public, he was a saint, always with a smile and a joke. The hard stuff went on behind the scenes. Bodies disappeared in the desert. Teeth got yanked, bones broken. The rat got fat, if you believed that kind of thing.

The Sheherezade was Boni's jewel. It was the first property he had built himself from the ground up, and when it opened in 1965, it attracted the top-line entertainers of the era. Boni had already figured out what later generations of Vegas entrepreneurs discovered, that the city had to be always new, always reinventing itself. So Boni never let the Sheherezade get stale. He found new shows, new stars. Like Amira and *Flame*. He found new ways to shock and tempt people. And the money flowed.

Stride had seen photos of Boni's late wife, Claire's mother, with

178

whom he had a short and tempestuous relationship. Eva Belfort was a beautiful, aristocratic blonde, a distant cousin to French royalty. Marrying her gave Boni an aura of European style. The truth was, like everything else in Boni's life, Eva was bought and paid for. Her family owned a chateau in the Loire Valley and was about to lose it for back taxes when Boni, on a tour of the wine country, met Eva. The family soon became rich again, and Boni had his trophy bride. It must have killed her, Stride thought, a wealthy child of the French countryside forced to live in a sand-swept version of hell. According to Rex Terrell, Eva was a spitfire, and she and Boni argued ferociously over Boni's penchant for affairs with his dancers. Stride wondered if Eva knew about Amira.

It didn't really matter, though. Their marriage, Boni's only marriage, lasted just three years. Eva lived only a few months longer than Amira. She died in childbirth, and Boni was left with his one child, Claire.

Stride and Serena waited almost ten minutes in the foyer of Boni's suite before the double doors suddenly opened with a click and swung silently inward. An attractive woman of about twenty-five, with pinned-up brunette hair and a tailored business suit, was there to greet them.

'Detective Dial? Detective Stride? Please come in. We're very sorry to keep you waiting.'

She waved them into a lounge that seemed to stretch the length of a football field. The whole of the north wall was windows looking out on the Strip, with views to the mountains on the west and east.

'Mr Fisso will join you in just a moment,' she told them. 'We have breakfast set up here, so please, help yourself.'

She left them alone, disappearing through a door in a leather-clad wall that led to the rest of the suite. Stride eyed the buffet and realized he was hungry. The spread on the mahogany bureau could have served twenty people. He took a plate, spread cream cheese over half a bagel, and layered it with pink lox. He poured a glass of orange juice and did the same for Serena.

The room, which had a rough Western feel to it, featured cowboy artists like Remington. There was sculpture, too, with a rodeo motif. Stride had a hard time imagining Manhattan-born Boni Fisso in a cowboy hat. He was about to make a joke to Serena, but was glad he didn't when he realized that Boni Fisso himself had made a silent entrance into the room.

Fisso read his mind. 'All men are cowboys at heart, Detective. Me, I'm an Italian cowboy. You've heard the term spaghetti Western? That's me.' He laughed, a loud, deep-throated bellow that echoed in the large room.

179

He moved with remarkable grace and speed for a man in his eighties. He shook both their hands and maneuvered them toward the full-length windows, where he pointed with a sweep of his arms at the view. 'Look at that city! God, what a place. You know what they say, every world-class city has a river running through it. Fuck 'em. We've got dust and yuccas and rattlesnakes running through ours. Only river here is money. I'll take that over all the sewage and fish heads floating through the Missouri or the Hudson.'

'You don't miss the old days?' Stride asked him. 'Everyone else from back then seems to think Vegas was better in the sixties.'

'Hell, no!' Boni exclaimed. 'Sure, I wish I had the body and half the energy I did in those days. We all think that, right? I've lost a lot of friends, too. Everybody gets old. You know the saying. Tempus fuck-it. But that's the beauty of this town. It's always young. Bulldoze the past, and get on with it. Magic is what you grew up with, Detective. I guarantee you, forty years from now, old people will be talking about how they miss Vegas in the two thousands.' Boni poured himself a glass of champagne from the buffet. 'Come on, you two, eat, eat. God, I sound like my grandmother.'

There was no way around it. Boni was charming. Stride had to work to remind himself that the man wouldn't think twice about ordering a killing if it suited his purposes. He thought about Walker in the wheelchair, having been beaten nearly to death by Boni's goons. About Amira and her crushed skull.

Boni fixed him with sparkling blue eyes, and Stride thought that the man knew exactly what he was thinking. It was probably the same thing that everyone thought when they came into this room and met the man for the first time.

'Fill your plates, and then let's sit down,' Boni told them. He took a red leather armchair for himself, and Stride noticed that it had been designed low to the ground, so that Boni's feet lay flat on the floor. He was short, no more than five foot six. The chair itself was on a slight riser, higher than the sofas around it. His throne. Stride half expected a ruby ring to kiss.

Boni was dressed all in black. He wore a turtleneck, a tailored ebony blazer, and creased black dress pants. His shoes were patent leather with a mirror finish. He still looked very much like he did in the photos from decades ago, when he already had a balding crown of black hair. The hair was gray now, and his forehead was mottled with liver spots. He had sunken crescent moons under his eyes and five o'clock shadow that a razor couldn't scrape away. But he was fit and strong, and his eyes were piercing and alert. He still had movie-star teeth.

180

Assuming the movie was *Jaws*, Stride thought to himself.

'Mr Fisso,' Serena began.

'Oh, please. It's Boni, Boni. Don't make me feel so goddamn old.'

Stride saw that Serena was uncomfortable being on a first-name basis with the man, but she struggled to spit out the name. 'Boni then. My name is—'

'No need, no need,' Boni interrupted her again. 'Serena Dial. You're from Las Vegas by way of Phoenix, if my sources are correct.' His tone was light, but Stride had the feeling that Boni could have rattled off every detail of Serena's past, maybe more than he could have done himself. 'And you're the new kid on the block,' he continued, turning to Stride. 'From Minnesota? Lots of lakes there. I'd ask what the hell you're doing in the desert, but that's pretty obvious.' He winked at him and glanced at Serena, and it was clear that he knew all about their relationship. Stride wondered if it came from Sawhill.

'I have to thank you,' Boni told Serena. 'I haven't talked to my daughter in years. It was good to hear her voice. Once upon a time, I thought she'd be living here, running my empire right beside me. Girl had a business sense like no one I've ever met. Hell, she must get it from her old man, right? I mean, Eva, her mother, she could cut you a new one, but her gift was spending money, not making it. No, my baby Claire, she's the talented one in the family, I can't hold a candle to her.'

'Why are you estranged?' Serena asked.

Boni's face hardened like concrete. 'A police detective concerned about my family values. That's very nice. You didn't really come here to help me patch things up with Claire, did you?'

'No, it's just that—'

'Look, Claire and I didn't see eye to eye about my business ventures. So she went off to sing her sad songs, just to spite me. And to live in that little apartment, when I know perfectly well she's made millions in the market.' Boni watched Serena, who couldn't keep the shock off her face. 'She probably told you it's because she likes to sleep with girls. That's not the Catholic way. Well, I'd have been happier if she married some strapping fellow like Detective Stride here. I made her go on a few dates with some good-looking guys. Any sin in that? But no, I have to deal with Claire in confession every Sunday, God help me. Father D'Antoni always asks about her, to see if she's come back to God's way. I think he just likes hearing the details, if you ask me.'

'Have you heard her sing?' Serena asked.

'I have. She's primo. That girl would *run* Nashville if she moved out there. It'll never happen, though. She's all Vegas at heart.' Boni settled back in his chair and took a sip of champagne. 'But we have other things to talk about, don't we? Claire says you two wanted to have an off-the-record conversation with me, no goddamn lawyers around. I have to respect that. I'm a lawyer myself, and I have to tell you that most of them might as well stick a talking parrot on their desk that says, "No, no, no." And they'd bill the parrot out at a thousand dollars an hour. So there's no lawyers here, Detectives. Just the three of us. This conversation never happened. Got it?'

They both nodded.

'The reason we're here—' Stride began.

'The reason you're here is you're trying to catch a killer. And you want my help.'

Stride nodded. 'That's right.'

'I saw the sketch in the paper. I can't help you. I'm sorry.'

'He worked for your company,' Serena retorted. 'David Kamen hired him at Premium Security. I'm sure you know that, because I'm sure Kamen called you.'

'Yes, he did,' Boni said. 'But that doesn't change a thing. I never met this Blake Wilde, and I don't know how you can find him. I wish I could help.'

'You realize Claire could be his next target,' Serena said.

'I'm not a fool, Detective,' Boni said sharply. He fixed Serena with his blue eyes and added, 'I always have people watching Claire. Even when she doesn't know it, I'm always protecting her.'

Serena fired back. 'Was Blake one of the people you had *protecting* her?'

Boni didn't reply, and Stride thought she had hit a nerve.

'Mr Fisso, may I speak candidly?' Stride asked.

'By all means, Detective.'

'It hasn't been in the papers, but you probably knew even before we did that these murders have one thing in common. The Sheherezade. Or more specifically, Amira Luz. Blake Wilde, whoever he is, seems to be bent on avenging Amira's death, because he thinks it didn't go down the way the papers and the police said it did. He may very well be right about that. But we're not here to reopen the investigation into the murder of Amira Luz. That case is closed.'

'Really? I understand you've been making a lot of inquiries about it, Detective. I hear you even paid a visit on my old friend, Walker Lane.'

'You know he's in a wheelchair,' Stride said. 'He has been since that night.'

'Terrible thing. A car accident, wasn't it? A good lesson about not driving while intoxicated.'

'That's not what Walker says.'

'Oh?'

'He says you had him beaten. Crippled. As payback for trying to take away your mistress.'

'I suppose he also accused me of killing Amira,' Boni replied placidly.

'Yes, he did.'

'Naturally. I liked Walker very much, Detective, but his behavior was reckless. When you make mistakes that have awful consequences, you often try to blame someone else.'

'So you didn't have Amira killed,' Stride said.

'Of course not.'

'No? Wasn't she your property? Didn't you own her?'

Boni tut-tutted him like a child. 'No one owned Amira. No one. Least of all Walker. I believe that frustrated him enormously.'

'So you're saying Walker killed Amira?' Stride asked.

'As far as I know, a deranged fan killed her. Walker wasn't here when Amira was killed. He had already left to drive back to Los Angeles. Coincidentally, I believe that's when he had his accident.'

'And I'm sure we'll find a police report about the accident if we go back far enough,' Stride said.

'I'm sure you would. Then again, in forty years, things get lost.'

'What about employment records from the Sheherezade back then? Did they get lost, too?'

'Why?' Boni asked. 'Who are you looking for?'

'A kid who worked at the hotel during the summer as a lifeguard. His name was Mickey.'

Boni cocked an eyebrow at Stride. 'And why would you care about someone like that?'

'He called your casino boss Leo Rucci about a fight outside the night of Amira's death. I want to know more about it.'

'Well, I'm sorry, Detective. I'm sure the old employment records are in a warehouse somewhere in the city, half eaten by cockroaches. But when we had college kids working here over the summer, I usually had Leo pay them in cash. It was more hassle than it was worth to worry about the paperwork and taxes.'

Stride felt like he was battling an old elk with a massive set of horns and the willingness to bang heads all day.

'If there was nothing unusual about Amira's death, why is Blake Wilde so intent on avenging her?' Serena asked, clearly tired of watching the boys play a game of which one's bigger.

183

'He's a serial killer. You know the mind of that kind of man better than I do.' Boni couldn't keep a small smirk off his face.

'If we knew *why* he was doing this, it might help us find him,' Stride said. 'And I think you know why.'

'You already said it, didn't you, Detective? He has some misguided ideas about what happened to Amira.'

Stride shook his head. 'Look, I know you want him first. You want to get him and deal with him your own way.' Stride paused and noted that Boni didn't disagree with him. 'But the main thing is that one of us catches him, soon, before he kills anyone else. If you catch him, OK, we'll never know. But I don't think there's a downside for you if we get him first.'

'Think harder,' Boni said. The mask slipped. A glint of steel.

Stride knew he was right. It was a race, and Boni needed to win. Not just to squeeze Blake, but to make him disappear quietly and quickly from the headlines. In custody, who knew what Blake might say? Or what he knew. His allegations alone would keep the heat on Boni and might drive investors away from his Orient project.

He wasn't going to help them.

'What if you're too late, Boni?' Serena asked. 'What if he gets to Claire first? Is it worth the risk?'

There was silence as Boni chewed on that thought.

'Where did Kamen find him?' Serena asked.

'That won't help you,' Boni said. 'Wilde was a mercenary in Afghanistan. David used him sometimes for ops that weren't on the books. He was good. Fearless. Ruthless. But that's all shadow stuff. Fake names. No backgrounds.'

'Were there others Kamen worked with who might know him?'

Boni shook his head. 'No way I'm giving you that. No way David gives you that.'

Stride knew there were military channels he could pursue, but if Wilde was a rogue player, the brass wasn't likely to give them any more information than Boni. 'Then tell us why,' he said.

He watched Boni grinding through calculations. It was all mathematics to him, debits and credits. The value of information. Stride thought at first Boni would stiff them again, but the old man leaned forward, his hands on his knees.

'I tell you this, and we're done.'

They both nodded.

'Amira, she wasn't celibate, you get the picture? She came to town, and she started sleeping with Moose. Smart girl. Moose had juice. Pretty soon she was lead dancer in one of out T&A shows. Then she went to Paris, OK? Special engagement. That's where she came up with the idea for *Flame*.'

Boni seemed to enjoy the confusion on their faces.

'The thing is, she didn't go to Paris,' he went on. 'She was pregnant. She wanted to keep it under wraps. So I sent her away for a few months, and she had the kid.'

A baby, Stride thought. A secret baby. Sometimes the hardest problems were really the simplest. Blake Wilde was *Amira's son*.

'What happened to the baby?' Stride asked.

'Adoption,' Boni said. 'Amira couldn't get rid of the baby fast enough. It killed her stuck up there all alone. She couldn't wait to get back. She knew *Flame* would be a huge hit.'

'Moose didn't know?' Serena asked.

'No one knew.'

Something niggled in Stride's brain. A plate shifted, and like an earthquake a piece of the puzzle fell into place.

'You said "up there",' Stride said. 'Where did you send her?'

'An associate of mine had resort cabins in Reno near the lake,' Boni replied. 'That was where a lot of the girls from Vegas went when they had problems like that.'

Stride and Serena looked at each other. 'Reno,' they said.

PART THREE

BLAKE

Thirty

'I get to see you twice in one week,' Jay Walling said as Serena got out of her rental car outside the retirement home near downtown Reno. He was wearing his black fedora at a cocky angle. 'How blessed I am.'

'Stuff it, Jay,' Serena said pleasantly.

She zipped up her leather jacket. It was cold in the city, with a stiff wind off the mountains and snow flurries in the air. A fall heatwave was firing up the temperatures in Las Vegas, but up here, it felt like winter. The sky overhead was a somber charcoal, and the mountains looked angry.

'His name's William Borden,' Walling said. 'Alice Ford's brother.'

Once they knew about Blake's connection to Reno, it hadn't taken them long to find what they had been missing from the beginning – something to tie the murder of Alice Ford at her Reno ranch to the other deaths in Las Vegas. They discovered that Alice's brother had spent thirty years as executive director of a non-profit organization that delivered family services in the northern half of the state. That included arranging confidential adoptions for knocked-up showgirls like Amira.

'Did you find out any more about the agency?' Serena asked.

'They're saintly, as far as the folks in Carson City are concerned. Modest budget, lots of small annual gifts, no significant complaints. They do good work.'

'Was Borden running the agency when Amira Luz had her baby?'

Walling nodded. 'He took over in nineteen sixty. Ran it until he retired. He's terminal now, with a heart condition. Moved into this place last year.'

Serena studied the three-story senior facility, a concrete box in dirty white, and felt herself getting depressed. They weren't far from the huge old homes that looked down on the rushing waters of the Truckee

189

River, but they may as well have been in another universe. It got worse when they went inside. The nurses tried hard, decorating the walls with children's art and wearing wide smiles, but it was still a place where used-up people went to die. They passed a diabetic man with amputated limbs. A woman trembling in the grip of severe Parkinson's. People with empty stares, their minds gone. Serena felt a sense of claustrophobia.

They found William Borden in the lounge on the second floor. There was a television in one corner, and a dozen people were on sofas and in wheelchairs around it, watching a rerun of *Friends*. A nurse pointed out Borden for them. He was off by himself in an armchair on the far side of the room, a book in his lap.

They introduced themselves and pulled over chairs to sit in front of him. Serena took off her coat. The room was a furnace.

'I'm very sorry about your sister,' Serena told him. She noted that the book in his hands was entitled *Families Making Sense of Death*. She wondered how anyone ever did make sense of it. Particularly violent death. Borden's eyes were far away.

'I feel terrible guilt,' Borden replied. He had a professorial voice, self-reflective and somewhat pompous. He was a small man, with a gray beard and silver hair badly in need of a cut. He wore light blue pajamas and slippers. 'I guess that was this man's intention all along. To inflict guilt and pain. I haven't seen Al yet. I wonder if he'll even visit me now, since I took his wife away from him.'

'You didn't do that, Mr Borden,' Walling pointed out.

Borden shrugged. 'Didn't I?'

'We'd like to see if you can identify the man we think may have killed your sister,' Serena said. She began to hand him a copy of the police artist's sketch, but Borden waved it away.

'No need. I know who it is. When Mr Walling called me, I knew exactly who it had to be.' Despite the warmth in the room and a wool blanket over his legs, Borden shivered.

'He calls himself Blake Wilde,' Serena said.

Borden shook his head. 'That name doesn't mean anything to me. But I'm sure he's changed it many times over the years. When I knew him, he was Michael Burton. But that was more than twenty years ago.'

'I really would like you to look at the sketch,' Serena said.

Borden sighed. He took it and stared at it with obvious discomfort. Finally, he closed his eyes and nodded. 'He was only sixteen when I last saw him, but it's definitely him. Those eyes. The rest of his face is older, but those eyes are just as they were.' He heard a titter of laughter from the crowd gathered around the television set. He frowned. 'This is what it comes down to, you know, this place. Gather the dying like cattle and wait for them to peel off one by one. It's ironic. I spent my whole career trying to better the lives of children. I never found time to get married and have kids myself. Instead, I wind up here with a decaying heart, no one to visit me except my sister. And now she's gone. Thanks to the mistake I made. One terrible mistake in thirty years.'

'Was Blake – or Michael – the son of Amira Luz?' Serena asked.

'I really don't know. I never did. I never met the mother.'

'Tell us what happened,' Walling suggested gently.

'A man came to me,' Borden explained. 'This was spring of nineteen sixty-seven. It was after hours. He had a baby with him, very young, no more than a couple days old. He told me that the mother was unable to care for him and asked if I could find a home for the boy.'

'Do you know who the man was?'

Borden shook his head. 'He didn't give a name. He was big, neck like a redwood tree. Intimidating.'

Serena thought it sounded like Leo Rucci, although there were plenty of muscle men working for the casinos in those days. 'You took a baby, just like that? No questions asked?'

'Things like that happened all the time back then. Girls in Vegas had relationships with high rollers and got pregnant. They wanted it to go away quietly. No papers. No inheritance problems. Every month it seemed there was another girl, another baby. Everyone has such nostalgia for the Rat Pack times, but that was mostly if you were rich and white. Nobody wanted to look at what was behind the curtain. Virulent racism. Women abused. Children thrown away.'

'So you took the baby?' Serena asked.

Borden nodded.

Walling leaned in and whispered. 'Not that I don't think you're a fine citizen, Mr Borden, but did any money change hands?'

Borden looked up at the ceiling. 'Yes, yes, there was money, too. These people always paid handsomely. But I assure you, not a dime of it went into my pocket. It all went into the agency. It pulled us through some difficult times.'

'What about the family?' Serena asked. 'Didn't they ask questions?'

'Everything was anonymous back then. To them, there was nothing unusual. It's not like today, where many birth mothers stay in touch with their children long after they've been adopted.'

Walling smoothed his fedora as he held it in his hands. 'I'm a little confused, Mr Borden. If you didn't know where the baby came from, and the family didn't know either, how did this man figure out that Amira Luz was his mother? And why did he start this nasty little game by murdering your sister?'

Borden looked pained. He took a few deep breaths, and Serena noticed that they didn't come easily. 'How he found out about Amira, I don't know. But the vendetta – well, that began a long time ago.'

'Explain,' Walling said crisply.

'I told you I made a mistake. An awful mistake. I don't mean accepting the baby or taking the money. If I had it to do over again today, I would do the very same thing. My mission was protecting children.'

'Then what?' Walling asked.

Serena looked into Borden's eyes, and she began to realize what had really happened. She had been there, too. She felt the warmth in the room begin to smother her. The word hung between them, waiting to be spoken.

Abuse.

'My mistake was in the family I chose,' Borden said.

Walling saw it now too. 'What did they do to the boy?'

'You have to understand,' Borden said. Serena thought he was trying to rationalize the decision to himself. 'Placing children with adoptive parents is not an exact science. We make our best judgement based on interviews. But occasionally there are problems. I confess, I was young and overconfident in those days. I have a doctorate in child psychology. I thought I could size up an adoptive family and tell you in a few minutes whether they were suited or not. I didn't know then all the things I didn't know.'

'The Burton family wasn't suited,' Serena said.

Borden shook his head. 'The husband, maybe. He was a decent man, hard-working, lower middle class. They had been married for five years. Desperate for a child. His wife, Bonnie, she was very eager. I thought they would do fine as parents. I simply missed the signs. Based on what I know now, I'm sure Bonnie herself had an abusive parent. She picked up right where they left off. Although, if the boy was telling me the truth, Bonnie was singularly cruel.'

'Don't you do follow-up visits?' Walling asked.

'Of course. Everything looked fine. You have to understand, Mr Walling, I'm not talking about physical abuse. Beatings. Violence. I'm talking about sexual abuse. Bonnie Burton was intimate with her adopted son from a very young age.'

Serena felt as if the ceiling were getting lower, as if it would begin pressing her into the floor. She had a flashback of her own mother and Blue Dog, over her on the bed. Her body became bathed in sweat.

'It wasn't just sex,' Borden continued. 'She terrorized the boy in order to dominate him. She had complete control over his psyche. When he resisted, she would do unspeakable things.'

'Such as?' Walling asked.

Serena really didn't want to hear the details.

'The boy told me that Bonnie would sometimes lock him in the bathroom, naked, in the dark. And then she would release – things – under the door.'

'Things?'

'Cockroaches mostly.'

'Shit,' Serena said involuntarily. 'You didn't know any of this at the time? The husband didn't know?'

'No, I didn't know a thing. Our contact with the family ends at an early age. And the husband – if he knew, he didn't stop it. I hope he didn't know.'

'How did you find out?' Serena asked.

Borden's face twitched. The crowd in front of the television laughed again. 'It wasn't until years later. The boy broke into my home while I was sleeping. He tied me up. I had no idea who he was at first. I thought he was going to rob me. Then he sat down by the bed, after I was tied up, and explained who he was. He wanted to find his mother.'

'So he was obsessed with her even then,' Serena said.

'Oh, yes. In his mind, his birth mother was a victim, like he was. Through the abuse, he had built an imaginary bond with her. He told me that she came to him and whispered to him sometimes. Told him everything would be fine. Told him to find her.'

It's OK, baby, Serena thought to herself and felt the room spin again. She was angry at herself, letting her own past creep into the present. It was infecting her.

'He told you about the abuse while you were tied up?' Walling asked.

Borden nodded. 'In detail. If you're wondering whether he made it up, I assure you, he didn't. I've interviewed thousands of children. I know lies and fantasies, and this wasn't either of them. Whatever he's done since, whoever he's become, the boy suffered indescribable torture in that house.'

'What was he like?' Serena asked. 'Was he violent?'

'Violent, yes,' Borden replied. 'But it wasn't an uncontrolled violence. He wasn't angry or confrontational. He was simply calm and cruel.

I don't even think it was deliberate cruelty. He had dealt with suffering by shutting himself off from pain and decoupling his emotions from what was happening around him. He was – I know this sounds strange – very focused. Very professional. For his age, he was quite mature. Violence was just a tool to get what he wanted.'

'And what he wanted was his real mother,' Serena said. She thought about Blake as a boy and realized she understood how he had reacted. He had become a kind of Barbed Wire, as she had. Frozen himself. Gone inside.

'Exactly. Unfortunately for me, I couldn't give her to him.'

Walling's eyes narrowed. 'What did he do to you?'

Borden unbuttoned his pajama top and calmly pulled aside the fabric. His wizened chest bore the zipper-like scar of open-heart surgery. But there were other scars, too, dozens of them across his chest, circular disfigurements like pencil erasers. 'He started asking me questions about the adoption, what records were kept, where he could find them. I told him lies at first, that we didn't have records from back then, that records had been lost in a move. He knew I was lying. He was smoking a cigarette while he questioned me, and with each wrong answer, he used the end of the cigarette to brand me. I can't even describe the agony of it. He didn't take any pleasure in hurting me, though. It was clinical. Inflicting pain to get what he wanted. Answers.'

'You told him the truth?' Serena asked.

'Very quickly. It took a long time for him to believe that there were no records on his adoption, that I didn't know anything about his birth mother. I described the man who brought the baby as best as I could remember, but sixteen years later, that wasn't going to help him. I told him what I had always suspected, that it smelled like the mob. But a sixteen-year-old runaway in Nevada wasn't going to crack the wall of silence among the casino bosses.'

'So you don't think he found out about Amira back then?' Serena asked.

'I don't see how. I still don't know how he found out. I didn't know myself until you people told me.'

'Well, let's assume he found out somehow. Why do you think he's doing this? What's his plan?'

Borden stared down at the sketch in his hand. He didn't say anything for a long time, and Serena realized that a tear had slipped out of his eye. He wiped it away. She wondered if it was for himself, or for his sister, or for the boy he had accidentally sentenced to a tormented life. Maybe all three.

'Part of it is certainly vengeance. Not just on his behalf, but on his mother's. He's getting justice for her.'

'But why family members?' Walling asked. 'Why not just off the people he thinks played a role in Amira's death?'

'In his mind, it hurts more to lose a family member,' Borden said. 'That's his own pain. It's something he can relate to. He wants the people who took away his mother to know what it's like to lose your family. Like he did. And like Amira did, too.'

'From what we hear, Amira was happy to be rid of the kid,' Serena said.

'Maybe so, but he doesn't know that. I'm sure he wouldn't believe it anyway.'

'But you didn't kill Amira,' Walling pointed out. 'Why start with you?'

Borden shook his head. 'It's not just the people who killed her. It's everyone who *betrayed* her. In his mind, I was the first. I split up mother and child. That was obvious when he first came to me. He blamed me for taking him – and for placing him with the Burtons.'

'We should talk to the Burtons,' Serena said to Walling. A part of her hated the idea of coming face to face with another abusive mother, and a part of her wanted to lash out at the woman.

'That will be difficult,' Borden said, interrupting them. 'When the boy came to see me that night, he was running away, leaving the city. Before he left, he burned down the Burtons' home. With them in it.'

Thirty-one

Blake remembered vividly the first time he learned the truth about Amira.

It was an accident. A miracle, some people might call it. There were a million reasons why he should never have known. But he was there, and the magazine was there, and he felt the truth shudder through him like acid burning in his veins. Life hangs on a slender thread.

Several months ago, he had been in the waiting room of a dentist in Cancun, whose specialty was not root canals or cavities, but connecting American tourists with hits of cocaine. The dentist had made the serious mistake of skimming cash from people higher up the supply chain, people who didn't tolerate theft. Blake's job was simple. Separate the dentist from two of his incisors.

While he waited for the man's last patient to leave, Blake found that the dentist had another passion. Gambling. That was probably why he needed to take an extra slice off the top. His waiting room was filled with magazines from Las Vegas, Mississippi, and Monte Carlo, including a recent issue of *LV*. It happened to be the issue with Rex Terrell's article about Amira Luz and the Sheherezade.

A slender thread.

He opened the magazine, and there, staring out from a forty-year-old photograph, was his mother. There wasn't a shred of doubt in his mind. To him, looking at Amira was like looking in the mirror and seeing his own eyes. He didn't need anyone to tell him. He didn't need DNA. He *knew*. The connection between them seemed to leap off the page and into his bones.

When he read the article, the pieces fell into place, confirming what he saw in the photo. The missing time in her life, when Amira was supposedly dancing in Paris, was the same stretch of months in which Blake had been born. *But you weren't in Paris, were you? You were in Reno, a lost girl having a baby.*

Even the mob connection was there, just as the man from the adoption agency had warned him.

Boni Fisso.

Right there in the office, his mother called him back home, to Nevada, where he had once vowed never to set foot again. She cried out for justice.

He left the Cancun dentist on the floor, passed out from pain, his face bathing in the puddle of blood that streamed from his mouth. Blake washed the teeth and kept them in his pocket as good luck charms. Reminders of the day his old quest ended and his new quest began. He was already developing the list of people who needed to pay for their sins. Sins against Amira and her son.

He slipped back into the US across the Mexican border in Texas. It wasn't hard. He had spent most of his life finding ways across borders, in countries like Colombia, Afghanistan, Nigeria, and Iraq. He had adopted dozens of identities, all of which came naturally to him, because he felt he had no true identity of his own. His own past stopped in Reno, when he had tied up his adoptive parents and doused them and the house in gasoline. And then, outside, he lit the match and watched the house of horrors erupt explosively into flame, and heard their last pitiful screams as the fire streaked up the stairs to find them, like a bloodhound on a strong scent. He took a deep breath, smelling the air as their flesh cooked, and then he ran.

A new life. Almost twenty-five years of running.

He had been shattered when the search for his mother turned into a dead end. The man from the adoption agency had begged him, in tears, his chest scalded, to believe that he had been a Mafia baby who came from nowhere. And ultimately Blake did believe it. A part of him even liked the mystery that came with it. It felt appropriate, being a nowhere man, someone literally with no past. But the desire for the truth never went away, just like his mother never went away. Inside, in his head, she still talked to him. Guided him. There was still an umbilical cord that connected them and never went away.

Blake didn't linger in the US. He was sixteen but could pass for early twenties. When the US invaded Grenada, he went down there with a couple of other mercenaries from Louisiana who smelled money. He found that there were always people ready to pay for someone to do a job. He didn't need an identity, because no one wanted him to have one. He was smart, ruthless, and anonymous. That was all they asked, and they paid well.

From Grenada he went to Nicaragua. And then to Africa. He circled the globe, moving in the shadows. For most of the past decade, he had been in the Middle East, where the risks were infinitely higher, but so were the rewards. He enjoyed the challenge, but eventually he tired of working with fanatics and suffering the desert heat. He relocated to Mexico, hooked up with the cartels when he needed cash, and found himself enjoying the gulf breezes and bronzed women that came to the coast.

He thought of himself as semi-retired. There was plenty of money in an offshore bank. He still took jobs from time to time, usually jobs that kept him on the coast. For someone who had always been homeless, he felt at home in the sun and by the water. A parade of anonymous young women, some tourists, some locals, kept his sex drive fully satisfied. He bought a house. He taught himself to cook and fish, and he drank Corona and played poker with dock workers and waiters on Wednesday nights.

But the empty black corner of his soul stayed dark. The light never shone there. Things moved invisibly, rustling and clicking. And always, from the darkness, he heard her voice. His mother, whispering to him and telling him of unfinished business. He realized he had become lazy and content. He was in danger of losing his edge, and he couldn't afford that, not yet. After a summer not working, drinking too much and fucking a different woman every night, he stood on the beach outside his home and realized he wasn't ready to retire. Something egged him on, and later he realized it was a hand somewhere, guiding him. Unfinished business.

A few months later, he found himself in the dentist's office, staring at his mother's face. If he had stopped working, he never would have found her. When he read the article, and felt his rage growing, he knew that he had been led to that place and that moment. It was meant to be. He was going home.

In Las Vegas, Blake found a cheap apartment in a sorry neighborhood on the wrong side of a crumbling stone wall that separated the lower class from well-funded Cashman Field. He could have afforded better, but he wanted a hideaway where the person next door never remembered your face, and no one talked to the cops.

There was a code in the mean streets. Keep your eyes to yourself. Mind your own business.

He devoured everything he could find about Amira Luz. He spent hours reading about her. He surfed the web and found a pirated film on eBay with a grainy record of one of Amira's performances in *Flame*. Blake re-ran the film over and over, watching transfixed as his mother stripped off her clothes in front of the leering crowd. She seduced him, along with everyone else. He memorized every detail of the performance and even began to recognize other people lurking in the showroom and other dancers on stage. It was like watching the magazine story come alive.

Helena Troy. There was a look she gave Amira at one point, a nasty glimmer that came and went. Sheer jealousy and hatred were written on her face.

Moose Dargon. Drunk on stage between the dances. His eyebrows furling and unfurling like black sails. Making nasty jokes. *When God made Amira, he didn't rest on the seventh day. He jerked off.*

Walker Lane. Just the top of his head, taller than the others around him in the front row. But Blake could feel him panting when Amira came on stage. Lust was like that. You could see it in how a man cocked his head.

Leo Rucci. Hovering stage right, like a wolf. Blake could feel his hunger, too, in the way he eyed the girls. *A man with a neck like a redwood tree.* He had been the one to strip Blake out of Amira's arms.

He began to feel as if he knew them all. As if he could crawl through the screen and find himself in the showroom, smelling perfume, brilliantine, and smoke. As if he could mingle with them, wearing a tux that made him stand a little straighter and strut a little cooler than the rest. As if he could swoop Amira off the stage and drive with her into the desert in a Coronet convertible, her raven hair flying in the wind. As if the whole world was a black and white movie.

The more he buried himself in the past, the easier it was to map out the game in the present. There was a bonus, too. David Kamen was in town, the marksman from Kabul who had his fingers in every black market in the Afghan theatre. Blake had done plenty of wet work for Kamen, and the man owed him. Soon, Blake had a job that gave him access to the very people he wanted to reach out and touch.

Piece by piece, it all fell into place.

The night before he went to Reno, he sat in the dark, watching the film of *Flame* again. He kept the dentist's teeth, his lucky charms, in a box on top of the television, but he took them out and juggled them in his hand as he watched. He was restless and anxious to get started. As he watched the film, he thought about himself, a baby, already in the vicious hands of Bonnie Burton while Amira was on stage. Blake didn't feel any anger now. The next day, he would begin to even the scales.

But he knew he wouldn't sleep that night. His nerves were on edge, and he needed to calm them, to deaden himself for what lay ahead. The long drive to Reno. The few seconds of violence at Alice Ford's home. He left his apartment and went out for a drink and a smoke at a club he had already visited several times before. The Limelight.

It was hard to believe, weeks later, that the game was almost over.

He sat in his car, a nondescript brown sedan, in a parking lot one block north of a popular strip club near the Stratosphere. It was night, but neon lit up the street. He could see the other car, the convertible, in his rear-view mirror, parked behind the club. Ninety minutes had passed, and Blake figured it wouldn't be long before the man would re-emerge. He kept a close eye on the customers who came and went.

His window was open. He was smoking. Every few minutes a hooker drifted by, leaned her tits into the car, and tried to pick him up. Blake just blew smoke in her face and stared at her until she backed away, nervous and scared. He wondered if any of them recognized him from the sketch on television. In the shadows of the car, he doubted it. He also didn't think any of the girls would be rushing to find a cop.

At eleven thirty, the man came out of the club. He was impossible to miss. Young and fat, his belly hanging over his gray slacks. A white shirt and a bright tie loosened so far it dripped between his legs. He was tall, dwarfing a tiny blonde girl who clung to his arm. Her assets were squeezed into a pink form-fitting dress. Both of them walked like they were drunk, but that didn't stop them from climbing into the convertible.

Blake saw a bodyguard, who had been holding up the wall of the club while the man was inside, take a gander up and down the street. He was inexperienced and stupid and didn't even pause to study the sedan. Blake could have walked up to the convertible with a crossbow and this guy would have kept chewing his gum.

Blake pulled out of the lot and into the Strip traffic in the right lane. Behind him, he saw the fat man and the blonde peel out in the convertible. The bodyguard climbed into an SUV, but he was slow. Blake let the convertible roar past him, then accelerated and kept them in sight. A minute later, the bodyguard's truck flew past him too. Blake stayed a few car lengths back.

They drove past wedding chapels, donut shops, bail bondsmen, and psychics who read palms and tarot cards. Traffic was heavy. Hot, dry air blew in through the window as Blake followed the convertible. He figured they were heading for one of the casinos on Fremont Street.

Blake had a wireless Bluetooth device hooked to his ear. He punched in a number on his cell phone, and a few seconds later he heard a gruff voice answering through the earpiece.

'Yeah?'

'Good evening, Leo,' Blake said.

'Who the fuck is this?'

'This is Blake Wilde. Do you know who I am?'

There was a long stretch of silence.

'OK, yeah, Boni told me about you,' Leo Rucci said. 'So did the cops. You're the guy who thinks he can bring his mama back to life by running down little boys. So what? I should be scared of you?'

'Yes, you should, Leo.'

'Well, you don't scare me, you little prick. Why don't you come over to my house right now and talk to me face to face? You won't, because you know you won't walk out of here alive.'

'I just want to know if it was you,' Blake said. He accelerated, closing the distance to the convertible. He passed a limousine and slid back into the right lane. The convertible with the fat man and the blonde was on his left.

'Huh? What do you mean?'

'You were Boni's right-hand man in the Sheherezade. I want to know if you were the one who actually killed Amira.'

Rucci laughed. 'Some dipstick fan bashed her skull in. Let it go.'

'We both know that isn't what happened,' Blake said.

'Yeah? How do you know that? You were shitting your diapers when it went down.'

'Just tell me if it was you, Leo. If it was you, then this is between us. You and me. No one else.'

'I don't owe you nothing, fuckhead.'

'OK, if that's the way you want to play it.' Blake took a deep breath and let it out slowly. 'I'm driving beside a white convertible,' he said, eyeing the car next to him. 'License plate YA8 371. That's what your son Gino drives, isn't it?'

There was silence again, longer and more deadly.

'Don't you fucking dare,' Leo whispered.

The convertible with the fat man and the blonde stopped at a red light just ahead. Blake pulled next to it in the right lane and rolled down his driver's side window. 'Pay attention, Leo,' Blake said into the phone.

Leo's voice screamed in his ear. 'You fucker! Don't you do this, you fucker!'

The blonde was cuddling up against Gino Rucci's side. Blake figured her hand was in his lap. In his wing mirror, he saw the bodyguard in the car behind, lazy and unconcerned.

'Hey, baby,' Blake called out to the blonde. 'How much?'

She wheeled round. 'Shut up, you creep!'

'Come on, baby, I said, how much?' Blake repeated. 'How much is fatso paying you for a hand job? Can't be worth more than five bucks.'

Wing mirror. The bodyguard was paying attention now. He was opening the driver's side door. Blake saw Gino's beefy arm push the blonde back into the seat. Gino leaned forward, his face black with rage.

'That's a pretty sorry excuse for a hooker,' Blake told him. 'Is she the best you can do, you loser?'

Gino's cheeks pulsed red. Blood vessels popped like fireworks. 'I hope you enjoyed your last walk, creep,' he hissed. ''Cause you ain't ever going to walk again.'

'You listening, Leo?' Blake murmured into the phone.

Leo screamed, '*Amira was a whore! She was a fucking cunt!*'

The bodyguard shouldered his way out of his car. Gino was getting up too, his huge torso lifting off the seat like a hot air balloon. The blonde cowered with her head buried in the leather cushion.

'Want to say goodbye, Leo?' Blake said.

'I WILL FUCKING DESTROY YOU.'

A cell phone began ringing in Gino's convertible. Blake knew it was Leo on another line, trying to reach his son. He casually picked up the Sig Sauer from between his legs and pointed it out the window. 'Listen up, Leo,' he said.

The bodyguard's hand began diving into his jacket. Gino got the same stupid look on his face that M.J. had when he opened his eyes. Blake pulled the trigger twice, firing two neat rounds into Gino's skull. Flicking his arm back, he fired again, catching the bodyguard in the throat. Both men collapsed. Through the earpiece, Leo let fly with a guttural scream. The blonde joined in.

'Say hi to Boni for me,' Blake said as he accelerated calmly through the green light. 'Tell him he's next.'

Thirty-two

Sara Evans again. Restless.

When Stride fished his cell phone out of his pocket, he saw a 218 area code on the caller ID. He had spent his whole life in that area code, which included most of northern Minnesota. He answered the phone and heard a familiar voice say, 'How's it going, boss?'

'Mags!' Stride exclaimed. 'God, it's good to hear your voice. I miss you.'

'Same here.'

Maggie Bei had been his partner for more than a decade. She was a Chinese girl the size of a Kewpie doll but with the best brain he had ever encountered on the force. Shortly before Stride left for Las Vegas, Maggie had announced that she was pregnant and was giving up her shield. It helped make it easier for Stride to leave.

'What's the weather like up there?' Stride asked. Only a Minnesotan could appreciate that every conversation had to begin with a review of the weather.

'Sucks. Rain. Cold. How about there?'

'Heatwave,' Stride said. 'We had a couple weeks in the seventies, and now it's in the upper nineties again. I thought we were done with that after August.'

'You gone Vegas on me yet, boss?' Maggie asked. 'Silk shirts? Shades? Bubbly drinks with little umbrellas?'

'Yeah. I'm coloring my hair, too. Got it slicked back.'

'Right, and I'm blonde now. Got implants.'

Stride had to pull his Bronco over to the curb and park. He was laughing too hard. 'I really do miss you, Mags.'

'Who wouldn't?' Maggie paused and added, 'Listen, I've got some news. Not good, I'm afraid.'

Stride sobered up immediately. 'What is it?'

'I lost the baby.'

He heard the crack in her voice. 'Oh, no. I'm so sorry.'

'Yeah. It was actually a couple weeks ago, but I didn't have the guts to call and tell you.'

'Shit, Mags, you should have told me right away.'

Maggie sighed. 'Nothing you could have done.'

'Are you OK?' He shook his head in disgust. That was the kind of stupid question reporters asked victims on the evening news.

'So-so. Doc says it's real common, we can try again, blah blah blah. That doesn't make it any easier. Eric's taking it hard. He says he's not so sure he wants kids now. Like God's trying to tell us something.'

'That's crazy.'

'I know.' She hesitated. 'I'm wondering about going back on the force. I didn't really want to leave, you know, it was Eric's idea.'

'Is that what you want?' Stride asked.

'I don't know. It's not the same without you.'

Stride didn't know what to say to that, so he kept quiet. He didn't know where Maggie was going. Once upon a time, there had been history between them. Maggie had been in love with him for several years, and she had made a play for him shortly after Cindy died. It didn't work out. She didn't hold a grudge, not even when Serena entered the picture, but Stride always wondered if the emotions were entirely dead. Even after Maggie married Eric, there were hints sometimes that she would have gone over the edge if Stride had ever given her a reason.

'But I suppose you're happy in Sin City,' Maggie continued.

'Oh, yeah. I fit right in here. You'd expect that.'

She ignored the sarcasm. 'What's it like being a working stiff again and not the big boss?'

'I just do what you always did. Complain about the lieutenant.'

'Nice. Good one. How's Serena?'

'OK.' He knew his voice sounded like lead.

Maggie took a long time to reply. He could never fool her. 'You guys having problems?'

'I don't know what we're having,' he admitted.

'Serena's got ghosts, boss. You knew that going in.'

'This isn't a ghost.' He took a deep breath and told her about Serena and Claire. And about his secret fear, which he had barely expressed to himself, that this would all end in him losing her.

'She says she still loves you?' Maggie asked.

'She says that.'

'What about you? How do you feel?'

Stride thought about the old joke. Ask a Minnesotan how he feels

204

on the day his dog dies, his wife leaves him, and he loses his job. 'Fine,' he said.

'Real funny.'

'I love her, Mags. You know that.'

'So what's the problem? Hell, boss, this could be your ticket to a threesome.'

Stride laughed. 'Sure.' He added, 'OK, the thought did cross my dirty mind. But come on. Me?'

'It's a lot stranger world than you know,' she replied, in a voice that didn't sound like Maggie at all.

'Don't tell me that you would get into anything like that.'

'Let's not go there, boss,' she retorted.

He felt like he was walking in quicksand and decided to change the subject. 'So what about you? Are you going back?'

'I haven't decided. It's too soon after the baby, you know?'

'I know.' He was so accustomed to thinking of Maggie as a rock that it was difficult to hear pain radiating from her. 'I really am sorry, Mags.'

'Thanks. You know, there was another reason I called.'

'Oh?'

'K-2 asked me to do it. He was too chicken to call himself.'

Deputy Chief Kyle Kinnick was Stride's old boss in Duluth. 'What does he want?' Stride asked, feeling a tingling in his chest.

'The search for a new lieutenant in the Detective Bureau washed out,' Maggie said. 'He wanted me to feel you out. See if you might be interested in coming back.'

'Libraries,' Amanda said. 'I think that's our best bet.'

She stood by the open window in Sawhill's office. There was barely a whisper of a breeze. A portable fan whined on his desk, directing its air at the lieutenant's face. Part of the downtown area had lost power earlier in the afternoon, and though the station had a backup generator, it didn't extend to air conditioning. The office was stifling.

'This guy had to find out about Amira somewhere,' she went on. 'We're talking about Vegas forty years ago. Sure, he could surf the web, but wouldn't he go to the library, too? That's where he'd find old newspapers, old magazines, anything like that. It may be one way he built his list of targets.'

'Check it out,' Sawhill said. He had a glow of sweat on his face, but his tie was tightly knotted at his neck. His one concession to the heat was removing his black suit coat. 'We've got this guy's description all over the papers and television, but we can't find him. And he

205

still manages to gun down Gino Rucci and his bodyguard right on the Strip. Explain that to me.'

'We know he can disguise himself,' Stride said. 'If he doesn't want to be recognized, he won't be. But we've got uniforms and casino security people on the lookout for him. Witnesses last night pegged him in a brown sedan, but no one got a plate. We've added that to the profile.'

'Are we getting calls to the hotline?'

'Lots, but nothing you could call a break,' Stride said.

'What else do we know about this guy?' Sawhill asked.

'He's pretty much an unperson,' Serena replied. 'He was called Michael Burton in Reno until he was sixteen. Jay Walling dug up some school records, but nothing that will help us here. After he torched his parents, he fell off the grid. There's no record of who he became or where he went.'

'I checked with the military,' Stride added. 'I was able to contact two other men from David Kamen's unit in Afghanistan. One of them remembered Wilde and confirmed Kamen's story that the guy was essentially a mercenary. But he didn't know anything that would help us find him.'

'We haven't gone public with the connection to Amira,' Serena said. 'Maybe we should.'

The political wheels turned in Sawhill's mind. 'How would that help us?' he asked.

'Wilde might have talked to someone about Amira or the Sheherezade. They might remember him or know something about him.'

Sawhill shook his head. 'Not strong enough. The casino connection would generate a lot of headlines, but I don't think it will help us catch this guy. It'll just be a distraction.'

In other words, people might start asking Boni Fisso some embarrassing questions, Amanda thought. 'Someone's going to make the connection soon,' she said. 'Either it will leak, or some writer like Rex Terrell will put it together.'

'Let them worry about that, and we'll worry about catching this guy before he kills someone else.' Sawhill pulled a handkerchief from his shirt pocket and wiped his brow. 'What are we doing to prevent another hit?'

Serena glanced over her shoulder at Cordy. 'Did you get the list?'

Cordy nodded. 'Uh-huh. We got another ten people who worked at the Sheherezade back then and had jobs that had something to do with Amira and her show. Dancers, choreographers, the kind of folks this Wilde thing might decide to have a grudge against, you know? We've told them to make sure their relatives keep an eye out.'

'But Wilde seems to be moving up the food chain,' Stride said.

'Meaning?' Sawhill asked.

'Meaning Boni,' Stride said. 'Wilde wouldn't let us know what he looks like if he wasn't in the last stages of his game. He wants Boni to know he's coming after him.'

'Why announce his intentions?'

Stride shrugged. 'Pride. Ego. Confidence. He wants Boni to squirm.'

Sawhill rocked back in his seat and frowned. 'Except he's not likely to tackle Boni directly, is he? In every other case, he's gone after a relative. His daughter, Claire, she's got to be at the top of our list, doesn't she?'

'No question about it,' Stride said.

Sawhill leaned forward, jabbing a finger at Serena. 'You know her, don't you? I want you to take charge of her protection. I want you all over her, Detective.'

'I'm not a babysitter, sir,' Serena said.

'No, you're a detective trying to save a life,' Sawhill retorted. 'Do you have a problem here?' He didn't wait for an answer but added immediately, 'I want you to oversee security for Claire Belfort. Under no circumstances are we going to let Wilde get near her. You got that? I want you with her now, and I want you glued to her side until we catch this guy. Have her stay at your place.'

'Understood,' Serena said. She looked as if she was wilting in the heat. Amanda was surprised. She had always thought of Serena as cool and unflappable.

Amanda's cell phone vibrated. She quickly excused herself and left the office. She ducked into an empty cubicle. 'Gillen.'

'It's Leo Rucci.'

Amanda sat down. Even the seat felt warm, as if the heatwave had worked its way inside the cushions. 'I'm sorry about your son,' she said.

'Save it. I'm not looking for sympathy.' Gino's death hadn't softened Rucci at all.

'I'd like to talk to you about the murder,' Amanda said. 'Maybe you can help us find this guy before he kills anyone else.'

'I got nothing to say to you. I'm not talking about the past, OK? And what happened to Gino is between me and this Wilde fuckhead. I don't need any help. I just wanted to tell you that if you want to catch this guy, you better do it quick.'

'Oh?'

'Yeah,' Rucci growled. 'Because I'm coming after him too.'

Thirty-three

Blake blew out a cloud of acrid cigarette smoke that billowed around his face. Picking up his drink, he took a hit of salt from the rim and a sweet-sour sip of margarita. In reality, he despised the lime drinks that all the tourists sipped in Cancun. He preferred beer or Scotch. But a red-headed lawyer from the bankruptcy attorneys convention in town, with shades, a name tag, and a margarita, didn't attract special attention. He was just another shyster soaking up the blues and hoping to get lucky by flirting with the twenty-something waitress.

He sat at a circular table in the last row of the Limelight show-room. Other people squeezed around him, clinking ice, talking too loudly, coughing, and passing gas. It was hard to see faces with the lights low and bodies shifting in their seats, blocking his view, but he had already pegged the security before the show began. Two bulky detectives squirmed at a table in front of the stage, painfully obvious in suits and ties. An Hispanic cop, a smooth piece of work with slicked black hair and a permanent leer, hovered in the back, constantly scanning the crowd. He was almost close enough to touch. On the east and west walls, standing, were two of the boys from Premium Security. Blake knew them. Enormous, probably part gorilla. Walnut-sized brains. He had actually waved at one, and the man just stared dully back, not penetrating the disguise. Blake couldn't help but laugh.

Claire was on stage. It was her second show, and midnight had already come and gone. He didn't usually care about music, but he enjoyed her voice. She had a throaty country drawl, and there was something sad about the way she sang that made him remember the suffering he had experienced as a boy. He rarely visited that room in his soul, but Claire's voice made it seem like a good thing to do, as if she could march you inside and make you believe that loss was what made you alive, that yearning for something could be more beautiful than having it.

Not that he really believed it.

He thought about his adoptive mother. Bonnie Burton. She could still make his flesh crawl two decades later. It was crazy back then, how he had loved her and wanted to please her. He had actually hated his adoptive father more, because he was the one who let it all happen and did nothing to stop her. Blake even enjoyed cuckolding him at first, when he began having intercourse with Bonnie. He could still feel her hands. It infuriated him that when he thought of her, he sometimes got an erection. That she still controlled him like that. She used to tell him that he was her best lover, that she would never hurt him, that her body belonged to him. Her body with its drooping breasts and doughnut-shaped middle.

Once, she told him what a good idea it would be if he killed his father and the two of them could be alone. His father, who knew what went on in the bedroom, who didn't care or was too scared to do a damn thing.

He said yes, that would be a good idea, and didn't add that the best idea of all was to kill them both. A month later, he stood in the dark yard and watched the fire consume them.

He thought about the boy in the Summerlin street. Peter Hale. That was a lesson for him – that he wasn't the rock he imagined himself to be, that the fury could come back and temporarily blind him. He had watched the boy throwing the ball against the garage door. Hypnotic, the ball going back and forth, bang bang, over and over. It wouldn't be hard to smile at the kid, go inside, slit Linda Hale's throat and go back to the car. Maybe toss the ball a couple times with the boy. But then he thought about leaving this kid with no mother, and he realized he couldn't do that. He sat there, paralyzed. Bang bang, back and forth. Happy kid. A kid who had everything Blake never had, for no reason at all, who didn't have any Bonnie in his life, who hadn't had his real mother stripped away and killed by Las Vegas. The anger rose up like a dust devil, spinning out of the sand. Insane jealously. Disgust. It grabbed him so hard he thought he would break the steering wheel in half. That was when, without any more hesitation, he put the car in gear and slammed the accelerator down, gunning for the boy, wanting to erase him, wanting to see him disappear into nothingness under his tires.

Sometimes nothingness was a blessing.

In the Limelight showroom, Blake blinked. He had been gone for too long, not concentrating. The memories did that to him. He blamed it on the seduction of Claire's voice, which was somehow lazy but still as sharp as a razor blade on his wrist.

Focus, he thought to himself.

Amira.

Blake had to move quickly. He had been to Claire's show several times, and he knew there were three songs left in her second set. He had to go now, or risk getting caught in the sweaty mass of fans elbowing their way for the exits. In a few minutes, he could use the chaos of the crowd to spring Claire loose from the blanket of security protecting her.

He knew how to do that. With Claire's help.

When she finished her next song, a searing cover of Mindy Smith's 'One Moment More', Blake stood up during the applause and picked his way through the tables to the nearest door. He wore a sport coat, shirt and tie, jeans, and dress shoes. Back in the casino, he stubbed out his cigarette at one of the slot machines and proceeded to the glass doors that led to the parking lot. He surveyed the small lot quickly. The Boulder Strip was on his left, and a two-way middle lane in the lot led to a series of rows where the cars parked diagonally. His own brown sedan was in the rear, where he could jump the divider and head straight to the highway.

A plainclothes cop was leaning on the hood of a red Caprice Classic near the middle lane, eyeing the people who came and went from the casino. Blake felt their eyes meet and experienced a moment's uneasiness, wondering if the man recognized him. With a friendly nod, Blake sauntered past him, heading for his sedan. He didn't look back, but he listened carefully for the sound of footsteps following him. None did.

He got in his car and got out his cell phone. He waited ten minutes until he saw people flowing out of the casino, exiting the showroom, then dialed a number. Claire answered immediately. Even when she was talking, not singing, he loved her voice.

'This is Detective Jonathan Stride,' he told her. 'I work with Serena.'

He could hear her breathing and imagined her still flushed from the show. 'I see,' she said calmly.

'We need to get you out of there right away, Claire.'

'Where's Serena?' she asked. 'I thought the two of you were coming to pick me up.'

Blake frowned. He didn't have much time and had to think quickly. 'Serena's tied up. We don't think we should wait. I'm outside in the casino parking lot now. It's a red Caprice Classic in the second row. The sooner you can get here, the better.'

'Is that safe?'

210

'We'll have people watching your every move.' He added, 'Candidly, if this guy is here, we want to flush him out, not scare him away.'

'In other words, you want to put me on a hook and let me wriggle like a worm?' she asked.

Blake smiled. 'Something like that.'

Claire waited a few beats before replying. 'OK. If that's how you guys want to play it. I'll see you in five minutes.'

Stride pulled into the crowded porte cochère in front of the Limelight. He drove past the convoy of cabs and parked at an angle on the sidewalk.

'The show's out,' he said.

They got out of the Bronco. Stride used his shield to wave off a valet, and they marched inside, pushing past people who were on their way into the hot night air.

'Are you sure about this?' Serena asked him.

Stride knew what she meant. Sawhill had suggested that Claire stay at their place while they hunted Blake. He thought: sure about letting Claire into their home? Sure about letting her seduce his girlfriend in front of his face? No, he wasn't sure.

'We need to babysit her,' Stride said. 'Sawhill's right. It'll be easiest to do it at our place.'

'I didn't think she'd agree,' Serena said. 'She's pretty independent.'

'It must be your charm,' Stride told her and watched Serena flush.

The showroom was almost empty. Waitresses were gathering half-empty wine glasses and wet napkins from the tables. Serena flagged down Cordy, who was on stage near the performers' door. He was talking up a member of Claire's band, a two-tone blonde with a nose ring and a tattoo of an eagle on her upper arm.

'Is Claire in back?' Serena called.

'You got it, mama.'

They clambered up on stage. 'Any sign of Blake?' she asked.

Cordy shook his head. '*Nada*.'

'No one's been in or out through this door except the band?' Stride asked.

'You got it. I also put guys on the casino door and the emergency exit, checking anyone who tries to get back there. They gave us a staff list. Nobody gets in unless they're on the list and they got a photo ID to back it up.'

Stride nodded. He and Serena exited through the stage door, winding up on a small landing, and then took a few steps down to a dingy corridor. On his left, he could hear the clatter of china from the kitchen. Serena led him the other way, to a wooden door near the emergency exit. There was a crudely cut paper star taped to the door and a black and white publicity still of Claire. Stride had never seen her before, and he was a little disturbed to realize how attractive she was. Like Serena, she was weak-in-the-knees gorgeous, with teasing lips that were all about sex, and haunted eyes that made you want to take care of her.

Serena knocked on the door. 'Claire!'

There was no answer. Serena knocked again, louder. 'She could be in the shower,' she said, but Stride had a bad feeling. He tried the door handle. It was locked. He thumped heavily with his fist.

'Shit,' he murmured.

He crouched down on his hands and knees and put the side of his head on the floor, so he could look through the crack under the door. He didn't see what he was afraid he would find – a body. But the dressing room looked empty and dark.

'I'll check the casino,' Stride said.

Serena nodded. 'I'll do the other side. She may have gone out for a smoke.'

Stride took off back down the hallway. He heard Serena bolt through the crash door behind him. He nimbly dodged a cocktail waitress who was emerging with a tray of drinks, then ducked briefly inside the warm, humid kitchen to make sure that Claire wasn't there. He continued through double doors at the end of the hallway into the pinging noise of the casino.

A house security man barely looked at him. Stride felt sick. He grabbed the man's shoulder.

'Did Claire come through here?' he demanded.

'Who?'

'*Claire Belfort*. The woman we're all trying to keep alive.'

The man shrugged. 'Oh, her. The singer. Yeah, she came through here a minute ago.'

'Alone?'

'Yeah, just her.'

'And you didn't try to stop her?' Stride retorted.

'Hey, no one said to stop anyone going out. I'm just here to make sure some guy doesn't get in. Besides, she said she was meeting someone from Metro.'

Stride began to sweat. 'Who?'

'Some guy named Stride.'

Stride cursed and reached for his gun. 'Which way did she go?'

212

The guard pointed at the glass doors to the parking lot. 'Through there.'

Stride hid his gun under his sport coat and ran for the doors, attracting annoyed glances from the gamblers. There was still a crowd of people from the show clustered around the doors, spilling into the parking lot. Safety in numbers, Stride thought. Murder, chaos, an easy escape.

He struggled past people to get to the door, feeling each second stretch out. He knew that seconds were all he had, the difference between life and death. In the glass, his reflection mocked him. He couldn't see through it to what was happening outside.

Blake eased the body of the policeman into the back seat of the Caprice Classic. He wiped his knife on the man's pants and put it back in his pocket. He closed the car door and gave a broad smile to a couple getting into an SUV next to him.

'Few too many,' he said, making a drinking motion with his hand.

They nodded, uninterested.

He strolled to the front of the car and watched the people emerging from the casino door. Women in clinging killer dresses. Men lighting up cigars and tugging at their collars in the sweaty weather. The couples strolled, in no hurry, holding hands, kissing, laughing. No one paid any attention to him.

He kept his eyes on the door. Two minutes later, he saw her. Claire glided outside, her hair tossed as the wind caught it. She stopped on the sidewalk, looking around with her blue eyes. She wore a long-sleeved red silk blouse and jeans, with high heels. Her skin glowed fresh under the light.

She saw him standing by the car. He nodded at her, and she took a minute to size him up. Then she stepped off the curb, walking toward him. He stripped off his sunglasses and smiled. Their eyes met.

She stopped, hesitating, still too far away.

'It's me,' he called.

She began walking again, but slowly.

Blake saw a flurry of motion over her shoulder, a man fighting to get through the casino door, and he scowled as he saw who it was. Stride. The real Stride. The detective had his hand inside his coat, hiding a gun. Blake began reaching for his gun, too.

'Come on,' he urged Claire.

She stopped again and followed his eyes. She looked over her shoulder and saw Stride. When she turned back again, she was frozen, paralyzed. Her eyes traveled up and down Blake's body and came to rest on his hands.

Shock and fear filled her face.

Blake looked down at his hands and saw what she saw. Blood.

Stride finally burst from the crowd onto the sidewalk. She couldn't be far away. He studied each face as snippets of conversation floated past him.

'What a voice.'

'She made me cry. When's the last time that happened?'

'Hot. God, she's hot.'

He didn't know Claire and hoped he'd recognize her from the photograph on the door. Did she even still look like that? Stride took a few steps onto the asphalt. He thought about calling her name but didn't want to draw attention to her.

A blonde brushed past him. He spun her around, then apologized when he saw it wasn't Claire.

'Jerk,' she hissed at him. He didn't care.

Where was she? His eyes traveled back across the crowd. Claire. Blake. He knew they were both here.

She was meeting someone from Metro. A guy named Stride.

He heard another fragment of conversation on his left, a low whisper.

'Is that her?'

'Who?'

'The singer.'

Stride followed their eyes. He saw her then, turning toward him, and his first impression was of strawberry-blonde hair catching the neon light, and then blue eyes reaching out to him. He felt a huge relief, but it only lasted a moment. Over her shoulder, he glimpsed a man with red hair, in a shirt and tie. His mind processed the man's face and didn't perceive a threat, but as he turned his attention to Claire, his head snapped back automatically.

It wasn't the face. It was the eyes.

The eyes that had stared at him from the sketch.

The man smiled at him. He knew. His hand was reaching into his jacket.

Stride ran straight at them. 'Claire! Get down!'

She froze for an instant, torn between the two men, then ducked behind a parked car and rolled away. Stride drew his gun into plain sight and squatted in firing stance, both hands on the barrel, but he was too slow. Blake moved like a ghost. The man dropped to the ground, spun to his left, and came back up with his own gun ready to fire. All Stride could do was leap to the asphalt, feeling his clothes tear and his shoulder burn on the pavement. A rain of bullets streaked past him and into the casino window, shattering it into popcorn shards.

Bedlam erupted around him. People dropped to the ground, and others ran for the street. Screams wailed through the parking lot.

'Police!' Stride shouted. 'Everyone take cover and stay down!'

He stole a glance at the lot and saw bodies scrambling between the cars. Blake had vanished. Stride crab-walked to the first row in the lot, where Claire was sitting by the rear tire of a truck, her arms wrapped around her knees, her eyes staring vacantly at the ground. He came up and put a hand over hers.

'I'm Stride,' he said. 'Don't move. Stay right here.'

'There was blood,' she murmured.

'What?'

'On his hands.'

Stride swore. He risked a glance through the windows of the truck and didn't see anyone. The people in the lot had disappeared, as if they had been lifted off the planet, some hiding in the rows, others heading for the Boulder Strip. There was still a sea of potential hostages.

'Stay here,' he told her again.

He slipped between the cars and darted across the open row without drawing fire. He recognized the red Caprice in front of him as a Metro undercover vehicle, and he rose up high enough to look inside. A body was slumped across the back seat, half on the floor of the car. Stride pulled the door open, and blood dripped out, puddling on the ground and staining his pants. He grabbed the man's wrist, feeling for a pulse, but there was nothing.

Stride backed away. He heard footsteps behind him, running for the opposite side of the lot. When he twisted round, he caught a glimpse of Serena, just as another series of gunshots exploded from the rear of the lot. He watched her dive behind the cars and saw sparks as the bullets bounced on metal.

'*Serena!*' he screamed.

There was an excruciating pause. 'I'm OK, I'm OK!' she shouted back.

Stride felt his heart start beating again. He ran to the next car in the row and rose up behind the hood in firing position. He spotted Blake three rows away and got off two shots before the man ducked under cover. His bullets took out the windshield of a Cadillac.

Sawhill would chew out his ass for that.

He moved again, using a minivan for cover. When he tried to cross the next row, Blake spotted him, and another flood of bullets chased him across the open space of pavement. Just as he reached safety, he felt a stinging pain in his chest and looked down to see a two-inch tear in his shirt that was oozing red. He tore his shirt open and concluded that he hadn't been shot, just cut by a metal fragment that had ricocheted off one of the cars. Even so, it hurt like hell.

He heard the muffled chiming of his cell phone in his pocket. He retrieved it and heard Serena's voice. She was whispering.

'Are you all right?'

'Slightly damaged, but nothing serious,' Stride said.

'Backup's on its way. We should have ten cars here in two minutes. If we can keep him pinned down, we can surround him.'

'We've also got a shitload of civilians.' Stride listened to the silence and didn't like it. 'Can you get over to Claire?'

'I think so.'

'Do it. I'll cover you. Then stay with her. I don't want this guy doubling back on us.'

Stride scooted to the end of the Grand Am he was crouching behind. He came up in firing position, wincing as the skin on his chest tore further. He balanced his elbows on the trunk of the car. Behind him, he heard Serena running across the middle lane, and he saw a flash of movement a few rows ahead of him. He couldn't tell if it was Blake, so he fired high in the air. The person went down again.

Serena shouted. 'Clear!'

Stride ran, dodging between the cars, his body bent over as he sped through three rows. Blake couldn't be far away.

Blake was low on ammunition, and he could hear sirens in the distance. Lots of sirens. In another minute, the Limelight would be overrun with police, and even though he knew he could escape in the confusion, it would be ugly and violent.

He saw the female detective, Serena, bolt for the opposite side of the lot, where Claire was hiding. Stride gave her cover. Blake didn't have a shot, and he knew tonight's plan was a bust. Claire was out of reach.

Time to fold.

He heard running footfalls and knew Stride was making his move, creeping closer.

Blake silently slipped back into the last row, where his brown sedan was waiting. He came upon a couple huddled by the side of a Toyota RAV4. The woman, overweight with curly black hair, stared at him and his gun with terrified eyes and buried her face in her husband's chest. The man put on a brave face, staring angrily back. He had a round face and a double chin.

'Not a sound,' Blake hissed. He extended his arm and pointed his Sig Sauer into the man's face.

The sirens were almost on top of them. The first police car fishtailed as it swerved into the parking lot. The people who had been hiding in the rows began running for the protection of the squad car.

Stride jumped when he heard another explosion, then realized it wasn't a gunshot, but a car backfiring. Two rows ahead, at the far back of the lot, a car engine screeched and roared to life. His heart lurched – he knew what it was.

He started to run again and saw a brown sedan leap the shallow landscaping that divided the lot from the Boulder Strip. He squatted, preparing to fire and aim for the car's tires. Then he realized that the car's dome light was on, and he could see two silhouettes inside. He couldn't risk taking the shot.

'He's got a hostage!'

The sedan headed north at extreme speed. Stride gave up on cover and sprinted for the highway. He waved his arms, flagging down three of the police cars converging on the casino, and pointed them toward the sedan. Its tail lights were already disappearing as it weaved through the other traffic on the road.

The chase began.

Stride jogged back to the other end of the parking lot. Cordy was there, along with half a dozen uniformed officers and another two police cars that had blocked the exits. They were taking names and phone numbers from the people still lingering in the lot, but Stride knew the scene was blown. Most of the people had melted away.

He asked about Serena, and Cordy jerked his thumb inside. The two women were back in the casino, well away from the shattered window, with several armed police officers standing watch around them. Claire had both arms around Serena and her head on Serena's shoulder.

He came up to them. Serena pointed at his chest. 'You need a doctor.'

'It's nothing. A band-aid, that's all.'

'What about your legs?'

Stride studied the splashes of red on his pants and frowned. 'Not my blood.'

'Blake?' Serena asked.

217

Claire looked up, expectant, waiting for his answer. 'Did you get him?'

Stride shook his head.

Wearing a baseball cap, a Running Rebels T-shirt, and gym shorts, Blake strolled out of the Limelight parking lot. No one tried to stop him. His other clothes were stuffed into the back seat of a Mustang convertible. He waited for the traffic to clear before crossing the highway and scanning the streets for a cab.

He could still vaguely hear the distant sirens. They'd be catching the brown sedan soon, running it off the road. He hoped the round-faced man and his overweight wife would be smart enough to keep their hands in the air and not draw fire.

It had been easy – hand the man his keys, tell him to drive as fast as he could and not stop for at least ten minutes. He also told them there was a bomb in the trunk that he could detonate by cell phone if they stopped early for the police. Complete nonsense, but people will believe anything when there's a gun in their face and someone is giving them a chance to stay alive.

So off they went.

He could have driven the sedan himself, but he put the odds of surviving the chase at no better than fifty-fifty.

Not good enough. He still had work to do.

Thirty-four

Stride lay naked on their bed. The ceiling fan spun above him, circulating the stifling air that crept in through the open window. It was three in the morning. They had finally come home from the crime scene at the Limelight to find the power out in their town home. The bedroom was pitch black and hot as he lay there, eyes open, seeing nothing.

He was in pain. His whole body hurt. It was bone pain, the worst kind, deep and aching, not like muscles that could be stretched and massaged. Everywhere he had tumbled and rolled on the pavement, he felt it now. There was a time, in his twenties, when he didn't pay a price for that kind of punishment to his body. No longer.

The abrasions on his skin stung. The cut on his chest was bandaged, but there were others, scrapes and burns, that he hadn't discovered until he stripped off his clothes and found places where the slightest touch made him wince. He forced himself to take a shower, and the hot pounding water felt like knives. But it made him feel better to wash away the dirt and then to stretch out in bed.

He heard the bedroom door open and close softly as Serena came in. She crossed to the open window and stood there, looking out. She was a tall, lovely silhouette.

'Claire?' he asked.

'Sleeping. I gave her an Ambien.'

She came and sat down on the bed.

'I was afraid you were going to get yourself killed out there,' she told him.

'Right now, I wish I had.'

He felt her fingertips moving, tracing circles on his chest.

'Do you hurt?' she asked.

'All over.'

'Let's see if I can make it better.'

219

Her hands put gentle pressure on his skin, pushing, looking for the erotic nerve ends that let him feel her there.

'Claire's in love with you,' he said. 'It's obvious.'

'I know that.'

Claire had made no effort to hide it. It was there in how she looked at Serena, how she hung on her on the ride home.

'What about you?' he asked.

Serena touched a sensitive spot, and he sucked in his breath in pain.

'Oops,' she said.

'You did that on purpose.'

'Then don't ask me silly questions like that.' She cupped her hand over the skin as the pain faded, and then began again, touching him.

'I've been keeping something from you, Jonny, but not about Claire.'

He made a low sound, questioning her. It didn't matter what she told him now, not while she was doing this.

'Deirdre and I were lovers,' Serena said quietly. 'Back when I was a teenager. I'm sorry, I should have told you before.'

She picked up one hand and rubbed along his fingers with her thumb, then sucked each fingertip into her mouth. A moment later, he heard the drawer of her nightstand open. She retrieved something from inside.

'A lot of men find it exciting,' she said. 'Two women together.'

'I know.'

'Do you?'

'What do you think?' he said.

She didn't need to ask. She could feel the effect she was having on him.

He had always suspected there was more to the relationship between her and Deirdre than she had let on. He wished he had pushed her harder. It was such an important piece in the puzzle that was Serena.

Her hands came back to his body, on his legs this time, massaging the muscles in his thighs. She ran them up onto his stomach and then down all the way to his toes.

'My shrink would say it's transference,' Serena said. 'I'm guilty about Deirdre, so I'm attracted to Claire.'

'What do you say?'

'She's hot, and she turns me on.' Serena laughed.

She pulled back, and he heard a strange plastic sound, like a cap being popped, and then he quivered as a stream of cool liquid dripped down his shaft. Her hands were back, both of them, and suddenly he was slippery, and her hands rubbed up and down as if gliding over soapy skin.

220

'It's your fault,' she told him. 'You turned me into a damn sex addict.'

He tried to speak, but he wasn't sure he knew how any more. His body seemed to lift off the bed. The pain evaporated.

'Feel better?' she asked, and he knew without seeing her that she was grinning.

When the spasms began coursing through his body, he found himself holding his breath, and the lack of oxygen spun images into his head. Cindy, his first wife, in bed, making love. Maggie, his partner. Amanda. Serena. He thought about being homeless and about being, at that instant, disconnected from his body, rising above it, looking down into the darkness.

He wasn't sure how long had passed before she went into the bathroom and then came back with a warm, damp towel that she used to clean him off. She slid into bed next to him and was asleep almost immediately, her head lying on his arm, her breath blowing on his face. He thought he would sleep too, but he didn't. His mind was too full of her, and of Minnesota, and of what it meant to be home. Long minutes later, he finally felt himself slipping away, but he thought, or maybe he dreamed, that he heard Claire's footsteps in the hall, and he wondered if she had been there the whole time, listening to them.

Thirty-five

Sawhill put down the phone. His face was purple. The lieutenant who kept an iron lock on his emotions was losing control, and Stride thought the man was ready to stroke out right there in front of them.

'That was Governor Durand,' Sawhill said, his voice pinched. 'He's wondering why this perpetrator is still alive, when one of my detectives had him in his gun sights last night. He's wondering why it took half a dozen squad cars to surround a honeymoon couple from Nebraska, while a serial killer was able to walk away from a crime scene where he murdered a police officer without so much as someone asking for identification.'

Stride was reminded of why he hated politicians. 'No offense to the governor, but he wasn't there. This guy is shrewd. He used a ruse to draw Claire out into the open, and he had all of us in a situation where we needed to be concerned about citizen casualities. It's not like we could fire randomly.'

'Yes, yes, I've read the report. He out-dueled you, Stride. You had the drop on him, and he turned it back on you.'

'That's true enough,' Stride admitted. 'He's a trained mercenary.'

'Well, I'm sorry if we have a more sophisticated criminal than you're used to dealing with in Minnesota,' Sawhill shot back. He reached for the stress ball on his desk and began squeezing it furiously. 'But I expect my detectives to be better trained than the people they're trying to collar. All you managed to do was shoot up an Escalade, which, by the way, happened to be owned by a senior vice president at Harrah's who is a good friend of my father. My rule of thumb is, if you've got the shot, you take the shot, and you make the shot.'

Stride wondered if Sawhill had read that in the *Seven Habits of Highly Effective Detectives*. 'Agreed,' he said.

'Then the perp pulls a simple switch and manages to fool all of you,' Sawhill continued. 'This couple owns a Subway franchise in

Lincoln Falls, and we nearly blew the husband's head off because you told a team of squad cars the man was a serial killer who had just killed a cop.'

'It was the perp's car,' Stride said, but he was loath to make excuses. He knew he had screwed up.

'And once again he proved he was smarter than the people I've got trying to catch him. Tell me at least we got something from the car.'

Stride shook his head. 'Fingerprints, but we already had those. He bought the car for cash three months ago. Fake name and address. There's not a scrap of paper inside to suggest where he might be living. We're doing a forensic examination to see if there's dirt or other trace evidence that might give us a clue, but that's going to take time.'

'We don't have time,' Sawhill said. 'Is Claire under wraps?'

Stride nodded. 'Serena's babysitting her.'

'So what do we do to find this guy?'

Amanda, who had been quietly watching the ping-pong game between Stride and Sawhill, spoke up. 'We could set a trap. Put Claire back in the game in a setting we control.'

Sawhill snorted. 'We do not use Boni Fisso's daughter as bait. Period, end of discussion. Serena's on top of her, and the perp doesn't know where she is. Let's keep it that way.'

'We've been checking libraries all over the city,' Amanda added. 'Nothing so far.'

'Half the force is working on this, and they're hot to catch him,' Stride said. 'He killed a cop, and he killed a kid. Everybody wants him.'

'So do I. So does the governor. This is bad news for the city. What do we think this guy is going to try next?'

'I think he's going to go after Claire again,' Stride said. 'We need to catch him before he does. We've also redoubled security around other people who might be on his hit list, but the fact that he tried for Claire last night makes me think he's at the end of his list.'

'Do you think he might go after Boni directly?' Sawhill asked.

Amanda nodded. 'It's not his pattern, but he might.'

'Boni's not an easy target,' Stride said. 'But the Sheherezade comes down next week. That's the link to Amira.'

'Great. Just great. The implosion is going to be televised nation-ally, you know.'

'Maybe he'll take out Boni at the ceremony,' Stride said. 'Good for ratings. Tourism will climb.'

Sawhill leaned forward. 'Is this a joke to you?'

'You don't need to tell me how this place works,' Stride said. 'In six months, we'll have a daily bus tour of the murder sites and a new ad campaign. "We've Put Sin Back in Sin City."'

'You've been here a few months, Detective. I've lived here nearly my whole life. My father has devoted *decades* of his life to this town. This is our home. You *serve* this city, so treat it with respect.'

Amanda stood up and dragged Stride's arm until he was standing too. She nodded to Sawhill. 'We're both tired, sir. Don't worry, we take this perp very seriously.' She began pulling Stride out of the office.

Sawhill stood up and laid his hands flat on his desk. 'See that you do,' he called after them. He and Stride exchanged icy glares, and then Amanda had them back in the corridor, with the door closed behind her.

Amanda leaned back against the wall and wiped her brow. The air conditioning was back on, and the office air was frigid, but she was sweating. She gave Stride a smile and a low whistle. 'That wasn't too tactful.'

'I know. Sorry. I didn't mean to put you in the middle of it.'

'This is a corporate town,' Amanda pointed out. 'Image matters to these guys.'

Stride shook his head. 'Money matters.'

'You're not going to change the city, Stride.'

He nodded. 'I know.' Before he could stop himself, he added, 'I'm not sure I'm going to stay.'

Amanda looked shocked. 'What?'

'They want me back in Minnesota,' he explained. 'I'm thinking seriously about it.'

'What about Serena?' she asked.

Stride didn't say anything. That was the question, he knew. The one on which his life hung. What about Serena?

'Nothing's set in stone,' Stride told her. 'Let's catch Blake Wilde first.'

Thirty-six

Amanda pulled into the parking lot of the downtown library and got out of the car, the heat searing her lungs. It was late afternoon, when the October weather in Las Vegas should be perfect, but the sun still felt like an oven cranked to the broiler setting.

She had been stewing about the idea of Stride leaving since he told her. There was no reason to be angry at him, but she was angry anyway. For once, she had a partner she could work with, and suddenly she might lose him. She hated the idea of starting all over again with someone new. Anyone she got would probably be like Cordy, making jokes behind her back, ogling her tits, looking for ways to drive her out. It made her wonder again what she was doing here, and whether she and Bobby would both be better off if she followed Stride's lead. Get out. Head for San Francisco. Leave the city and all its craziness behind.

She was in no mood for games. Her patience was worn down, like a T-shirt washed so many times you could see through it. When she looked across Las Vegas Boulevard, she saw the car again. A steel-gray Lexus SUV. She had seen it twice before that afternoon and had already run the plates. She knew who was driving.

Amanda crossed the street. The car windows were smoked, so she couldn't see inside. She rapped her knuckles on the driver's window and waited.

The window rolled down. She felt a blast of cold air.

'Hello, Leo,' she said, trying not to boil over. 'You following me?'

Leo Rucci was wearing sunglasses. The red veins in his neck bulged like barbells. 'It's a free country, ain't it?'

'Sure is. Where any shithole hood like you can become a million-aire. God bless America.'

'Hey—'

'Don't play games with me, Leo. I'm having a really bad day. Now get out of here, and don't let me see you behind me again, or I'm going to haul your ass downtown.'

'For what?'

'For obstruction of justice and being really annoying to a police officer.'

'I can help you,' Leo said. 'My way's a lot quicker than some monkey trial. You get a lead on this guy, you call me. I take care of the rest.'

'Go back to the golf course, Leo. Let us worry about Blake.'

Amanda turned on her heels and stalked back across the street to the library. She heard Rucci's car start up and roar away. Inside the library, she made her way to the reference desk.

'I'm looking for Monica Ramsey,' she said.

The librarian pointed at a tall woman in her fifties who was re-filing microfiche boxes from a cart. Amanda approached her.

'Ms Ramsey? I'm Amanda Gillen. You left a message on my voice-mail?'

Monica had owlish glasses and long black hair tied in a pony tail. She was built like a walking stick and wore flimsy plastic gloves on her hands. 'Oh, yes. You're the detective. You're looking for that man.'

'That's right,' Amanda said, feeling a tiny glimmer of hope after hours of frustration. 'Have you seen him?'

'Well, I think so, yes, although it was a number of weeks ago. I don't see what help I can be.'

'You'd be surprised. Please tell me about it.'

'Oh, of course. Let's sit down.'

They sat at the corner of a long reference table near the book-shelves. Monica peeled off her gloves. 'I always wear these, you know, when dealing with fiche. The film is so delicate and so old.' She tapped her finger on the sketch that Amanda placed between them. 'This man, he was so rough at handling the fiche. I had to ask him to be careful.'

'You're sure this is the man?'

'Oh, yes. Those eyes are quite unforgettable.'

'No offense, but can I ask why you didn't call me earlier?'

'I'm so sorry. We've been away. A Caribbean cruise. I just got back to the library today.'

'Tell me what you remember about the man,' Amanda said.

'Well, again, this was quite a while ago. Midsummer, I think. July? Maybe August. He came in on successive days, three or four days in a row, looking up all sorts of material related to Las Vegas in the nineteen sixties. I pulled fiche, magazines, books. He wanted it all.'

'Did he tell you specifically what he was looking for?'

'Well, he had me run a Lexis search on one of the old casinos. The Sheherezade, I think. Yes, that's right, because he was also reading about Boni Fisso, and as you can imagine we have *quite* a lot of material about him.'

'Did he say why he wanted this information?'

'Oh, no. He really didn't say much at all. Not a very talkative type. We get lots of requests for archival information so it wasn't at all unusual.'

'Did he ask you to research any other individuals? People besides Boni Fisso?'

'Not that I recall.'

'Monica, I really need your help here. We need to find this man right away. I'm going to ask you to think back, think real hard, and remember anything distinctive about him. What he wore, what he said, what he carried, what he did. Anything that might give us a clue about who he is and where we can find him.'

Monica sat up very straight in her chair, and her neck looked elongated. The librarian's tongue slipped out to wet her lips. Amanda was reminded of a giraffe at the zoo, reaching to get a leaf from a distant tree branch.

'He had a blue backpack with him,' she said. 'That was where he carried his materials. I really don't remember how he was dressed. Jeans, maybe? Otherwise, there wasn't anything special about him. I'm very sorry.'

Amanda was disappointed. 'How about a car? Did you see him come or go, or see what direction he might have headed?'

Monica shook her head.

'Have you seen him since then?'

'No, he never came back, not when I was here.'

Amanda stood up. 'I appreciate your time, Monica. Thanks very much for calling me. If you remember anything else, please let me know.'

'Of course, I will.'

As Amanda turned to leave, she heard Monica giggling. She reversed her course. 'What is it?'

Monica blushed. 'Oh, I'm sorry. It's very silly. I was just thinking, if you want to catch this man, you should stake out doughnut shops.' She laughed again.

Amanda looked at her, wondering if this was a stupid police joke. 'Why?'

'Well, I remember now, the man was obsessed with Krispy Kreme doughnuts. I caught him eating a doughnut at the fiche machine, and I had to tell him that he couldn't eat in the library. I told him I couldn't resist those things either, and he said they were addictive.'

Amanda felt her heart race. 'Thanks again, Monica.'

Son of a bitch, she thought. Krispy Kreme doughnuts.

Thirty-seven

Claire sat with one leg tucked beneath her and the other leg dangling from Serena's sofa. She cradled a warm mug of coffee in both hands. Her hair was loose and uncombed, and she wore a roomy, extra-long T-shirt that stretched to the middle of her thighs. Her feet were bare, the nails painted red.

She glanced at the wall clock that tick-tocked behind them, counting away the minutes. 'It's late,' she murmured. 'Past eleven. Where's your lover?'

Serena looked up from the computer on her lap, although she could barely concentrate on the screen. Her eyes were tired.

'He's still out trying to find Blake,' Serena said.

'You resent it, don't you? Being here with me.'

'No, I don't resent being with you. But sitting around isn't my style. I want to be where the action is.'

'That's right,' Claire said with a grin. 'You're tough, aren't you?'

'That's me.'

In fact, it had driven her crazy, being shut up in the town home all day. She had made calls, hunted down leads on the internet, and gone back through her notes to find something she had missed. But none of it was the same as being on the street. She felt isolated, cut off from the investigation.

'He's attractive, your man. I see what you see in him.'

'Thanks.'

'He loves you. It's there when he looks at you.'

Serena remembered that Jonny had said the same thing about Claire the previous night. 'I love him,' she said.

'I've been with men too, you know,' Claire said.

'Meaning?'

'It's not like I don't understand the attraction.' Claire unfurled her legs and climbed off the sofa. She padded to the white wall and

229

examined the desert photographs hung there. 'Did you take these?'

Serena nodded.

'They're striking. You have an eye for the land. That's what they can't teach, you know. The eye. A lot of people understand the mechanics, but they can't see the picture.'

'You're pretty calm about it,' Serena told her.

'About what?'

'About almost getting killed.'

Claire shrugged. 'I wasn't calm last night. But I feel safe with you.'

'I could take you to Boni's place. It's like a fortress there.'

'That's not safe. That's a prison.'

'He wants to make up with you,' Serena said. 'He was glad you called him.'

'Oh, are you a family therapist now?'

'No. But I know what it's like to be an adult without parents. There are a lot of times when I wish things were different.'

Claire continued to stare at the photographs on the wall, but Serena thought she had touched a sensitive spot. 'I wish things were different too, Serena. But they're not.'

'He says he doesn't care that you're gay.'

'Catholics never care if you're gay as long as you're celibate,' Claire said.

Serena watched Claire smile and realized it was false. She thought Claire might cry.

'It has nothing to do with your being gay, does it?' Serena asked. 'The split between you and Boni.'

'No.'

'What is it then?'

Claire shook her head. 'It was a long time ago. I don't want to go back there.'

She could hear it in Claire's tone. The secret was profoundly horrible, whatever it was. 'I've got monsters like that too.'

'I know you do. That's why we click. We both have pasts we're trying to run from.'

'Did you get therapy?'

'No.'

'Why not?'

Claire sighed. 'Please, Serena. Let's drop it. I couldn't talk about it then. I can't talk about it now. Not to anyone. Not when my father's name is Boni Fisso.'

Serena let the silence stretch out while Claire stared blankly at the photographs. She could see raw pain in her face.

'Boni says you've got millions in the bank,' Serena said.

Claire smiled, a real one this time. 'Are you after me for my money now?'

'I was just curious.'

'When I left, I wanted to be independent. I am. Boni didn't give me a stake. I built it myself. So yes, I've got a lot of money. I'm Boni's daughter; genes count for something. Plus all that time I spent in business school.'

'But you're happy living in a small apartment? Singing your songs?'

'I've learned a lot being on my own,' Claire said. 'I'm free, and no one owns me. But I'd be lying if I said I don't have any ambition. There's a part of me that still longs to be in charge of the hotels and run them *my* way.'

'You still could be.'

Claire shook her head. 'Not if it means going back to my father.'

'How would you run them?' Serena asked. 'If you had the keys to the kingdom.'

'Me? I'm tired of all the bigness. Big shows. Big names. I think people want intimacy. They don't want to get lost in a crowd. They want to see singers, not shows. Talent, not names. And glamour, like in the old days. The huge resorts have glitz, but not much character.'

'You could start your own place.'

Claire was wistful. 'Maybe someday. It would be nice to show Boni that I can do it without him. And that you don't have to sell your soul to the devil to be successful.'

Serena heard bitterness creep back into her voice. 'You want to tell me what he did to you?'

'It wasn't him,' Claire said. 'It was someone else. But Boni let it happen. The business came first, like it always does.' She looked as if she was about to say more, but she clapped her arms around her body and shivered. 'I don't want to talk about it.'

'OK.'

'It's in the past. I don't worry about it. I like to sing and drink and talk about life and make passionate love.'

'I like two out of the four,' Serena said, laughing.

'Which two?'

'Well, we know I don't drink.'

Claire laughed too. She came over to where Serena was sitting and knelt by the side of the easy chair. She leaned forward, her bare arms on the cushion. 'I'm going to bed,' she said.

'OK.'

'How about you?'

231

Serena didn't want to look into Claire's eyes, but there seemed to be no other place in the room to stare. Her blue eyes teased her. 'Is that an invitation?' Serena asked. As if it was a joke.

'Yes.'

'I don't think Jonny would be too happy to come home and find us in bed together.'

'You might be surprised.'

'I'm sorry, Claire. If things were different, you know? But they're not.'

'I understand.'

Claire used one fingertip to glide along Serena's forearm with a silky touch. Serena was so on edge that she almost jumped.

'Are you going to catch Blake tonight?' Claire asked.

'If not tonight, then soon. Half the police in the city are looking for him. The valley isn't so big. We'll get him.' Serena wanted to believe it.

'Don't kill him,' Claire murmured.

She spoke so softly that Serena wasn't sure she had heard her right. 'What?'

'Don't kill him, I said.'

'Why not?' Serena asked. 'Why do you care?'

Claire looked down. Some of her blonde hair fell across her face. 'You really don't know, do you? It's so obvious to me.'

'What is?'

'Look at me,' she said, looking up, holding Serena's stare again. Serena did. 'So?'

'Blake is my brother.'

'*What?*'

'I knew it as soon as I saw him,' Claire said. 'I can't believe you don't see it. Those eyes. There may be a lot of Amira in him, but that's not all. It's more than that. It's Boni, too. Boni's his father.'

Thirty-eight

Ten minutes to midnight, Amanda thought.

She could have been home with Bobby. Making love to him the way she liked best, on their sides, face to face, rubbing together. Warm and safe under the blankets. Or they could have been in the Spyder right now, on the desert highway to California, leaving Las Vegas behind forever at a hundred miles an hour through the black night of Death Valley. A new life.

But no.

She sat alone in a Krispy Kreme doughnut shop a few blocks from downtown. Her coffee was getting cold, and she looked up every now and then, hypnotized, as rows of glistening doughnuts streamed along the conveyor belt, getting drenched in icing. There was a steady stream of late-night patrons in and out. She was one of just a handful of people who waited inside, her back to the door, a newspaper in her hands, a half-eaten doughnut on a napkin in front of her. She had nursed it for an hour.

All right, it was actually her fourth.

The reality was that adrenaline was pumping through her veins, along with the sugar. It had taken her several hours to find this place, going from shop to shop in the city, before the little Asian man behind the counter here took the sketch and nodded vigorously.

'Yeah, sure, he come here. Day, night, couple times a day like. Always the same. Half a dozen original and Sprite.'

'You're sure?' Amanda asked. 'This guy changes his appearance a lot.'

'Oh yeah, he look different. Sometimes blonde, sometimes beard, sometimes old, sometimes young. Order always the same, though. Half dozen original and Sprite. It's him.'

'You didn't think it was odd, him looking different all the time?'

The Asian man shrugged. 'This Vegas.'

233

That was enough for Amanda.

She was waiting for Blake. The manager said he hadn't been in yet tonight, so there was a good chance he'd arrive for a late-night fix. She sat so he couldn't see her face, and she had a baseball cap on her head, with its brim pulled down. She didn't know if he knew her face, but she had to assume he did. She wanted him in the store, in a confined space, not out on the street where he could run.

It was the most dangerous thing she had ever done, and she tried not to think about that. She radioed in that she was taking a break for an hour and then switched off her walkie-talkie. She was all alone.

She knew she should have called for backup. That was procedure. They could have surrounded the place and mounted a stake-out, but Amanda wasn't sure they'd let her inside the store, and that was where she wanted to be. She also thought Blake was savvy enough to spot a stake-out from six blocks away, and he would disappear and never come back to the store again. They had only one chance to get it right. Her, by herself.

She could have called Stride. But he'd want to follow procedure. Never in a million years would he expose her to this danger alone. Or he'd want to be there with her, and she knew that Blake would spot him.

A part of her wanted to prove herself. Bring Blake in herself and then extend her middle finger as she walked out the door.

She put down her newspaper and picked up her coffee. Cold. She thought about getting a warmer-up, but she didn't want to draw attention to herself. The Asian manager buzzed behind the counter, busily attending to the doughnuts. She had told him to be cool, not to betray any reaction, not to look at her when Blake came in. She hoped he could do it. She hadn't told him that the man in the sketch was wanted for multiple homicides.

Almost midnight.

The bell on the door signaled another customer. She took a bite of doughnut and picked up her paper. She didn't glance at whoever passed by, just listened to heavy footsteps and knew it was a man. Whoever it was beat a steady path to the counter.

Amanda heard the Asian manager. 'Hey, boss.' And then he added, 'Same as usual, huh? Half dozen original and Sprite?'

Mistake. She hoped Blake didn't recognize the tip-off.

Amanda put down the paper and reached for her coffee at the same time, with the barest glance at the counter. The man wasn't looking at her. She saw blond hair. The height was right, and so was the lean and strong physique.

234

She watched the manager use a straw to pick hot doughnuts off the assembly line and put them in a box. He didn't look at her. He filled the box, then opened the refrigerator and pulled out a plastic bottle of soda.

'Here you go, boss.'

'Thanks,' the man said.

Was that the voice she had heard through the static on Stride's cell phone?

He was paying now. She had to be ready when he turned around, with her gun in her hand, pointed, ready to fire. He's lightning fast, Stride had told her. She thought about Sawhill: *If you've got the shot, take the shot, and make the shot.*

Amanda reached behind her, taking the butt of her Glock in her grip, wishing there were no sweat on her palm. She silently extracted it and kept it in her lap under the table.

Her eyes never left Blake. If it was Blake.

'You got eleven cents?'

'No.'

'OK, boss.'

The little Asian man counted out change. He extended a palm to the man at the counter.

Time began to freeze.

The man reached for his change, but then he slid his arm past the register, took the Asian man by the throat, and in an instant yanked him up bodily by the neck and catapulted him over the counter. Coins sprinkled across the floor. Amanda's mouth fell open in shock; she bolted back in her seat, the chair tumbling behind her. She sprang up, swinging her gun.

'Police! Don't move!'

She took aim, but Blake already had the Asian man suspended in front of him. Blake's pistol was at the man's head. The manager's eyes bulged with fright, and he wet himself, urine dripping from his pant leg as Blake held him in the air.

Amanda and Blake stared at each other. He had a beard again. Fuller cheekbones. Glasses. But it was him. His lips curled into a smile.

'Very nice, Detective,' he said. 'I wondered if my doughnut addiction would get me into trouble eventually. But they are so good, aren't they?'

'Put the gun down, and let him go. The building is surrounded, Blake. You're not going anywhere. Let's end this thing without more violence, OK?'

Blake shook his head. 'There's no one out there, Amanda.'

235

He knew her name. It was scary.

'We held back until you showed up. As soon as you came in, I gave them the signal on the radio. There's no way out.'

Blake nodded. 'Excellent. Signal on the radio. That's a nice touch, Amanda. But I've spent years working with military personnel trained far better than any police force. There was no one in the area. It's just you and me. I've been watching you drink your coffee and make your way through five doughnuts for the past hour.'

'It was four doughnuts,' Amanda said. 'Put the gun down.'

'Don't follow me, and you stay alive,' Blake said. 'So does this nice man here.'

He began backing down the corridor that led to the restrooms and the crash door that led outside. Amanda had checked out the exit earlier. It led to a vacant lot, strewn with glass, backing up near 8th Street.

Amanda followed cautiously, keeping her gun trained on him. She wished she had called for backup now. She knew there was no one on the other side of the door, and if Blake got away, he would disappear through the downtown streets. Slip through their fingers again.

Take the shot. Make the shot.

But she couldn't. She didn't have it. And she couldn't risk Blake getting off a shot first and killing the manager.

Blake was almost to the door. 'The two of us are leaving now. Don't make me kill him. Stay where you are.'

'Go through that door, and they'll split your head open like a watermelon, Blake.' Bravado. Lies. They both knew it.

She was six feet away from him. Blake's back was at the crash door. He waited there, hesitating, and she wasn't sure why. Did he believe her? Was he wondering if there really was a SWAT team poised out back?

The bell on the front door clanged again. A new customer entered the shop. Amanda flinched, and Blake threw the Asian manager at her, his body wildly flying through the air and tumbling both of them to the ground like bowling pins. As Amanda fell, she heard the crash door bang as Blake spun through and vanished. She cursed, disentangled herself from the manager, and scrambled back to her feet.

She charged down the corridor.

At the door, she froze.

Was Blake running or waiting?

Amanda raised her gun and kicked the door open with her foot. It slammed round into the wall of the building.

*   *   *

236

When the door swung open, banging against the wall, Blake knew she was smart.

He recoiled and almost fired. His finger twitched on the trigger, instinct taking over, and he realized at the last instant that she wasn't coming through behind the door. She wanted him to fire, betraying his position.

His bullet, then her bullet, and he would be dead. A nice ruse.

He knew enough to respect his enemy.

But he didn't fire. She didn't know where he was. Now, he knew, she had to choose.

Damn. He didn't fire.

Left or right? she thought.

She had to make a choice. Either he was on the left side of the door or the right. Or he was running, getting away, and each second she hesitated gave him more time to escape.

She would roll through, pivot, and fire. Make the right choice, and it was even odds for both of them, gun to gun, man to . . . woman.

Make the wrong choice, and she was dead. Simple as that. Left or right.

Left was the only direction that made sense. The door opened left. On the right, he was exposed. To the left, the door gave him cover, blocked her view for a crucial millisecond, gave him an advantage. She had the edge if he was on the right. And he knew it – unless he could see into her head and anticipate what she was thinking, and realize that being on the right gave him the edge if she went to the left first, offering him her back. A gamble. A risk. Vegas.

But she couldn't overthink. She was up against a tactician. He'd give himself the maximum odds for survival. That meant he was waiting for her on the left.

Or running.

She needed to move.

Amanda thought about Bobby. She could taste his last kiss.

Then she kicked the door a second time, and as the light spilled out she dived and rolled onto the pavement and came up in a crouch to her left with her gun aimed. She had just enough time for the image to reach her brain, to see the empty stretch of wall behind the door, to realize her mistake. She reacted instantly. Didn't fire. Began to twist, turn, duck, shift.

Fast. Blindingly fast. But not fast enough.

He waited for her on the right, his gun poised. She had to go left,

237

because all her training told her to go left, and cops were creatures of training. There was no surprise, no pleasure, no sadness, when she did. In every fight there was a winner and a loser, and it was no disgrace to lose with dignity.

She was very fast. He was impressed.

Most cops would have frozen, hesitated, but she turned seamlessly, recovering from her mistake and spinning back the other way. If she had gone right, she might well have got the first shot.

But no.

Blake pulled the trigger.

It was such a short moment, but it felt so long.

Amanda was on a precipice, a slim tower of rock. Around her were other peaks, a chessboard of granite kings, many of them grand, cloud-swept mountains climbing into the sky. She stood on the edge and looked down, but there was no bottom to the world, no emerald earth, just mist. She knew she could fly.

When she glanced behind her, Bobby was there, tears streaming down his face, and she didn't understand how he could be so sad when there was such joy to be had here.

Amanda smiled at him, blew him a kiss, and then with her arms spread wide she stepped into the air.

Thirty-nine

Blake ran. The night gave him cover. He sprinted through the empty lot, feeling broken glass crunch and scatter under his feet. When he reached 8th Street, he headed northeast, toward the downscale neighborhood surrounding the overpass for Highway 95. He slowed to a walk as he crossed Stewart Avenue, then ran again when he was beyond the glare of lights from the street.

He abandoned his car, which was parked three blocks in the opposite direction; it was stolen and he could readily steal another. His apartment was only half a mile away, and it was safer now to get there on foot.

There were a handful of strangers around him. It was after midnight, and they were mostly ducking the law themselves, selling drugs or using drugs. They glanced in his direction as he ran, to make sure there were no cops in hot pursuit, but otherwise they didn't care about him. The deeper he penetrated into the neighborhood, the fewer people he saw, until he was alone. He walked again.

He saw the concrete overpass ahead. The houses around him were sunk into decay, with collapsing fences, cracked pink stucco, and gates hanging open. A few dusty cars were parked haphazardly in the yards. He passed a couple of old shopping carts on the sidewalk, their wheels stripped off.

Sirens erupted in the surrounding streets. Blake ducked back into the shadows near one of the houses. He eyed the traffic behind him and saw the flashing red lights of a patrol car as it streaked toward the cafe. Word was out. It wouldn't be long now, just a few minutes, before the neighborhood was engulfed by police trying to lay a net over the area.

He walked faster. When he passed a house with laundry hung out on a sagging clothes line, he slipped inside the fence and grabbed a denim shirt off the line and shrugged it over his white T-shirt. A baseball cap was lying in the dirt, and he put it on. He began peeling at the false beard on his face. He kept a small bottle of spirit gum remover in his jeans for emergencies and quickly got as much of the hair and glue off his face as he could. It wasn't perfect, but at least at first glance he was again a man without a beard.

Blake thought about strategy. He had always expected the police to get close to him eventually, but he had been hoping for a couple more days and a little more breathing room to put his plans in motion. He didn't have that now. He had to move immediately. Tonight.

That was when he realized the crush of police searching for him in the dirty streets could actually work to his advantage.

He only needed a few hours.

Blake made his way under the overpass. The freeway traffic roared overhead, thundering in his ears and causing the ground to vibrate under his feet. His eyes darted around the concrete superstructure, on the hunt for muggers or gangs. It was easy to get trapped here, with no way out to the sides and an easy path to block in front and behind. But he didn't see anyone except a young hooker, sitting with her back to one of the pillars.

He didn't know why she was there. There was no business to be had in this area. Then he saw she was smoking a cigarette and taking an occasional snort of cocaine from a wrinkled piece of tin foil. Blake stopped and looked at her, his mind grinding and coming up with a plan. She was young, trying to look twenty-one, but he suspected she was no more than fifteen. She wore knee-high boots, a fake leather jacket, and had poorly applied lipstick and platinum-blonde hair that was almost white. She saw him watching her and gave him a drugged smile. When she spread her legs, he saw that she was naked underneath her skirt. She reached down with two fingers and spread her pink lips.

'Twenty bucks, baby,' she murmured.

Blake reached down, grabbed her by her blonde hair, and yanked her to her feet. Her cigarette fell smoldering to the pavement.

'Hey!' she screamed. 'Fuckhead, that hurts!'

He slapped her hard. 'Shut up.'

She took a look in his eyes and tried to run, but he had a lock on her shoulder and spun her back around. Her face filled with fear, and she touched her red cheek tenderly. Her voice became like a kid again, weak and scared. 'Don't hurt me.'

'I'm not going to. Shut up and listen. I've got two hundred bucks. It's yours if you spend the night with me.'

The expression on her face changed. Greed took over. She smiled a fake seductive smile at him. 'Two *hundred* bucks? Sure, baby, you got it. But look, I don't do ass, OK? I do everything else, but not that.'

Blake took her elbow and pushed her to walk beside him. 'Fine. Come on, my place is a few blocks away.'

'Your place?'

'My apartment.'

The girl struggled to keep up with him in her high-heeled boots. She looked nervous at the idea of going to his apartment.

'Three hundred bucks,' Blake said, pulling her faster.

'Three hundred! Yeah, OK, yeah.'

He led her from the overpass and continued along 8th Street to where it ended at 9th Street and turned north. His eyes were constantly moving. He could hear sirens everywhere now. Police cars were beginning to fan out around him.

'Lot of cops tonight,' the girl said.

Blake saw a flash of yellow on the street ahead of them. He knew what it was – one of a corps of policemen in neon-colored shirts who patrolled the area on bicycles.

He turned to the young prostitute. 'Kiss me.'

Before she could react, he leaned down and pressed his lips firmly against hers. She responded hungrily and put her arms around his back. She smelled of little-girl perfume, and her lips tasted like smoke. Her breathing was rapid, and he could feel her pulse racing in her throat, accelerated by the drugs.

Behind him, he heard the cop on the bicycle slow, watching them.

Don't stop, Blake thought. He didn't need another dead body and a screaming, hysterical hooker on his hands.

'Hey, buddy,' the cop called.

Blake pulled his mouth free from the girl and turned just far enough toward the street to see the cop, with only a shadow of his own profile showing. He hoped the cop couldn't see the traces of spirit gum clinging to his face. 'What's up?' Blake replied.

'Look, buddy, we both know what she is. All I can say is, make sure you use a condom, all right?'

The girl wrenched away from Blake's arms. 'Hey!' she shouted.

The cop laughed.

Blake grabbed her waist and picked her up and began carrying her away up 9th Street. The girl shouted an obscenity and spat in the cop's direction.

'A feisty one,' the cop called. 'Just remember what I said.'

'Thanks, officer,' Blake replied without looking back.

He exhaled in relief when he heard the bike squeaking as the cop rode away. He put the girl down and locked her jaw in his fist. 'You say another word before we get to my place, and the deal's off. If we

241

see another cop, you act like my girlfriend, and you shut the fuck up. Got it?'

'Did you hear what he said?' the girl retorted. 'Acted like I had some kind of disease.'

'You probably do.'

The girl reared her hand back to slap him, but he snatched her wrist and twisted it until she grimaced in pain. 'Not a word,' Blake repeated. He tugged her along beside him.

She stayed quiet now. Her lower lip jutted out as if she was pouting. They crossed Bonanza and passed Metro's downtown command building. It was the middle of the night, but there were cops coming and going past the palm trees that lined the entrance. He felt the girl tense, and he whispered to her, 'Don't worry about it. Just keep walking.'

It was like hiding in plain sight. He wondered what Jonathan Stride would think when he discovered that Blake had been living only a couple of blocks from his headquarters. True to form, no one looked at him or the girl as they sauntered past the building and continued to the end of 9th Street. They reached a narrow alley bordered by a graffiti-strewn stone wall. On their left was a bone yard of abandoned casino signs, the place where the city's old neon went to rust and die. He pulled her into the alley, which was dark and deserted, and she looked up at him, afraid again. She began twisting to get away, but he held her tight in his grip.

The area was a honeycomb of dead-end streets. He saw the occasional glow of cigarettes in the black spaces between decrepit houses. There were other signs of life. Coughs. Mutters of conversation. People who didn't want to be found. He stayed in the middle of the alley, and the girl clung close to him now.

Four blocks down, he turned onto his street. He stopped, watching it carefully, listening, smelling. There was no stake-out here yet, and he hadn't expected one, but it paid to be careful. He made his way to the two-story chocolate-brown apartment complex, which was halfway to becoming a wreck. He saw clothes hanging over the balconies. A motorcycle was parked near one of the doors. A sorry palm tree drooped near the sidewalk.

'Come on,' he told her.

Blake pulled her inside the building, and they went up the stairs to the second floor. His apartment was at the rear. He stopped in the corridor again and listened. A television was on in the first apartment, and he heard the canned laughter of a sitcom. A couple was having sex in another apartment, and he heard exaggerated moaning.

'Hey, I think I know her,' the girl said brightly.

'Shut up, let's go.'

He took note of the tells he had left on the door of his apartment – a thread on the hinges, a hair stuck near the floor. They were all undisturbed. No one had been inside. He opened the door and pushed the girl inside ahead of him. With the door closed, he flipped the light switch.

'The bedroom's in there,' he said, pointing to a doorway to the right. 'Go in and take your clothes off.'

'What about my money?' the girl asked. Blake sighed, dug in his wallet and peeled off eight fifty-dollar bills. The girl's eyes lit up. *'Four hundred bucks?* Cool! You're great! I'll ride you as long as you can keep it up, you know?'

'Get inside, strip, and wait for me.'

'You don't need to wear a condom, really, I don't got anything.'

Blake waved his hand toward the bedroom, and the girl rushed inside, clutching the money in her hand.

He studied the apartment, assessing what he needed. He already had his gun, which he reloaded quickly, and his knife and a stolen cellular phone. He grabbed a new roll of duct tape to replace the roll he had left behind in the stolen car. He looked around to see if there was evidence he needed to destroy, but decided it didn't matter now.

He wouldn't be coming back.

Blake picked up the plastic case he had taken from a gumball machine. Two human teeth rattled around inside it. He juggled them, looked at their spiked roots, and thought about Amira again. He had come a long way since the day he first saw her in the magazine and finally put a beautiful face to the voice he had heard in his mind his whole life.

He could see her there, on the roof of the Sheherezade. Her naked body in the cool water of the pool. He imagined her desperate screams for help, which went unanswered.

He was ready to answer them now.

There was just one last thing to do.

Blake went into the bedroom. The girl was stretched out on the bed, her nude body squirming on the rumpled sheets. Her breasts barely swelled from her chest, and her nipples looked like mosquito bites. She flapped her spread-open legs.

'You ready, baby?'

Blake sat down on the bed beside her. She gave him a big teeny grin, and then he clapped his hand over her mouth and stuck the barrel of his gun onto the skin of her forehead between her terrified eyes.

243

Forty

Stride closed his eyes and wanted to scream.

The call had come in. Officer down. The store owner who phoned it in had fingered Blake as the shooter, and Stride and a dozen other cars had responded to the scene within minutes. It wasn't until he arrived at the shop that he learned the identity of the officer who had been shot.

Amanda.

He wanted to throw up. The pain felt like someone had taken a serrated knife to his stomach and hacked their way up his rib cage until they found his heart.

Stride had lost cops before in the line of duty, sometimes good friends, but never a partner. In the short time they had been together, Amanda had developed a special hold on him, as if she were filling the void that Maggie had left in Minnesota. He didn't understand her sexuality, but he didn't care. She was smart. Funny. An underdog. Stride liked underdogs. He felt more for the prostitutes and cocktail waitresses in this city than for the casino bosses in their five-thousand-dollar suits or the drunk tourists and convention rats looking for an easy score.

Amanda.

He felt depression crash down through his brain. He leaned against the wall of the shop and felt all his losses replay in his head like a sad movie.

If he had been faster than Blake. If he had taken the shot in the parking lot at the Limelight.

That had been his problem all his life. He couldn't let go of guilt. His regrets clung to him forever and gathered into a stony shell.

He hadn't been fast enough to see her. The paramedics were already shutting the ambulance door when he streaked up to the curb. Their faces told the story. Ashen and tight. Fighting time, fighting death, and losing both fights. She wasn't expected to survive the ride to the hospital.

He found himself angry at Amanda for being there. It was brilliant, tracking Blake via the doughnut shops. The little things always brought down the smartest criminals, even if it was something simple like a sweet tooth for Krispy Kremes. Stride wished he had thought of that himself, and he half wondered if that had been the point of leaving the receipt behind from Reno. A taunt. A clue. To see if they'd pick up on it. *But why didn't you call for backup, Amanda?* It was such a basic lesson, all the way back to the academy. Never march into a high-risk situation alone, never be a hero. She knew that.

But Stride knew why, too. She knew Blake was smart, that he would have spotted them long before they saw him coming. Anyone who had survived the extremists in Afghanistan could smell out a trap by the local police. They had only one chance, one visit to the shop, to grab him. She didn't want to blow their best shot, so she did it on her own.

There was the other part, too – the chance to rub it in the faces of the cops trying to force her out. To prove who she was and what she could do. Ego. He couldn't blame her for feeling that way, but he blamed her anyway.

'You could have called me, Amanda,' he whispered aloud. *But Blake knows you,* he could hear her saying right back at him.

The door to the shop opened, and two uniformed cops walked out. They didn't see Stride on their left. They stopped outside and lit cigarettes, and the aroma of the smoke wafted to him and filled his lungs with a longing more intense than he had felt in a year. He looked at his hands, which were trembling. The craving was a need, as if his soul was bone dry and nothing on earth could fill it up again except a cigarette. He could taste it on his lips, inhale it into his chest.

'Can you spare one?' he asked.

He didn't recognize them, and they didn't recognize him. The taller cop, about Stride's height, with black hair and a mustache, nodded and shook an extra cigarette out of his pack. Stride took it and bent down to catch a flame from the man's lighter.

'Thanks.'

The first drag was paradise. Like angels singing. He couldn't believe he had gone a year without this.

'You knew her?' the cop asked.

Stride nodded. He pursed his lips and blew out a cloud of smoke. God would forgive him, even if Serena didn't. He needed this.

'Tough break, but at least it gets the freak off the force, huh?' the cop added.

Stride heard a roaring in his head. He watched the man grin. He looked at the cigarette in his hand, and suddenly it was something ugly and foreign. A sick, hacking cough waited deep in his lungs, ready to spew out and leave him breathless. He dropped the cigarette on the ground and crushed it with his foot.

'Shit, man, those are expensive,' the cop said.

Stride grabbed the man's shirt and threw him so hard his feet left the ground. The cop slammed backward into the wall of the shop, his head and shoulders colliding with the stucco. Dazed, he shook his head and crumpled to his knees. Stride squeezed his fingers into a fist and was ready to send it like a piledriver into the man's face. He reached down to grab him again, but the other cop sprang between them.

'Back off, back off!' he shouted at Stride. 'Are you crazy?'

He pushed Stride square in the chest, but Stride didn't move. His feet were rooted to the ground. The cop hesitated, and Stride knew he was wondering if he should pull his gun.

'Listen,' the cop told him. 'He's got a big mouth. He can be an asshole. OK? It was a stupid thing to say.'

Stride walked away. He was about to cross the street, but there was a crowd of gawkers on the other side. He walked to the corner of the block instead. There was a vacant lot there with a truck parked on the gravel, with back-lit photos of stunning women on the truck's panels. It was the kind of truck that did nothing but drive up and down the Strip, advertising escort service phone numbers for tourists. Escorts who looked nothing like the women in the photographs.

It was one more shell game in a city of con artists.

Stride sat down on the truck's bumper. He wished to hell he hadn't thrown away the cigarette. He pulled out his cell phone and dialed Serena, who answered immediately.

'Amanda's been shot,' he told her.

'No.'

He filled her in on the details. They were canvassing the surrounding blocks, looking for witnesses, hunting for Blake.

'Is she – I mean, what's the outlook?' Serena asked.

'Not good.'

'I'm sorry, Jonny.' She added, 'Don't blame yourself. There isn't anything you could have done.'

'I know.'

'Shit, I wish I was there. This is driving me crazy.'

'I'll keep you posted.'

He hung up. He tried to slough off his feeling of despair. When he pushed himself off the truck, he saw someone jog around the corner. It was Cordy. He was breathless. The detective spotted him and shouted.

'Stride! I've been looking for you.'

Stride thought about the hatred that Cordy had shown toward Amanda, and he felt his rage building inside him again. His jaw was clenched so tight he wasn't sure he could speak.

'What?' Stride hissed.

Cordy stopped short. He could read Stride's emotions. His mouth was pulled into a thin line, and he seemed genuinely remorseful. 'Hey, I know. I know. I'm sorry, man OK? Sorry about a lot of things. Makes me feel like shit, it does. She bleeds blue like the rest of us.'

Stride nodded. He took a deep breath. 'What is it?'

'We got a 911 call. Some hooker over near Harris Avenue. You know, the shithole hood near HQ? She says she saw our guy taking another of the street girls into an apartment building.'

Stride frowned. 'A hooker? Blake? That doesn't sound right.'

'Maybe he figures he needs a hostage.'

'Is she sure?'

Cordy nodded. 'Yeah, yeah, swears up and down it's the guy. Says she's seen the sketch all over town.'

'Did we get an address? An apartment number?'

'Not the number, but we got the building, yeah.' He rattled off the address. 'Takes balls, huh? Guy's been holed up so close to us we could have pissed out the window and drowned him.'

'How long ago did she see them?'

'Five minutes, maybe ten.'

Stride began to understand what Amanda felt. The desire to go it alone. To take Blake on *mano a mano*, just the two of them, where he could exact revenge for Amanda and all the others who had died. The cop in the parking lot at the Limelight. Peter Hale. Tierney Dargon. M.J. Lane. Alice Ford. Stride could see Blake's face and the arrogant smile as their eyes met. He wanted to drive over to the apartment building and storm inside, riding a wave of fury and adrenaline.

Fifteen years ago, he might have made that mistake. Like Amanda did.

'I'll call Sawhill,' Stride said quietly. 'We need to get him over here.'

Cordy nodded. 'Uh-huh. We should get a cordon around the scene.'

'Right. Let's get squad cars two blocks from the apartment building on every major intersection. But *no* lights, *no* sirens. Silent running, OK? And let's keep them *off* the actual street. We don't want anyone in that building seeing a cop anywhere.'

247

'We'll need to move fast. We don't know how long he's going to stay put.'

'Exactly. Let's establish a base down on Harris in ten minutes, and we can meet Sawhill there to map out our plan.'

'Shouldn't we do some recon?' Cordy asked.

Stride thought about it. 'Yeah. See if we can get one of the undercover cops from vice. Someone already dressed like a hooker. We'll have her do a walk-by on the building and then stake out a place where she can keep an eye on the front. But nothing too close. If Blake is eyeing the street, we don't want him spooked.'

Cordy already had his phone in his hand as he took off.

Stride retreated toward the doughnut shop and found his Bronco. He wanted to be on the scene as the cordon took shape at Harris. If Blake was in for the night, if he thought he was safe, then maybe they could take him quickly, with a minimum of violence.

Why the girl? Stride wondered. He knew there were killers who wanted sex after a murder, but he didn't think that fitted Blake's profile. Maybe Cordy was right, and Blake wanted a hostage. Whatever the truth was, it complicated their assault. It would slow them down, deciding how to proceed with a third party in the room. Maybe that was what Blake was counting on.

Forty-one

Normally, Serena loved the silence of their town home because it was a respite from the noise of the city. That was one thing about Las Vegas – you couldn't escape the din of people and machines. At home, she and Jonny sometimes turned off the stereo and sat in the darkness to relish a few moments of quiet.

But tonight the silence felt like a threat. It got under her skin.

When she put down the phone, she thought about Amanda. She had heard the pain in Jonny's voice. She had never really known Amanda, not well, but she of all people knew the effect that Jonny had on women. How they fell in love with his caring, his humanity. And how he in turn wanted to wrap his big arms around them and be a protector. Some women hated that. Most wanted to get lost in it. She knew that Jonny and Amanda had taken no time at all to bond as partners and that Jonny felt her loss as keenly as if it had been herself, or Maggie, under the gun. It made her a little jealous.

Serena went to the front door. She opened it and went outside onto the porch. Her senses were on high alert, and fear pricked along the nerves in her back. She listened carefully, and she spied every detail around her home. Nothing was moving. The overhead garage light shone down on her Mustang convertible in the driveway. The maze of streets through the gated complex was empty, except for the tall silhouettes of palm trees. No strange cars. No headlights. She studied the shadows on both corners of the house. It made her palms sweat to realize she had left her gun inside, that she was a target here, unarmed. But she was alone.

She returned inside and locked the deadbolt. She made sure the alarm was set. She thought about turning off the lights as she went upstairs, but decided to leave them on. Let anyone who was out there think she was still awake. This time, she took her gun with her.

She felt guilty being here, safe. Jonny was out on the street, chasing

Blake, and she should be with him. She said a silent prayer that he wouldn't let his emotions overrun him, that he wouldn't be foolish like Amanda and try to take Blake on his own.

Don't die, Jonny. Don't leave me. It was that simple.

But nothing was simple.

She passed the spare bedroom in which Claire was sleeping. She stopped there and listened. Her hand reached for the doorknob, and she turned it silently. To check on her, she told herself. To make sure she was OK. But that was a lie. What she wanted to do was go in and sleep beside her. Touch her. Make her spill her secrets. Serena realized she was like Jonny, wanting to wrap her arms around Claire and protect her.

She let go of the doorknob, and it clicked loudly. Serena winced. She continued quickly to her own bedroom and shut the door behind her.

The ceiling fan moved the cool air around the room. Even so, she was overheated. Flushed. She laid her gun on the nightstand beside her bed and put her cell phone next to it. She took off her clothes and went into the bathroom to get ready for bed and take a brief shower. Her skin was still damp as she returned to the bedroom. She draped clothes for tomorrow over the back of a chair, in case she needed to get dressed quickly overnight, and then she stretched out naked on top of the blankets.

Serena switched out the lamp on the nightstand. The room was dark. She lay on her back, her eyes open. The aloneness of the night felt oppressive.

Tap tap tap.

She froze, and it happened again, a scratching on the window glass. Tap tap tap.

Serena practically leaped from the bed, her heart pounding. She scrambled for her gun and ran to the window, where she tore the curtains open. Dim light streamed in from the lamps hung outside. Where the glow reflected on the window, a white moth was beating against the glass, its wings quivering. After a few seconds, it rose up higher and flew away.

Good, Serena, she thought to herself. Shoot a moth.

She left the curtains open and went back to bed, where the beam of light from outside played across her body.

As her heart slowed down, sleep began to catch up with her. She tried to stay awake, in case Jonny called again, but the harder she tried to keep her eyes open by staring at the ceiling fan, the more it hypnotized her until her eyes blinked shut.

Dreams floated in. Bad dreams. The kind where she was chased, where footsteps pounded behind her, and she ran from someone invisible. She was out in the desert at night, and she could hear rattlesnakes, and hawk wings, and the snuffling of javelinas, and someone's breathing in the darkness near her, measured and loud.

Something awakened her. She didn't know what. When she glanced at the clock, she saw that an hour had passed. Had she heard something? A click. Footsteps. Was it real? She glanced around the bedroom and saw a ghost, a shadow by the closed door. As she squinted and looked harder, the shadow moved. Someone was in her room.

Serena felt paralyzed and exposed, naked in the glow from outside. She started to reach for her gun again. 'Who's there?'

From the darkness, she heard Claire's voice. 'It's only me, Serena.' Claire stepped further into the room, where the light found her. She was naked too.

She came and lay next to Serena on the bed without being asked. They were both on their backs, staring at the ceiling.

'I'm sorry, I couldn't sleep,' Claire said. 'Did you hear something before?'

'I assumed it was you in the hallway.'

'No, something else.'

They waited and listened. Serena knew every groan and creak in the beams of her home, but there was nothing out of place.

'It's my imagination,' Claire said.

'Try to sleep.'

Serena turned on her side, away from Claire. She could see the time glowing on the clock. Almost two in the morning. She wondered where Jonny was and when he would be coming home to her. She wanted to close her eyes, but she was awake now, keenly aware of Claire behind her. She could hear her breathing softly; she was awake too. A fragile silence hung between them. Waiting for the next move.

Claire shifted onto her side. Without an invitation, she slid her body across the bed and spooned against Serena's back, molding her skin against her. She didn't say anything. Serena felt Claire's breaths in short puffs on her neck and her blonde hair tickled her ear. Claire's nipples were erect. Serena could feel them on her back. Her skin was smooth everywhere it touched her.

'Is this all right?' Claire murmured.

'Yes.'

Claire's arm came around Serena's body and rested lightly on her stomach. 'You feel good.'

'So do you.'

Claire's lips brushed her neck, kissing her. It was tender and erotic. They lay there like that for several minutes, connected, not moving or talking. Serena could feel warmth, love, and desire emanating from the woman behind her.

'I've never felt anything like this,' Claire told her.

'It's nice,' Serena said, closing her eyes at her lame reply. Claire was telling her she loved her. She didn't want to acknowledge it.

'You have a beautiful body. So strong. I can feel how strong you are.'

Serena didn't feel strong at all.

Claire's fingers came alive and began gently brushing Serena's stomach. She was testing, waiting to see if Serena would stop her.

'Do you want me to leave?' Claire asked.

'I don't know what I want.' Not saying yes. Not saying no.

'I think you do,' Claire said.

Her hand seemed to fly, and when it came down again, it cupped Serena's breast. Serena tensed, and Claire stopped.

'Too fast?'

'Too everything.'

'I can go.'

Serena felt the heat of Claire's hand over her breast. 'No, don't go.'

Claire's hand began to move downward. Serena realized she was holding her breath.

'Relax,' Claire said. 'Let it happen to you.'

Claire found her way between her legs.

'Do you like this?'

Serena heard herself sigh with pleasure.

There was only one thing to do next, to let Claire inside, where she would find her wet and wanting. To open her legs and let Claire bring her to climax with a few quick circular caresses. That was all it would take. That was how close she was.

She felt Claire's middle finger explore and could hear the rumble of satisfaction in Claire's throat as she discovered her arousal, her folds supple and damp.

Serena bit her lip and cried out.

Then she was blinded as the bedroom light went on.

Forty-two

The black van rumbled down the street, slowly, as if the driver was looking for something in the adjacent buildings. But its headlights were off. Flaking paint on the side of the van read MEADOWS CLOTHING AND CASINO SUPPLY, although several of the letters were missing. It drifted to a stop across the street from Blake's two-story apartment complex and waited there with its engine running.

Stride was squeezed into the back with eleven other cops in body armor. All men. Tension and pent-up adrenaline buzzed among them. Sawhill had made the decision to go in, and they were waiting for the green light.

He heard chatter on his headset.

'The street is clear. No civilians. We're good to go.' That was the driver of the van.

Sawhill radioed back. 'Tammy, you concur?'

Tammy was an undercover cop who had been staking out Blake's building from a complex across the street for more than an hour. 'Right, no civvies. Nice to do this in the middle of the night, guys.'

'Alonzo, any movement in back?'

'Negative.' Alonzo had slipped into position in a yard behind the building and was watching Blake's apartment.

'Lights from inside?'

'Negative.'

'OK, insertion team, stand by.'

In the van, they continued to wait, anxious to get started. The vests were warm, and their bodies were in close quarters.

They had caught a break shortly after the cordon was set up on the surrounding streets. A Vietnamese man returning from his job in a downtown casino had approached them about access to his apartment. It turned out that he lived in Blake's building. He was able to identify Blake from their sketch, pinpoint the location of

Blake's apartment on the second floor at the rear of the hallway, and give them a thorough map of the thirty-unit building itself.

The warrant had arrived fifteen minutes ago. They were ready to go.

Sawhill's voice crackled on the radio. 'One more time, people. We go with four in back, Rodriguez and Holtz on the north, Han and Baker on the south. The perp's balcony is in the dead center of the building, count three from the north or south, one two three. Got it? Be ready if he tries to go over the side.'

Several voices in the van grunted affirmatively.

'Lee, Salazar, Alexander, Odom, Stride, Cordy, you're the assault team. Down the hall quick and quiet, then Lee and Salazar, you take the door, Alexander and Odom, you go in first, Stride and Cordy, you're behind them. Remember you've got a potential innocent party in the room with the perp. You've got a living area straight in, with a bedroom and kitchen on the south wall.'

'Copy that,' Stride replied.

'Kwan and Davis, you're in the rear. Kwan, you take the upstairs hallway and keep any residents inside their apartments. Davis, you're backup in front of the building.'

'Roger.'

'We go on my signal in one minute.'

The seconds passed slowly. It gave Stride time to think about Amanda again. And Serena. He had been on a limited number of major raids in his career, mostly drug-related. They were always risky.

Sawhill's voice came over the radio without fanfare. 'Go.'

The van's rear doors opened on greased hinges, and the team piled out. For large men, they moved with grace and speed. The first four peeled off, two heading to the left side around the rear of the building, two repeating the maneuver on the right side. They all carried automatic weapons. Stride moved with his team of six across the street at a jog and up the sidewalk to the building entrance. The outer door was open. Alexander and Odom, carrying assault rifles, went first, moving inside the building and then signaling behind them an all-clear. The two policemen began slowly climbing the stairs to the second floor, their weight causing the wood steps to creak.

Stride heard a voice on his radio. 'We're in position in back.'

Two cops with battering rams followed up the stairs. Stride and Cordy went next. The last man held position at the top of the stairs while the others proceeded down the hallway, hugging the walls. Stride heard few sounds from the apartments they passed. It was the middle of the night. He counted five doors on either side, and ahead of them, less than a hundred feet away, was an identical door at the far end of the hallway.

Blake's door.

They tried to be silent. It was almost impossible. The complex was low-end construction, and the floors groaned as six bulky men made their way to the rear. If Blake was awake and alert, he'd hear them coming. Alexander and Odom had their rifles aimed at Blake's apartment, and they picked up the pace, knowing they couldn't make a quiet approach. Stride saw a spy-hole in Blake's door and wondered if he was there, watching them. But if he was, he had to know he was trapped and outgunned.

As Stride passed one of the apartment doors on the left, it suddenly opened inward.

He spun and was bringing his gun up when he saw an old woman in the doorway, her eyes bleary. She wore a tattered white robe. When she saw Stride, her mouth fell open in fright, and she was an instant away from screaming when he quickly pushed her back into the apartment and covered her mouth with his hand.

'Hold,' he hissed into his radio.

Then to the woman, 'Police, ma'am. It's OK. Stay in your apartment. Don't open the door.'

She nodded frantically.

Stride smiled at her and backed out into the hallway. He shut the door with a soft click.

'Go.'

Alexander and Odom took up positions on opposite sides of Blake's door. Stride went to the left, behind Alexander, and Cordy went to the right, behind Salazar. They waited. There wasn't a sound from inside the apartment, and no light shone from the crack at the base of the door.

Alexander held up three fingers. Then he made a fist and raised his fingers one at a time.

One. Two. Three.

The battering rams both hit the door at once, and it caved immediately. Alexander and Odom spun around the frame and ran crouched into the apartment with their rifles leveled. Stride and Cordy followed. They all shouted at once. 'POLICE!'

They made a circuit of the small living room in less than five seconds, but it was empty. One man shouted that the kitchen was clear. The only other room in the apartment was the bedroom, and the fragile veneer door leading there was closed. Alexander didn't wait for the battering ram but simply brought up his giant leg, which was

255

like the trunk of an oak tree, and kicked the door down, tearing it off its hinges and sending it flying into the room.

He stormed in.

'Hostage on the bed!'

Stride followed him into the room. A young teenager was tied to the four casters of the bed. She was naked and spreadeagled, with a T-shirt rolled and tied around her mouth. Her eyes were as wide as saucers. She tried to scream, and she struggled with the rope that held her.

'Clear!' Alexander shouted, having checked the closet and bathroom. 'The son of a bitch isn't here!'

Sawhill's pinched voice responded over the radio. *'He's not there?'*

'Negative.'

'Rodriguez, Holtz, tell me you've got him in back.'

'Sorry, sir, nothing here, no movement.'

Sawhill was exasperated. 'We had this place staked out five minutes after the 911 call! Where did he go? Start going door to door, check every apartment.'

'What about the warrant?' Alexander asked.

'We have a multiple murderer loose in the building, just do it!'

Stride interrupted on the radio. 'Give me thirty seconds, sir, let's talk to the girl.' He gestured at the closet. 'Alexander, grab me one of those dress shirts, OK?'

The big cop pulled a shirt off the hanger and tossed it to Stride, who used it to cover the girl on the bed. She was small, and the shirt stretched from just below her neck almost to her knees.

'Take it easy, OK?' Stride said. 'You're fine now.'

He drew out a small knife from his pocket and cut the twine that tightly bound her tiny wrists to the casters of the bed. Deep red welts gouged her skin, and the rope was bloody where she had struggled to get free. As soon as he cut her loose, she sprang up and threw her arms around his neck. She sobbed, and her nose ran on his Kevlar vest.

Stride let her cry out for a few seconds, then gently pushed her away.

'Where is he?' he asked her.

She shook her head. 'I don't know.'

'When did he leave the apartment?'

'A while ago. I don't know. More than an hour, I think. I was afraid he'd come back.'

Stride didn't think Blake was ever coming back here. 'What happened after he brought you into the apartment?'

'He made he undress. Then he tied me to the bed, and he made me make the call. He held a gun to my head, and he told me exactly what I should say. As soon as I made the call, he gagged me and left.'

'Call?' Stride asked. He suddenly understood and felt a sense of horror.

'The 911 call. He made me call and pretend like I was outside, you know?'

'*You* called 911?'

The girl nodded earnestly.

Stride shook his head. 'Shit.' He spoke into the radio. 'The 911 call was a hoax, sir. Blake made the girl do it. He bolted as soon as she did. He's been long gone, an hour or more, while we've been spinning our wheels.'

Sawhill, who never swore, sounded close to swearing. 'I don't believe this. Check the other apartments anyway, just to be sure.'

Alexander nodded. 'Got it, sir.'

'He's probably got a backup crib on the other side of the city,' Sawhill said. 'Keep an eye out for reports of stolen cars from this neighborhood. He may have snatched another vehicle to get out of here.'

Stride was about to reply, and then he thought about it. Blake had begun to get inside his head. He couldn't have expected to encounter Amanda in the doughnut shop, so he had to act fast to get out from under the heat. The net would be tightening, and sooner or later it would lead the police right here. He needed a diversion. An escape. Blake was buying time.

Too much time. Stride realized. He didn't need to invite the cops into a phoney raid in order to get away. He was trying to tie them down, keep them occupied.

So he could launch his last big play.

Stride felt his whole body run cold. 'That son of a bitch.'

He had spoken into the radio, and Sawhill responded. 'What? What are you talking about?'

Stride ripped off his headset. He clawed his cell phone out of his pocket and dialed. It took forever for the call to go through, a stretch of dead air and silence that went on and on. As he waited, he began to have waking nightmares.

The phone rang. His home phone. Where Serena and Claire were.

'Pick up,' he begged them.

The phone kept ringing. No one answered.

Stride ran for the door.

Forty-three

When Serena could see again after her eyes adjusted to the dazzling light, she knew she was about to die. Blake stood in the doorway with a Sig Sauer pointed directly at her head.

'Sorry to interrupt,' he said.

He had a hint of a cold smile. There was arousal in his eyes, looking at the two women entwined on the bed.

A flood of regrets ran through Serena's head. That she had never been to Hawaii. That she had never been able to have children, although she had persuaded herself over the years that it didn't matter. That Jonny would find them like this, naked, together, and realize she had betrayed him. That her weaknesses were stronger than she was. That he wouldn't know how much she loved him.

Her eyes flicked to the nightstand, and in an instant she measured the time it would take to leap for her gun and get a shot off. Too long. Much too long.

Blake watched her eyes. 'Please don't do that. Don't make me kill you.'

'Like you're not going to anyway.' Serena gave him a defiant look. She laid an arm across her chest, covering her breasts.

'Let's just stay calm,' Blake said. 'Claire, get off the bed and go to the other side of the nightstand.'

Claire hesitated, and Serena reached over and squeezed her hand. 'It'll be OK,' she told her. A lie.

Claire did as she was told.

'Good,' Blake said. 'Now, with two fingers, take the gun on the nightstand, and hand it to me.'

Claire picked up the gun as if it was a dead fish on the beach and let the butt dangle from her fingers. Blake kept his eyes and his gun trained on Serena the whole time. He took the gun from Claire and shoved it in his belt.

'Get dressed,' he told them.

Claire didn't move. She waited until Blake looked at her. His eyes traveled up and down her naked body, and then he blinked, as if he were embarrassed. Serena thought his reaction was remarkably human for a multiple murderer.

'Do you know who I am?' Claire asked.

'You're Boni's daughter,' he snapped.

'And do you know what that makes me?' she asked. She stared at him hard. 'You know, don't you? You have to know.'

Blake's composure developed a hairline crack. 'Yes.'

'Then how can you do this?'

Serena waited to see if Blake would answer. He seemed to be at a loss for words. 'Both of you, get dressed.'

'My clothes are in the other room,' Claire said.

'Use some of hers. Come on, let's go. No sudden moves.'

Serena wondered what the hell he was up to. Why get dressed? She had expected him to kill them both immediately, but Blake seemed to be following a more complex plan. That was fine. The more time she was alive, the more opportunity there might be to escape or over-power him.

She slid her legs off the bed, still trying to cover herself. Quickly, she pulled on the clothes she had draped over a chair – panties, T-shirt, jeans. She opened two of her dresser drawers and tossed clothes to Claire, who was shorter and smaller than Serena. The clothes fitted loosely, and Claire rolled up the pant legs.

'Where are we going?' Serena asked.

Blake didn't answer. He pulled a roll of duct tape from his rear pocket and tossed it to Claire. 'Bind her wrists together tightly.'

Serena looked at Claire, and their eyes met. Serena extended her hands, palms together.

Claire seemed to be frozen. She had the tape in her hands but didn't move.

'Do it!' Blake said.

Claire's eyes looked pointedly away at something behind and below Serena, then directly back at her. She did it again. And again. Directing Serena's attention to something.

It took Serena only a second or two to figure it out.

Her nightstand. Her *cell phone*.

'I can't believe I trusted you,' Claire said bitterly.

'I'm sorry.'

'You said you'd *protect* me!'

'Shut up!' Blake insisted.

259

'You?' Serena asked. 'You arrogant little bitch! You could have hidden behind all your daddy's money, and instead you get *me* killed, too!'

'FUCK YOU!' Claire screamed, stepping forward and laying both hands on Serena's chest, pushing her violently backward. Serena toppled off her feet, colliding with the nightstand as she fell, knocking everything on its surface to the floor. The lamp crashed, its bulb shattering, and books and keys littered the carpet. Serena twisted, landing on her face, but she already had the cell phone spotted as she hit her knees.

'Get up!' Blake hissed. 'Not another word!'

'Fuck you, too!' Claire retorted. She turned and partially blocked Serena from view as she bent over and began wrestling her back to the ground. Blake leaped forward and pulled Claire back by the hair.

'Enough!'

Blake pushed Claire away and fired his gun into a pillow on the bed. The explosion rattled the walls, and a huge cloud of feathers burst into the room, flying and floating over the two women.

'The next one kills Serena,' he said.

Both women froze. Claire was crying. 'I'm sorry.'

'Get up,' Blake told Serena.

Serena got back to her feet, her face flushed.

'Now *tie her hands*,' Blake repeated to Claire.

Claire nodded meekly. She began wrapping the tape round Serena's wrists.

'Tighter,' Blake instructed. 'Go higher up.'

Claire frowned and did the next loops more tightly and continued rolling the tape until it was almost to Serena's elbows. With a tilt of her head, she managed to raise one eyebrow at Serena, who replied with the barest nod. A whisper of a smile came and went on Claire's face.

Claire finished, and Serena's arms were locked in front of her, her hands dangling below her waist.

'Now her face. Gag her. *Do it.*'

Claire took a final strip of tape and placed it across Serena's mouth.

'Push her down on the bed,' Blake said. When Claire hesitated, he broke between them and roughly shoved Serena down. She landed on her back on the bed, her upper body strangled for motion. She watched as Blake tied Claire's wrists next and then gagged her, too.

'Come on,' he told them. 'Let's go. The two of you go first. If you try anything, you'll both be dead, and probably some other innocent people too.'

260

He took Serena by the shoulder and forced her to her feet. She left the bedroom with Claire immediately behind her. They proceeded down the hall and then downstairs to the first floor. Blake pushed past them and opened the front door. He went out onto the porch, his eyes darting back and forth. With a jerk of his head, he gestured them outside and then down the steps to the street.

An old white Impala was parked at the curb, blocking her Mustang.

Somehow Blake had managed to steal the car and the keys. Or maybe he had kept another car hidden away for the end game. He used the remote control on the key chain to pop the trunk. Serena's heart fell again, and she had visions of him taking the two of them out and dumping them in the desert to rot. Or burying them alive. His desire for revenge was so bitter that anything was possible.

'In the trunk,' he said. 'Fast.'

Serena tried to bend at the waist and ease herself inside, but with her arms bound, she could barely move. Blake came up behind her and grabbed her T-shirt and belt and lifted her bodily like a suitcase and dumped her into the trunk. The hard floor smashed her face, and she tasted blood in her mouth and tried to swallow it quickly so she didn't choke. Her head banged the roof as she tried to move. She rolled to the back, and two seconds later the car rocked as Blake threw Claire inside next. She heard a muffled cry of pain. Claire's body was wedged against her.

Blake slammed the trunk down.

A black, claustrophobic fog enveloped Serena. Barely able to move. Unable to talk. All she could do was hear.

And feel the cell phone wedged inside her jeans.

She heard the driver's door open, but then the next sounds made no sense. There was a shout, a gasp, a bang. A clattering as Blake's gun fell to the ground. The car bounced again as something large and heavy struck the Impala above them. Like something hitting, sliding, and falling.

It took her a moment to realize that the sound was Blake being thrown across the roof of the car.

Forty-four

Leo Rucci came around the front of the Impala, where Blake was on the ground, shocked and dazed. Blake realized his hands were empty, that his gun was gone. He reached into his waistband for Serena's gun and pulled it out, but the impact had dulled his reaction time. He wasn't fast enough. As he drew the gun, Leo kicked it out of his hand. It skittered down the street as if it was gliding on ice and wound up near one of the squat palm trees lining the curb.

'OK, you pussy, now it's the just the two of us. Think you can beat an old man?'

As the fog lifted from Blake's head, he felt Rucci's giant hands on his shirt, lifting him up off the ground and slamming him face first into the rear door of the car. Blood erupted from his nose, and his brain seemed to slap against the sides of his skull. The world spun again.

'You killed my son. You murdered him like a dog. Now I'm going to make sure every bone in your body is broken before I finally finish you off.'

Leo spun Blake around. The Impala window was streaked with blood. Leo's fist reared back and came streaking forward, but Blake had recovered enough to duck down. Leo hit the window instead and grimaced. Blake used the moment to try to squirm free, but Leo still had an iron lock on Blake's shoulder. He grabbed Blake's neck with his hand and yanked him off the ground.

Blake couldn't breathe. Leo's fat fingers squeezed off his air. Blake grabbed at the man's hand and tried to dislodge him, but it was like trying to peel away a boa constrictor that had coiled around his neck in a death grip. With a grin, Leo wound up and sent a hammering blow into Blake's abdomen. Blake felt his lungs balloon as the pent-up air tried to escape and had nowhere to go. He felt as if he had swallowed a hand grenade that had blown up inside him, as if his chest were being cut up from within.

262

He was beginning to lose consciousness. There was a roaring in his ears, and a million blood vessels felt like they were popping at once. Blake thrashed. He continued prying at Leo's hand and got nowhere.

'This is just the beginning,' Leo said. 'We're not even close to being done. Once you black out, I'll take you somewhere nice and private.'

An image penetrated Blake's brain. Something long and smooth. He couldn't see it but he could feel the cold touch of steel. His knife. It was still in his back pocket. Blake gave up trying to free his throat from Leo's grasp and instead used his last few seconds of awareness to squeeze his hand behind him. His limbs didn't seem connected any more. Whatever messages his brain was sending were scrambled. He kept reaching for his pocket and finding nothing, and his fingers began jerking spastically.

Finally, he touched the handle of the knife. He had an instant of crystal clarity, and his hand dug for it, grabbed it, and pulled it free. In a single, desperate swing, he buried the blade in Leo's forearm and heard the man roar in pain like a wounded bear. Leo's fingers unlocked from Blake's neck, and sweet air rushed in. As Leo stumbled back, Blake's mind cleared, and he kicked ferociously with his boot into the meat of Leo's knee. The old man toppled to his side, a tree falling.

Blake still had the knife.

He pounced, aiming the next thrust of the blade for Leo's chest. Leo saw it coming and grabbed Blake's wrist as the knife came down. His grip was slippery and loose from the blood on his hand, and Blake easily pulled away and jabbed again. The tip of the blade sliced Leo's shoulder, but before Blake could inflict further damage, Leo used his other arm like a baseball bat and swatted Blake away. Blake rolled several times and got up, shaken.

Leo pulled himself to his feet. Both of his arms were streaked in red. He was unsteady, but he waved Blake toward him.

'Come on, pussy. You need a knife to beat an old man? Come on. Try it again.'

Blake didn't let himself be goaded. He held back, breathing heavily, trying to nurse his strength back and drive the fog from his brain. He kept the knife poised in front of him.

Leo inched forward.

'Pussy, pussy. Gino would have crushed you in a fight.'

'You should have seen his head split when I shot him,' Blake retorted, taunting him. 'Like a hairy coconut.'

Leo charged, his voice bellowing in rage. Blake sidestepped him and swung his knife again, finding a target in the fleshy muscles under Leo's shoulder blade. He thrust the knife brutally inward all the way to the hilt. Leo threw his head back and screamed. Blake tried to cut his way downward into Leo's organs, but the man twisted away, and Blake lost his grip on the handle. Leo swung blindly and caught Blake on the side of his head with a massive curled fist. Blake felt the world spin again, and he collapsed to his hands and knees.

He felt something metallic under his fingers. His car keys, lying on the pavement. He cupped them in his hands and tried to get up.

Behind him, he heard a sucking, slurping sound. It was Leo, pulling out the knife. Blake turned around, lost his balance, and steadied himself against the side of the Impala. He and Leo eyed each other warily. Blood soaked Leo's shirt, and he looked weak and pale. But he still had a substantial advantage in size, and now he had the knife. Leo's hand was so big that the knife looked tiny in his grasp.

Blake crept backward, still leaning against the car. Leo matched him step for step. Blake's eyes scanned the pavement, looking for his gun, but he realized he had lost it somewhere on the other side of the car. Leo seemed to read his mind. As Blake retreated toward the trunk, Leo shifted, moving around toward the front of the car.

If the gun was in sight, Leo would get it first.

They stared each other down from opposite corners of the Impala, Blake on the right rear, Leo on the left front, near the headlight. Blake saw Leo's eyes sweeping the curb and driveway, and then a twisted smile formed on Leo's lips. Confident. Nasty. Their eyes met again, and Blake knew Leo had found the gun. He watched the old man edge away from the car toward the landscaping in front of Serena's home.

Blake pushed a button on the remote control of the car keys. With a soft chirp, the lock on the trunk unlatched.

Leo watched him with a puzzled expression, and then he understood. He turned away, and with a groan of pain he bent to retrieve the gun.

Blake swung the trunk open and ducked, expecting a bullet to tear through the metal. He saw Claire's blinking, terrified eyes looking up at him. With both hands, he pulled Claire out of the trunk in one smooth motion and then slammed it back down. He twisted Claire around and snaked one arm around her throat. He put his other hand on top of her head and held her skull firmly.

He didn't see Leo at first. He backed up, worried that the man would creep around the side of the car to ambush him. He kept Claire in front of him and could feel her fear. She fluttered in his grasp like a bird.

Leo straightened up. He hadn't moved. He was still near the front of the Impala, but he had the gun now, and he pointed it at Blake.

264

'Let her go.'

'You want to take the shot and risk killing her? Go ahead.'

Blake began to push Claire forward as he nudged toward the Impala. His keys were still in his hand. 'Drop the gun, Leo. Throw it away.'

There was hesitation in Leo's eyes.

'I'll crack her neck, Leo. One quick snap, and she'll be gone.'

Claire struggled frantically in his arms, panicking. He held her tight.

'And so will you,' Leo told him. 'You kill her, and I kill you.'

'And then Boni kills you for letting his daughter die. Is that what you want? Do you want to be the one to tell Boni that you let his daughter die right in front of you? Do you want to fail him like that?'

Frustration boiled over in Leo's face. Blake knew he wanted to shoot, and he couldn't. Blood was still flowing out of his wounds, too, and Leo wouldn't be able to stand much longer. Blake kept coming forward, moving up on the driver's door of the car.

'Throw it away, Leo. If you throw it away, she lives.'

With a hiss of hatred, Leo flung the gun behind him, out of range.

'Smart move,' Blake said. 'Now back off away from the car. We're leaving, Leo.'

Leo retreated. He backed up slowly, retracing his steps around the front of the car and taking a few steps down the street. His hands were in the air. His eyes were dark with anger and pain.

'You don't look good, Leo. Better call an ambulance after we leave.'

Leo kept backing away. Blake opened the car door and shoved Claire inside, pushing her across to the passenger seat. He clambered behind the wheel and pulled the door shut, keeping an eye on Leo. The old man seemed to be crumbling. His chest was heaving as he took labored breaths. His footfalls were erratic. He wasn't even looking at Blake or the car any more. He staggered back, bumping into a palm tree near the curb, and bent over, his hands on his knees. Blood began to spit from his mouth.

Blake started the car. He backed up and then turned for the street. As he spun the wheel, he saw Leo look up again, and with blood on his chin the old man smiled, his face coming alive. It had been an act. Gasping. Staggering. Nearly falling. Blake realized finally that Leo had come to rest at the palm tree, inches from Serena's gun. Leo ignored his pain and reached for it, and an instant later he had the gun in his hand and was swinging it up, pointing toward the windshield of the Impala.

'Get down,' Blake told Claire.

He aimed the car at Leo and jammed his foot into the accelerator.

The engine raced, and the car leaped forward, its tires squealing. Blake kept a hand on the wheel and jerked to his left, hearing the explosion of the gun at the same time that the windshield shattered and spilled glass into the car, covering him and Claire and the front seat with sharp confetti. The car shuddered as the front bumper struck Leo. A second later, the car jarred to a halt, and the air bags deployed, cushioning them as their bodies were thrown forward. The balloons collapsed, and he saw Claire jolt back against the passenger seat.

Blake looked through the shattered windshield.

The car was lodged against the palm tree. Leo was pinned between the car and the tree, his lower body crushed. The gun had fallen from his hands. He was still alive, barely, and he stared back at Blake with the ferocity of a man who has been defeated in a fight that meant everything to him. Tears of agony slipped down his cheeks, but he didn't cry out or say a word.

Blake got out of the car. He retrieved the gun where it had fallen to the ground. Leo watched him, impotent, unable to move.

'You played this well, Leo,' Blake told him with genuine admiration. 'Gino would be proud of you.'

Leo tried to spit at him. He couldn't.

Blake glanced into the car and saw that Claire was watching him. He found himself feeling something like mercy. He shoved the gun in his belt and went around to the other side of the Impala. He opened the door, and Claire seemed to spill out into his arms.

'Are you hurt?' he asked her.

He let her stand up, and she was unsteady on her feet, but she didn't seem to be injured. She was too stunned to walk, though, and Blake picked her up and carried her back to the trunk. He opened it and laid her inside next to Serena as tenderly as he could. He closed the trunk again and walked back to Leo.

'I know that the pain must be excruciating,' Blake said.

Leo didn't look at him.

'Eyes open or closed, Leo. It's your choice.'

Leo turned his head with what seemed to be a superhuman effort. His eyes were open. Blake nodded, brought the gun up to Leo's head, and fired.

Forty-five

Serena reached for Claire's bound hands and held them tightly. When the gunshot exploded outside the car, she knew that Claire was screaming behind the tape that gagged her mouth. She could hear the muffled cries as Claire buried her face in her shoulder in the dark, cramped confines of the trunk. She felt the dampness of tears through her shirt. Claire clutched her hands so fiercely that her nails were close to breaking the skin.

The car rocked as Blake got back inside, and then they were moving, their bodies bouncing loosely as Blake steered the Impala through the town home complex toward the street. Serena recognized the familiar turns. She hoped someone had heard the shots and called 911, but she knew they would be long gone by the time a squad car responded.

Serena was bruised and sore. She had flown forward when the car thudded to a stop earlier, and she had banged her head against the rear wall of the trunk. Her arms ached from being held stiffly in place, and something – a tire iron? – had struck her squarely in the knee. The bone throbbed with pain.

She disentangled her fingers from Claire's and rolled onto her back, landing hard on her shoulder blade. She had discovered earlier that she had enough play in her arms to bend them at the elbows and bring her hands up to her mouth. Her fingers clutched at the tape that was gagging her, and she peeled it slowly and painfully away. When her jaw was free, she rubbed it and took several long, deep breaths, gulping air into her lungs. She was sweating. The trunk was hot enough to make her light-headed.

The car rolled over a dip in the street, and her forehead struck sharply against the roof of the trunk. She cursed softly.

Serena braced her left foot on the floor and pushed herself back onto her side, facing Claire again. She found Claire's hands.

'Claire, listen to me,' she whispered. 'You can probably get your hands up to your face and get the tape off. Can you try it?'

She hoped Claire had enough strength, mentally and physically, to do it.

She let go and felt Claire squirming to reposition her arms and get her fingers near her mouth. Claire pulled the tape off quickly, and Serena heard her gasp.

'Shit, that hurt.'

They both laughed. Serena was pleased that Claire sounded calm now and not frantic. She nudged closer and put her mouth close to Claire's ear. 'We need to be as quiet as we can. What happened out there?'

'It was Leo,' Claire said. 'I think Blake killed him.'

'Did he hurt you?'

'No. But I was scared to death.'

Serena laid her cheek against the soft skin of Claire's face. 'It's OK. We're going to get out of this.'

It's OK, baby.

Serena felt a strange sense of freedom. Of strength. As if she had been given a second chance, a way to make up for the past. To save Deirdre by saving Claire.

'Do you know where he's taking us?' Serena asked.

'I have no idea.'

Serena didn't want to speculate. None of the alternatives was appealing. She had tried to keep track of the stops and turns once they made it onto the street, but the route quickly became too confusing to follow. They were still in a busy part of the city, because she could hear plenty of traffic noise, even late at night.

'I'm sorry I got you into this, Serena,' Claire told her.

'You didn't.'

Claire was silent for a moment. 'What was happening between us inside—'

'Let's not talk about that now.'

'I need to know if you regret it,' Claire said.

'No, I don't.' Serena knew she had to change the subject. 'That was smart, what you did inside with Blake. Pushing me. Yelling at me.'

'Did you get it? Did you get the phone?'

'Yes. You have to get it for me. I shoved it in my pocket.'

Serena shifted her arms as far as she could, and Claire's hands explored around the front of her jeans until her fingers pressed into the hard shell of the wafer-size cell phone.

'Can you slide down a bit?' Claire asked.

Serena pushed herself down, bending her knees to get more room when her feet bumped the side of the car. She felt Claire's fingers at her waist, slipping inside the tight pocket. It was strangely intimate, to be doing this in the dark, in the hot interior of the car. Claire's breasts were almost in her face. Her T-shirt clung to her skin like glue.

'Normally, I'd enjoy this,' Claire whispered.

'Hush.'

Claire found the cell phone and slid it between her palms. As she tried to pass it into Serena's hands, she dropped it somewhere between them.

'Shit!' she hissed. 'My hands are slippery.'

The car went through a sharp turn at that moment, and they found themselves sliding and rolling in the narrow space. The phone slid too. Serena lost her sense of direction in the dark and didn't know which way she was facing or which way was front and back. She was disoriented. 'Claire?'

'Here.'

Serena tried to roll back next to her. 'We have to find the phone.'

They performed an awkward dance as both of them tried to flip over and scour the black interior of the trunk. Serena brushed her legs along the carpeted floor, trying to feel the slim rectangle of the phone. Claire did the same. Serena began to feel the pressure of time, wondering how long it would take for Blake to reach where he was going. But the phone had seemingly vanished from the trunk.

'Anything?' Serena whispered.

'No.'

The car turned again, and their bodies shifted. Serena wasn't sure why, but she had an intuition that they were almost there, and she had learned to trust her sixth sense over the years. The road beneath them was bumpier, as if there was loose gravel on the pavement. The noise outside had quietened. They weren't on a busy street any more.

'We need to hurry,' Serena said.

'I've got it, I've got it,' Claire replied. 'It's near my face. It slid over here on the last turn.'

'Try to get your hands on it before we turn again.'

Serena heard Claire moving and maneuvered herself in the direction of Claire's voice. She bent her elbows again, bringing her hands near her face. She pushed herself closer and felt her fingers touch Claire's forearm immediately in front of her. She followed the soft skin up to Claire's hands and was relieved to feel the cell phone nestled between her fingers. Claire was holding it tightly.

'OK, loosen up just a bit,' Serena said.

She worked her own fingers into Claire's hands and curled them round the phone. It was small and familiar. 'I've got it.'

Claire breathed a sigh of relief.

The car swung through another turn, and Serena clutched the phone and tried to brace herself to keep from sliding. Claire bumped up against her. Serena almost lost her grip and bobbled the phone in her fingers, but then felt it sink back into her hands. She ran her fingertips over the keypad and tried to imagine the numbers laid out on the phone. The keys were almost flat, and she could barely feel them.

She pressed what she thought was the number two. The speed dial code for Jonny's cell phone.

Nothing happened.

Serena tried another key with the same result. Finally, she remembered that she had turned the phone off as she grabbed it from the floor in her bedroom, to make sure that an incoming call didn't give away what she was hiding in her pocket.

'Shit, it's off,' she said.

She hunted for the key that turned the phone back on and held it down. As she did, she felt the car turn onto a rutted stretch of pavement that rocked the vehicle up and down. The brakes squealed, and the car lurched to a stop.

The phone lit up. It began hunting for a signal. 'Come on, come on,' Serena urged.

She heard the driver's door open and Blake get out. His footsteps crunched on gravel.

'Hurry,' Claire said.

Serena punched the number two button again and held her breath. Blake was almost to the trunk. The phone began ringing.

Forty-six

Stride swung into the gated driveway of the town home complex and knew something was wrong. The gate was wide open. He hesitated and felt his horror grow as he heard sirens drawing closer through the surrounding streets.

He tried Serena's cell phone again, as he had been doing constantly on the drive west from downtown. There was no answer. He tried their home number again, too, and heard Serena's voice as the answering machine picked up. The pit in his stomach became an awful pounding in his head. He accelerated into the winding streets past the maze of homes.

When he reached their street, he saw a body lying under the glow of a street light. A big man, slumped like a beached whale. Stride got out of the car, the engine still running. The man was face down, half off the curb, with blood dripping in the gutter. Recently dead. The burnt smell of powder was still fresh in the air. Stride bent down and saw the hole in the man's forehead, and despite the red trails on his face, he knew it was Leo Rucci.

He had held out a faint hope that it might be Blake.

Stride ran for the house with an awful vision of what he would find inside. The front door was open. He drew his gun and leveled it as he crept through the doorway. He listened for voices or movement upstairs but didn't hear a thing. When he glanced automatically at the alarm box on the wall, he saw that it had been disconnected. His heart turned to lead and seemed to plummet to the floor.

He was about to scream her name, but he stopped himself. Blake might still be here.

Stride silently followed the wall to the stairs and waited, listening again. He scoped out the empty hallway and took the steps to the second floor. The three bedroom doors upstairs were all ajar. The first, their office, hadn't been touched. The second was the spare bedroom,

271

and he saw Claire's clothes on the floor. He checked the bathroom and the closet inside and didn't find anything amiss.

That left their own bedroom at the end of the hall.

He stared at it and didn't want to go through the doorway. Reluctantly, he sniffed the air, and he was relieved that he didn't catch the mineral scent of blood. He could see part of the bed ahead of him, its blankets rumpled.

If anyone was there, they would already have heard him coming. 'Serena?' he called, not expecting an answer.

Stride used the toe of his shoe to push the door open slowly. He led the way inside with his gun. His eyes swept the room in an instant, and his heart started beating again when he realized there were no bodies on the floor. But something had happened here. The nightstand lamp was on the carpet, and the nightstand itself was tipped against the wall. Debris littered the floor – a hairbrush, a hardcover book, lipstick.

A fight?

It didn't matter. They were gone.

Stride went back downstairs and tried to figure it out. If Blake hadn't killed them here, what had he done with them? His MO was murder, not kidnapping. If he had taken them, why? Where was he going?

Stride went out into the night air again. The sirens were closer. The police would find him soon, and he didn't want to be here. Every second put Serena and Claire at greater risk.

He went back to his Bronco. As he turned it around and headed for the street, he heard his cell phone ringing. He grabbed it from his pocket and saw Serena's number in the caller ID.

'*Where are you?*'

Serena froze. She heard Jonny's desperate voice in her ear as he answered. Blake was at the trunk, and she expected to feel a rush of air as he swung it open and see him looming above them.

'Wait, Jonny,' she hissed into the phone.

She listened and realized that Blake had continued walking past the trunk. He was somewhere close by, and she heard the jangle of metal, like a chain scraping through the links of a fence.

'Serena!' she heard in her ear.

'I'm here, I'm here,' she whispered.

'Where are you?' he repeated.

Serena knew their emotions were both running wild. She had to stay in control. Report the facts. They wouldn't have much time before Blake came back.

'I don't know yet. Claire and I are in the trunk of a white Impala.' She rattled off the license plate. 'We drove for twenty minutes or so, and we're stopped now.'

'Are you hurt?' Stride asked her.

'No. A little bruised, but we're both OK. He killed Rucci.'

'I know, I found the body. Do you know which direction he went?'

'I think we headed east, but I couldn't keep track.'

'Do you know what he's doing?' Stride asked.

'No. This feels like the end game, though.'

'How do I find you?'

Serena thought about it. 'I don't know.'

'If you keep the cell phone on, I might be able to have the phone company trace the signal,' Stride suggested.

'That'll take too long, Jonny.'

'I know.'

Serena listened. Blake was doing something outside. She heard a grinding of metal. 'It sounds like he's opening a fence now. I think we're going to drive inside. Hang on.'

She heard Blake's footsteps returning. She hesitated again, wondering if he would let them out of the trunk, but he continued back to the driver's door and got inside.

'He's back in the car,' Serena whispered. 'I don't think we have much time.'

'Can you keep the line open?'

'I'll try. We're tied up. I may be able to hold the phone without him seeing it.'

They were driving again. The Impala moved slowly, but the rocky ground caused the car to bump and jolt. Serena felt as if a prizefighter were delivering hammer blows to her kidneys. She heard Claire wince in pain beside her. They drove for less than a minute, and the car stopped.

'I think this is it. I have to go quiet now, Jonny. I don't know what you'll be able to hear. If he finds the phone, I'll try to shout something before he shuts it off.'

'I'll find you.'

The driver's door opened, and Blake came around to the trunk. Serena heard a click as the lock unlatched. The trunk opened, and she felt as if she could breathe again. The hot air outside felt cool compared to the stifling interior. Wherever they were, it was barely lit, but Serena still squinted, her eyes adjusting to something other than complete darkness. She saw Blake's outline above them. Behind him, stars in the night sky.

He reached in and took Claire by the upper body and lifted her out of the trunk. Her legs were rubbery, and she began to fall, and he had to support her. Claire turned and looked up and saw where they were, and she gasped.

Serena laced her fingers together, cupping the cell phone between her hands. She hoped she didn't accidentally cut the connection. Blake pulled her gun from his belt and pointed it at her. 'Please don't try anything.'

Serena nodded. 'It'll be easier if I roll over.'

'Do it.'

She shoved herself over on her stomach. Her face and breasts were squashed against the floor of the car, and her hands were between her legs, clutching the phone. She felt Blake take hold of her belt and T-shirt and drag her roughly over the edge of the trunk. She dangled there briefly until he took one of her legs and maneuvered it so it was outside the car and almost on the ground. He took her T-shirt and lifted her up again, and Serena was able to stumble out onto the gravel.

She turned around and looked skyward at the dark hotel.

'Welcome to the Sheherezade,' Blake said.

Forty-seven

It was a looted beauty, stripped bare, ready for the imploders to do their work. Where the grand entrance had been, a jagged hole was punched in the wall of the building, more than two stories tall, as if some comic book monster had fought its way inside. The windows on the lower floors were broken, leaving empty holes. Serena could see columns inside, their decorations gone, just rough concrete where carefully measured charges of dynamite would be inserted.

Higher up, the hotel looked as it always had. If they turned on the lights, it would be the same place she had driven by hundreds of times in the past two decades. It had been a jewel once, but that was long ago. Other towers dwarfed it now. Even before the wreckers had come, it was showing its age. Twenty stories held up by nostalgia and echoes. Sinatra's voice. The whine of the roulette wheel. Honeymooners making love. All of it about to become dust.

She had never been inside, never been this close. Until tonight.

'The Sheherezade,' Serena said as loudly as she could. *Did you hear that, Jonny?* She added, 'Why are we here, Blake?'

But she knew. This was Amira's house, where she danced, where she died. Blake was coming home.

He gestured them inside. Serena and Claire led the way. They had to make their way past rubble and glass. They walked right through the gaping hole into the lobby, as if they were checking in for the night.

'You can imagine what it was like, can't you?' Blake said.

Serena understood. It was easy to float back to the nineteen sixties here. Easier than it would have been a few weeks ago, when the hotel was still open and twenty-first-century guests were coming and going. Now they were alone with the ghosts. The furniture was all gone, the fixtures pulled off and sold at auction, everything taken away: chairs, wastebaskets, ashtrays, slot machines, paintings, craps tables, beer

275

taps. Only the skeleton was left. But even the bones of the building told a story. The geometric Arabian design in the wallpaper. The desert mural stretching across the ceiling. The etchings of Sheherezade herself in gold leaf on the elevator doors.

Blake pushed the button for the elevator.

'Where are we going?' Serena asked. She heard the singsong chime of the elevator as its doors slid open. It seemed odd to her that the elevator still worked in a hotel that was about to be destroyed, but then she realized it would probably work right up until the last day, as explosive experts checked their charges throughout the building.

She was afraid she would lose signal when the elevator doors closed.

'The roof?' she speculated loudly. 'Of course, that's where Amira was killed. In Walker's suite. That's where you're taking us.'

Jonny? Are you there?

The doors closed. The three of them were alone in the small compartment as it hummed upward. Blake pushed the button for the top floor, heading exactly where Serena had expected. But why?

'I don't see what you hope to accomplish, Blake. None of this will bring Amira back.'

'I'm here for the truth,' Blake said.

He didn't say anything else. The elevator was slow, or maybe it was just that her nerves were on a razor edge, not knowing Blake's next move. She watched the numbers for each floor illuminate one by one. Climbing higher and finally thudding to a halt. With another bird-like song, the doors opened again, and Blake forced them out into the hallway. They were opposite two double doors, painted gold.

There was no suite number on the doors. Maybe they had sold the room numbers at auction. Or maybe, if you were in the high roller suite, you simply knew where to go.

Blake twisted the handle. The door was unlocked. He pushed it open and waited as Serena and Claire passed him into the foyer of the suite. Without furniture, the room was vast, and it kept a lingering elegance, despite its barren appearance. Even the carpet had been rolled up and sold, along with the chandeliers. But there were stretches of delicate porcelain tile that had been left to be crushed in the demolition, presumably because it couldn't be safely removed for sale.

Serena had to imagine what the suite would have looked like when it was fully furnished. There were hints in the multicolored kaleidoscope of the tile and the pistachio colors of the painted ceiling. She thought of flowing draperies behind honey sofas laden with pillows. Wrought iron hanging lamps. Rich lapis vases. All that and a five-hundred-dollar hooker would make any high roller feel like a sultan.

'Keep going,' Blake said.

He pushed them through the deserted suite to the far wall leading to the outdoor patio. Serena slid through open stained-glass doors and stepped outside with Claire beside her. Blake followed. They were immediately bathed in a rainbow of light from the giant Sheherezade sign flashing above them. Each letter in the name was mounted on its own frame and must have been thirty feet tall. They flicked on and off in a rhythm of darkness and color that made Serena think of a nightclub dance floor.

There were twelve-foot walls on three sides of the huge patio, all decorated in Moroccan tile, leading up to the actual roof of the hotel. She could see a barbed wire fence on the roof, preventing trespassers from creeping down from the roof to the high roller suite. The fourth side of the patio, on her right, had a much lower wall, with a scalloped top. That wall faced the street and created the distinctive notch in the roof line of the Sheherezade.

The patio, like the rest of the suite, had been largely stripped of its decorations. There were still date trees that had been planted into stone circles cut directly into the floor, and marble fountains, now turned off, carved into the walls. The pool was filled with water that had turned dank and green from lack of care.

She noticed that Blake was staring into the murky water. Thinking of Amira.

'I'm sorry,' Claire said.

Blake looked up. 'For what?'

'That you lost your mother. I never knew my mother either. It's hard growing up that way.'

Blake was silent. Serena wondered how many times he had made secret visits to this place in the past few weeks. It wasn't his first time, she was sure of that. She could imagine him alone in the hotel, here by the pool, obsessing over his mother's death.

'I think I know what you want,' Claire continued. 'But you won't get it from him. I know him too well. He won't confess. He won't apologize. He'll never tell you the truth.'

'We'll see,' Blake said.

'He betrayed me, too, Blake. I hate him like you do.'

Serena thought again about the schism between Boni and Claire and wondered what terrible thing he had done.

'He hasn't rejected you,' Blake said. 'He hasn't denied your very existence.'

'No, it was worse than that.'

Claire's intensity made Blake hesitate. Then his face became a hard mask again. 'I guess we'll both find out how much you really mean to him,' he said. He pulled a phone from his pocket and dialed.

'Hello, Boni,' Blake said. 'You know who this is, don't you? I'm here where it all started. I'm home. If you go out on your nice penthouse balcony, you can see us all down here. By the pool. Where you had my mother murdered.'

Blake paused. 'What do I want?' he said. 'I want to see you face to face. Right here. You've got twenty minutes. Or else I kill your daughter.'

Forty-eight

Stride parked across the street, outside the hurricane fence. He stared through the windows of his truck up at the roof of the hotel, trying to see if anyone was watching from behind the parapet, but his eyes couldn't penetrate the shadows at night. He had to take the chance. He got out of the Bronco, pulled his gun, and crossed the street, taking cover behind the plywood wall that surrounded the property.

He made his way to the gate, which was unlocked now and open. He slipped inside the demolition site and took a quick survey of the lot. Other than Blake's Impala, there was nothing and no one around, just him and the eerie hotel shell marked for destruction. Stride jogged across the pavement. He stopped at the Impala, pulled a Swiss army knife from his pocket, and sliced through the valve on the right rear tire. Air began hissing out. He scuttled to the front of the car and did the same with the right front tire. Blake wasn't driving out of here.

The roof?

Those were the last words he had heard from Serena on her cell phone before the call died. But it was enough. He figured they were upstairs in the penthouse suite.

Stride made his way inside the hotel. He knew he was guilty of doing what Amanda had done, what he *never* did himself. He was going in alone, without backup, without calling Sawhill or anyone else to let them know where he was. This was different. Serena was up there. Stride didn't know what would happen if Blake felt trapped and surrounded, but he was deeply afraid that Claire and Serena would both wind up dead before they could mount a successful operation.

They might be dead now. But he couldn't afford to think like that.

He looked for the elevators and spotted the elegant bank of gold doors on his left. He headed in that direction, then ducked as he saw twin beams of headlights shining through the lobby as another car

279

drove into the hotel lot. When the car turned, he saw it was sleek and black, a limousine. Stride hurried past the gaping hole in the wall until he was out of sight. Across from the elevators he found a secluded hallway that had previously housed a bank of pay phones and waited there. Less than a minute later, he watched from the dark corner as a small, elegant old man strode purposefully for the elevators.

Boni Fisso.

'Boni!' Stride hissed before the man could push one of the buttons.

Boni turned around, startled. 'Detective Stride. Were you invited to this little party too?'

Stride shook his head. 'Serena's up there with Blake and Claire. She was able to let me know where they were.'

'Is Metro sending in an entire squad?' Boni asked, concerned.

'No, I haven't alerted anyone yet. I thought this might turn out better without a crowd.'

Boni inclined his head. 'My thoughts exactly. Thank you, Detective. I don't care what happens to Blake. The only thing that matters to me is getting Claire out safely.'

'Technically, I shouldn't even let you up there,' Stride said. 'You become another hostage as soon as you walk through that door. Blake wants you dead.'

'But you won't stop me,' Boni said. 'You want Serena back, just like I want Claire back. And after all, it's my hotel. Besides, if I'm not up there in five minutes, Blake will kill Claire and probably Serena, too. I think he's a man of his word.'

'Are they inside the suite?' Stride asked.

'No, on the terrace outside by the pool. That's where Amira was killed.'

'Tell me the layout.'

Boni described the high roller suite and the patio area in detail from memory, as if it were still 1964 and the hotel was brand new. The part that interested Stride was the fact that the roof of the hotel looked down on the patio area on three sides.

'Is there any access from the roof down to the terrace?' Stride asked.

Boni nodded. 'There's a locked gate and an emergency ladder near the parapet at the front of the hotel.'

'I don't suppose you have a key to the gate.'

Boni smiled. 'It's a combination lock. 1-2-1-6. My birthday. I like to make sure I have access to everything, Detective. Now we'd better go. The clock's ticking.'

They took the elevator up to the top floor of the hotel. Stride waited out of sight until Boni gave the all-clear sign that the doors to the penthouse suite were closed and Blake was nowhere to be seen. Stride followed Boni into the hallway. He noted a green EXIT sign at the far end of the hall to his left.

'The stairs are down there,' Boni said. 'You can go up to the roof. The door should be unlocked.'

'Try to keep him distracted. Keep him from looking toward the ladder.'

'I'll do my best. Good luck, Detective.'

'You too.'

Stride opened the door to the roof slowly and carefully, not knowing how well the sound would carry. He slipped outside and closed it behind him with a soft click. The hot wind off the mountains almost blew him over. He was exposed out here, with nothing except a few ventilator ducts to block the gusts.

The roof was bright, thanks to the massive Sheherezade sign stretching overhead, flashing its colors. A five-foot wall, capped by small onion domes, stretched all around the border of the roof, except for the segment where the roof dipped down and made a rectangular notch to offer a view for anyone on the elegant terrace one floor below. Stride saw the tall barbed wire fence completely surrounding the open area of the terrace and quickly spotted the locked gate near the front of the hotel.

He wanted to run, but he was afraid his footsteps would echo down to the patio. Instead, he walked as quickly as he could, putting each foot down softly. He stayed away from the fence until he was near the gate, to make sure no one could see him.

The gate was near the edge of the roof. The wind was even stronger there. Stride dropped to his knees and crawled closer. He inched his head up when he reached the fence and saw that the terrace itself was invisible from this angle. All he could see was the upper few feet of the patio wall, with its colorful miniature tiles. No one could see him here.

He checked out the lock, which was a combination lock, just as Boni had said. He hoped the old man was right about the numbers. The lock wasn't attached to the gate itself, but instead was looped through the links of a chain that was tightly wrapped between the gate and the frame. Stride carefully lined up the numbers 1-2-1-6 on the dials and tugged at the U-bar on the lock. It popped open. He slid the lock out of the chain and held the chain together with his fingers. After he hung the open lock on one of the holes in the mesh, he unwound the chain from the fence, taking care that the links didn't rattle together. It was hard to keep his hands steady while his body was being buffeted by the wind.

Finally, the chain was limp in his hands like a dead snake. He laid it carefully on the ground. The breeze began to open the gate on its own, and Stride froze when he heard the hinges squeal. He grabbed the gate and held it tight.

He stopped and listened. The fence creaked and whined in the wind. Slowly, he began opening the gate, moving it an inch at a time, trying to minimize the rusting grind of the hinges and blend it in with the other noises on the roof. When he had a few inches of clearance, he squeezed his body through and dropped back to his knees. He pulled the chain gently to the other side of the fence, then swung the gate shut again. He rewrapped the gate and the fence together with the chain and relocked it, so that the gate wouldn't swing wildly.

Stride was six feet from the sharp drop down to the terrace. He was at least twelve feet above the terrace floor. Immediately in front of him, almost butting up against the parapet, was a wrought iron ladder bolted to the roof. As Stride crept closer and examined it, he saw that the ladder appeared to be original equipment from 1964. So were the bolts. The metal was rusting.

He didn't know if the ladder would support his weight, and if it did, whether he could climb down silently.

But he didn't have a choice. There was no other way to the terrace, and it was too far to jump.

He lay flat on his stomach and stretched out his legs behind him as far as he could without colliding with the fence. He inched forward, pushing his face just past the edge so he could look down at the patio. His hair swirled in the breeze.

He heard voices below, by the pool.

Forty-nine

Serena saw Boni standing in the doorway of the suite. No matter how small or old the man was, he still carried an aura of power. It clung to him and fitted as neatly as his suit. Claire saw him too, and Serena tried to unravel the emotions in her face at seeing her father again. Love. Longing. And, most of all, contempt.

An unhappy family reunion.

Boni didn't even look at Blake. He looked right past him to Claire. Serena saw a father's love in his eyes, passionate and strong; he had missed Claire badly all these years. She saw something else, too, something she wouldn't expect from Boni Fisso. Guilt. It was everywhere in his face and how he held himself. He could barely look into her eyes, and he almost cringed under the fiery anger he saw Claire directing at him.

Not like Boni at all.

Blake scowled. 'I've waited a long time for this. To be face to face with you.'

Boni walked out into the open air of the terrace, the neon light playing on his features. He continued to ignore Blake. 'Are you all right?' he asked Claire.

'It's a little late to worry about that,' she answered.

'I'm sorry.'

'Don't even think about forgiveness. Not now. Not ever.'

Blake gestured at Serena and Claire with his gun. 'Both of you, get on your knees.'

'What are you doing?' Boni demanded.

'I think you know exactly what I'm doing,' Blake replied. 'You of all people.'

He was preparing to kill them, Serena thought. A tight ball of frustration and despair lodged in her heart again, just as it had when she first saw Blake in her bedroom. Serena knelt near the marble skirting

283

of the pool, with Claire right beside her. She kept a close eye on Blake, looking for a moment when he might be distracted and she could rush him.

Claire didn't look at Blake or the gun. She held her head high and stared angrily back at her father.

'Take off your coat,' Blake told Boni. 'I want to see that you're not carrying.'

'I always carry a gun for protection,' Boni said. 'It's in my right suit coat pocket. But I hope you don't think I can draw fast enough to shoot you.'

'Take the coat off,' Blake repeated.

Boni shrugged and complied. Serena wondered about the coldness of the man, that he could get a call in the middle of the night telling him that his daughter would be dead in twenty minutes, and he could still take the time to dress impeccably, right down to the perfect knot in his tie. Blake balled up the coat and threw it to the far side of the terrace, well away from them.

'I'm here,' Boni told Blake. 'What do you want?'

'What do I *want*? What the hell do you think I want?'

'I have no idea. You're nothing but a murderer.'

Blake shrugged. 'Like father, like son.'

Boni jabbed a finger at him. 'Don't you dare judge me. I've provided entertainment for millions of people. I've provided homes, food, and education for thousands of employees. I've built hospitals, parks, and day care centers. Right here on this ground, where we're standing now, the greatest resort in the city is going to rise up. So don't you try to compare your pathetic little life to mine, you worthless piece of shit.'

'You *made* me what I am!' Blake spat the words out.

'That's bullshit. So you got dealt a tough hand. Big fucking deal. I was born with nothing, and I built everything myself. If you're still a sniveling child hiding in the closet in Reno, don't blame me.'

Blake took a step forward and shoved his gun hard into the skin of Claire's forehead. Claire's eyes widened in terror, and she tried to back away, but Blake grabbed her by the throat.

'If you don't give a shit about your son,' he said, 'maybe you give a shit about your daughter.'

Boni's voice was like ice. 'Let her go.'

'*Tell me about Amira.*'

'Let go of my daughter,' Boni repeated.

Blake yanked the gun away and pointed it at Boni. 'Amira,' he said again.

'What do you want to know?' Boni asked.

284

'Why did you make her give up her baby?'

Boni hesitated. Serena could see it again – the calculations always spinning in his mind as he looked for the best odds. As he looked for a winning hand.

'*Our* baby,' Boni replied quietly. 'I was the father.'

'Do you think I don't know, *Dad*?' Blake said. 'That makes it even worse.'

Boni shook his head. 'I had no choice. Eva, my wife, knew about Amira. Eva hadn't been able to get pregnant herself, and she was furious to find out that Amira was going to have a baby. My baby. She wanted it to go away. I mean, really go away. An abortion. But I wasn't about to do that. So instead I sent Amira away to have the baby, and I led Eva to believe that Amira had had the abortion and was in Paris getting over it. Getting over me.'

'Amira wanted to keep me,' Blake said.

Boni hesitated, and his eyes flicked to Claire. 'Yes, of course, she was devastated to give up her child.'

Serena remembered what Boni had told them before, that Amira couldn't wait to be rid of the screaming brat. That she had no interest in the child at all. Had that been a lie? Or was he now trying to spare Blake's feelings and talk him down?

'Then Eva did finally get pregnant,' Boni went on. 'While Amira was away. It made me wonder if she'd been taking precautions all along and not telling me.'

'But Eva died,' Blake said. 'She died giving birth to Claire, and you had your daughter. And I was in the hands of a monster. Why didn't you come get me then? How could you turn your back on your own son?'

'No one *knew* it was my baby. Just me, Amira, and Eva. I couldn't very well admit it at that point. Particularly—' Boni stopped.

Blake finished the sentence. 'Particularly because you *murdered Amira*.'

Boni was silent.

'Tell me what happened,' Blake insisted.

'I have nothing to say about that.'

'*Tell me.*'

'It won't change a thing.'

Blake shoved the gun back in Claire's face. 'TELL ME.'

Blake was breathing heavily. Serena saw that he was focused on Boni and paying little attention to what was going on around him. She began to slowly move her feet, so she was in a better position to leap when he gave her the opportunity.

That was when she noticed something in the darkness over Blake's shoulder. She saw movement on the roof, in the corner of the terrace. For the first time, she realized there was a narrow ladder stretching along the tiled wall, and someone had appeared at the skyline, climbing onto the first step.

Her heart raced.

Jonny.

Stride knew this was the best time. Blake was absorbed in the intense argument with Boni, and he wasn't thinking about anything going on behind him or above him.

He thought about taking a shot at Blake from the roof. *If you've got the shot, take the shot, and make the shot.* That's what Sawhill would say. Put an end to it right now. But the distance, the wind, and the crazy neon light were working against him. Claire and Serena were both in the path. He couldn't see clearly. If he fired and missed, or if Blake moved, he could hit either one of them, and that wasn't a risk he was willing to take.

He crouched low and turned around so his back was to the terrace. He took hold of the iron railing of the ladder with one hand; his other hand held his gun. When he looked down, he thought he saw Serena glance his way and then turn quickly back to Blake.

The wind buffeted him. He felt the railing quiver under his touch. The ladder was loose and unsteady, and he didn't know what would happen when he put two hundred pounds of weight on the platform. He swung his right leg over the edge. His foot gingerly touched the topmost step. He tried to test it, leaning his weight back into the step, and he felt the ladder sway under the gusts and the bulk of his body.

But it held.

He gripped the railing tightly, looping his arm and wrist round the metal for more leverage. He kept his gun trained on Blake, but his arm kept jostling, losing his aim. He swung his left leg over now, and both feet were squarely on the top step of the ladder. He could feel vibration running up his body through his legs.

He took a step down, climbing backwards, one-handed.

Then everything fell apart.

The atmosphere seemed to yawn, taking a deep breath and exhaling it across the notch in the roof like a tornado. The gust slapped him in the back and drove his whole body against the fragile ladder. His wrist struck the railing, and it popped his gun out of his hand. He watched in horror as it tumbled downward toward the terrace. He lurched off balance as the wind shifted and sucked him backward.

The rusting bolt that held the ladder to the wall popped, and a moment later Stride was flying. The ladder spun in a lazy arc toward the parapet. He hung on with one hand, feeling the iron buck and swing as his weight crushed all of its pressure onto the last rusting bolt.

With an awful grinding, the bolt gave way.

The ladder began pitching forward at its middle, metal tearing and bending. Stride looked down, falling, and saw the onion domes stretched along the top of the wall and, beyond them, twenty stories of air.

Serena saw the gun fly out of Jonny's hands. She braced her left foot against the marble and stared at Blake, waiting. When the gun clattered to the ground, Blake instinctively twisted to look behind him, and in the same instant Serena sprang forward, shooting up from her knees. She rammed Blake with her fists clenched together and drove her arms up into his abdomen. The gun flew from his fingers and skittered away behind him. Blake tumbled backward, and the momentum carried Serena with him, both of them spilling off their feet. With her hands tied, Serena couldn't break her fall, and the hard ground flattened her arms against her chest, knocking the wind from her lungs. She couldn't breathe.

She tried to get up and made it to her knees. Her eyes searched the shadows.

Where was the gun?

She felt air coming back slowly. Her chest swelled. Blake's gun was only a few feet away, almost within reach. She clawed out for it and then tried to stand up, but before she could get to her feet, she felt an electric shock of light and pain through her skull. Blake's elbow crashed against her head, knocking her over. Then Blake was climbing over her, scrambling for the gun.

The parapet zoomed up into Stride's face. He hung onto the railing as the ladder disintegrated, swinging him over the big drop to the street. For an instant, he dangled there, his feet hanging free, and he felt his insides turn to water. The iron squealed and protested and dropped lower. His grip on the railing was slippery from sweat. Stride hunted for a foothold, feeling nothing but space, and then finally he scraped the edge of the wall with his shoe. He shifted his weight and managed to put half of one foot on the ledge.

For a few seconds that felt timeless, he hung on, caught between the back and forth swirls of the wind. Finally, a gust roared in, pushing him toward the hotel, and Stride let his hand slip from the iron. He bent and reached for one of the stone onion domes, but he was beyond that already, tumbling, falling, landing with a jolt and rolling onto the terrace.

The impact dizzied him, and he swayed as he got to his feet. He looked quickly for his gun but didn't see it. Then he saw Blake scrabbling across the marble and saw another gun lying almost within the killer's reach.

Stride charged, just as Blake curled his hand around the butt of the pistol.

With a flash of light and a deafening noise, Blake fired. Stride felt a searing pain streak across his leg, and he half dived, half collapsed across Blake. He heard a snap and realized it was Blake's wrist breaking as Stride's shoulder fell across his arm. Blake choked back a cry of pain, and the gun dropped from his hand. Stride twisted around, lunging for the gun, but Blake bucked like a bronco and threw Stride off his back. Blake picked up the gun again; he could barely hold it now. Stride rolled away and then stood up. Blake was still prone on the ground, trying to raise the gun, and Stride kicked his broken wrist hard with the side of his foot, causing a new bellow of pain from Blake and sending the gun spinning toward the pool.

Stride reached down and yanked Blake to his feet. The killer's body was like rubber, and his face looked bruised and dazed. Stride recoiled to send a fist across Blake's jaw, then realized he had been suckered as Blake brought a knee viciously up into Stride's groin. As hot pain raced through his body, Stride staggered back and saw Blake's left forearm slicing backhand toward his head. He tried to dodge the blow, but it connected hard on his cheek and sent him reeling, stumbling to his knees.

Serena saw Stride's gun lying on the ground a few feet from the roof wall, near the twisted remnants of the ladder. As Blake spun round, he followed her eyes, and he saw it, too. They both ran. Serena didn't have her wind back completely, and she realized that Blake was faster, that he would get there first. She turned and dived for him, trying to take him down. Blake saw her coming and swerved, then leaped to clear her body. His foot became tangled in her legs. He pulled free, but he lost his balance, stumbled, and fell.

She saw that Jonny was on his feet again. He was running for the gun too.

Then Serena felt a powerful arm snake around her neck and yank her up to her knees by her throat, sealing off her windpipe in a crushing grip. She fought and couldn't breathe. Blake had her locked in a stranglehold.

'Stride!' Blake shouted.

She saw Jonny freeze. She felt as if her eyes were bulging out of her head.

'I'll kill her.'

She wanted to tell him to *go for the gun*. Fuck Blake. Put an end to this. But she couldn't make a sound; all she could do was watch the world start to spin and darken. Her limbs felt as powerless as a marionette's. She wondered if it had been like this for Amira, dying here.

She heard Blake's labored breathing. His arm didn't loosen. He was killing her, choking her second by second. The blood began roaring in her brain, and her nerve ends exploded like firecrackers, causing a pain in her head powerful enough to burst open her skull.

Her eyes met Jonny's. He floated in her vision and did somersaults. *Go for the gun, Jonny.*

Jonny took a step toward the gun.

'I'll kill her,' Blake repeated.

Serena felt his other arm slide over the top of her head, grab her hair. He was going to twist her neck and snap her spine. But through the blackness that was falling down on her, Serena realized that Blake could barely hold her head with his other hand. *Snap.* His wrist was broken. Fragile. Vulnerable.

She hoped she could stretch her bound arms over her head. She told her limbs what to do, and somewhere between the confused impulses shooting from her brain, her arms obeyed. She reached up with her bound hands and took hold of Blake's wrist on the top of her head and clamped down on the bone as hard as she could.

Blake screamed. Serena jerked on his wrist. For just an instant, Blake's other arm came loose, and Serena wriggled free, gasping for air, feeling blood rush back to her head. She stumbled, unable to keep her balance.

Five feet away, she watched Jonny run for the gun. So did Blake.

Stride saw Blake coming and was on him before he could reach for the gun. He threw Blake against the parapet so hard the killer slammed into it and bounced off. Stride was waiting and threw a sledgehammer punch directly into Blake's face that snapped his head back. Blood sprayed from his mouth. He staggered back into the wall, and Stride followed, hitting him again.

Stride felt a stinging, bone-deep pain in his hand. He realized he had probably broken a couple of fingers.

Blake crumpled to his knees, and his head slumped forward. He teetered and then collapsed on the ground, not moving. Stride took a deep breath and reached around behind his back to snag his handcuffs.

He looked down. Something was wrong.

Behind him, Serena saw it, too, and shouted. *'Where's the gun?'*

Stride realized he couldn't see his gun any more. Blake had deliberately pivoted his body to fall on top of it. Stride saw Blake's arm moving and saw the man pushing himself off the ground, the gun in his other hand.

Blake aimed the gun, not at Stride, not at Serena, but at himself.

He pressed it to the side of his head. He could barely keep it steady.

'Drop it, Blake,' Stride told him.

Blake dragged himself to his feet. He staggered back to the wall. Stride and Serena edged closer from two sides.

'Give us the gun,' Serena said.

Blake gave them a bloody smile. He put his bad hand around one of the onion domes atop the parapet and braced himself, grimacing in pain, as he pulled a leg up onto the wall. The gun wobbled in his grip. He pulled his other leg up and stood, precariously balanced on the slim stone wall. Blake swayed, the wind toying with him.

He took the gun away from his head and casually tossed it off the top of the building.

Stride took a step forward, but Blake held up his hand, stopping him. Blake shook his head. He took a long look at the ground below.

'Amira,' he said.

Blake leaned into the wind. He spread his arms wide.

'Don't do it, brother.'

A sharp voice from the terrace stopped him in the moment before he let go. Blake looked around and steadied himself on the wall. So did Stride and Serena. Stride couldn't believe what he saw.

It was Claire.

She was standing by the pool, with Serena's gun in her outstretched hands. She was pointing it at Boni's head.

Fifty

'Claire, what the hell are you doing?' Serena demanded.

Claire didn't look at her. She stared down the sights of the gun at her father and walked toward him step by step, slowly, until the gun was an inch from his eyes. Her whole body was trembling. There was hatred in her face and a world of hurt gushing out like oil from a well.

Boni didn't even seem to notice the gun. His blue eyes and her blue eyes were locked in a duel. Claire was crying, and she struggled to keep the gun level.

'Now you know what it felt like for me,' she said. 'Powerless.'

'What do you want, Claire?'

'Tell Blake the truth,' she said. 'You owe him that.'

'I don't owe him anything,' Boni snapped.

Claire shook her head. 'You murdered Amira, didn't you? Because she had the fucking gall to try to get out from under your thumb. Because she didn't want to be owned and controlled any more.'

'I loved Amira,' Boni told her.

'Everything you love gets hurt,' Claire retorted.

'I can't talk about it.'

'It was forty years ago,' she insisted. 'No one can touch you now.'

'You may as well kill me, Claire, if that's what you want. I'm not going to say anything about Amira.'

'Is that what you want? You want me to pull the trigger?'

'For God's sake, stop this,' Serena pleaded. She started to move toward them, and Boni held up one hand to stop her.

'It's all right, Detective,' Boni said. He focused on Claire. 'Kill me if you want, sweetheart. I just wish you wouldn't throw away your own life to do it.'

'Does my life mean more to you?' Claire asked. She tilted her head back and shoved the barrel of the gun under her own chin. 'How about now?'

'Claire! No!' Serena shouted.

Boni looked at his daughter. Serena thought his eyes were filling up with tears. 'You're so beautiful. Just like your mother.'

'Do you think that kind of shit will work on me now?' Claire asked. 'What's next? You'll tell me how much you love me? That doesn't mean a thing.'

'I do love you.'

'Do you think I won't do it?' Claire demanded, pushing the gun harder against her skin. 'Is that it? I'm *your* child. You know I will.'

'If you thought it would give me enough pain, yes, I know you would.'

'Look at us!' Claire said. 'This is the family you've built. Look at your son on the wall. That's what you did to him. And you know damn well what you did to me.'

Boni recoiled as if he had been struck. 'Please, Claire, don't go there.'

'Oh, I'm sorry. Am I airing our dirty laundry in public? Am I embarrassing you?'

'Claire,' Boni begged her. 'No.'

It was as if Claire smelled a wound and steered for it like a shark. 'You *knew* what that bastard did to me.'

Serena didn't know who Claire was talking about. But Boni obviously did. He was visibly shaken.

'It was a terrible misunderstanding,' Boni said.

'Misunderstanding? You accused me of being drunk. You said I led him on. You knew that was a lie.'

'I didn't want to believe what he had done to you.' Boni raised his arms, reaching out to her, trying to touch her.

Claire stepped back and flung the gun into the pool, where it splashed into the opaque water. She screamed, '*He raped me!*'

'Claire, we can't talk about this. Not here.'

'Oh, no, no, of course not. It might endanger the empire. It might hurt *him*. My God, he raped your own daughter, and *you covered it up.*'

'I'm so sorry. So very sorry.'

'You had a choice. Me or him. But that was never a choice, was it? It's always been him. Everything you've ever done, it's been to protect him.'

Who? Serena wanted to shout.

'We talked about this,' Boni said. 'You told me you understood.'

'Of course I understood. I was asking you to expose a lifetime of lies. You would have lost everything. Gone to prison. So I was the good girl, and I shut up. I shut up, even though I had nightmares for

292

years. I shut up, even though I was sick and scared every time I saw his face. I shut up, and I saved you.'

'It was more than ten years ago, Claire,' Boni asked. 'What can I do? How can I finally make this right?'

'You can never make it right. But just once in your life, you can tell the truth. You can face up to something you've done. What happened to Amira?'

Boni looked stricken. 'I can't talk about that.'

'Why not? You say you don't owe Blake. But you sure as hell owe me.'

'I know I do. But you can't ask me that, Claire. You can't.'

Claire looked as if she would explode in frustration. If the gun had still been in her hand, Serena thought she would have killed Boni. Or herself. Or both. Claire turned away, and her shoulders wrenched as she sobbed.

Boni closed his eyes. His daughter's pain seemed to stab him and open up old wounds. 'It was him, Claire,' he said quietly. 'Back then. With Amira.'

Claire swung back in disbelief. 'No.'

Boni nodded. 'That was when it started between him and me. I made him. Like Frankenstein.'

'*Mickey* killed Amira?'

Boni's face contorted as if Claire had thrown open Pandora's box and all the demons had flown out and scattered. As if, by saying the name, she had taken the gun and shot him.

Serena's mind raced, and she mouthed the word at Stride. *Mickey?*

Claire stepped forward and slapped him across the face, so hard that the old man lost his balance. 'You knew what kind of monster he was. How could you let him near me? How could you ask me to go out with him?'

'So much time had passed, Claire. I thought he was different. I thought I could trust him.'

'He's still more important to you than I am, isn't he? After all these years. Of course he is. This is still about the empire. The Orient. The capstone to your life, and every brick of it built on suffering and violence and death.'

'Stop it, Claire.'

Claire shouted in his face, her lip curling in contempt. '*Mickey!* That's our big secret, Daddy. He's been hung around your neck – and mine – for forty years.'

Boni shook his head. 'He's still there, Claire. This doesn't change a thing. You know that.'

'Yes, it does. It's over. There's going to be a trial. Blake's trial. It's all going to come out. Amira. Mickey. You. Everything.'

'I can't let that happen.'

'It's out of your control now.'

Boni's voice was weary. 'Nothing is out of my control, Claire.'

He reached into the back pocket of his pants and pulled out a pack of European cigarettes. He slid one into his hand, and then hunted in another pocket and emerged with an old-fashioned Zippo lighter.

'Nothing,' he said.

He flicked the lighter, and even in the wind, it threw up a tiny flame.

A second later, on the ledge, Blake jerked like a toy dancer jolted with electricity, his eyes growing wide. Serena saw him stagger in confusion. A stain of red opened up on his shirt, dripping in trails down his chest. Another instant later, the sound wave of a distant crack rolled across the terrace. Blake seemed to fold in on himself. He sagged, his face went pale, and he vanished backward on the long fall that led to the parking lot below.

PART FOUR

MICKEY

Fifty-one

Stride knew they had problems when no one took their statements on the roof.

It was a crime scene. Shots had been fired. A man, however evil, however many others he had killed, lay dead on the ground far below them. Deliberately murdered. They should be spilling their guts now, explaining what happened and how it happened for the inevitable investigation and trial to follow.

It didn't work out that way.

Sawhill arrived and took charge of the crime scene personally, which meant, for the most part, keeping people out. He spent the first twenty minutes talking to Boni Fisso, not his own detectives. The two men hugged like old friends. That was the first bad sign. Then Sawhill asked a uniformed officer to take Claire home to her apartment. Not Serena. Not Stride. Claire looked longingly back at the two of them but allowed herself to be led away.

'You two,' Sawhill finally said. 'Why don't you go get some sleep?'

The next bad sign.

'You need our statements,' Stride protested blandly.

'It can wait until tomorrow. You've both had a hell of a night. Job well done. You got a mass murderer off the street. Now get out of here, and we'll talk in the morning.' Sawhill smiled at them, trying to act like the proud parent, but Stride knew it was a politician's smile. He was in damage control mode. The whitewash was coming down, painting over the sins, preparing to detonate them once and for all next week along with the Sheherezade. But Stride was too tired to complain. The bandaged flesh wound on his calf was throbbing. He hurt all over. He was happy to leave.

He and Serena went home. They didn't have the energy to talk. They fell into bed and were soon unconscious, and the only sensation that managed to penetrate Stride's brain was that the tangled sheets smelled

297

of Claire's perfume. He drifted away and had erotic dreams that were interrupted by violence, by people falling, by screams of rape.

They slept for ten hours.

It was early afternoon when they made it into the station. There was a buzz of exhilaration inside the building. Case solved. Cops came up and clapped them on the back, congratulated them. High fives all around. *Blake took a dive. Way to go.* Sawhill was there too, still smiling as he ushered them into his office. It was the same politician's smile he had worn last night, and Stride knew they were about to be rolled.

As he closed the door, Sawhill said the unthinkable to his assistant. 'Hold my calls.'

Stride and Serena settled into the chairs in front of Sawhill's desk. The lieutenant didn't pick up his stress ball; he seemed to be stress-free today. 'Congratulations, both of you,' he told them. 'Governor Durand asked me to extend his personal thanks.'

They didn't reply.

'I don't need to tell you how sorry I am about Amanda,' Sawhill continued. 'But you got the guy. Good for you. And the taxpayers don't have to pay his room and board for the next forty years. Even better.'

'Who's running the investigation now?' Stride asked.

'What investigation?'

'Into Blake's death.'

'Oh, we wrapped that up last night,' Sawhill replied. His smile grew wider, as if it was his nose growing longer.

'Wrapped it up?' Stride asked. 'Who killed him?'

'The head of Boni's security agency. David Kamen. He's a sharp-shooter, as you'll recall. Fortunately, Boni thought to take precautions when Blake called him, and he had Kamen take position in the Charlcombe Towers opposite the Sheherezade.'

Stride nodded. He had figured that. 'Is Boni under arrest?'

Sawhill looked shocked. 'Whatever for?'

'He had Blake killed. This was an assassination. Blake was *secure*, sir. Boni gave a green flag for Kamen to kill him, because he didn't want dirt coming out at Blake's trial about Amira's death.'

'You're mistaken, Detective. I talked to Kamen personally last night. He had Blake under his scope the entire time, and he shot him when Blake began reaching for a backup gun he had in an ankle holster.'

'Blake never moved,' Stride said.

'Are you absolutely sure about that? I understand you were focused on Boni and Claire at the time. Good thing Kamen was there, Detective. This could have been another mistake on your part. A fatal one. Blake could have had his gun out and taken you both out in less than a second.'

Stride frowned. He couldn't swear in court that his attention hadn't wavered, at least for a second, during the confrontation between Boni and Claire. A tiny space of time was all Blake would have needed.

Except it was a lie. They all knew it.

'We found a gun on the ground near the body,' Sawhill continued. 'A Walther. Small but deadly. Blake still had the holster strapped to his ankle.'

Isn't that convenient, Stride thought. 'So that's it?' he asked.

'That's it.'

'Who's Mickey?' Stride asked. He watched Sawhill's eyes but couldn't read anything in the man's level stare.

'Mickey? I don't know what you're talking about.'

'What about Amira?' Stride persisted.

Sawhill smiled. 'Like I told you at the very beginning, Detective, Amira Luz was killed by a deranged fan.'

Stride lit a cigarette. Serena looked at him, frowning.

They sat in a park a few blocks from the station. It was late afternoon. The heatwave had finally broken, and the October sunshine felt like another day in paradise. Mid-seventies, endless blue sky. The smog was taking a day off, leaving the mountains sharp and crisp on the horizon.

He was half hooked again, and he knew it. The smoke in his lungs felt like an old friend he had missed. He didn't look back at Serena. 'I wouldn't say anything if you had a drink,' he said.

'Like hell. You'd rip it out of my hand and pour the bottle down the sink.'

'OK, yeah, I would,' he admitted.

Serena reached over and grabbed the cigarette from his lips. She flicked it to the ground and crushed it under her foot. A few embers fizzled in the dirt. Stride felt an immediate longing and wondered if he could win the war twice.

'You haven't asked anything about me and Claire,' Serena said. She squinted into the sun, and Stride saw her tongue flick over her dry lips.

'That's true,' Stride replied flatly. It had been in and out of his thoughts all day. The sweet aroma of Claire in their bed. But he wasn't going to say anything. He waited, needing a cigarette.

'I get it,' Serena said. 'It's up to me. Tell you or not tell you. A lot of guys couldn't live without knowing.'

'I'm not saying I can,' Stride said.

She studied her fingernails and looked incredibly nervous.

'We had sex,' Serena told him.

The words hung there between them, and Stride tried to read Serena's face. She was embarrassed. Guilty. Scared. Proud.

'I mean, we were going to have sex,' she rushed on. 'Blake interrupted before anything could really happen. But that doesn't matter. We had started. I was going to let her make love to me. I was going to make love to her. That's the truth.'

She wanted him to tell her everything was all right. He hoped the blankness on his own face didn't register as disapproval.

'Are you going to say something?' Serena asked.

Stride said the first thing that occurred to him. 'I have a raging hard-on.'

Serena burst out laughing. Stride did, too. When the laughter died away, she kissed him hard and then whispered, 'What about the rest of you?'

'It doesn't change anything for me. The real question is you.'

'I feel like I purged a demon. But I was afraid I'd lose you because of it.'

'That wasn't going to happen.'

'I'm sorry,' she told him.

'You don't need to be, not for this.'

'I need to tell Claire the truth. Let her down gently.'

'Have you talked to her?' Stride asked.

Serena shook her head. 'I'm worried. I tried her home, her cell phone, the club. Nothing. I don't know where she is.'

'Boni has her under wraps.'

'That's what scares me.'

'I don't think he'd actually harm her,' Stride said.

'No? He killed his own son. I don't want her winding up as a so-called suicide. "My daughter was upset, couldn't handle the stress", that kind of shit.'

'You really care about her.'

Serena hesitated. 'Yes, I do. I could love her. But I don't.'

Stride was surprised at the depth of relief he felt, hearing her say those words. 'She wanted the truth to come out. Now it's probably not going to. Can Claire live with that?'

'Boni won't give her a choice.'

'How about us? Can we live with the whitewash?'

Serena shrugged. 'It's not the first time, is it?'

Stride heard and understood the message. They had resolved the murder of Rachel Deese, the case that had brought them together, in a way that left part of the truth hidden. At Stride's request. It was their secret.

'Sometimes politics and money win out, Jonny,' she added.

'In Vegas?'

'Everywhere.'

'The bigger question is whether he'll let *us* live,' Stride said. 'We heard things we weren't supposed to hear.'

'Mickey.'

'Exactly. Whoever he is, he's at the heart of Boni's power.'

'But he must have been a kid back then,' Serena said.

'Helen Truax said he was a pool boy. A lifeguard, looking to get lucky with gamblers' wives. Maybe he tried to seduce Amira, and things got out of hand.'

Serena shook her head. 'No way. He was with Amira because Boni wanted him there. He called Rucci when the job was done. The fight story was just a ruse.'

'And from that day forward, Boni owned his soul,' Stride said. He took out his cell phone and began dialing. 'Let's find out who the bastard is.'

'Helen didn't know.'

'Maybe Moose does.'

Stride heard the big comedian's voice on the phone, and he re-introduced himself. Moose began to fall over himself, congratulating Stride on catching Tierney's killer. Stride let the man gush. He could imagine his eyebrows dancing with joy.

'I have a question for you,' Stride said when Moose finally took a breath.

'Anything.'

'Do you remember a lifeguard at the Sheherezade back in nineteen sixty-seven named Mickey?'

There was a long pause on the phone, and Moose began to back-track. 'There were a lot of college kids around back then.'

'That's not an answer, Moose. Did you know him?'

'Why? What's this about?'

'It's just a loose end we're trying to clear up.'

He could hear Moose breathing. 'Well, I don't think he makes a big secret of it. He put himself through law school working at the Sheherezade. A lot of the big shots did.'

Stride began to feel uneasy. He wondered if he had made a mistake that would get him and Serena killed. 'So you've stayed in touch with him?'

'Of course. Mickey Durand is the best damn friend the entertainment industry has ever had in this state. God and the voters willing, he'll be re-elected as governor next month.'

Fifty-two

Beatrice Erdspring punched the volume button on the television remote control repeatedly, but it didn't make any difference to the sound. The newscasters kept whispering, and she couldn't hear a thing.

'Oh, for heaven's sake,' she grumbled, pulling the cream-colored blanket up around her nightgown.

She tried several channels, but the sound was all the same, so she went back to the local CBS station, where that nice Hispanic man with the black hair read the news. Raul was his name. He looked strong and trustworthy, and he had an attractive mustache. Her husband, Emmett, had always worn a mustache.

It wasn't like Raul to whisper, but even when Beatrice craned her neck and cupped a hand behind her ear, she could barely make out a word.

'Speak up, Raul,' she said to the television.

Beatrice was frustrated, because she recognized the attractive woman in the old photograph on the screen, and she wanted to hear what they were saying about her.

'Can you hear that, Rowena?' Beatrice called to her roommate. 'I think the television is broken again. Or maybe the remote control needs batteries.'

Rowena was in the other bed in the one-room studio they shared in the assisted living facility in Boulder City. Beatrice looked over and saw that Rowena was sleeping again. She slept most of the time. Beatrice had gone through three roommates in the past year, and she was afraid that Rowena would be gone soon too. It was too bad, because when she was awake, Rowena was a stitch. She had raised six children on a dairy farm in Iowa, and the stories she told could keep you laughing for hours.

Like the one about her eight-year-old daughter trying to 'milk' a bull. Well, wasn't that a surprise for both of them!

Beatrice stared at the television again and sighed. Raul had moved on to another story.

She looked out the window at the main street of Boulder City. Cars whizzed by, heading off to Lake Mead or Hoover Dam. Flora had taken the residents on an outing to Lake Mead the previous month, and although the wind had mussed her hair, it had been lovely to see the water again. Not that Lake Mead was as pretty as Lake Tahoe, where she had lived for so many years. But it was good to be outside again. She enjoyed the heat, although she did miss the chill of those winter nights long ago, when she and Emmett would snuggle under the quilt together. But she couldn't handle the cold any more. That was why she had retired in the southern part of the state.

Flora came running into the room, her hands over her ears. She made a beeline for the television, clicked it off at the switch, and then put a hand over her heart, breathing heavily. She wagged a finger and said something that Beatrice couldn't hear.

'You're mumbling again, Flora,' Beatrice told her. 'Speak up, will you?'

Flora came up to the side of the bed. She looked as if she was shouting, but the words were far away. 'Bea, honey, you forgot to put in your hearing aids.'

'Oh, dear.'

Flora rustled in the nightstand drawer by Beatrice's bed and triumphantly produced two beige-colored plugs. Flora helped Beatrice insert them in her ears and then stood back, laughing. Flora was a three-hundred-pound Filipino woman, and her body jiggled all over when she laughed.

'Is that better, honey?'

'You don't need to shout, Flora,' Beatrice said, which made Flora laugh again.

'Do you want the television back on?' Flora asked.

Beatrice shook her head. 'No, I missed the story I wanted to see.'

'What story was that?'

'Well, I missed it, so I don't know! But they were showing a photograph of a lovely girl I knew back when I was a nurse.'

'That's nice,' Flora said. She was bustling around the room, straightening up, and had stopped paying attention. 'Did you see they caught that terrible man? The one who killed all those people? Shot him off the top of a building. Bang, bang.'

Flora fussed at the bedside. She nudged Beatrice forward, then grabbed and fluffed her two pillows with a meaty brown fist. 'It's romantic, though. He killed all those people to get revenge for his mother. His mother! My boys, it's hard enough getting them to show up for my birthday party.'

'Who was his mother?' Beatrice asked.

'What? Oh, one of those showgirls from the sixties. She had to give up her baby. Isn't that tragic? Can you imagine? I would go crazy giving up one of my babies. I'd be happy if they were living here when they were fifty. Of course, the way my boys are going, they might well be!'

Beatrice frowned. 'Are you talking about Amira Luz?'

But Flora was already on her way out of the room and didn't look back. Beatrice was alone again, except for Rowena, who was snoring. She remembered now – that was why she had taken her hearing aids out. Rowena snored like a 727 on take-off.

Beatrice thought about Amira Luz and smiled. It had been so funny to see the beautiful, pregnant woman on the balcony of the suite, trying to do these strange, erotic dance moves while her bulging stomach got in the way.

Flora must have been talking about Amira. Why else would her picture be on television after all these years?

It didn't make sense, though. Flora must have got it wrong.

Beatrice turned on the television again and quickly lowered the volume with the remote. She waved at Raul, then began switching channels to see if someone else would have the story. Amira? No. They had made a mistake.

Fifty-three

The invitation came, just as Stride expected. The following night at ten o'clock, they found themselves back in the bone-white foyer of Boni's penthouse suite in the Charlcombe Towers. Boni himself let them in through the double doors and guided them into the mammoth cowboy room. The light was low, just a few pale lamps and the glow from the tower outside.

Boni wore a dark suit again. Stride caught the aroma of cigars and cologne. He still had an easy, charming smile, and Stride wondered if he was like the Cheshire cat, who could disappear and leave only the smile behind to fool people. He used a two-handed grip to shake both their hands.

'You saved our lives, Detectives. Me and Claire. I felt I owed you a celebratory drink.'

'That's why we're here?' Stride asked, suspicion in his voice.

'Of course. You will drink with me, won't you? You're certainly not on duty now.'

Message received and understood, Stride thought. This was all off the record.

'Ms Dial, I know you'd prefer mineral water or juice, of course. Detective Stride, what about you? Brandy?'

Stride nodded.

'I have an excellent brandy I think you'll like,' Boni told Stride. He retired to the bar to pour a glass, as well as three fingers of whiskey for himself.

Stride took a sip. It seemed to melt on his tongue.

'Good, huh?' Boni asked.

'Outstanding.'

'Where's Claire?' Serena asked.

'I thought she needed a break,' Boni said. 'These last few days have been stressful for her. I flew her down to St Thomas. She'll be back soon.'

'I'd like to talk with her,' Serena said.

'Of course. I'll give you the number for the resort before you go. I'm sure she'd love to hear from you.'

Stride took another sip of brandy. He wondered how this game was played. Who would start? How would they dance? What it really got down to was who would say the name first. It was foolish to pretend they didn't all know what this was about.

As it turned out, Boni moved the first pawn.

'There's someone here who would like to meet you,' he told them. 'I bet you'd like to meet him, too.'

Stride heard a swish of movement behind them, and when he turned he saw the silver-haired governor of Nevada joining them from one of the interior rooms of the suite.

'Mickey,' Boni called. 'Come on in here. Meet those detectives who saved my neck.'

Mike Durand was tall and imposing. He was heavily suntanned, but his ageing skin was tight and unblemished. A facelift, probably, with laser surgery to burn off the blotches of sixty-five years. And capped teeth, too, that gave him a huge alabaster smile. He was dressed in a black tuxedo that practically glowed, and he already had a whiskey in his hand, twice the size of Boni's. Stride also noticed something that he hadn't spotted before when he saw the man on television or in photographs. Durand had the meanest, most cutthroat eyes he had ever seen, worse than any hardened criminal. He could smile as he slit your throat. A perfect politician.

Durand extended his hand. Stride and Serena didn't smile back or take his hand, and Stride could see a barely contained fury in the governor's face.

No more pretenses.

'I don't think they're going to keep this quiet,' Durand told Boni, as if they were alone in the room. 'I thought you said you had this under control.'

Stride watched Boni and realized to his surprise that the old man hated Mickey Durand. There was undisguised contempt in his stare. As if Mickey was a parasite that fed off him, but one that had wrapped itself around his entrails until he couldn't tell any more where one organism ended and the other began. Kill one, kill them both.

'They're police, Mickey,' Boni replied calmly. 'Police don't stop until they know the truth. So you and I, we're going to tell them the truth. Then we can all put this behind us.'

'They'll talk. Hell, they could be wired.'

Boni shook his head. 'I have scanners in the foyer. They aren't

306

wired. As for talking, don't worry. I think we can come to an arrangement that keeps us all happy.' He took a slug of whiskey and nodded at Stride. 'You already know about Mickey. I know you talked to Moose. What else do you want to know?'

Stride looked at Durand. 'Amira,' he said. 'Why did you do it? We both know Boni put you up to it. What did he have on you back then?'

Durand didn't answer. Boni said smoothly, 'I saved Mickey's mother from some problems she was having with the district attorney. She was one of my casino employees. She murdered her sister when she found her in bed with her husband, and I got the charges dropped. So there were debts to be paid, you see. I was already putting Mickey through law school. I saw the kind of potential he had.'

Durand shrugged. 'He really didn't have to convince me, you know. Have you seen what Amira looked like? I would have volunteered.'

'Were you supposed to kill her?' Serena asked.

'No,' Boni said sharply, with another glance at Durand that suggested how much he loathed the relationship between them. 'It was just supposed to be a lesson in loyalty.'

'She was a fighter,' Durand said. 'It was an accident.'

'An accident?' Serena retorted cynically. 'Crushing her skull?'

'These days I guess we would call it rough sex,' Durand said, laughing.

'These days we call it rape and murder,' Serena told him coldly.

Stride saw that Boni wasn't laughing. 'I'm amazed you didn't kill him for what he did.'

Boni took a moment to rein in his temper. 'I'm a businessman, Detective. Sometimes you make difficult choices for the greater gain. Amira was already dead to me, and Mickey was a prime investment.' He added with a glance at Durand, 'But don't think it didn't occur to me.'

'We're blood brothers,' Durand said, seemingly unconcerned with the powder keg that stood near him. 'Both climbing the heights of power. It's been a hell of a ride. Congressional aide, state assembly, speaker, then governor. Who knows, maybe the Senate in two years. I love DC. And they're making noises about tighter gaming regulations, all those fucking preachers.'

'What about Claire?' Serena asked. 'Was raping her an accident, too?'

For the first time, Stride saw nervousness in Durand's cold eyes. 'That was miscommunication,' he murmured. 'We had both been drinking. Boni knows I would never deliberately hurt her.'

307

Stride didn't think Boni knew that at all. He wondered how far it went, being a businessman. Making difficult choices for the greater gain. Durand was a psychotic, and Boni had the keys to the cage. Stride saw Boni struggling with it, as he must have struggled his whole life. Tolerating the intolerable. He didn't think Boni had lied to Claire. He had loved Amira. And this man had killed her. Had raped his daughter. All for power.

'You know the truth now,' Boni told them, his voice tight. 'It's time to walk away.'

Silence lingered in the room. One of the light bulbs in a lamp on the nearest desk flickered. Somewhere outside, in the darkness over the valley, Stride saw the blinking of a plane climbing from the city.

'What if we don't?' Stride asked.

Boni sighed. 'Let's not go there.'

'Hypothetically,' Serena said.

'You can't prove anything,' Boni reminded them. 'You have no evidence. Your superiors won't investigate. The two of you are smart enough to know how power works in this city. Sometimes you're the fly, and sometimes you're the swatter.'

'We might go to the press,' Stride suggested.

Boni shrugged. 'Don't make me spell it out for you. You'd be discredited. Your lives would be ruined. I really don't want to do that. I mean that sincerely, Detectives. I respect you both. But things would come out.'

'Things?' Serena asked.

'Such as your sleeping with my daughter, Detective. In the middle of an investigation? It wouldn't look good.'

Serena didn't bother asking how he knew that. 'You wouldn't do that to Claire,' she said.

'Like I said, difficult choices. There's more. You'd lose your jobs. Probably go to prison, too. Obstruction of justice.'

'What the hell are you talking about?' Stride asked.

'I imagine the Minnesota police would be interested in how you resolved your last case. The murder of Rachel Deese and what really happened to her. So you wouldn't be the only one to suffer, would you, Detective?'

Stride couldn't help it. His mouth fell open in disbelief. *How did he know?* And then it was obvious. Boni had bugged their town home. He had been listening in on everything. Their secrets. Their sex. The investigation.

'So, really, it would be better for all of us if this just remained a story that the four of us know about and no one else. OK? Because that would just be the beginning. That would be just the things that are *true*. Once the media sinks its teeth into you, they'll believe anything, won't they? You know how it works.' Boni spread his hands.

The governor was smiling as he stood by the window. The lights illuminated half his face and left the rest in shadow.

Stride's mind was working furiously, wondering if they had talked about their plans inside the town home in the last day. Had they exposed their hole card? He couldn't remember, but it didn't matter. He had to play it and hope for the best.

Stride looked at Serena, and she nodded.

'Leo Rucci wanted it to stay a secret too,' Stride said.

Boni didn't say anything. He simply arched a curious eyebrow.

'But he wrote it down,' Stride said. 'He wrote down what really happened to Amira.'

Boni laughed. 'Don't be ridiculous. Really, Detective, that's a weak gambit. Leo Rucci was as loyal to me as anyone in my life.'

'We searched his home this morning,' Stride said. 'But you know that. You already had people there to clean it out. Make sure there was nothing incriminating. His office, too. They had already been rolled.'

Boni shrugged, not bothering to deny it.

'The trouble is, they missed something. A safe deposit box. The key was on the key chain in his pocket when he was killed. Not in his home. Not in his office.'

Stride thought he saw a glimmer of unease in Boni's face.

'We opened it today. There was an envelope addressed to his son Gino inside. But of course, Gino's dead.' He pulled an envelope out of his pocket and held it casually in his hand, so that Boni could see the one word written on the outside. *Gino*.

'Leo would never do this to me,' Boni said.

'He didn't. He just wanted an insurance policy for his boy. In case something happened to him. Leo knew that Gino was the kind of kid that might need a Get Out of Jail Free card down the line. Literally.'

'Give it to me,' Boni said.

Stride extended a hand, and Boni snatched it away. He studied the envelope, which was yellowed and looked to be more than a decade old. It bore the logo from Rucci's quick-lube business. Boni yanked the letter out from inside and unfolded it.

'This is a copy,' he said.

'The original is in a lawyer's office outside the city,' Stride said. 'Just in case.'

Boni began reading it. Stride knew how it began.

Gino,

If you're reading this, it means I've croaked. Hope it was quick, you know? Bullet to the brain, that's the way to go. Or maybe a heart attack while I was doing some blonde. Listen, kid, I've got a few secrets from the old days. When me and Boni were on top of the world. You share any of this with anybody, so help me God, I'll come back from the grave and kick your ass. If you get into trouble, call Boni. He'll help you, no questions asked. But if Boni's not around, there's somebody else to call. His name's Mickey . . .

They waited while Boni finished the letter. Stride saw his hand was trembling. The rosy flush in his old face drained away until he looked fragile and pale. When he was done, he looked up, his eyes vacant, his mind hard at work. Looking for a way out. An escape. A way to turn it back.

'This won't ever stand up in court,' he said. 'You can't touch either of us.'

Stride nodded. 'True enough. But it's plenty for the press. And the voters.'

Boni chewed on this thought. He knew they were right.

'You'll go down, too,' Boni said. 'The information about Rachel will come out. It will be war. You'll be destroyed.'

'We'll take that risk,' Serena said.

'We're a lot closer to the ground, so it doesn't hurt as much when we fall,' Stride added.

He watched Boni taking their measure, assessing the steel in their eyes. It was a game of poker, and both of them stared back without blinking, daring him to call. This was the moment where it all rose or fell, Stride knew. He knew Boni couldn't believe he had been outsmarted. That he might actually play and lose. He had built his empire for half a century, and just like that, in the space of a few seconds, it would be gone.

Stride realized he was holding his breath. Waiting.

There was only one thing Boni could do. Fight. That was the nuclear option. Destroy all of them on the way down. Stride hoped the old man was too shrewd for mutual annihilation.

'What do you want?' Boni asked quietly.

Stride kept the relief off his face. His expression was stone. 'The governor resigns. You give up control of your company.'

'Give up control? To who?'

'To Claire,' Serena said.

Stride hoped that Serena was right and that Claire would agree to take over.

'The empire stays in the family,' Stride explained. 'You're out, Claire's in.'

'This is *bullshit*,' Durand burst out from across the room. 'Kill them, Boni. They disappear, this goes away.'

Stride shook his head. 'If we disappear, this letter goes to the press.'

Boni had a look of admiration on his face, as if he appreciated how they had played the game. 'Nicely done, Detectives. It's a good plan. You're not suggesting I go in the Black Book, are you?'

'No, not at all. This is clean and simple. You're giving up the Orient project to someone younger, who can see it all the way through. Someone you trust. It may not be justice, but it's closer than we'd get in court. And if you live long enough, you still get to see your last dream realized.' He hoped Boni didn't realize that the whole point was *not* to make any of this public. To get it all done in private. Before questions started getting asked.

To get Durand out of office. That was the main thing.

Durand saw it too. 'Boni, you're not buying this, are you? These two are nothing. We can beat them.'

'Shut up, Mickey.'

Durand's tan face grew red with rage. 'Don't you talk to me like that, old man. I could have brought you down any time I wanted. We are *not* going to give in to these fucking cops.'

'You've forgotten who's really got the power, Mickey. I pull the strings. You dance.'

'No, we *both* dance. I'm not resigning.'

'The only reason you stay alive is because I want you where you are. Think about that.'

'You need me,' Durand shouted. 'You're nothing without me.'

'Tomorrow you'll release a statement,' Boni replied calmly. 'You're resigning immediately and quitting the campaign because of a serious knee injury. It's left you incapacitated and unable to perform your duties.'

'What the fuck are you talking about?' Durand said. 'What knee injury?'

Boni reached into the right-hand pocket of his coat and extracted a gun barely larger than his hand. In one smooth motion, he aimed and fired perfectly, not flinching at the explosion, drilling a bullet through the ball of Durand's knee cap. 'That one,' he said.

Durand screeched in agony and lurched forward, toppling to the ground.

311

Boni held up his hand and stopped Stride, who was reaching for his own gun. 'It's over, Detective.' He slid the gun back in his pocket. 'That was for Claire and Amira.'

Stride and Serena both recoiled as Durand wailed, rolling on the floor, grabbing his leg and crying like a baby animal caught in the claws of a crow. Blood seeped through his fingers. The pain was monstrous, and the horrible look in the man's eyes begged for unconsciousness. For death. For anything that would make it stop.

Stride felt frozen, as if he should do something to intervene. He looked for a phone to dial 911, but realized there was no phone in the room. He glanced at Serena, who was looking back at him. The seconds stretched out. His heart hardened. He realized he had no sympathy at all for Mickey Durand.

It was part of the city, Stride realized. Violent. Immoral.

Boni didn't even look at Durand. 'Don't worry, I'll get my doctor here in a few minutes. He'll live.'

He reached into his pocket and took out a piece of paper and scribbled something on it. He handed the paper to Serena. 'This is Claire's number in St Thomas. You can tell her she's in charge if she wants it. I won't go to the ceremony next week, but I figure you won't mind if I watch from up here as she blows up my hotel.'

Fifty-four

When they visited Nicholas Humphrey the next morning, the retired detective was in a deckchair on his lawn, still wearing his green terry robe. He had furry slippers lying near him in the grass. His decades-long lover, Harvey Washington, was in a matching chair next to him. The two men were holding hands. It was strangely sweet.

Their little Westie was a blur of white motion, running around the chairs and stopping long enough to roll over to be petted. Humphrey and Washington took turns rubbing the dog's belly with their feet. The noon sun made the shabby neighborhood around them look bright. A small airplane whined overhead, floating through the blue sky.

Humphrey waved as Stride and Serena climbed the driveway. The sour detective looked happy this morning. As if a long overdue debt had been paid.

'Heard it on the radio,' he called to them. 'I can't believe you actually pulled it off.'

Stride nodded. 'It may not be prison, but for Boni it may be even worse, not to be calling the shots any more.'

'And our governor? How did he take the news?'

'He wasn't kidding about a knee injury.' Stride explained what had happened in Boni's suite, and both men on the lawn winced, hearing how Boni had calmly shot Durand.

'Ouch,' Harvey said. 'Man, that must be like getting your balls in a vise.'

'Worse,' Humphrey said. 'I've seen guys who've been through it. They say that's the most excruciating pain you can inflict on someone. Well, too bad, so sad. Payback's a bitch.' He was tossing his Willie Mays autographed baseball from hand to hand. Finally, he tossed it to Stride, who caught it and smiled. 'Harvey and I, we thought you should have this.'

'Just don't go selling it on eBay,' Harvey added, with a crinkle of his brown lips.

Stride looked at the signature on the ball. If it had been genuine, it would have been worth a lot of money.

Of course, it was a fake, courtesy of Harvey Washington's magic hands. Like everything else in Humphrey's celebrity archives. Like his note from Dean Martin. Like his photo of Marilyn Monroe and her sexy message.

Like the letter from Leo Rucci to his son Gino.

Fake.

'I was nervous when Boni pulled the letter out,' Serena told them. 'I was sure he was going to realize we were conning him.'

'You have to have faith in me,' Harvey said, as if the very idea that one of his forgeries would be detected was an insult. 'Course, you hunted down that old envelope from Leo's office. That helps. If the package is authentic, people just assume that what's inside is genuine too.' He pronounced it *gen-yoo-ine*.

'It would have fooled me,' Stride said.

'But Boni knew Leo,' Serena added.

'So did I,' Humphrey retorted. 'That was how the son of a bitch talked. No, we had those bastards nailed. They were going down. Thanks for letting me and Harvey be a part of it. Feels good to make up for what I did all those years ago, you know?'

The Westie jumped in his lap. Humphrey scratched his head and let it kiss him all over his face.

'We couldn't have done it without you,' Stride told them. 'Boni had all the cards.'

Harvey laughed. The dog scampered from one chair to the other and nestled in his lap. 'Well, hell, this is Vegas, baby. When you don't have the cards, you bluff.'

It was later the same day. Stride had dropped Serena back at the station.

He hated hospitals. The antiseptic smell reminded him of the days he had spent in the Duluth hospital in January several years earlier, holding Cindy's hand as she grew weaker and weaker, until finally she slipped away. Dying in front of his eyes in the warm room, as the snow hissed and whipped outside. He tried to force the memories away.

He saw patients stretched out on beds in their rooms as he passed through the maze of corridors. Nurses tending to them. Anxious family members sitting beside them. As he had done.

He got lost and had to ask for directions, and the nurse was pleasant and patient, pointing him to where he had to go. When he found it, the door was closed, and Stride hovered outside nervously, not sure if he should knock, or go in, or wait in the corridor. He wasn't used to being indecisive, but places like this sapped his strength.

The door opened suddenly, and a man appeared in the doorway, almost filling it.

'I'm sorry,' Stride said, feeling stupid, holding flowers. 'I was looking for Amanda Gillen.'

The man nodded. He was at least six foot five, and Stride had to confess he was one of the most strikingly handsome men he had ever seen. As if he had come to life in the pages of an Abercrombie catalog. Early thirties. Perfectly featured, in clothes that fitted as if they had been sewn for him.

'She's in here,' the man said. 'I'm Bobby.'

Stride tried not to gape. 'You're Bobby?'

He wasn't sure how he had pictured Amanda's boyfriend, but certainly not like some male god.

'Are you Stride?' Bobby asked. 'It's great to meet you.'

They shook hands. He had a rock-hard grip.

'I want to thank you for being so supportive of her,' Bobby said. 'I don't have to tell you, you're the first.'

'She's a great cop,' Stride said. He found himself adding, 'A great woman, too.'

Bobby smiled. 'That's nice.'

'Can I see her?'

'Sure, go on in. I was going for coffee.' He added, 'She's better than she looks. It'll take her a while to get back on her feet, but she's going to make it.'

'I'm very relieved.'

'She's a little groggy from the morphine, but she can talk.'

'I won't stay long,' Stride said.

Bobby headed off down the corridor, and Stride noticed the nurses' eyes following him.

Stride went inside. He was careful to close the door behind him. When he went around the other side of the curtain, his heart seized. He knew Amanda was going to recover, but the sight of her there, motionless and pale, was an instant reminder of Cindy. A battery of devices measured her vital signs and fed them back on LED monitors. A tube across her face blew oxygen into her nose, and another tube was buried in her chest. She had an IV drip taped to her hand. Her hair was limp against the pillow, and her eyes were closed. The wrinkled white sheet was bunched at her waist.

He sat down on the chair next to the bed. He didn't say anything, because he didn't want to wake her. Tears filled his eyes. It was an automatic reaction; he choked up, consumed by the past.

'Hey.'

He saw her watching him. Her voice was weak, as if it was a struggle to draw the air into her lungs and push it out. She had tired, heavy eyes.

Stride reached over and squeezed her hand.

'Bobby tells me you're going to be OK.'

'Hurts like hell,' Amanda said.

'That's God's way of telling you to call for backup next time.'

She was able to move her hand enough to give him the finger. Stride laughed.

'I hear two of the nurses fainted when they stripped you for the OR,' he added.

Her lips puckered into a smile. 'Ha ha.'

He squeezed her hand again. 'You had me scared.'

'Sorry.'

'Bobby told you we got him?'

She nodded and gave him a thumbs up with a loose fist.

'There's more,' he said. Stride glanced at the door to make sure it was closed, then spent the next few minutes explaining everything else that had happened. About Boni. About Mickey. About the confrontation that he and Serena had had with them the previous night. She deserved to know the secrets.

When he was done, Amanda pointed a finger weakly at him and whispered, 'You got balls.'

'So do you.' Stride laughed so hard he thought he would fall off the chair, and he felt a surge of happiness and relief. It sank in. She was really going to be fine. Amanda couldn't laugh, but she smiled along with him, enjoying it.

'Wanna see?' she asked, like she had asked him the first time they met.

'No thanks, Amanda.'

'Chicken.' Her eyes were fluttering closed. She was getting tired.

'I'll let you rest,' Stride said, getting up to leave.

'Serena?' Amanda asked groggily.

'She's fine.'

Amanda took a deep breath, and Stride saw her flinch in pain. A few seconds passed, and then she held herself awake long enough to say, 'You?'

There were many ways to take that. How was he after nearly losing his life and coming face to face with the sins of the city. How was he after his lover had slept with another woman. How was he dealing with the choice that was eating away at his gut. To stay or go.

Stride didn't answer. It was easier that way. He let her fall back asleep, her chest rising and falling, her heart rate slowing on the monitor behind her. He crept from the room silently, closing the door behind him. Bobby was seated in a lounge across the corridor, with a cup of coffee in one hand and a magazine in the other. He looked up as Stride came out, and Stride mouthed the word, 'Sleeping.' Bobby nodded.

Stride heard his cell phone ringing. One of the nurses looked at him sharply, and he nodded in apology. 'I'm a police officer,' he said.

He found a quiet corner to answer the phone. 'Stride.'

'Detective, my name is Flora Capati,' a woman said, her voice bright and foreign-accented. 'I run a senior care facility in Boulder City. The Las Vegas police gave me your number.'

Stride was puzzled. 'How can I help you, Ms Capati?'

'It's one of my residents. Her name is Beatrice. She's been beside herself the last couple days, and I promised I would call you in order to calm her down. She insists you're making a terrible mistake.'

'A mistake?' Stride asked. 'About what?'

'Well, Beatrice claims she knew Amira Luz.'

Fifty-five

The crowd gathered like bloodthirsty witnesses to a hanging, ready for the Sheherezade to fall. Thousands of them trampled on the parking lot and green lawns of the Las Vegas Hilton, their eyes riveted on the old hotel across the street. They pushed and shoved for a better view and kept checking their watches. It was almost high noon. Hanging time.

The street was closed, traffic re-routed to the east and west a quarter mile away. The gawkers were cordoned off at a safe distance, away from the danger zone, but close enough to see the action. Helicopters hovered overhead with their cameras poised, delivering a live feed for the lunchtime news. Stride could smell steak grilling and realized that dozens of people in the Charlcombe Towers were giving barbecue parties and staring at the spectacle from their balconies. Everyone was a voyeur today.

No doubt Boni was up there too, alone on the top floor, with a drink in his hand, missing the spotlight. Waiting for his little girl. Saying goodbye to Amira one last time.

It was a beautiful day for an execution. The wind was still. The faces on the demolition team showed nervous excitement. They were pros who had done this dozens of times before, but the last few minutes before that little spark of electricity jumped through the wires had to be nerve-wracking, no matter how much planning had gone into the job.

Radios chirped. The site was clear, ready to go.

'Where is she?' Serena asked, standing beside him. She looked around at the crowd with unease.

'She'll be here,' Stride said. 'It's part of the show.'

As if on cue, a ripple of noise ran through the crowd. There was a car on the closed-off street, a limousine slowly rolling down the center of Paradise Road. It eased to a stop, and the driver hurried around to open the passenger door.

318

Claire climbed out of the limousine and blinked. Flashbulbs popped. Voices cheered. She seemed taken aback for a moment, and then she smiled and waved, looking every inch the performer. The new executive, cool and confident, who was probably wondering if she could make it to the stage without throwing up.

She glided through the roped passageway that led from the street to the riser constructed on the parking lot opposite the Sheherezade. There was a red carpet along the route, and she took long, easy steps in her heels. People called her name from the crowd, and she beamed at them, warm and friendly. A man in a dark business suit hurried down the steps of the stage and met her halfway and whispered instructions in her ear. She nodded and looked unfazed.

The head of the demolition team met her too. Stride could hear what he said. 'Everything is ready for you, ma'am.'

Claire followed them to the riser, but she stopped when she saw Stride and Serena off by themselves, between the stage on one side and the flocking crowds of people on the other. She whispered to the man in the suit, who looked pained and pointed to his watch. Claire calmly shook her head.

She came over to join them. All eyes followed her.

Stride noticed that Claire stared at Serena the whole time.

'Look at you,' Serena said.

Claire smirked and gave them a mock curtsy. She was dressed in a burgundy business suit, custom tapered to her curves, with diamond accessories adorning her wrist and neck. Her flowing strawberry-blonde hair was carefully pinned up and styled.

'Do you like it?'

'You're beautiful.'

Claire blushed. 'I don't know if I'm ready for this.'

'You'll do fine.'

She soaked in the atmosphere around her. The sights, sounds, and smells. Her new world. 'I haven't had time to properly thank you both. For everything that happened with Mickey and Boni. I don't know how you did it.'

'No thanks needed,' Stride said.

'A part of me wishes I was back at the Limelight. It was easier then. Singing my songs. Before all of this happened with Blake.'

Stride and Serena looked at each other.

'Do we tell her?' Stride asked.

He and Serena had talked about it through half the night, and they were genuinely torn. Maybe the truth wasn't necessary. Maybe it was good enough to leave the lies in place that had been there so long.

'Tell me what?' Claire asked.

Their conversation seemed loud, but it was drowned out by the crowd. Stride felt exposed, talking about it here. But they had decided she needed to know before she pushed the button. Before the Sheherezade became dust and debris. So that she knew, as the building fell, what she was losing.

Except now, when they had to say it, Serena looked as if she couldn't find the words. Stride knew there was a part of her that was in love with Claire, in a part of her soul that he couldn't reach. She didn't want to hurt Claire. But Serena had spent enough time running from the truth herself to know that there was no finish line.

'Blake wasn't Amira's son,' Serena told her.

Claire opened her mouth but didn't find any words. She looked around as if everyone had heard. She stared at Serena, certain that she was joking, and then shook her head. 'That can't be.'

The dead seriousness in their faces was enough to convince her.

'But I could see it in his eyes,' she protested. 'He was Boni's son. He was my brother.'

Serena's voice was sympathetic. 'You saw what you wanted to see, Claire. So did Blake. You wanted to believe you weren't alone. He wanted to believe that he'd found the mother he had been looking for his whole life. But he was wrong.'

'You mean everything he did was for *nothing*? All those innocent lives?'

'You're here,' Stride said. 'Boni's not. Mickey's not. So maybe it wasn't all for nothing.'

'You can't be sure about this,' Claire said.

'I'm sorry. We are sure. We talked to a woman named Beatrice who was Amira's nurse during the pregnancy. She knew what happened to the baby. It wasn't Blake.'

'Then who was Blake's real mother?' Claire asked.

Stride spread his hands. 'We'll probably never know. He was one of the throwaway babies from back then. Off the record and under the radar. He had the bad luck to wind up in a terrible home.'

Claire looked up at the Sheherezade, remembering, and Stride thought she was anxious now for it to be gone. She would push the button, and the memories would be rubble. He also wondered if her mind had leaped ahead of them and was dragging her places she didn't want to go.

'Boni *told* you about Blake,' she said. 'He sent you to Reno. Boni had to know Blake wasn't Amira's child.'

Serena nodded. 'He did.'

'Then why?'

'He knew that Blake believed it,' Stride said. 'As far as Blake was concerned, he *was* Amira's son. Boni was happy for us and everyone else to believe it too.'

'He could have stopped it,' Claire whispered. 'That son of a bitch. He could have told Blake the truth. How many people could he have saved?'

'I don't think Blake would have believed him,' Stride said. 'Blake was too far gone.'

'But he could have tried,' Clare insisted.

'Never,' Serena said gently. 'There was no way Boni was going to tell the truth about Blake. Or Amira.'

'Oh, Serena, don't protect him. He's my father. I know what kind of a man he is. This time, he could have done the right thing. He could have told the truth.'

'It would have meant giving up the most important secret in his life,' Serena said.

Claire's voice was bitter. 'Mickey. I know.'

Serena shook her head. 'No, not Mickey. He would have had to admit what really happened to Amira's baby.'

Claire looked back and forth between them and read the discomfort in their eyes. 'Why was that so important?'

Serena leaned forward and murmured in Claire's ear. 'Amira was *your* mother.'

Claire reacted as if she had been stung. She took a step back and shook her head violently. 'No.'

Serena simply stared at her with sad eyes.

'I was born months later,' Claire told them. 'My mother died giving birth to me.'

'Boni's wife died in childbirth,' Stride said. 'So did her baby.'

'That was *me*,' Claire insisted.

'Boni went to Reno and found the family that had adopted Amira's child,' Stride said. 'Not a son. A *daughter*. You.'

'You're wrong.'

Serena put both arms on Claire's shoulders and pulled her close. 'The nurse in Reno was the one who delivered you to them. She knew the story. She knew what happened. Boni wanted his daughter back. His only child.'

'He never wanted you to know,' Stride said. 'He was afraid you'd find out the rest. That he was the one who had your mother murdered. That's why he couldn't let the truth about Blake come out.'

She took a step away from them. There were eyes and cameras

on her everywhere, and for a moment, Stride thought she might run.

'I'm Amira's daughter?' Claire said, as if she were wrapping her mind around the idea. She was struggling not to cry. Then, in the next instant, her eyes sparked like flame. Amira's eyes. 'She wanted to be free. Just like me. God, I hate him. I hate what he did to us.'

'So did Blake,' Serena said. 'It destroyed him. Don't let it destroy you, Claire.'

'Are you saying I should forgive him? How can you say that?'

'I'm not saying that at all,' Serena told her. 'I just don't want this to consume you.'

Claire looked up at the riser, where the politicians and money men were gathered, waiting for her, watching her. It was her world now – Boni's world – and Stride could see her questioning whether she really wanted it. Whether the prize meant anything at all.

And whether, knowing her past, she was different now from what she had been moments before.

'You could have kept this from me,' Claire said.

'That's true,' Serena said. 'But you're tough.'

Claire laughed and touched her shoulder. Something intimate flowed through their skin. 'I don't feel very tough right now.' She took a deep breath, steeled herself, and added, 'Time to do what we do best in Vegas. Bury the past.'

'It's just a building,' Stride said.

'Maybe, but I'll be glad when it's gone,' Claire said. 'The ghosts can die with it.'

Serena shook her head. 'It's not that easy.'

'I know that.' Claire approached Serena and whispered, loud enough for Stride to hear. 'I'd like you in my life.'

'I'm already in someone else's life,' Serena told her. 'I'm sorry.'

Claire smiled sadly. She looked at Stride. 'You can't tell me you haven't thought about what it would be like. The three of us together. Can't we share?'

Serena answered for him. 'There's only one of me.'

Stride knew the truth. Sure, he had thought about it. But it was nothing but a wild fantasy. There would have been physical moments, ecstasy, like a drug, lingering for a few seconds that felt like forever. But in the end, it would have been a cancer eating them up and splitting them apart. Some lines you can't cross.

Claire knew it too. She kissed Serena's cheek and told her, 'You're deeper than Vegas.'

The crowd was restless. Impatient. They wanted a body.

Claire retreated to the riser, climbed the steps, and waved to the crowd, which cheered wildly. She made the rounds on the platform. The mayor. The demolition team. Investors from New York. All of them taking her measure and studying her suspiciously, this *girl* who would oversee the rising of the Orient, a gleaming red tower to replace the old, tainted past of the Sheherezade. Stride could see behind their eyes and toothy grins and knew what they were thinking. It was OK to let her handle the ceremony. But behind the scenes, she would flounder, and others would grasp the real power.

Stride thought they were all going to be surprised. Claire *was* tough.

She didn't give any speeches. She just placed both hands on the plunger that would trigger the explosion, and the crowd instantly fell silent. The hush lingered for several seconds as faces turned expectantly toward the hotel. Strange, Stride thought, how we're so fascinated with destruction, with the tearing down of idols. Maybe because it was so fast. Years to put it up, years to visit, pass by, and play, seconds to bring it all to the ground.

No one was watching Claire any more, except himself and Serena, who saw the smile fade from her face as she stared up at the sign. *Sheherezade.* It looked tired in the daylight, not like the multicolored glow that washed over them at night. Tired and ready to fall. Claire's eyes were wet. He saw her lips moving, whispering silently to herself.

Goodbye.

She pushed the plunger down. Electricity sparked through the wires and made its way to the dynamite packed inside the columns.

There was a long moment when nothing happened, and people held their breaths and wondered if it had all gone wrong.

Then bang bang bang bang, the charges detonated in a staccato rhythm like cannon fire, shooting from top to bottom with flashes of orange fire. The ground rumbled and shook under their feet, as if massive tectonic plates were grinding together somewhere beneath the earth. The hotel stood proudly for another few seconds, defying the dynamite, as if it could stand forever suspended against gravity. But it couldn't. Deep inside its bowels, the hotel had been eviscerated, its supports gone, leaving only the crushing weight behind to go down. From afar, as it began, the implosion looked as easy and graceful as a puff on a dandelion, not like the rape of thousands of tons of rock and steel. As if they were of no more substance than paper, the walls caved in on themselves, and the glamorous hotel collapsed like a body that had bled out. The force of the fall caused another earthquake under the street, strong enough to feel as if they might all be lifted from the ground.

The crowd gasped and then cheered nervously, as if it were a little dangerous to spit in the face of so much power. They knew what was coming, too. Fearsomely, a mammoth white dust cloud billowed up from the earth, growing like fallout from a bomb. People began backing up, wondering how far it would spread, and Stride was anxious for a moment that there would be panic. In the towers across the street, voyeurs scurried nervously inside from their balconies, shutting their glass doors against the wave of dirt. Forty years of it, an accumulated exhalation of grit, detritus, and skin. There was probably a little bit of Frank Sinatra in the cloud. And Amira, too.

The dust began to rise long before it reached the crowd, bubbling up toward the sky. As it climbed higher, wind off the mountains caught it and carried it northward, sprinkling its ashes in particles over the city. The haze on the ground began to clear, revealing the remnants of the hotel – a forty-foot jagged pile of rubble, walls, roof, floors, tiles, porcelain, wood, and gold leaf, all of its elements jumbled together. Earth movers and dump trucks were waiting a few blocks away, engines thundering, to begin picking at the mountain and hauling it away.

The party began to disperse. The show was over. Curtain down.

Stride took a last look at the tower of debris and saw that a little piece of the hotel sign had somehow wound up on the top of the heap, a bent fragment of neon. He couldn't even identify the letters. Something made him think of the old days, of the faded newspapers he had read, of the photographs of young people back then who had since lived their lives and died. Of 1967. The sun glinted on the lost fragment, and for an instant it was as if the neon flashed one last time, giving up a burst of color that came and went, winking at him.

Fifty-six

They left the demolition site along with thousands of people, struggling through the crowded streets. Haze lingered in the air. Serena suggested that they take the afternoon to go back home, relax, swim, and make love. And then lie in the shadows of their bedroom and talk through the evening and the night. About nothing. About everything. She seemed aglow with his presence, and he felt it right down to the bottom of his soul.

He turned right on Las Vegas Boulevard, along with half the city, heading north. The Stratosphere tower loomed ahead of them. There were only two types of traffic jams on the Strip, bad and worse. Today was worse. They crawled forward, watching pedestrians make faster progress on the sidewalks. The street was a ribbon of steel, stretching through the stop lights. Horns blared, accomplishing nothing. When they reached the Stratosphere after what seemed like endless time, he looked up through the windshield, seeing the saucer of the tower more than a thousand feet above them.

When he had come here from Minnesota a few months earlier, he had found Serena there in the middle of the night, staring at the city. The cool wind had enveloped them, and the neon everywhere had been dazzling. They had embraced. Kissed. He had thought then how their relationship was homeless, how it could never survive in this place, how sooner or later they would be forced to choose. But at that moment it hadn't mattered. The future held no sway over them. Nothing had been real then except how they felt for each other.

This was a different moment.

Real and dirty and crowded, with no escape. The future wasn't the future any more; it was the present. It was here and now.

He left the Stratosphere behind them. The traffic eased a bit. He drove another block and then swung the car into the driveway of a vacant motel, shutting off the motor. His hands lingered on the steering wheel. He didn't look at Serena, but he felt her looking at him. Felt her anxiety grow the longer they sat there in silence.

How to begin. Just say it.

'They've asked me to come back to Minnesota.'

He heard her sharp intake of breath. And then, calmly, slowly, 'You want to go, don't you?'

He turned and looked at her finally, and the pain in her face made him feel as if the weight of the Sheherezade were falling on him. 'Yes.'

She got out of the car. Just like that, she was gone, slamming the door behind her, hurrying down the sidewalk with her arms tightly folded across her chest. He got out too and chased after her.

'Serena, wait!'

She didn't want him to catch up with her, but he did, and he spun her round and saw the river of tears on her face. Her black hair stuck to her skin. She was angry at herself. Blaming herself.

'I'm sorry,' she told him. 'I cheated on you. What the hell did I expect?'

'You didn't let me finish,' Stride said.

'I always knew you would leave. That you would wake up one day and say you were going away. Don't you think I know you're not happy here?'

'You're right. I'm not.'

'I knew you'd wind up going home.'

He shook his head. 'Minnesota isn't home. When I lived there, home was Cindy. I was restless for years after I lost her.'

He reached out and took her hands.

'Until I found you. Home is *you* now.'

'But you still want to go back to Duluth,' she said softly.

'That's true. I'm a snowman here. I melt.'

She summoned up her courage, ready to set him free. 'I don't want to keep you where you don't want to be. Not even for me.'

He said the words he had been longing to say for days. 'Come with me.'

'To Minnesota?' she said. She looked down at herself, as if she were taking stock of who she was. She looked around at the Vegas street, the traffic flowing back and forth, the big sky, the lights. 'Jonny, you know that would never work. I'd be as much a fish out of water there as you are here.'

'I don't think so. Claire said it too. You're deeper than Vegas.'

'But this is my—' She stopped. He knew she had been about to say *home*. Maybe she was thinking about what he had said. Or maybe

326

she had begun to realize the depth of what he was asking, to uproot herself, to commit.

People were passing by them on the sidewalk, but they were alone.

'What do you want us to be, Jonny? Partners? Lovers?' She had a quiet intensity in her face, feeling her way, as he was. 'Or something else?'

He was afraid of saying the wrong thing. Every word felt like a landmine. 'I've been married twice,' he reflected. 'One was a perfect match. The other was a terrible mistake. I'm not scared of trying again, but I want us to be ready.'

'I have a long way to go,' Serena said. 'Not because of you, but because of me.'

'I know that.'

'And you still want me to come with you?'

'That's what I want.'

He watched the emotions battling behind her eyes and knew he had thrown her into a deep pool and asked her to swim. He knew what he was asking her to give up, the chance he was asking her to take.

It had been easy for him. A few months ago, when he had chosen to leave Duluth, his life had been in transition. His identity had been spirited away. In his short time in this electrified city, he had been forced to re-examine everything that had made him who he was. And who he was not.

Suddenly, he had a chance to rebuild what had been stolen from him. To go home again and make it something new.

Serena wandered away from him, back toward his truck, parked askew on the sidewalk. She stood there, one knee bent, with her hands jammed in her pockets, staring southward at the chaos on the Strip. He wished he could be inside her mind. He wondered whether, as she absorbed the madness of the city through her green eyes, she was staring at her past or her future.

She shook her head, as if laughing at an old joke. Then she opened the truck door, got in, and leaned back out the window. 'Hey, Jonny,' she called to him. 'You coming or what?'

Stride smiled and went to join her. He took a glance at the warm blue sky and thought that on the shores of the great lake in Minnesota, the colored leaves had already fallen. Winter would be shouldering down from the north. Soon, the snow would fly.

Acknowledgments

My thanks as always go to the five amazing women who have been so instrumental in my career: my agents Ali Gunn in London and Deborah Schneider in New York; my editors Marion Donaldson in London and Jennifer Weis in New York; and my wife Marcia.

There are many others, too, who have made this journey possible: Carol Jackson, Diana Mackay, Kate Cooper, Stephanie Thwaites, and the entire team at Curtis Brown; Beth Goehring, Gary Jansen, Victoria Skurnick, Carole Baron, and their colleagues at Bookspan; Brigitte Weeks; Sally Richardson; Peter Newsom; the tremendous sales and publicity staff at both Headline and St Martin's; and the creative web team at Designstein (Nathan, Rob, Cat, Ed, Mark).

I have also worked with many wonderful overseas editors and sales people at publishers around the world. Thank you all for being early and enthusiastic supporters.

This life would be impossible without great friends, such as Barb and Jerry, Keith and Judy (and the entire Bath mafia), Janean, Janice, Kris, Cindi, our friends at HSCA and Faegre & Benson, and many more.

I'm blessed to have parents who have always supported and believed in my dream, along with a great family of supporters. We may not always be near each other, but you're all close to me in spirit.

Finally, I must thank the many booksellers who have embraced my work and the thousands of readers who have joined me, Jonathan Stride, and Serena Dial on their adventures. (Special thanks to Gail F., Bonnie B., Tim S., Eric S., Ed K.)

So far, I have always been able to reply personally to everyone who has written to me at brian@bfreemanbooks.com and I hope you will, as they say, keep those cards and letters coming. You can also visit my web site at www.bfreemanbooks.com for more information about me, my prior and upcoming books, and my blog.